NON SUSPICIOUS

A DETECTIVE BROOK DEELMAN MYSTERY

ED CHURCH

DOUBLE TIME

Paperback ISBN: 978-1-9163246-0-2
.mobi eBook ISBN: 978-1-9163246-2-6

www.edchurch.co.uk

Produced in United Kingdom

Cover Design and Layout by SpiffingCovers

Chapter 1

Thursday, 21st April 2016
North London

There was something compelling about the scarred old man drinking on his own. At least, there was to the young Australian barman, watching him between pulling pints. The rest of the north London pub was more interested in Arsenal's Premier League game – shunted to a Thursday night due to fixture congestion. Sixty thousand fans may have been watching it live half a mile away, but big screens and beer meant few in the pub felt hard done by. At a small table at the edge of it all, the old man sat impassively.

The table's position against a side wall offered the double advantage of a decent view up to an overhead screen and a clear path to the end of the bar – a fact not lost on the venue's oldest customer. It was as he returned for a third time that the young Aussie finally got a chance to serve him.

Around 5'8" tall in his tweed suit (maybe touching 5'10" back in his prime), what remained of his white hair was neatly parted at the side of a sun-spotted scalp, while rheumy blue eyes looked out from a deeply lined face. The barman's colloquial inner voice was already calling him 'Gramps'… but it was the injuries that had really caught his attention.

The top third of Gramps' left ear was no longer there and his nose had suffered multiple untreated fractures. Most striking of all, his neck displayed the sort of cartoonish scar – horizontal with clumsy vertical stitches – that made one think of Hallowe'en. It looked like the guy had been guillotined then knitted his own head back on.

With a degree of embarrassment, the barman realised he'd been staring at the neck for too long. The ancient blue eyes were now looking straight at him, patiently waiting for service.

'Sorry, mate. Miles away. What can I get you?'

Gramps was standing close enough to his draught of choice to touch the top of the pump, then raise a single finger.

'Sure thing.'

The barman selected a dimpled pint glass and began pouring, now wondering whether the man in front of him could speak at all. Although still vivid, the scar looked like it had happened a long time ago, somehow now at home in the creases and folds of the ageing skin.

'You're getting through a few of these tonight.'

He gave a nod towards the pump, still not sure if Gramps was capable of answering.

'It's my birthday,' came the reply, causing sufficient surprise to send beer spilling down the sides of the glass. Far from being non-existent, the voice was still clear. It had a clipped, old-fashioned quality that reminded the barman of black-and-white movies.

'Well good on yer, Sir,' he said, swapping his usual *mate* for a slightly clunky attempt at deference. He wiped the concave dimples with a paper napkin and placed the pint in front of his intriguing customer, noticing a neat pile of correct change already stacked on the bar.

'Can I ask how old you are?' he added, genuinely curious (Gramps could have been anything from ninety to a hundred). The old man raised both hands, palms facing forward, fingers splayed, like a magician showing the crowd he wasn't hiding anything.

'I lost count,' he replied, wiggling the stump that was all that remained of his left little finger.

The barman winced. 'Ouch! How'd that happen?'

It seemed faintly ridiculous to be asking about the finger before any of the more obvious injuries, but the opportunity had presented itself. He had read a book about London's gangsters of the 1960s and was starting to wonder if this guy had been one. Or at least on the receiving end of one.

Gramps placed his hands flat on the bar and leaned in a little closer.

'Mousetrap.'

He maintained a poker face just long enough to see a moment of confusion in the barman's eyes – not sure if it was meant to be a joke. Then the old man threw his head back and laughed. For one absurd moment it was possible to imagine the neck tearing open and his head toppling off altogether.

A Glaswegian accent interrupted the strange thought: 'Oi! Danny! Fuck's sake. You still serving here or what?'

The junior employee acknowledged his bar manager and scooped up the pile of coins.

'Well, I hope you got some nice birthday cards,' he said, trying to sign off breezily but instantly cringing at how patronising it sounded.

'Cards?' replied Gramps, carefully ferrying his pint. 'I don't like cards.'

It was five minutes after the final whistle when Danny saw his strange new friend readying himself to leave. He was holding a walking stick and patting the pockets of his tweed jacket, as if confirming the contents. The barman watched as 'Gramps' made his way to the exit, glad to see an outstretched arm holding the door open for him. He was already pouring his next pint by the time a tanned man in a navy sports jacket took the same route.

Just like Danny, he was interested in the old man.

He was interested in killing him.

Chapter 2

Stick in hand, the scarred old man clacked his way through the pub's courtyard and headed out into some of the nine million randomly colliding souls with whom he shared the city. He began making his way up Holloway Road. There were a couple of routes home he could have taken, but something he had seen in the pub made him choose this option. He hoped he was wrong.

The rumbling, horn-filled traffic was even denser on match days, while those leaving the stadium on foot provided flashes of colour among the pedestrians – their red Arsenal shirts weaving hurried paths to favourite post-match drinking holes. After a few minutes' slow progress, the old man joined a group waiting at a pedestrian crossing, taking the chance to look around under the pretence of checking the traffic… No sign of the man who had caught his eye in the pub. Perhaps he had been mistaken.

Just in case, he would stick to his plan. After all, if his gut feeling was correct, then making it home safely would only delay the inevitable – he would merely be picked off at some later date. No, the only way to stay alive… if it came to it… was to strike first. And make it count.

He had first noticed him while eating breakfast in a café the previous day. It wasn't so much that he looked out of place – people often do – it was a quiet determination to *not* look out of place through some observe-and-mimic approach. That, and a few surreptitious glances the old man had caught in the café's vintage wall mirrors. Adverts for Oxo, Marmite and Cocoa. Easy for someone to think they could hide their eyes among the elaborate fonts and rosy-cheeked characters that adorned the silvered glass.

In any case, his sixth sense had pinged loudly enough for him to make a rare phone call of warning to the only other person who might be on the same 'list'. The only other person who knew the truth. He doubted he would have to do so again. The man on the other end of the line had sounded weak. Nature would surely take him before any human killer.

The café incident had still been playing on the old man's mind when he spotted the same face in the pub. Something told him he was there even before he saw him. Nothing magical, just peripheral vision relaying a perceived threat straight to the subconscious (he believed in the raw survival instincts of evolution over the mystical guidance of the cosmos).

Either way, there he was. Keeping his target in sight while trying to make himself look like one of the locals again. The old man's instincts refused to bow to age, even if his body had to. Yes, he understood. Both what was happening and what needed to be done. He had killed before, of course – on many occasions. But not for a long time. And certainly not in his tenth decade. He hoped the pints of Dutch courage would settle nerves and loosen arthritic limbs…

Accompanied by high-pitched beeping, the dozen or so waiting pedestrians began to pour across to the opposite footpath. A boy racer in a souped-up hatchback was forced to stop and showed his disapproval by revving his engine. He was met with a volley of abuse and hand gestures from fans still pumped up by the match.

On reaching the far side, the walkers had a choice of sticking to the main road or cutting through Madras Place – past the grounds of St Mary Magdalene Church. The old man took a different option. He headed straight into the shadows of the churchyard.

A paved area was illuminated well enough by nearby streetlights but, beyond this, mature trees and the imposing church itself cut any ambient glow to a minimum. The smattering of lights within the church grounds were mainly broken or missing. He stuck to a cinder path down the side of the 200-year-old structure – the black perimeter railings and undecorated windows creating an institutional feel better suited to fire-and-brimstone preachers than smiley vicars with guitars.

On he clacked. The church to his left. To his right, among the ancient trees, a grassy area dotted with 19th century family tombs (stone and coffin-like – the sort that scrape open in bad horror movies). Straining to listen for footsteps behind him, the traffic noise and his naturally diminished hearing made it hard to tell. Still, if he could just make it to the other side without incident, he would write the whole thing off as a false alarm. Hell, he might even reward himself with an extra large nightcap for still being so alert after all this time.

It was as he neared the front of the church that he heard the footsteps. Faint, but real. He stopped thinking about that extra large nightcap. Of course, there was still a chance that the footsteps weren't for him, even if in his heart of hearts he knew otherwise.

Just to be sure, as the path reached the corner of the church and turned 90 degrees to the left – towards the pillars and steps of the front elevation – the old man continued going straight. Onto the grass. The footsteps behind him stayed regular for a few seconds then, as expected, they disappeared. His follower had stepped off the path too. There could be no doubt now. He didn't have to wait long…

'Victor Watson.'

A voice filled the void left by the muted footsteps. The old man stopped and leaned heavily on his cane but didn't turn round. There was no surprise. Just the grim sense of inevitability that comes with a long-awaited and unpleasant appointment.

'It's a nice name,' the voice went on.

Victor sensed his follower move closer. Their shoulders brushed as he passed. Then the man in the navy sports jacket was standing in front of him.

'Victor… The winner… But not today.'

The accent was not native British, but nor was it one you could place. That kind of pan-European English with an American twang. Victor stared at his younger adversary. He stood close. In the dim light, he was still able to see tanned skin and dark hair, cut short and sensible. With pale chinos and a light blue shirt under the sports jacket, he had the air of a well-dressed tourist. Yes, that was it. A tourist. But something about the squareness of jaw and shoulders, and the well-worked muscles of the neck, hinted at less leisurely pursuits.

'I know what you are,' said Victor.

'Then you know what happens next,' said the Tourist.

Victor broke off the staring contest and gave a shrug to signal his acceptance.

'Well, if this is it, old chap, then at least let me have a cigarette.'

He patted an outer pocket of the tweed jacket with his left hand, frowned, and repeated the action on the other side – hooking the walking stick over his thumb as he patted the right pocket. A short 'Ah' and confirmatory nod indicated he had found what he was looking for. All of it a little piece of theatre.

Awkwardly trying to dip his hand into the pocket, the cane still hooked over his thumb, he soon gave up. Instead, he stood the stick back on the ground and leaned the handle a little towards the younger man, gesturing for him to hold it.

'Would you mind?' he asked.

With no offer of help forthcoming, Victor simply let go of the handle and put the now free hand in the jacket pocket. The cane stayed upright for a second then began to topple forward…

Resisting the urge to catch it, some deep-rooted suspicion still made the Tourist glance down at the object moving towards him.

As soon as he did, something felt wrong.

Without even waiting to look back up, he thrust out his left hand to where memory told him Victor's right wrist would be. He caught it, just as the hand was emerging from the jacket pocket. With a mixture of relief and annoyance at himself, the Tourist raised his eyes.

'You don't smoke,' he said.

Maintaining a vice-like grip of the wrist, he lifted the hand fully out of the pocket. The blade in Victor's grasp was so well maintained that it glinted even in the half-light. A flick knife, neatly disguised as a fountain pen when not in use. A nice bit of kit, in fact. He had to hand it to the old guy. Nearly a century on Earth and still prepared to fight, stab and kill for just a little bit longer.

'You were meant to catch the walking stick,' said Victor.

'I see that now.'

The Tourist squeezed hard on the slender wrist to make Victor loosen his grip on the weapon. It had little or no effect. He was strong. Not as strong as the younger man, of course, but far stronger than expected. At last there was a crack as an old bone gave way and the knife fell to the ground. Victor blinked once, slowly, but otherwise gave no reaction.

'Good,' said the Tourist. 'Now, I think you have something else for me.'

Keeping hold of the broken wrist, he snaked his free hand into the inner pocket of Victor's tweed jacket. It emerged holding a gold medal. The Tourist briefly examined it, keeping the four-and-a-half fingers of Victor's left hand in view in case he tried anything else.

'Why do you still carry this?' he asked.

'It reminds me of the second chance I was given,' said Victor.

The Tourist allowed his gaze to flicker over the old man's injuries. The missing top section of his left ear, the pummelled nose, the gruesome patchwork of his neck. Then he looked into those rheumy, blue eyes… For a moment, it felt like he was looking straight through them, back into the depths of violence and brutality that had brought them both to this point.

'Well,' said the Tourist at last. 'I have a message for you.'

He spoke briefly. Fewer than half a dozen words. Apart from a distant police siren, and the fatal thud of his head against a tomb, it was the last thing Victor Watson ever heard.

Chapter 3

Friday, 22nd April 2016

The radio message brought a swift halt to the good mood that had been threatening to creep over DC Brook Deelman. There were two hours left of his final night shift and he had breakfast beers on his mind. Now there was a body in the way. One in a churchyard, no less. Talk about cutting out the middleman.

A dozen years ago, nearer the start of his career, Brook would probably have put his selfish thoughts on hold and offered some cliché about how 'that puts things in perspective'. After a while, he had stopped really feeling it, but carried on saying it. Now he did neither. He was just annoyed about the beer situation.

The silence coming off him filled the unmarked police car to the extent that his senior colleague in the passenger seat felt the need to try and lighten the atmosphere.

'Fucking hell, Brook. Chin up, son,' said DS Kev Padmore. 'A dead drunk in a churchyard? This'll be squared up in world record time. Guaranteed.'

The CID attitude towards rank did away with many formalities of the uniform approach, though it could still be found in certain quirks. Like a 36-year-old Detective Constable being called *son* by a Detective Sergeant just a few years his senior.

'I hope you're right.'

The audible traces of Brook's childhood in Botswana had faded a little over the past couple of decades. But not nearly as fast as his current enthusiasm levels.

'Course I'm bloody right. Set your stopwatch if you like.'

Brook managed a half-smile at Kev's quick-fire East London patter and glanced at the dashboard clock… 5.16am. Still plenty of time to be sipping on his first Guinness in the Fox & Anchor at 7am as planned – as long as there were no complications.

'Deal,' he said.

'Good. You fucking miserable lump.'

After Kev's brief attempt to lift the mood, the pair drove wordlessly to the scene; their coffees from the 24-hour Starbucks at St Pancras making steamy circles on the windscreen. As a crime-fighting vehicle, the high-roofed, silver Ford C-Max scored low on stealth. But its array of adjustable coffee cup holders still made it the most popular CID choice on nights. Brook wasn't sure if the person who had ordered it for the fleet knew nothing about policing or everything.

He flicked the wipers a couple of times as misty rain added a shine to Pentonville Road and the night buses lumbering up and down it like giant oxen.

'Control receiving from 262…'

A female voice came over the radios both men carried in their jackets (Brook's an army-green workhorse from a military surplus store, Kev's a branded product from an overpriced camping chain). She waited for the acknowledgement.

'Go ahead,' replied the operator at last, her slightly muffled words betraying the hurried mouthful of cake.

'We've got a scene set up now at St Mary Magdalene Church. I'm here with 548. I'll give you an update once CID have been.'

Kev pressed the button on the side of his radio.

'We're en route.'

At a red light, Brook reached for his coffee and glimpsed the effects of nocturnal living in the rear-view mirror. His white skin was a little paler than usual – the perma-tan of his youth long gone – while some fresh crinkle lines were emerging at the edges of his grey-blue eyes. The dark hair had a mind of its own as always, but there were definitely more flecks of silver around the temples. Heavy stubble had also crept up over the week of nights. The whole assessment took about three seconds (longer than Brook usually spent looking in the mirror, but the female PC at the crime scene sounded nice).

It took less than five minutes to get there. A patrol car was facing them as they turned into Madras Place, the reflective elements of its Met Police livery appearing to twinkle in greeting as the C-Max's headlights played across the bodywork. Brook pulled over to the kerb and rolled to a halt in front of it. To his right, a low wall marked the edge of the church grounds beyond.

The patrol car had one occupant – an overweight male PC in the driver's seat. Brook recognised his chubby features from a few previous encounters. Baz or Daz. Something like that. He had never been very impressed. The uniformed cop had the car's internal light switched on and was laughing into his mobile phone while simultaneously shovelling a Snickers into his mouth. *Brilliant*, thought Brook. *Illuminate yourself, reduce your external visibility, eliminate your ability to hear anything and pay no attention to your surroundings. What a cop.*

Kev reached the same conclusion via a less analytical route.

'Not that fat prick.'

Brook hauled himself out of the car and into the light drizzle. At 6'2" and 230 pounds, he wasn't the biggest officer at the station, but he looked every inch the former rugby player he was. He had the sort of broad shoulders and thick arms that had more to do with big Dutch genes and ignoring red meat guidelines than powdered supplements and gym regimes.

Any medical scan of the numerous rugby-related repairs – of varying success – to tendon, ligament and bone would confirm the initial impression. It was why he rarely exited a vehicle without at least a couple of non-specific clicks and twinges in his back and knees.

Despite being slightly older, Kev had no such difficulty. Just an inch or two shorter but with far less bulk and accumulated damage to contend with. Fit enough, in a weekly five-a-side kind of way, he denied dying his light brown hair – in a gelled style that was a bit too young for him – but Brook had his doubts.

Both detectives ignored PC Snickers.

They stepped over the low wall and into the churchyard…

The side elevation of St Mary Magdalene Church loomed large ahead of them. In front of it, blue and white cordon tape and a torchlight scanning the ground. A little closer and they could make out the form of a female constable holding a white A4 scene log. Her torch beam raised its angle and settled on them for a second before flicking off out of courtesy. Brook and Kev flashed their warrant cards as they drew near.

'Nice to have some company,' said the PC, leaving it open as to whether it was a comment on her work-shy colleague in the car. Tied up blonde hair was visible beneath the never-flattering female version of the police hat. The fact it was still in its factory shape – the bowler hat-style rim not yet bent up at the sides – marked her out as a probationer.

Kev scanned the area within the cordon but saw no sign of a body. 'Has the dead guy got up and fucked off then?'

'Behind there,' said the blonde PC, nodding at one of the tombs. Kev lifted the cordon tape and ducked under.

'Can I just..?' The female officer showed the open scene log and waved a pen in Kev's direction, but he was already striding off. Brook shook his head at his colleague's rudeness.

'That's DS Padmore,' he told the probationer. Up close, he realised he had seen her a couple of times around the station. A little taller than average. Pale blue eyes. She had a pleasant way about her, though her youthful looks made him feel old.

'Thanks,' she replied, checking her watch and carefully writing the time and DS Padmore's name into the log. Brook took the opportunity to glance at the Velcro name badge on the left side of her waterproof. '*Constable Sanderson*'. Maybe some Scandinavian in there, way back.

'And you're DS Brook, aren't you?' she asked, looking up, pen poised.

'DC. But thanks for the promotion.'

He was glad Kev hadn't been there to do the inevitable routine of '*DS? God help us!*'

'And it's Deelman,' he added. 'D, double E, L, man.'

'Oh, sorry,' said the probationer, writing the correct name. 'Where did I get Brook from?'

Her unaccented voice had a certain warm, friendly quality to it.

'Well, that's my first name. So you're forgiven.'

'Ohhhh,' came the elongated reply, a wrinkle of the nose and self-deprecating smile. 'Like Brooke Shields?'

'Without the 'e'. Or the Hollywood mansion.'

'Shame.'

'I agree.'

Brook was enjoying talking to her, but thought it was probably time he looked at the corpse. He produced a torch and lifted the cordon tape.

'Come over, if you like,' he said. It didn't look as if there was about to be a rush of names to add to the scene log. PC Sanderson hesitated for a moment, no doubt remembering some dos and don'ts about scene management from training school, then joined him in heading over to the body.

'Any sign of the informant when you got here?' he asked.

'None. His phone just rings out. The call handler said it sounded like someone on their way home drunk from a party.'

'Lucky devil.'

They joined Kev on the far side of the tomb. It was about eight feet long, three feet high and a similar width – a few yards beyond the point where the footpath turned left towards the church's front steps.

The three officers found themselves looking down at the lifeless body of a white-haired old man in a brown tweed suit. He was lying on his front, perpendicular to the long side of the Victorian family grave, his legs awkwardly splayed and his arms giving the appearance of reaching for the stone monolith.

His head was the only part of him that wasn't flat to the ground. It was pressed against the tomb, right cheek against the stone, neck broken. Damage to the forehead marked the fatal point of impact. The eye nearest the tomb was still open, giving the odd impression that the dead man was looking down the side to check it was vertical. A zombie surveyor.

'Shouldn't have gone for that diving header,' said Kev, chuckling at his own joke.

Brook shone his torch on the dead man's right hand, its fingers pressed against the lichen-covered stone. The slender forearm protruding from the tweed sleeve was lying on top of a near-empty 50cl bottle of supermarket own brand whisky. Bruising around the wrist suggested something might be broken. He sniffed the air. A stale odour of cheap whisky filled his nostrils.

The two detectives crouched closer to the body and worked their way through the old injuries – the partial ear, the battered nose, the gruesome scar *('Fuck me. It looks like Sweeney Todd shaved that neck').* Then they looked more closely at the new ones. The neck break and the head wound. Brook suspected there might be a skull fracture under there.

Finally, he angled the torch beam at the left hand that had landed just shy of the tomb. He noted the missing half finger. A walking stick lay a couple of feet away at a haphazard angle. It was just possible to imagine the old drunk falling badly, putting an arm out to arrest his descent – even letting go of his precious whisky at the last second – only for his efforts to be in vain. Wrist and neck both breaking. The latter fatally so.

'Well, that all seems pretty straightforward,' said Kev, standing up from his crouched position. 'Looks like he's got injuries galore from getting pissed and falling over before.

Luck has to run out at some point, I guess. I don't know how these fuckers last so long.'

PC Sanderson had been quietly watching them, the scene log now tucked into her waterproof.

'Horrible scar on his neck, isn't it?' she said to no-one in particular.

'Funny thing with chronic drinkers,' said Kev, 'is they often let some fucking horrendous injuries go untreated. Either because they're so off their face they hardly feel it, or they know they're Wanted for their latest booze theft and don't want to risk getting nicked at hospital. I wouldn't be surprised if one of his mates did those stitches. Maybe even the one who slashed his neck in the first place. They're forever falling out and making up.'

'He looks really old, doesn't he?' she added.

'Yeah, these drinkers always look a lot older than they really are. Look at Brook. You wouldn't think he was eighteen, would you?'

Kev was clearly enjoying grandstanding in front of his attractive, young audience. His points weren't entirely without merit but he was definitely using some pretty broad brush strokes, while Brook hadn't finished looking for the details.

'Come on then, Brook. Let's have it.' Kev gave him a thump on the arm. 'You've gone all quiet. Spit it out. What's on your mind?'

Brook was still looking down at the body, absent-mindedly stroking his chin. Apart from a slight regret at having invited PC Sanderson over to witness Kev's masterclass of assumption, there was indeed something on his mind. Or rather two things. Shoes.

'He's got some nice new brogues on,' he said, using the torch to make his point. 'Even got a bit of polish on them.' It didn't seem to fit the quickly accepted narrative of a down-and-out succumbing to a booze-related accident. Kev was unmoved.

'It's amazing what people throw out these days,' he said, barely glancing at the shoes.

'Anyway,' said Brook, not pushing the point for now. 'We need to find out who is. Has he been searched yet?'

'I had a quick check for other injuries, but I haven't looked in his pockets,' replied PC Sanderson. 'They always give you horror stories at Hendon about missing the big knife sticking out of their back.'

Kev muttered something cynical about the police force knowing all about sticking a knife in your back, while Brook pulled on some blue latex gloves and began going through the dead man's pockets. There wasn't much. A few quid in loose change and a betting slip didn't cause much surprise. Brook opened the blue receipt from Ladbrokes.

'Didn't Arsenal win 2–0 earlier?'

He knew Kev had a season ticket at West Ham which, by definition, meant he followed the other London clubs in the hope they would lose.

'Yep,' he replied, joylessly.

'Two goals from Alexis Sánchez,' confirmed PC Sanderson.

Both men looked at her, impressed. She smiled and shrugged.

'Poor bastard never collected his winnings,' observed Brook, holding up the square of paper with the correct prediction.

He carried on his search.

'What's your first name, by the way?' he asked in the direction of PC Sanderson, his blue latex fingers going from pocket to pocket.

'Caroline. But everyone calls me Sandy.'

'Sandy Sanderson. That's easy to remember.'

He plucked an old wallet from a rear trouser pocket. It didn't contain much. Promotional takeaway voucher, £10 note, local library card with a membership number rather than a name and, finally, a slightly battered Post Office account card. This time, there was a name: Victor Watson.

He moved on to the tweed jacket. An outer pocket gave up the only other item. A couple of house keys on a simple ring. One for a Yale lock and one for a mortice.

'A hostel,' said Kev, seeing the keys and clinging to his narrative. 'Bet you anything.'

Brook put all the items in a clear property bag except for the Post Office card. Then he placed both hands just above his knees and pushed himself upright, momentarily self-conscious of the un-athletic action in front of PC Sanderson.

'So, that's Victor Watson,' he said, holding out the Post Office card.

'Vic Watson?' said Kev, with unexpected gusto. 'Vic Watson? Fuck me. West Ham legend. Three hundred league goals. Can you believe that? Three… hun… dred. Mental.'

After rugby, Brook took an interest in all sports, but he couldn't compete with Kev's football trivia. Especially when it came to his own team.

'This guy?' asked PC Sanderson. An incredulous tone.

'Well, no. Not this guy,' replied Kev. 'Vic Watson's era was the twenties and thirties. Been dead a while. I've just never met another one.'

'He doesn't look as thrilled as you,' said Sandy.

Brook was already on his radio, passing on Victor Watson's name and description for a support operator to search police databases for an address. It was a long shot without a date of birth but still worth a try.

'No cameras around here, are there?' he asked PC Sanderson once he'd finished.

'Nothing covering the churchyard. I had a look around. Holloway Road and Liverpool Road will be the closest.'

Brook thumbed his Nokia radio to the 'CCTV' channel and asked for someone to acknowledge him. A Welsh accent answered his request…

'Go ahead, Number One.'

He immediately recognised the booming baritone of 'Jonboy' – an old friend from his uniform days, and legendary boozer, shuffled into CCTV following something of a meltdown. From the moment he discovered Brook was from Botswana, he had called him 'Number One' in honour of his only other reference to the country – a book he had read called *'The Number One Ladies' Detective Agency'*. Since they shared a love of beer and rugby, Brook had always let him get away with it. Jonboy listened to the location and description of the deceased.

'Right you are. What sort of time frame are we looking at?' he asked.

'Well, he must have placed the bet before kick-off. I think that was 8pm. The body was called in thirty minutes ago, so that's a window of about eight hours for you to try and find out how he got here. Not busy are you?'

'Rushed off my feet,' said Jonboy suppressing a yawn. 'But I'll try and squeeze you in. You *do* know it's one doughnut per hour of footage checked, don't you?'

'I thought you had a fast-forward button.'

'Right. Just for that, it's two doughnuts now.'

'Let's call it performance-related,' said Brook.

'You have yourself a deal, Number One,' said Jonboy. 'Performance-related. On top of the flat rate of two doughnuts per hour.'

He signed off just as Brook became aware of someone new for PC Sanderson to add to her scene log – a task which would have been far easier had the new arrival not been totally ignoring her to address Kev over the PC's shoulder.

'Night Duty SCD1 skipper,' he said, flashing a warrant card. SCD1 meaning Homicide. Skipper meaning Sergeant. A murder squad DS.

He was tall and thin in a trench coat buttoned all the way up. Clean-shaven face. Clean-shaven head. Totally smooth. The long darkness of the coat and pale skin of the head made him appear completely bereft of colour. A black-and-white photo of a person.

'Did someone call you?' asked Kev, getting straight to the point.

'No-one. We were just on your borough grabbing a coffee. Heard this come out over the local channel and thought I'd see if we were needed.' His voice was as expressionless as his face. A monotone, monochrome man.

Kev was still standing near the body. He had been secretly looking at the nice shoes.

'Be my guest,' he said.

The tall murder detective stooped under the cordon and walked round to the far side of the tomb, taking out a torch and illuminating the dead man.

'I was thinking of putting in an application for your lot,' said Kev, never one to miss an opportunity.

'You should do it. Might be a few vacancies coming out soon. We're definitely under quota. How many years have you got in?'

'Coming up to twenty.'

'Perfect. A bit of experience. We've got too many kids at the moment. Make sure you do it.'

'Nice one.'

The two fell quiet once again. Kev smiling a little, the bald man without any discernible expression.

'He was found by some drunk party-goer on his way home,' said Kev to break the silence.

'CCTV?'

'None around here.'

'Witnesses?'

'No.'

'Any calls to do with a disturbance?'

'Not that I know of.'

'Anything taken?'

'Doesn't seem to be. Money's still there. Old wallet. Doubt there was ever a phone.'

The Homicide officer let his torch beam fall on the bottle of whisky, then the walking stick, then the broken neck, as if leading someone through the A, B, C of what happened.

'Cause of death seems pretty clear,' he said.

His phone buzzed and he answered it on the second vibration.

'Hello? Tell them to keep it warm. Nothing for us here. See you in two minutes.'

He hung up and waited for an indication that everyone was on the same page…

'Yeah,' said Kev, obligingly. 'I don't think we'll be needing you on this one, but thanks for coming down. Think we can go with 'Non-suspicious' on this.'

Correct answer, thought the bald DS. Now he just had to reinforce the point.

'I mean, to be honest,' he said, 'everyone could faff around for ages, calling it 'Unexplained'. But I guarantee it would end up being bounced back to you and called non-suspicious anyway.'

'Nah, you're right. I'm not going to argue with any of that. I was just telling this lot the same as it happens. I'll let you get back to your coffee.'

'Thanks. Listen, I'll try to let you know a couple of weeks before the next openings come out. Give you a bit of a heads-up. See if you can come down for a few shifts.'

'That would be brilliant. Cheers,' said Kev. 'It's Padmore. Kev Padmore.'

The black-and-white man nodded and gave his first hint of a smile. He didn't write the name down.

'Got it,' he said.

Brook had been observing from a short distance. He hadn't warmed to the new arrival. More importantly, a little voice in his head was giving him a hard time. Much as he wanted this to be a straightforward, non-suspicious death – to facilitate his swift departure to the pub – the little voice wasn't going away.

'Quite an impact though, isn't it?' he said, walking back to the body. The tall DS had already started to walk away. Kev flashed Brook a look that told him to shut up and stop ruining his networking. When it came, there was a hint of annoyance in the reply – the first deviation from the monotone.

'Well, I imagine it would be. If your walking stick goes from beneath you while you're pissed out of your skull on shit whisky. A metre and a half of free fall then it's game over.'

Brook felt no need to rise to the more confrontational tone.

'What do you make of his polished brogues?' he asked, calmly.

This time the murder detective answered over his shoulder, stooping under the cordon tape to leave the crime scene.

'People throw out all sorts these days.'

'So people keep telling me.'

The black-and-white man stopped on the other side of the tape and turned to face Brook (PC Sanderson glanced between the two with raised eyebrows, intrigued by the sudden tension).

'South Africa?' he asked.

'No,' said Brook, without further explanation.

The DS looked him up and down.

'Huh,' he said dismissively, before walking away.

PC Sanderson waited until he was safely out of earshot.

'He was rude, wasn't he?'

'Very,' agreed Brook.

'You didn't have to fuck things up for me though, did you?' said Kev.

Brook shrugged. 'I didn't like him. Did someone get his name anyway?'

Kev suddenly realised his networking skills weren't quite as good as he thought.

'I… Fuck…' He looked at PC Sanderson. 'And he just walked straight past you, didn't he?'

'It's okay. I got it when he flashed his warrant card.' She checked her scene log. 'DS… Chris Beckford.'

'Well done,' said Brook, staring in the direction in which DS Beckford had walked off, even though he was now long gone.

The radio in his jacket beeped twice and a voice came over it.

'DC Deelman receiving?'
He took it out and hit the talk button.
'Go ahead.'
'I think I've got an address for your Victor Watson.'

Chapter 4

Brook headed back to the C-Max to write down the new information out of the drizzle. The support operator explained that after ruling out a few Vic or Victor Watsons of the wrong age or ethnicity, he had just one possible hit. It was old. Over a decade old. A short intel report from 2005. It did, at least, contain a pretty good description of the subject.

'Has your man got any scars?' asked the operator.

'Where do I start?'

It was him.

The report related to a call from a local resident about a man in her block, drunkenly singing shortly before midnight. The caller said they were concerned for his welfare, which was a clever way of saying 'Can you come and shut him up?'.

Officers had attended and satisfied themselves with some words of advice to the drunk man, before one had written the brief intel report and attached some flag to do with 'Elderly Welfare Concern'. That was it. No mention of his circumstances. It had all the hallmarks of a report banged out at the end of a shift. But at least there was an address: 64 Duke Crescent. It was close.

'What was the date on that report?' asked Brook.

'Funny thing. Yesterday's date. Minus eleven years. Twenty-one, four, oh five.'

21st April 2005.

Brook raised an eyebrow. He had a healthy mistrust of coincidences.

'I take it they got a date of birth for him?'

'Negative. Seems he was a bit rambling. Sorry.'

Not very useful.

'Okay, mate. Cheers for your help.'

The exchange came to an end just as Kev stepped back over the churchyard wall. He banged on the marked police car as he passed it, causing PC Snickers to jump and drop his latest chocolate bar in the footwell (the light blue wrapper suggested he had moved on to a Bounty). Kev settled into the C-Max passenger seat and gave him a little wave.

'So is it a hostel then?' he asked.

'We'll find out in about two minutes.'

Brook swung the C-Max around, turning away from the first glimmers of dawn in the east and back into the night.

'Why did you tell that guy you weren't from South Africa?' asked Kev.

'Because I'm from Botswana.'

'Which is in South Africa.'

'*Seri*ously, Kev.'

'What?'

'How many times?'

Brook's estimate of two minutes was accurate to within a few seconds. The address was part of a Georgian terrace, the windows getting smaller on each floor until the old servants' quarters at the top. Wide stone steps led up to a communal front door with a chrome panel of buzzers beside it.

'My money's still on a hostel,' said Kev as they climbed the steps. He sounded like a man trying hard to convince himself.

Brook didn't reply. He was already reading the little nameplates that accompanied the buzzers. Eight in all, split into two columns from 1A to 4B – some neatly typed, others in Biro or felt-tip, the remainder blank or broken. Nothing indicated either Victor Watson or a hostel.

As Kev started hitting buzzers at random, Brook asked the support operator if there was a flat number to go with the 64 Duke Crescent address. Nothing. Then he tried Victor's keys in the communal door. No good. The intercom stayed resolutely silent.

'Going to be a job for Early Turn at this rate,' said Kev, rattling the door in its frame. As a last resort, he took a battered Oyster travel card from his wallet and began sliding it up and down the narrow gap between door and door frame. It always looked easy on TV.

Brook left him to it. He forced his knees into a crouch and peered through the letter box to see a dimly lit communal lobby – white walls and a tiled floor resembling a diagonal chessboard. To the left and right were the front doors of the first apartments, while a stone staircase at the rear led up to the higher floors, turning clockwise at each landing. He allowed the letter box to snap shut and descended the steps to street level before looking up at the windows.

'Oi. Don't quit now. I've nearly got this,' said Kev.

Brook could see only one flat with a light on. He imagined climbing the internal stairs. The turns to the right. The first flat on each floor an A, the second a B…

'Hit 3B again,' he said.

Kev allowed the momentary interruption, pressed the requested buzzer, then returned to his manipulation of the Oyster card, as obsessive as it was fruitless.

After a few seconds, a face appeared at the sole illuminated window – a neat-looking man in his 30s. Black framed glasses, white shirt with the collar still up, a tie draped loosely around his neck. Early start at the office, perhaps.

Brook raised his warrant card in his left hand and gave an open palm of acknowledgement with his right. Then he pointed at the communal door and made his middle and forefinger walk through the air. The neat man disappeared from view.

The detective went back up the steps and heard the universal buzz of admission as he reached the top. The heavy door swung effortlessly open on the first push, Kev's ineffective Oyster card immediately falling from his grasp.

'I was so close,' he said, scrambling for it in the shadows.

Inside the lobby, a domed button at shoulder height activated the main lighting, over and above the low-level glow of the standby setting. At the foot of the stairs stood a pot plant and a small table that clearly served as a dumping ground for the local postman. The two of them sifted through a dozen or so letters, ignoring the reams of pizza and kebab advertising. Nothing for a Victor Watson.

Somewhere above them, a latch clicked and a door scraped open over a rough mat.

'Can I help?' came a voice. The Good Samaritan who had let them in – well-spoken and hushed. Wife and kids still asleep maybe.

Brook and Kev made their way up a couple of flights until the angles allowed them to crane their necks and see him standing outside his doorway, one hand stopping the door closing behind him. The tie was still loose around his neck.

'Thanks for buzzing us in,' said Brook. 'Sorry for the early hour.' He held out his warrant card for the man to take a closer look as both detectives reached his landing. 'I'm DC Deelman and this is DS Padmore. From the police station down the road.'

Always try to make it sound friendly.

The neat man looked at the warrant card, then at Brook, then at Kev, then back at Brook. He was a few years younger than the officers. Apart from the black-framed glasses, he had perfectly maintained designer stubble and cropped hair, beginning to recede at the sides.

'Can I help?' he said again.

'We're trying to establish if there's an old guy in this block by the name of Vi–'

With a loud click, the main lights switched themselves off, returning everyone to the low glow of the standby setting. An energy saving timer system. Without needing to look, the neat man extended a hand to the side of his front door and pressed another domed button to reactivate them. He must have done it a million times.

'That would drive me mad,' said Kev, receiving a look that said *I paid a lot for this place.*

'Yeah, Victor Watson,' continued Brook, trying to get things back on track. 'White hair. Walking stick.'

'Right… Well, I couldn't tell you his name, but there's an old man who lives on the ground floor who sounds like that. The first on your right as you come in. He's got… erm…' He waved a finger at his own neck and then at one of his ears. Brook saved him the trouble of searching for the socially acceptable way to say a fucked up neck and a fucked up ear.

'That's him.'

'Is it some kind of hostel down there?' asked Kev. 'Bail hostel? Halfway house? Charity thing?' He wasn't going to give up easily.

'I don't think so,' came the reply, along with a repeat of the *I paid a lot for this place* look. 'As far as I know he just lives there on his own. I've never seen him with anyone else.'

'Bit of a loner, yeah? Bit of a drinker?'

Brook clenched his jaw and blinked. Kev's contributions were proving less than helpful.

'I... I wouldn't... Is everything okay?' asked the neat man.

Kev was already heading back down the stairs, bored of a conversation that was failing to confirm his assumptions. He called his answer in the questioner's general direction.

'If I tell you we're looking for his next of kin, you'll know he hasn't won the fucking lottery.'

Brook was glad to hear Kev's footsteps retreating down the stairwell. He allowed his eyes to emerge from their long blink and noticed the black-framed glasses were now topped by a deep frown. Just one more unimpressed taxpayer.

'I'm afraid your neighbour died a little earlier,' said Brook. 'We found this address for him and we're just trying to establish some basic facts. Date of birth, family circumstances...'

'Oh, I'm sorry to hear that,' came the standard reply. Brook doubted the news would ruin his day, but at least the frown was disappearing now that Kev had gone.

'You said you used to see him on his own. Do you know of any relatives? A carer perhaps?'

The resident puffed out his cheeks and exhaled.

'Well, I never saw any family or friends. And I never had a real conversation with him, so I can't say that he mentioned any. I mean, he certainly seemed to be fully independent. I knew him to say hello to but that's about it.'

'Okay, thank you. And thanks again for letting us in.' Brook hoped he had smoothed over any damage done by Kev. 'We've got his flat keys, so don't worry if you hear someone in there on your way out. We'll just see if we can find some next of kin details.'

'Of course.' The neat man nodded and pushed his front door fully open, before pausing on his way back in. 'I hope he wasn't too lonely.'

Maybe the news would spoil his day a little bit after all.

Brook headed down to the ground floor and found his colleague waiting outside the door indicated by the early riser in 3B *('The first on your right as you come in').*

'You took your time,' said Kev.

'Just getting you out of a complaint as usual.'

'Come on then, let's have those keys.'

'I thought you would have got in with your Oyster card by now.'

They knocked and buzzed first. Just in case. No reply. The mortice key worked smoothly, sliding the unseen deadbolt out of the door frame.

'It's the right place then,' said Kev.

The Yale key completed the job.

The communal lighting clicked off once more as Victor Watson's door eased open.

Chapter 5

For a moment the detectives' unadjusted eyes registered only darkness. Fumbling fingers eventually settled on a light switch and revealed the space before them.

'This isn't screaming *hostel* to me,' said Brook.

The front door led straight into a pristine living room. Dated but immaculate. Vintage wallpaper, maroon curtains and a patterned carpet provided the backdrop, while a Chesterfield sofa, antique armchair and landscape paintings completed the heritage effect. There were only two nods to modernity – a television and a push-button telephone. Neither was exactly cutting edge.

Kev didn't respond to Brook's hostel comment. Nevertheless, it seemed fair. He was having trouble marrying the meticulous room with the idea of a shambolic drunk.

'Let's just find some next of kin details,' he said. At least that bit hadn't changed.

Two doorways led from the living room – one into a kitchen that was old enough to have become retro cool again (duck egg blue cabinets and bevelled wall tiles), the other into a modest dining room with formal table and dresser.

The dining room wall also displayed the only photograph in the flat – a black-and-white image of some kind of raucous stage production. Half the cast were in outrageous drag, while a piano provided the music and a boisterous crowd roared their approval. Brook read the caption at the foot of the blown-up image:

'Stalag IV-B, Christmas 1944, 'The Empire' Theatre'

It was easy to be mesmerised by the scene… he eventually tore himself away.

A dated green bathroom suite and unfussy bedroom completed the tour. Brook returned to the main room where Kev was finishing his search of the telephone stand.

'Nope,' he said, shutting the drawer and looking around.

The kitchen offered few opportunities. No notice board or calendar. Brook soon moved on to the dining room where the dresser gave up the first find – a small pile of bills. Utilities, council tax and telephone.

'Got something here,' he said, laying out the paperwork in Victor Watson's name. The council tax included a 'single occupant discount' – confirmation that Victor lived on his own – while the BT phone bills for the last two months showed just six calls and four separate numbers. Brook tapped each one into the chipped screen of his ageing iPhone. All local takeaways.

'I'll take a wild guess his next of kin doesn't work at the Phoenix Golden Dragon,' said Kev. Victor Watson was proving a hard man to pin down.

While Kev disappeared into the bedroom, Brook looked again at the phone bills. The most recent covered a period ending seven days ago. The place may hardly have been a hive of activity, but there was still a chance a call had been made in the past week. He went through to the landline. With its rectangular screen above the keypad it was not dissimilar to the ones in his CID office.

Lifting the receiver, he hovered his iPhone's camera over the grey screen and hit Re-dial. A number flashed up… his iPhone made a shutter noise… he cut the call before it could connect. The whole thing took less than half a second. Brook looked at the photo, memorised the digits, then tapped them into an internet search:

'Peak View Care Home, Sheffield, S. Yorks'

Better. Much better… Was Victor calling to speak to a friend or relative? To talk to staff and discuss a place for himself? Either way it was progress.

'I don't know what you'd do without me,' he called to his colleague.

Kev emerged from the bedroom a few seconds later but didn't respond. He was holding two bits of paper.

'You'd better see this,' he said. 'From the bedside drawer.'

Brook followed him into the dining room where he placed the two pages on the table. Neither was particularly easy to read. In both instances, cursive handwriting filled boxes on administrative forms faded by the passing of time.

It was the birth certificate that Brook recognised first. He could make out '*Victor Watson*'… '*The Foundling Hospital*' (some kind of orphanage, he guessed)… '*28th April 1923**'. Whatever the asterisk stood for wasn't made clear.

'Christ, he was ninety-two years old,' said Brook, a finger resting on the date as if to confirm it was real. Kev nodded without offering any more. He knew that his own recent words were running through both their minds. *'These drunks always look a lot older than they are…'*

Brook turned his attention to the second bit of paper. The basics were the same – densely swirled handwriting on some archaic piece of officialdom. After a couple of seconds, he had figured out the nature of it. A record of overseas internment. A POW record:

'L. Cpl. Victor Watson'... 'Middlesex Regiment'... 'Stalag IV-B, Mühlberg, Germany'... '11th Feb 1944 – ? Apr 1945'... 'no. 211251'

'And these too,' said Kev, adding some battered metal dog tags on a chain to the collection. They were embossed with details of the same camp and prisoner number:

'STALAG IVB 211251'

Brook turned to the framed photo of the Stalag IV-B stage show and looked at it more closely, wondering if the face from the churchyard could possibly be there, young and re-animated. Allied prisoners in a variety of patched up uniforms were crowded onto benches with pockets of smart German guards among them. All were united in bawdy laughter at the antics of those on stage. After a while, he gave up. Maybe it was too much to ask.

Using his phone once again, he took photos of all the documents, then one of the theatre scene for no other reason than it intrigued him. He found Kev back in the living room, staring blankly at a landscape painting, lost in thought.

'I think the whole street-drinker theory may be up for review,' said Brook.

'Mmm,' replied Kev, distantly.

'I mean, if there's any chance of foul play, and this guy is a 92-year-old war hero, then we'd better play it safe. Even if it means calling baldie from Homicide back to the scene.'

'Mmm.'

Brook glanced down at a glass-fronted drinks cabinet. Then he looked a little closer.

'And why was someone with a taste for 40-year-old single malt necking Tesco Value whisky in a churchyard?'

Kev finally snapped out of his trance. He looked at the whisky that was the same age as him.

'For fuck's sake. You were right. Those shoes… I'll tell them to keep the scene up.'

He took out his personal radio to hail PC Sandy Sanderson, only to hear her voice already emerging from it…

'Control from 262.'

'Go ahead.'

'Update from St Mary Magdalene Church. The Coroner's officer has now left and this crime scene is closed on the authority of DS Padmore. We're available for any outstanding calls.'

Coroner's officer has left. Crime scene is closed.

The words hung in the air as Kev searched for the appropriate response.

'Fuck!' That did the job… 'I told her to treat it as non-suspicious while you were in the car. I mean, it fucking *was* non-suspicious. Even Homicide weren't interested… And how fast was that fucking Coroner's officer? He must be the Ayrton fucking Senna of Coroner's officers.'

Just a few minutes earlier Kev had been smooth-talking his way into a job with Homicide while dealing with the routine death of a routine drunk. Now it was the increasingly strange death of a war veteran, the body taken away and the scene closed down on his authority. No forensics, no photographs, no thorough search. He could hardly get the Coroner's officer to return the corpse, re-arrange the limbs a bit, put the cordon tape back up and say: 'Okay, people. As you were.'

A familiar voice broke the awkward silence in the flat.

'CID receiving from 262.'

Sandy Sanderson was still doing all the updates. Maybe her partner was locked in mortal combat with a Twix.

'Go ahead,' replied Brook, since it didn't look like Kev wanted to talk to anyone. For once, the probationer's radio protocol deserted her.

'There's been a… I mean… We've had…'

Whatever it was, she was struggling to say it. In the end she kept things simple.

'Can you two just come back to the church? You'll see when you get here.'

Chapter 6

The dashboard clock showed 6.23am as Brook rolled the C-Max into the same spot as before. Dawn had broken while they were in the flat. The marked police car was still in front of them, but it was empty now. Brook and Kev stepped over the low wall and back into the churchyard.

The misty rain had disappeared with the night and the wet grass now shimmered in a hazy morning light. Ahead of them, both uniformed officers were standing on the far side of the tomb that had – in one sense, at least – been Victor Watson's final resting place. They were staring at the exact spot where the body had lain.

'Don't tell me his head fell off,' said Kev. He was now officially having a bad night.

While Kev made his way around the tomb to PC Sanderson – who, he presumed, would be doing most of the talking – Brook skirted the opposite end, towards her colleague. There was something he quickly wanted to address.

PC Snickers was leaning on Victor Watson's walking stick. 'Just messing around' no doubt, but Brook didn't like his attitude towards the dead man's property. As he joined him, he made sure his foot nudged the bottom of the stick, moving it a few inches on the wet grass. The uniformed PC stumbled forward as his centre of gravity shifted, just about managing to avoid propelling himself head first into the tomb. It seemed to be a popular pastime around here.

'Sorry, Baz,' said Brook.

'It's Daz.'

'Right.'

The little sideshow meant Brook was the last of the four to turn his attention to whatever was making everyone else stare. The fact that Kev was yet to deliver a one-liner should have told him to expect something out of the ordinary.

Victor Watson was definitely gone (and his head hadn't fallen off). But in his place was another man. He was sitting on the damp ground, shoulders against the tomb and chin resting on his chest. He was also snoring loudly.

The gatecrasher had dark matted hair, a thick beard in similar condition and a padded lumberjack-style coat – black and red checks with a few rips where the fluffy internal padding was poking through. Dark grey trousers with a couple more rips and black trainers with lopsided soles completed the Spring Collection. He was mid-50s maybe – not that Kev would be guessing any more ages for a while. The overall impression was of a homeless, hibernating bear.

'Well, Victor's looking better these days,' said Kev at last. The gallows humour of a man who had decided things couldn't get any worse. He was wrong about that too.

'Who's this?' asked Brook. Less funny, but probably more important.

Over the course of the next couple of minutes, PC Sanderson explained how she'd been taking down the crime scene tape when she heard groaning, then coughing, coming from the bushes a few yards away. Before she could investigate, the 'lumberjack' had lurched from the undergrowth and collapsed to the ground in front of her.

'He gave me the fright of my life,' she said (Brook rather liked the slightly old-fashioned phrase – ninety-nine percent of officers would have said 'it scared the shit out of me').

The Lumberjack had apparently tried to get back up a couple of times, without any great success, and eventually decided he was better off having a snooze against the tomb. The same smell of cheap whisky that had emanated from Victor Watson was now mixed in with all manner of other odours.

'He's got a bit of a cut on his forehead too,' explained Sandy, some curls of matted hair having flopped over the injury.

'Right,' said Kev. 'If that's everything, then call for a paramedic to check him out if you like. Up to you. You don't need CID for any of this.' There was a hint of annoyance in his voice that Brook thought was a bit harsh on the probationer.

'No. That's not everything,' said PC Sanderson. 'Before he fell asleep, he said the old man was murdered.'

To Kev's frustration, there wasn't much PC Sanderson could add to the few words that had just ruined his night. The Lumberjack had not gone into detail before succumbing to the snoring. Nevertheless, Kev wanted to know exactly what had been said.

'Well, he pointed at the ground where he's sitting,' said Sandy. 'And he said… 'The man here. Killed. He was killed'. That's it, word for word. I wrote it in my pocketbook.'

Killed. He was killed.

Shit.

There was probably only one thing worse than prematurely shutting down the scene of a possible murder. And that was prematurely shutting down the scene of a definite murder. Unfortunately for the Lumberjack, he was going to have to be woken. Brook placed a hand on his shoulder and began trying to shake him awake.

'Can you hear me, mate? Open your eyes, fella.' A big paw tried to swat his hand away. It lacked any real co-ordination, but it *did* give Brook a bargaining chip.

'I'll stop shaking your shoulder when you open your eyes,' he said.

'They're open,' grunted the Lumberjack, without a flicker of movement in his eyelids. At least he had a sense of humour.

'Have to be wider than that,' said Brook, shaking the shoulder a little harder. After a few seconds, the eyes finally opened and the shaking stopped. Deal done.

'There was an incident here. Can you tell us anything about it?'

The Lumberjack opened his mouth a few times in different shapes, as if repeatedly on the brink of starting a sentence but unable to decide upon the first word. Maybe the question was too broad.

'Where were you?' asked Brook, keeping things simpler.

'The… that… the bench,' said the Lumberjack, nodding towards the bushes. What was that accent? Cornwall? Devon? Sure enough, cut into the bushes that bordered the church's front approach was a bench, facing away from them. From the officers' position, it was just about visible through the foliage, which, logic suggested, meant Victor Watson's last moments might have been just about visible from the bench.

'And did you see anything?' asked Brook.

'Heard… first… heard.'

The man may have been fighting some pretty extreme effects of alcohol – both short and long-term – but he was switched on enough to specify which sense had alerted him.

'A voice… voice said… 'Victor'.'

That got their attention.

'Someone said 'Victor'?' asked Brook.

The Lumberjack either nodded slowly to confirm or slipped into a micro-sleep. Whichever it was, his head came back up after a moment and he answered.

'Umm… younger… younger man…' He waved a finger around the area in front of him, as if to say *this is where it happened,* then tried some more words.

'Victor… was… Victor was… he was… old.'

Thanks for bringing that up, thought Kev.

The more he heard, the more Brook thought he was right about the Cornish accent. It had that piratical twang.

'And what happened?' he asked. It was slow progress, but progress nonetheless. The Lumberjack made some actions with his hands, as if his faltering speech was again letting him down. In the end he settled for one word.

'Knife.'

The single syllable prompted an exchange of glances between the officers. Kev's face – already pale from a week of nights – was rapidly turning paler. He could see it all panning out before him…

'War hero killed by knife-wielding attacker'… 'Victim dismissed as accident-prone homeless drunk'… 'Police missed witness only fifteen feet away'…

A career in the property store beckoned. He may as well report straight for duty.

'The younger man had a knife?' asked Brook, looking for clarification.

The Lumberjack wagged a finger in the air again. What did that mean? There *wasn't* a knife? Or was he *waving* the knife? He shook his head. Okay. They had got something wrong.

'The old… the other… had… had the…'

He stopped and composed himself for a few seconds before charging at the sentence again.

'The old man had… the knife.'

A hiccup served as an exclamation mark.

Colour returned to Kev's face.

'Ha! Wow! Oh, thank fuck for that. He's just talking nonsense. Jesus, he almost had me for a moment there. So Victor was lurking around the churchyard all tooled up, was he? That's a good one. I guess he was only in that old suit because his hoodie was in the wash. Fuck me, this guy's good.'

Brook wasn't sure what to make of it. At face value, it seemed every bit as ridiculous as Kev's little rant was taking such pleasure in pointing out. But the Lumberjack had shown all the signs of someone trying to help. In the end, it was Sandy who spoke first.

'He heard the name Victor though,' she offered. Fair play to her. Despite her lack of service, she wasn't afraid to put her point across to a ranting DS.

'Of course he heard it,' said Kev. 'From us! After we found the wallet. How many times did we say the name Victor Watson? Christ, I was even going on about Victor Watson the footballer. I'm sure he heard all of that while lying on his fucking bench.'

Sandy looked a little crestfallen.

'All right, Kev,' said Brook.

'What does *all right* mean?' came the spiky reply.

'It means I think you've made your point.'

'Well… Good.'

A few more hiccups aside, the Lumberjack had gone quiet – happy to close his eyes while the officers argued amongst themselves. Kev began clicking his fingers in front of his face… 'Hey!'… The heavy eyelids began to open.

'So the old man is the bad guy?' he asked.

The Lumberjack gave a slow shake of his head.

'Victim… victim… theft… and…' He paused for a second, then made a fist of his right hand and swung it against the tomb with a ferocity that made everyone jump. It could have been frustration at the struggle to get his words out or a demonstration of what happened to Victor's head.

'Oi! Don't bloody wake them up,' said Kev, nodding at the tomb.

'Did you say theft?' asked Brook.

A nod.

'From the old man?'

A nod.

Kev wanted to remind everyone that this was nonsense.

'From the old man with the knife, lurking in the churchyard?'

For the first time, the Lumberjack raised his eyes above the horizontal and fixed them on Kev.

'What was taken?' asked Brook.

The Lumberjack kept his eyes on Kev as he spoke.

'Big… gold… coin.'

The combination of the piratical Cornish accent and the treasure-like description gave the words a certain pantomime quality. Kev wasn't about to turn down such an opportunity.

'A big gold coin? Ha! Fucking hell. I'll start putting up the Wanted posters for Long John fucking Silver, shall I?'

He glanced around at the others, his big grin slowly fading – disappointed they weren't joining in the hilarity.

'Fuck it. I've heard enough. I'll be in the car.'

He set off, shaking his head – the relief that the witness wasn't sober and credible replaced by frustration at his colleagues for not being equally dismissive.

'Hey!' Brook shouted after him.

'What?' snapped Kev.

Brook tossed something through the air in a looping underarm throw.

'Keys.'

Kev caught them, the simple gesture seeming to cut through his anger. He took a breath.

'Thanks.'

After a couple of seconds, he carried on walking.

The remaining officers shared a look of mutual relief that Kev's mania was no longer around. Brook turned back to the man sitting on the ground and aimed for a friendlier tone.

'What's your name, mate?'

Despite his intoxication, the Lumberjack had come to the very reasonable conclusion that he was heartily sick of these officers. A whole bunch of ridicule and not a single 'thank you'. That was all he got for trying to help. Fuck 'em. He had never liked them anyway.

'Jud–' he said.

'Jude?'

'Judas… Iscariot.'

Brook had met a few Mickey Mouses and Jesus Christs in his career. Even a couple of Elvis Presleys. But this was the first

Judas Iscariot. The withdrawal of co-operation was confirmed by way of a 'V' sign and a loud raspberry.

The detective came out of the stoop in which he had been trying to converse – a grimace of disgust at the raspberry and a wince at his straightening back blurring into one generally pained expression.

'Well, I think that's the end of that,' he said to Sandy. 'Are you going to get him looked at?'

The cut on his forehead was still there.

'I think so. I should probably have sorted that out first but, well, it's been a strange one.'

'Good way of putting it,' said Brook.

'Yep,' said Baz or Daz.

Brook and Sandy both looked at him.

'What?' he said.

'Nothing,' said Brook. 'I was just going to say thanks for your input.'

'S'okay.'

'So, what's your favourite – Snickers or Bounty?'

'Umm. Snickers.'

'I knew it. Me too. What do you like best about it?'

'The nuts.'

'Oh yeah, they're good.'

'And the caramel.'

'Oh my God, that caramel!'

Sandy bit her lip. Brook was glad to have at least made her smile after all the problems that he and Kev had caused.

'Brook!' As if on cue, Kev called over from the car.

'What?'

'Get a fucking wriggle on. I'll update you on the way to the pub.'

Sandy raised an eyebrow.

'The pub?'

'Well, you know. They all serve coffee these days, don't they?'

'I think I'd rather have a pint,' said Sandy.

Chapter 7

DS Kevin Padmore took over the driving duties while DC Brook Deelman slumped his big frame into the passenger seat.

'Did he have any more to say?' asked Kev, turning the C-Max around.

'Not really. I think you upset him with your Long John Silver comment.'

'Yeah, well. He started it with his big gold coin nonsense.'

Brook thought it was time to move on.

'You said you had an update.'

'An update and a favour to ask, I suppose.'

'I'm all ears,' said Brook, realising too late he had teed Kev up a treat.

'I bet Victor Watson never said that! You know, with the missing top bit of–'

'I get it.'

At least it cheered Kev up. Brook allowed his colleague a moment to savour his punchline while the C-Max bounced gently over the endless speed bumps.

'Anyway,' continued Kev, 'I just got off the phone to the on-call DCI. I wanted to keep him up to speed on this one.'

You mean you wanted to get your version of events in first, thought Brook.

'That was quick,' he said instead.

'Yeah, we were at Hendon together.'

The silent training school bond that cut across rank.

'What did he say?'

'Well, he thinks it's borderline, but he's happy enough to go with a call of non-suspicious.'

Brook doubted Kev had gone into too much detail about the various anomalies that he now seemed content to wish away.

'He's just a bit concerned with the whole war veteran thing,' Kev went on. 'Wants us to make sure we do things right in case there's any extra interest.'

'Right.'

'Look, the job's going to have to stay with CID until we find his next of kin anyway. And, while we've got it, he's just keen we make sure it's a cast iron non-suspicious. Make sure there's nothing weird on any CCTV, no related 999 calls that have been missed, no pattern of similar incidents, no witnesses – genuine ones, I mean. All simple stuff. What do you think?'

It wasn't hard to read between the lines. A DCI who was far from comfortable with the death being classed as non-suspicious, but was doing his best to back his old friend while simultaneously 'covering his arse'.

'I think it sounds like the DCI wants someone to tick a few boxes without looking too hard,' said Brook. For the sake of harmony, he avoided saying 'the DCI and you'.

They came to a halt at a red light where Liverpool Road met Upper Street. The pause allowed Kev to turn to his passenger.

'Well, if there's something there then we can re-assess, and if there's not then… there's not,' he said, somewhat meaninglessly.

Brook looked straight ahead. On the far side of the junction, early morning commuters were silently disappearing into Angel tube station like worker ants returning to a burrow.

'I can guess what the favour is,' he said. 'You need someone to do the honours with the investigation.'

'Well, you do have a head start on everyone else by knowing the case.'

'I'm also about to start four days off.'

'Hey, no-one can force you to do it. But, on the plus side, it's all red ink. Authorised by the DCI. Most people would bite my hand off.'

Red ink – another way of saying overtime paid at double time. From the days when the overtime ledgers were filled out by hand.

Brook nodded.

'Does that mean you'll do it?'

'It means the lights have changed.'

'Oh…'

Kev raised a hand of apology to the car behind and moved off through the junction, past the burrowing commuters. The C-Max was heading south now, towards Smithfield meat market and the morning pubs.

'It's easy money, that's all I'm saying. Milk it for fuck's sake. It'll take you no time at all to find a next of kin and bottom out those extra enquiries. Then you're getting paid double bubble for putting your feet up and drinking coffee. As for whether it's ticking boxes or looking hard, well, there's no need to overthink it. What you find is what you find.'

'And that will be that there was no foul play.'

'If that's what you find.'

Which I'm sure you will, in exchange for all that lovely red ink.

The coded request was clear. Brook chose not to address it directly. While far from a model officer, he retained enough integrity that being paid handsomely to find nothing was not really his thing. That said, the whole incident was increasingly… intriguing. And when most workdays were of the Groundhog variety, that simple fact had a value all of its own.

Neither detective spoke again until they were rumbling over the cobbles in front of Smithfield's vast 19th century halls – still standing in defiance of the property developers keen to turn it all to dust. Dotted all around, historic pubs that had grown up to slake the thirst of meat trade night workers. Pubs and workers that, for generations, had enjoyed a symbiotic relationship with night duty coppers in search of an after-work pint.

'You going to do it then?' asked Kev, trundling to a stop by the kerb.

Brook was busy removing the radio, handcuffs, baton and CS spray from his jacket.

'Yeah, I'll do it,' he said. He couldn't deny it any longer – the case and its curiosities had piqued his interest. Just enough to overcome the white noise of apathy and exhaustion that accompanied most of police life.

'Great,' said Kev.

'You sure I can't tempt you with a quick one?' asked Brook. It seemed the polite thing to do, even though he already knew the answer.

'Nah, you're okay. School run in a couple of hours.'

Brook nodded. He always found it difficult to picture Kev as a husband and father. He hauled himself out of the passenger door, turning to drop his kit onto the seat.

'There's a spare key taped to the back of my office pod if you can throw that lot inside. I'll just have a couple here then get my head down for a few hours at the station. Not much point going home just to come straight back in.'

'Okay, mate. Give me a bell if there are any problems.'

Kev left it vague as to what *problems* meant.

'Will do. Cheers for the lift.'

Seconds later, Brook was pushing open the door to the Fox & Anchor and entering a pub that had changed little since his thirsty predecessors crossed the same threshold in an age of smog and street urchins… Polished oak, brass, leather, glazed tiles and ornate mirrors. Half a dozen customers were inside, a couple in yellow tabards, one in the process of taking off a long white coat covered in the bloody smudges of his trade.

Brook ordered a Guinness and downed half of it instantly… Decompression. Vasodilation. A wave of endorphins. God, it felt good. Taking a seat along the back wall, he flicked through the pub's copy of *The Sun* – about as challenging a read as he wanted at the end of a night shift – then took out his phone and tapped on the internet icon. He was curious to look up the 'other' Victor Watson. The West Ham United legend that Kev had been waxing lyrical about in the churchyard.

As it turned out, he had not been far off with his claim of three hundred league goals. The exact figure was 298, scored between 1920 and 1935. For someone as prone to hyperbole as Kev, the addition of two goals was definitely acceptable – especially as 'Vic Watson' had bagged a load more in FA Cup matches, and four in five games for England. He had died in 1988 at the ripe old age of ninety. These Victor Watsons seemed to live a long time.

Two more pints and a fried breakfast later, Brook found himself blearily entering a combination code and opening the grey metal door of his police locker. He removed a foam camping mat, sleeping bag and pillow, then took his little bundle to the furthest corridor of lockers and laid them out. With any luck, uniform Late Turn wouldn't disturb him until around 2pm.

DC Brook Deelman left his jacket, jeans and shoes in a pile at the end of his makeshift bed. Then he turned off his phone, lay flat on his back and closed his eyes. The events of the last few hours flickered through his mind, over and over, like an old *Pathé* newsreel on a loop. At last, the repeating images came to an end, the grainy numbers counted down from ten to one, the screen went blank and sleep claimed him.

Chapter 8

He hadn't slept well.

The encounter with his first target was still playing on his mind.

He adjusted the mirrors of his hire car and checked his documentation was all in order, on the off chance he got pulled over. Getting your fake IDs mixed up might not get you shot by the British police, but it wouldn't exactly keep you under the radar either.

He was cross with himself for not putting the events of yesterday behind him and focusing on the second target. Little things had been bugging him all night. Rather than continue the losing battle to draw a line under it, he decided to allow himself a few minutes to indulge the thoughts that had been eating away at him. Maybe then it would be easier to move on…

He chose to think about what had gone well first. No point being entirely negative. He was satisfied that nobody in the pub had cause to remember him. He was also confident that no-one could tell he was following his target in the street. And, yes, he was as happy as he could be that nothing in the churchyard had been captured on camera. So that was three little ticks.

A bigger tick was the relative ease with which he had got his hands on the thing he wanted – other than the target's demise. That gold medal. Or whatever non-precious metal it really was. The target had unwittingly been very helpful in always having it on him.

Then there was the whisky. Yes, he was happy enough with that. A pre-planned decision to splash some cheap whisky over the dead target and leave the near-empty bottle under his hand. In his experience, cops tended to stick with their initial assessment of a scene through a mixture of pride and laziness. If it helped paint the picture of a stumbling alcoholic then it had done its job.

His decision to remove the key to the communal door was a little more 'left-field' but he had a hunch it might help. The item itself was obscure enough that its absence would never look like a theft. At the same time, if frustrated night duty officers left the task of gaining entry to the day shift, then there was a greater chance of bored cops simply going through the motions. Apathy accompanied any task handed down from a previous shift – it was human nature. And he hadn't been in the target's home so couldn't be sure what secrets it held.

Anything else in the 'plus' column? The broken wrist. That had worked out surprisingly well. In fact, it fitted so well with the story he had presented with the whisky and the nasty fall that he was almost annoyed with himself for not thinking of it in the first place.

That was about it on the positive side of things. Now for the stuff that had been bothering him. The stuff that had prevented him getting a good night's sleep in his anonymous chain hotel.

It started with the fatal blow. The hybrid martial arts move by which he had slammed the target's head into the side of the tomb. At first he thought it had gone well – death was certainly instant. But a closer inspection suggested he might have overdone the force by a newton or two. The break of the neck looked a bit too severe. It tested the boundaries of accidental impact. Maybe adrenalin had got the better of him.

Then there was the main thing he had to mentally address. He couldn't avoid it any longer. The fact he had come within half a second of being knifed by a target in his nineties. How could he have let his guard down so badly? The target's calmness alone should have alerted him. Even if no-one else had given him a second glance, the target must have spotted him. In the pub, maybe even in the café the day before. How else could he have shown so little surprise at their meeting?

All that sang-froid should have told him he might come up against a plan – basic, but very nearly effective. He tried telling himself to focus on the fact he had reacted in time, taken care of the threat. It provided scant comfort. A younger version of the target would surely have killed him.

He looked again at the target's fountain pen flick knife. It was nicely crafted – unrecognisable as a knife to the untrained eye. He had considered keeping it. Posting it to a safe address to pick up at a later date. The spoils of war. But the more he looked at it, the more he thought of his mistake. No, it would be disposed of. Perhaps he could make his negative thoughts disappear with it.

There was just one more thing in the 'minus' column. Nothing comparable to the previous mistake, but he may as well complete the self-analysis. His clothes. The pale chinos, light blue shirt and navy sports jacket, purchased after arriving in the country two days ago.

He preferred to kill in locally bought clothes – ones that would never have to pass through an airport's myriad security measures on the way in or out – and he had thought these would be pretty unremarkable for spring in London. But everyone in the pub had been wearing either 'smart' (variations on the office suit) or 'casual' (Arsenal tops and polo shirts). He seemed to be the only one wearing 'smart casual'. There was a difference. He looked like… like a tourist.

He chastised himself one more time for everything he had done wrong, took a deep breath and made his peace with it all. It had gone okay. That was enough. And he was now glad he had allowed himself a couple of minutes to work through it all in his mind.

Besides, on a brighter note, his police contact had been in touch to say he couldn't see anything to worry about. One of his men had made sure any prospect of Homicide involvement had been nipped in the bud and the whole thing was now being handled by a couple of local detectives – 'an idiot' and 'a drunk'. That made him smile.

He took out his phone and called up the map option, ignoring the hire car's satnav that could be downloaded and linked to him. He was going to do things right today. The 'From' box at the top showed 'Current Location'. He clicked on the 'To' box and typed his destination…

'Peak View Care Home, Sheffield'

Chapter 9

As a general rule, Brook avoided police station canteens. A passing superior wanting 'a quick word' about a case was a great way to make your food go cold. It was why he now found himself at the back of Alfredo's. An over-keen new recruit had scuppered his plans for five hours' sleep at around the four-and-a-half hour mark. But a shower, strong coffee and fresh t-shirt from the outdoor market (plain black, XL) were all helping the process of making him feel human again.

He thumbed the passcode into his phone and checked the home screen – two texts, one missed call and one voicemail. Not bad (zero was the ideal). He listened to the voicemail first, which turned out to also be the source of the missed call. The voice of a Safer Neighbourhoods PC explained that DS Kev Padmore had sent an e-mail requesting some door-to-doors in Victor Watson's block – to see if anyone knew a next of kin – and had asked him to update Brook. The enquiries were drawing a blank. Fair enough.

Text messages next. The first was from Jonboy, sent just after Brook turned his phone off:

'Number One! I trust you are sinking a few in the early house by now. Think I might have found your dead bloke. Before he was a dead bloke, I mean. Seems to leave The Junction at 9.52pm and enter the churchyard at 10.04pm. All wide angle stuff obviously. Might not be him but matches your description. Off home now. Have asked day shift to download it for you. P.S. Donuts.'

This was better. The footage would all be fairly distant – from the street cameras fixed high up on lampposts – but Brook was confident he would be able to tell if it was Victor. Plus, the timing made sense if he'd been watching the match on which he placed a bet. Yes, this was progress.

The next text was not so positive. From a colleague in Robbery Squad – Brook's regular gig when not working nights. It told him one of his prolific offenders awaiting sentence had received *'two years'*. Brook tossed the phone down. Two years for three violent robberies? Knock off half for the time he would spend out on licence and the little shit was looking at just one Christmas behind bars.

'One Christmas what?' said a Polish-accented waitress looming over Brook's shoulder.

'Hmm?' he replied, looking between the brunette and the plate of pancakes, maple syrup and crispy bacon she was placing in front of him.

'You say *One Christmas*,' she explained.

'Really? Wow. Talking to myself. Bad sign.'

'Polish Christmas is best Christmas,' she said matter-of-factly, before moving away to another table. Brook couldn't help but smile at the deadpan delivery. And the smell of his second breakfast was lifting his spirits still further.

He caught the waitress's eye as she headed back into the kitchen and silently ordered another coffee (Brook was well aware that hard-bitten detectives were supposed to drink black coffee, but since his stomach was usually recovering from some kind of alcoholic excess, he preferred the balancing alkaline effect of a splash of milk).

As usual, he enjoyed the café's vast array of sports photos as he set about the pancakes. Ali, Foreman, Frazier... Maradona, Pelé, Bobby Moore... Jonah Lomu, Francois Pienaar... James Hunt, Niki Lauda. Then there were the teams: Brazil 1970... A.C. Milan 1994. He found himself pausing on the Uruguay World Cup winning side of 1930. The sepia tint and fixed expressions gave the image a 19th century feel, yet Victor Watson would already have been seven years old at the time. It felt as if his long life had spanned two worlds before its unceremonious ending last night.

The pancakes did not enjoy such a long existence.

'It was good?' asked the Polish waitress, removing the empty plate.

'As good as a Polish Christmas.'

'Is not possible,' she replied, poker-faced. Brook wondered if she realised how funny she was.

He picked up his phone – it had been in the doghouse long enough – and double-checked the search result for the last number dialled from Victor Watson's landline. It remained the same:

'Peak View Care Home, Sheffield, S. Yorks'

He tapped on the number that accompanied the care home's website and waited for a receiver to be picked up 150 miles to the north. It was answered on the third ring.

'Ello-Peak-View-ow-can-I-elp?' A female with a broad Yorkshire accent made her greeting sound like a single, high-scoring Scrabble word.

Brook introduced himself and received a similar courtesy in return (he was speaking to 'Debbie') then gave his best summary of the situation: Trying to find the next of kin of a gentleman in his nineties who passed away… He appears to have called this number in the past week… May have been contacting a friend or relative or just making an enquiry… Would you have a moment to help?

A slight pause at the other end made him wonder if he'd been speaking for too long and Debbie had zoned out of the conversation. He needn't have worried.

'Ooh, don't you just love a good mystery?' she said with unexpected enthusiasm. 'I mean, of course you do. Being a detective an' all.'

'I like solving them,' said Brook.

'Ooh, me too,' she agreed.

They established that the name Victor Watson didn't ring any bells – and that there were no residents with that surname – then began approaching the riddle from different angles.

'How many residents do you have there?' asked Brook.

'Forty-two at minute. That's our capacity, like. Though it does go up and down as you can imagine in a place like this. Well, down and then back up I should probably say.'

'And how does it work if someone wants to speak to one of your residents on the phone?'

'Then they'll come through this number first.'

'Any kind of log?'

'Nothing like that, I'm afraid.'

'How about any residents with London links? The guy who died was born in London in 1923. He also served in the Middlesex Regiment in the war.'

'Oh, right. I'm happy to ask around, like. Though, obviously, some aren't quite 'all there', bless 'em. I know we've got a few old soldiers, mind. And I'll see if others on staff know 'owt… Ey, you might have to give me a job after all this.'

'I can't say I would recommend this one.'

'You should try mine for a day.'

They exchanged friendly farewells. There were just two more calls Brook wanted to make before leaving his temporary workplace and its pancake aromas. The first was to the CCTV office to check on the street camera footage Jonboy had identified – Victor Watson's final walk from The Junction pub to the churchyard. A civilian employee explained that the download to disc was on his to-do list behind a backlog of urgent jobs (a *non-suspicious* status didn't exactly help when it came to queue jumping).

The second call was to The Junction itself. Brook learned that the only two people who knew their way around the CCTV system were the manager and a barman called Danny. The manager was off today, but Danny would be starting at 6pm.

And that was it. The last of the phone calls… Peak View Care Home, the CCTV office and The Junction. The outcomes had all left Brook with an empty few hours ahead of him. He began absent-mindedly scrolling through the photos he had taken in Victor's flat and paused at the birth certificate. Those words again: *'The Foundling Hospital'*.

He came out of Photos and typed the name into an internet search. The result told him the establishment had stopped functioning as an orphanage in the 1950s, but he could still visit *'The Foundling Museum'* – next to the site of the original building – which was its successor of sorts. He checked the location… Bloomsbury… Russell Square was the closest tube station. Not far at all. Then he tapped the phone number on the screen. A male voice answered, chirpy and polite.

Once again, Brook introduced himself and gave an overview of the situation. This time he gave all the details from Victor Watson's birth certificate. Would a file exist from 1923? Would it have any family information? Most importantly, would it show if he had any siblings – either biological or in an adoptive family? Brook had definitely never gone back over ninety years to search for a next of kin. The fact he was doing so now showed just how little of himself Victor Watson was giving up.

'Gosh. Well. It goes without saying, I would be more than happy to have a look for you, detective,' said the voice at the other end. It had those hints of academia and friendly awkwardness that often go together. 'Records were indeed kept for every child, though some have been lost over the years as a result of moving or accidents. Still, what remains has just been digitised by some diligent souls so, if anything *is* there, one should be able to find it without too much exertion. Are you nearby by any chance?'

'Can be.'

'Well, if you would like to drop by in, say, forty-five minutes, I'll be more than happy to show you what we have.'

'Perfect. Who should I ask for?'

'If I'm not at reception, just say you're here to see Theodore.'

Great name, thought Brook. He was feeling a bit better about life as he settled the bill. Some wheels had been set in motion at least. The Polish waitress offered a 'Thank-you-bye'; her pretty face and Slavic cheekbones still practising for that poker game.

Chapter 10

The Foundling Museum turned out to be a three-storey building with large sash windows and some ornate stonework giving a touch of grandeur. Brook approached it through Brunswick Square Gardens, one of the historic oases he had always liked about the capital. It wasn't hard to picture strolling socialites of a bygone age discussing society scandal beneath parasols. No doubt secret liaisons between servant girls and their masters had accounted for some of the babies left on the Foundling Hospital's steps (there were probably plenty of foundlings with half-siblings in the House of Lords).

Raucous cheering from the AstroTurf football pitches that now adjoined the square brought an end to the train of thought. The strolling socialites had surely never had to contend with heated five-a-side matches.

Inside, a redhead at reception greeted the detective with a smile.

'Hi. I'm here to see Theodore. The name's Brook.'

'Ah, yes. He did mention you,' came the reply. 'I think he's still fetching that information you asked for, but feel free to have a look at the permanent display and I'll send him your way.'

Brook followed her directions to a series of exhibits telling the story of the Foundling Hospital from its creation in 1739 for *'the education and maintenance of exposed and deserted young children.'* One glass cabinet in particular caught his eye – a mix of buttons, brooches and assorted trinkets left with abandoned children as an identifier…

'Each child accepted by the hospital was given a new name; if a relative later claimed a child, the tokens helped prove the claim was genuine'.

He found himself staring at the items, each one a sad little tale that would never be known. The entirety of the end wall was covered in names given to the new arrivals. They ranged from the commonplace (John Gower), to the eccentric (Nancy Lovely) and the frankly criminal (Norman Conquest and Julius Caesar).

'Sorry to have kept you waiting.'

Brook recognised the voice from their phone conversation. He turned to see a friendly-looking man in his sixties with a shock of white hair and an open-collared floral shirt. It all reminded him of a British version of Doc from *Back To The Future*. Maybe he could jump in the DeLorean and sort out a new name for poor Norman Conquest.

'Theodore?' enquired Brook, extending a hand.

'Indeed. I've been neglecting you, I'm afraid,' said Theodore, shaking it.

'Not at all. I've been having a look around. Some interesting names.'

'Ah yes. As if the poor mites didn't have a hard enough start in life. So, did you like the displays?' He waved an arm towards everything Brook had walked past to that point.

'Very good,' said Brook, feeling a little bad that Theodore's enthusiastic smile dipped a bit at his generic answer. He tried to recover. 'Did I read the original building was where those AstroTurf football pitches are now?'

'Quite right,' confirmed Theodore, smile restored. 'Completed in 1752, sadly demolished in 1926. After that, the children were moved to a nunnery in Surrey and then to a new site out in Hertfordshire in 1935. It was thought the country air would be good for their little lungs. All that remains of the original building is the entrance gates, but if you go back through Brunswick Square and bear left you'll bump into them. I always find it amazing to think what they've seen.'

'I'll make sure I do that.'

Theodore nodded his approval. For a moment, the conversation dried up. Brook saw his host was carrying a few crisp sheets of A4 paper.

'Is that the–'

'Goodness, yes, sorry. Completely forgot the purpose of your visit for a moment there.' He gave a little chuckle and raised himself on the balls of his feet.

'Thanks for helping me with this,' said Brook, though he imagined Theodore had probably rather enjoyed the task.

'Actually, I'm the one who should be thanking *you*,' replied the older man. 'You seem to have stumbled across one of the most fascinating cases I've seen for a long time.'

Brook wasn't sure if that was good news or bad news.

'Maybe we should sit down,' suggested Theodore, 'and all will be revealed.'

He made the last remark with a playful hint of drama. Brook wondered what it must be like to be that happy at work. He followed Theodore past some TV screens showing old Foundlings talking of their memories and into a grand room with several immense oil paintings.

'Please,' said Theodore, inviting Brook to sit on one of the chairs around the edge. He took a seat next to the detective and held Victor Watson's file between them – the dense cursive writing reminded Brook of the birth certificate and POW record he'd been looking at earlier.

'Victor Watson,' began Brook's host, jabbing a finger onto the text. 'Remarkable.'

'In what way?'

'Well, by 1923 things had moved on a great deal with the way babies were accepted into this place. Rather than the earlier practice of little bundles being left on the steps, a mother had to make a formal application, be interviewed, provide references and be shown to be of good character. Then arrangements were made for the handover of the child. Plenty of applications were rejected, in fact. It wasn't the open door policy of the early days.'

'Okay,' said Brook. He was waiting for a *but…*

'But Victor's mother appears to have paid no heed to that whatsoever. It's really quite astounding that the child should have been accepted at all.'

'So why was he?'

'Well…' Theodore's finger traced some of the writing to remind himself of the details. 'He was left on the steps of the Foundling Hospital on the morning of Saturday, 28th April 1923 – the date you told me was on the birth certificate.'

Brook thought that might explain the asterisk. An official date of birth rather than an actual one. His host continued…

'It just happened to be the day of the first ever FA Cup Final played at Wembley Stadium. Bolton Wanderers versus West Ham United.'

'Interesting. Why would that change anything?'

'Good question,' said Theodore, raising an index finger then returning it to the page. He was in his element. 'It would appear the little fellow was wrapped in a West Ham scarf amongst other things. Could have been Aston Villa, I suppose, but a bit far perhaps. In any case, the staff took it to be West Ham and looked upon him as something of a curiosity, you see – like finding a little mascot on their doorstep on Cup Final day. They seem to have bypassed the new admission process and even named him after West Ham's star striker – Vic Watson.'

'Two hundred and ninety-eight league goals,' said Brook.

'I… Goodness, that's very impressive knowledge… I can see that young Victor weighed six pounds when he arrived here and was estimated to be two weeks old.' His finger traced some more text. 'No additional information could be obtained from the mother who was seen running away. And that's about it for his arrival. He moved with the Foundling Hospital when it went to Surrey, and again when it went to Hertfordshire. Left in 1939 aged sixteen. You can see the final entry here…'

He pointed to a note written in a different hand and lighter ink:

'Mdx Reg?'

'Middlesex Regiment,' said Brook. 'Like on his POW record.'

'Indeed. So that's it. No mother ever came back. He was never adopted out, no mention of any siblings. Probably not much use to you, I'm afraid. Even if such an unusual case *is* rather exciting for an oddball like me.'

Brook shrugged. 'It was always a long shot. Do you think I could have a copy of all that for the Coroner anyway? It can't hurt.'

'Of course. I'll meet you in reception with it.'

The pair stood up and Theodore made his way to the exit.

'Just before you do that,' said Brook, 'how about those trinkets that some of the babies were left with? Like in your cabinet through there. Did he have anything like that when he arrived?'

'I rather doubt it,' said Theodore. 'That practice had died out far earlier.'

Nevertheless, he held the pages close enough to read and delved back into the impenetrable writing. After a few moments, he gave a loud 'Ha!' and looked up.

'I can't believe I missed it. Gosh, this admission really was a throwback.'

'He had something?'

'He did indeed. And it might explain why they chose a player named Victor to name him after. It seems the baby was left with a keepsake bearing the motto *'Ad Victoriam'*. That would mean *To Victory* in Latin.'

'What type of keepsake was it?'

'It's described as a gold-coloured medal.'

'Like a big gold coin?'

'Yes, if you like. Like a big gold coin.'

Brook's pulse went up a notch. He could hear the Lumberjack's voice in his head.

'Would he have kept it when he left?' he asked.

'It's such an unusual case. I can only say it's possible.'

The corners of Theodore's smile dipped once again as he struggled to make sense of the distant look in the detective's eyes.

'Is there a problem?' he asked.

'I need to find Judas Iscariot,' said Brook.

Theodore's smile returned as if he had just heard the most normal thing in the world.

'Judas… Iscariot…' he repeated, walking past Brook and squinting at the far wall with all the outrageous names… 'Now, whereabouts is he?'

Chapter 11

Sunday, 15th April 1945
Stalag IV-B, Mühlberg, Germany

Victor Watson stood as close to the outside world as he dared and stared out through wire mesh at the surrounding fields and distant line of trees. The grey sky and flat landscape were each competing to be more featureless than the other. Escape was not an option. At least not by conventional means. The single wire in front of his shins was still twenty yards from the barbed wire-covered perimeter fence. One step over it and the sentry in the nearest watchtower would put a bullet in him before he even reached the impenetrable main barrier. He had seen it happen twice before, though neither could exactly be called an escape attempt.

The first poor fellow had simply cracked. A young Ulsterman. He went charging across the little 'no man's land' and, already full of bullets, flung himself into the tangle of razor wire at the foot of the main fence. The *coup de grâce* had been horribly long in coming – the guards wanting to make sure his helpless cries were heard by as many of the inmates as possible.

The second transgressor was a Polish chap. Having not eaten for days, he put one foot over the wire to try and reach a wild strawberry that was growing in the mud. The end result was the same. He died with the tiny fruit in his hand and a bullet in his head. This was Victor's world. It had been for the past one year, two months and four days. Some poor sods had been here three or four times as long.

He looked up at the sentry in the nearest watchtower and raised a hand of greeting. The German stared back, motionless. Then Victor tilted his raised hand forward and tapped an imaginary watch on the back of his wrist. Not long now, Fritz, old chap. The end of the war was coming and they both knew it.

Behind Victor a heaving throng of his fellow prisoners was facing the other way, absorbed in a football 'international' between POWs from Wales and Scotland. The dirt pitch was set back from the rows of overcrowded huts that formed Main Street in this ramshackle city of misery. Most prisoners of other nationalities had picked a side to support, though a number of Englishmen preferred to pour scorn on both teams. A Frenchman was refereeing while a Dane and Ukrainian performed linesman duties with flags made from sacking.

The match itself was not high on skill, but nobody watching seemed to mind. If they focused on the general ebb and flow of play, and lost themselves in the cheers, jeers and cigarette smoke, then – just for a moment – they were back at the football grounds of their youth with fathers, brothers and uncles. What they would give for a half-time pie and Bovril now. The simple pleasures of free men.

One of the spectators in the back row glanced over his shoulder and saw Victor tapping his imaginary watch. He peeled away from the crowd.

'Careful, Vic! You'll get your other bleedin' ear shot off!'

Victor ended his Nazi-baiting charades and turned to see a familiar face approaching. Harry Wilson – his 'mucker'. The term had a semi-official meaning in a prisoner of war camp. It was the person you looked out for and who, in turn, looked out for you. In its more general sense of mates or pals, Victor Watson and Harry Wilson had been muckers since joining the same regiment on the same day in 1940, with surnames that ensured they were paired together throughout their training. They were even captured in Italy on the same day. Now they counted the days to freedom together.

'As long as he makes the ears match,' said Victor. 'I wouldn't want to look silly now, would I?' He returned to staring out over the flat, hopeless landscape while his friend joined him.

'Not gonna do a runner, are yer?' asked Harry in his broad Cockney. Born within a stone's throw of the Boleyn Ground, he was always destined to be an avid West Ham fan. It was why turning up at Mill Hill Barracks at the same moment as someone bearing the name of his childhood hero had struck him as highly serendipitous (or *'What are the bleedin' chances?'* as he put it).

'No danger of me doing a runner, old chap,' replied Victor. 'Even if you removed all these fences and the guards had sponge rifles. Spot of unfinished business for me in this God-awful place.'

Unlike Harry, there had been no overriding influence on the young Victor's accent during his formative years at the Foundling Hospital. Largely isolated from life beyond the institution's walls – whether in Bloomsbury, Surrey or Hertfordshire – the key moment for Victor's accent had been the day he discovered he could sneak out to The Rex picture house on Berkhamsted High Street and return to his dormitory without being missed.

The 1930s movies of his adolescence had nourished previously neglected parts of his mind. They filled his head with a thrilling universe of idealised father figures, derring-do and escapism. It was only natural that he should start taking on the vocal traits of his new screen friends. The shiny citizens of his brave new world. If the ensuing voice had once seemed a little 'old' for him, the war had taken care of that. No-one in peacetime would have placed Victor and Harry at a few days either side of twenty-two.

'You really wouldn't go? Even if there was bugger all stopping you?' asked Harry, already aware of the reason why. 'All because Fritz has got your little trinket that says *Sad Victor* on it?'

'*Ad Victoriam*,' replied Victor, well-accustomed to the friendly teasing.

'You're a strange one, Vic. I'll give you that. Who else manages to lose 'arf a finger and 'arf an ear to one bleedin' bullet?'

Old jokes re-told had a unifying familiarity in prisoner of war camps. It also allowed both men to deal with an unpleasant memory by wrapping it in the comfort blanket of humour…

The Battle of Anzio. Early '44. The second week of attritional stalemate. Victor scrambling to treat the wounded Harry and their pal, Sidney, while pinned down by enemy fire. Vic in the process of replacing his dislodged tin helmet, one-handed, when the magic bullet removed helmet, ear and finger in one '*zip*'. When his humour was at its darkest, Harry liked to say that at least Sid had died laughing at Victor's sudden confusion *('I'm sure I had an 'elmet round 'ere somewhere… And a finger… AND a fuckin' ear!')*.

Harry's own injuries had healed pretty well, leaving a thick mop of dark hair and a general dishevelment as his most notable features. Victor, by contrast, had learned all about maintaining appearances on basic resources at the Foundling Hospital. His hair was always combed and his uniform as presentable as possible. He was also reminded daily – by the sight of less fortunate prisoners – that he couldn't be too upset about the dent to his good looks. Apart from the ear and the finger, he didn't have a scratch on him.

'Anyway, you know that medal wouldn't fetch two bob down 'oxton Market,' said Harry, giving his mate an elbow in the ribs. That was an old one too, but Victor still smiled.

Beneath the individual shouts and catcalls of the crowd, both men became aware of a secondary level of noise. A murmur among the back row of spectators on their side of the pitch. The two pals turned to see the most brutal of all their Nazi captors walking down the rear of the crowd.

Blondie.

At least, that was the name he was known by.

A non-commissioned officer. And a psychopath.

Those he had already passed turned their heads to see what he was up to. A few among those he was yet to reach glanced back down the line, curious at the murmur, then quickly reverted to 'eyes front' and shuffled their heels further in.

Whereas some of the older guards – the weary veterans of the Great War who just wanted a quiet life – were referred to with the adjective 'German', Blondie was a proper 'Nazi'. A believer right to the end. Even his barrel chest and rosy cheeks seemed to mock the very physical form of the skinny inmates.

He had once delighted in the bloodlust of kicking to death some poor Russian who dived too near his feet, clawing up a splash of thin soup spilled in the mud. The talk in the huts was that Blondie had got a sexual thrill out of it. The sick Kraut bastard. Depending on who you believed, he had killed between five and seven prisoners and maimed ten times that number with fists, boots and pickaxe handles…

His eyes settled upon Victor and Harry. Away from the crowd. Two gazelles detached from the herd. He made his way over to them. Hands behind his back. Barrel chest thrust out. Slow, strutting strides. A murderous, 6-foot, Aryan peacock.

'Was ist ihr los?'… *What's going on?*

With the help of the more talkative guards, and popular lessons given by a Canadian prisoner – a schoolteacher before the war – Victor had picked up far more German than Harry. He took it upon himself to speak for both of them.

'Reden nur'… *Just talking.*

'Und?'… *And?*

'Und nichts'… *And nothing.*

Blondie took his time looking the Englishmen up and down with his icy blue, master race eyes beneath his light blond, master race hair. Victor and Harry were both now aware that the rearmost rows of the crowd had all turned to silently watch the encounter. The only football-related noise now came from the other three sides of the pitch.

The Nazi's penetrating gaze eventually came to rest on Victor's disfigured ear. He leaned closer to examine it like a doctor. Victor looked straight ahead, into the eyes of several hundred fellow prisoners now looking his way, transfixed. Blondie raised his right hand and began flicking the remainder of the ear. Two, three, four times. Victor blinked once, slowly, only opening his eyes after the final hard flick.

Blondie lowered his hand. He was bored by that now. Instead, he inhaled to the full capacity of his massive lungs and leaned in so his big lips were within half an inch of the ear. Then he roared with every ounce of his considerable vocal strength.

'KANNST DU MICH HÖREN?'... *Can you hear me?*

Spittle covered the side of Victor's head. Blondie dissolved into fits of laughter at his own joke, his big chest heaving and his red cheeks turning even redder. It took a full twenty seconds for him to compose himself and straighten up from his doubled over position. When he did, his contortions of hilarity had turned him 180 degrees and he found himself facing row after row of silent, staring prisoners.

'Was?' said Blondie, calmly... *What?*

He tried to look as many in the eye as he could. A few turned back to the football. Others carried on staring.

'WAS?' he bellowed at the remaining eyes with his caveman lungs, throwing his arms out to the side in challenge. The remaining observers began turning back. The show was over. Victor began to think perhaps he and Harry had got through it.

He was particularly relieved Harry hadn't done anything silly. If his mucker had one fault, it was that he'd spent over half his camp time in the cooler for 'insubordination'. It began in their first week, when a St George Legionnaire had been sent in to try to recruit other defectors. Harry had thrown a full latrine bucket over the English Nazi with a shout of 'De faeces are defecting'. Both were swiftly hauled out of camp. Albeit at arm's length.

Victor's silent gratitude that Harry hadn't tried anything silly did not last long. The chance to play to such a large audience was simply too much to resist. As the final one or two brave and curious souls turned their attention back to the football, Harry took a deep breath and threw himself to the ground behind Blondie. The match seemed to hit a lull at just the right moment. Pushing his mimic skills and knowledge of German to the limit, he shouted:

'Wales scheisse! Schottland scheisse! Deutschland Meister!'

Wales shit! Scotland shit! Germany champions!

It wasn't exactly sophisticated satire, but it did the job. The crowd erupted, turning to face the big Nazi, half of them hurling insults at him – the other half realising the role of the skinny Cockney and responding with laughter and pointing. The anonymity provided by a wall of noise emboldened the prisoners to give full vent to their feelings about Blondie's parentage and the exact nature of his relationship with Hitler and other animals.

The colour rose higher in Blondie's cheeks and his massive chest began heaving once again – now through rage rather than laughter. He tried, impossibly, to stare down every one of his hecklers. He wanted to kill them all and enjoy every second of it. In the end, he realised he would have to settle for just one kill…

Turning round, he bent at the waist and thrust a hand down towards his ventriloquist. The plunging fingers grabbed a fistful of Harry's shirt and hoisted him into the air – a human version of the mechanical pincer grabbing a cuddly toy. The noise level from the crowd went up another notch while play on the pitch ground to a halt. Spectators on other sides were now rushing round to find better vantage points. Then the players and officials joined the stampede.

As soon as Harry's feet were back in contact with the ground, Blondie spun him round to face 'no man's land' and grabbed a fresh handful of shirt between his shoulder blades.

The weight loss suffered by every prisoner meant there was plenty of material to get hold of. The Nazi was in complete control – six inches taller and twice as heavy as his prey. He took a step towards the low wire and the death zone beyond it, forcing Harry ahead of him. A fresh roar went up from the crowd. Blondie was using Harry to play a land-based version of walk the plank.

The nearest watchtower guard – so motionless in the face of Victor's taunting moments earlier – was now fully engaged, beginning to raise his rifle. He needed no reminding of his orders. Anyone stepping over the wire was to be shot. There was nothing in the small print about whether or not they were forced over.

Victor lunged in and grabbed hold of Harry's collar, trying to pull him back towards safety. He may have been a few inches taller than his friend, but he was similarly weakened by prison life. Blondie smashed him out of the way with his free hand then drew his service revolver and pointed it at him on the ground.

The sheer weight of numbers joining the crowd meant those at the front were being forced closer to the action. The gap had closed from twenty yards to six or seven, the mob now numbering several thousand. Every watchtower guard had their weapons trained on the front row. A mixture of rifles and fixed machine guns. Fingers on triggers.

Blondie waved his own revolver back and forth along the line in a 'keep back' motion. He looked like a lion defending his kill from hyenas. Then he shoved Harry another step forward. The wire was against his shins now. The nearest watchtower guard closed one eye – he had him perfectly lined up.

'Murderer!'... 'Hun bastard!'... 'You'll bloody hang for this!'... The individual shouts merged into one pulsating mass of hatred.

The wire began to strain against Harry's shins, his centre of gravity moving further and further over it. He was on the very tips of his boots now, ankle tendons straining to keep toes on the ground, physics making him desperate to take a little step. Blondie was savouring every moment of having the Englishman's life in his hand – it was the ultimate God-like power. But it would only be truly God-like if it ended in the *taketh away* bit. He gave Harry a final shove.

The right boot came off the ground first, passing over the top of the wire. As it neared its fatal appointment with the ground on the other side, Harry felt a despairing tug on his shoulder – Victor. It yanked him back and spun him at the same time. The new impetus was not quite enough to bring him upright, but the spin might yet save him as he tried to swing his right leg back to safety, like the arm of an unstable crane.

Victor's desperate lunge to save his mate earned him a backhanded bludgeon from Blondie that sent him face first into the ground. With the last few joules of rotational energy, Harry managed to get his right leg back over the wire, then found himself bent forward at the waist, windmilling both arms in a desperate attempt to stop himself toppling forward. The fourth or fifth whirl of arms brought him vertical, finally restoring his balance.

Amid the profanities being hurled at Blondie were simpler, instinctive reactions – the audible gasps of circus spectators who had just witnessed a death-defying trapeze act. Even Blondie thought it was good sport to see a life hanging so literally in the balance. But every show needed a grand finale… As soon as Harry was upright, he felt himself being lifted by the waistband.

Blondie was simply going to throw the English wretch over the wire.

Felled and stunned, Victor could only look back at the fate of his mucker and try to make his voice heard above the cacophony behind him.

'Machen Sie es nicht!'... *Don't do it!*

He reverted to English.

'For God's sake, man!'

As Blondie completed his backswing before launching Harry, a new voice cut through the chaos, away to Victor's left.

'SCHMIDT!'

The big Nazi paused and looked towards its source. Victor and the crowd did the same. Harry, suspended in the air, kept his eyes screwed shut. A tall German officer in crisp grey uniform was striding along the narrow strip that still existed between the mob and the wire. He was flanked by half a dozen uniformed underlings. The few prisoners in the crowd who had seen him before muttered his name.

'Oberst Lührsen'... *Colonel Lührsen*... The head of the camp. Even without a detailed knowledge of German army insignia, his status was self-evident thanks to the usual rule (the more ornate the epaulettes and the more dramatic the hat, the higher the rank). And Oberst Lührsen was *the* big cheese around here.

'Das ist genug, Schmidt.'... *That's enough, Schmidt.*

At least they all knew Blondie's real name now.

With visible disappointment at being denied another kill, the psychotic polar bear of a man dropped Harry flat on his face (having his eyes screwed shut didn't work in his favour as the unseen ground slammed into his nose). Three of the underlings ran over and roughly dragged him to his feet –

dazed and with blood trickling from a nostril – before hauling him away past Oberst Lührsen and towards the main gates.

'What about Blondie?' came a shout from the crowd followed by more on a similar theme. 'Get the bastard in bloody shackles!'... 'Court martial the ape!'

No underlings approached him. Like a sulking child, Blondie trudged past Oberst Lührsen with a half-hearted salute and set off back towards his quarters, the crowd whistling and jeering him on his way. His blood was still up and now he had a seething sense of injustice. Maybe he would bump into a Russian on the way.

Victor was still sprawled in the dirt, heart racing, cheek and forehead throbbing from their meeting with Blondie's mighty paw. He rolled onto his back, closed his eyes and waited for mind and body to find some calm. The thin chain with his prison dog tags was lying across his face. He was too exhausted to move it.

'Du auch'... *You too.*

He allowed his head to roll in the direction of Oberst Lührsen's voice and let his eyes fall open. Two more underlings were running his way. Victor offered no resistance as they pulled him to his feet, the crowd again giving their opinion at seeing another victim detained while Blondie went on his way. The dazed prisoner was roughly ushered across the short distance to the Colonel before being presented to him.

'Ich habe nichts gemacht,' said Victor... *I haven't done anything.*

'Es hat nichts damit zu tun. Es geht um etwas anderes'
... *It has nothing to do with that. It's something else.*

Chapter 12

Friday, 22nd April 2016
Holloway Road, North London

Brook could feel a sheen of sweat on his brow by the time he neared St Mary Magdalene Church. The natural place to start looking for the Lumberjack, aka Judas Iscariot, was where he had last seen him – the same place Victor Watson had died. The detective stepped off Holloway Road and into the now familiar grounds, scanning for a distinctive red-and-black checked jacket as he went. He doubted the homeless Lumberjack would have selected a different ensemble for today (if nothing else, it would spoil the new name that Brook now seemed to be assigning to him).

The churchyard had a different feel this time. Restored. Normalised. Like a car when a dent is beaten out. The dent may only be a tiny area of the vehicle, but it still defines the whole of it to the observer. The same was true of a dead guy in a churchyard.

Brook stood in the same spot as his earlier visits and turned full circle. A couple of dog walkers and a mum with a pushchair were the only other people in the grounds. Then he tried casting his mind back to the strange events of that morning – Kev, Sandy Sanderson, Baz or Daz and that weird DS from Homicide. He soon realised he was looking at the bushes through which the Lumberjack had stumbled to give Sandy 'the fright of her life'. There was something he wanted to check about the bench he had been on.

Approaching it from the path side – rather than using the Lumberjack's more direct route through the bushes – Brook could see the remnants of free newspapers and magazines strewn across the wooden slats of the seat. He crouched to try and recreate the view the Lumberjack would have had while lying here… Even in daylight, it didn't amount to much.

The wrought iron swirls of the back of the bench, the weave of twigs and foliage behind – it was just too much of an obstruction. Brook stood back up. Maybe Kev had been right about this guy being full of shit. But that detail he had mentioned about someone stealing Victor's 'big gold coin'. Could it be coincidence? Maybe. Though Brook's natural suspicion of coincidences hadn't changed.

He looked again at the tomb, barely fifteen feet away, then down at the bench. And, this time, beneath the bench. The ground was covered with bark chippings. He forced himself into another crouch and pressed a flat palm onto them. Dry, a little spongy, with a firmer base of compacted earth beneath. Then he stared at the newspapers on the bench, still showing the crumpled signs of drying out from an earlier soaking.

He silently berated himself for taking so long to realise it. The Lumberjack hadn't been lying on the bench at all. He had been *under* it – the bark chippings his mattress, the newspapers and magazines his flimsy roof against any showers in the night.

The detective got down on his hands and knees and observed the tomb from the new angle. The dense foliage of the bushes didn't reach all the way down to the ground. It stopped about ten inches shy. The only obstacles now were the sporadic… what were they? Trunks? Legs? Do bushes have legs? Brook's botanical vocabulary was letting him down. More importantly, however, the line of sight to the tomb was clearer. *Much* clearer. Yes, if the Lumberjack had been lying beneath this bench when Victor Watson met his demise, he may have had an excellent view.

Before he stood up, something else caught Brook's eye. A few drops of something that looked like blood. He wasn't sure how it fitted into the grand scheme of things (had the Lumberjack already had that head wound when he was lying here?). Brook took two photos on his phone – one of the tomb from the new vantage point and one of the blood-like substance. Then he clicked himself upright.

'Stems,' he said to himself. 'They're called stems, you idiot.'

One more quick scan of the grounds. No Lumberjack. He looked at his watch – 5.55pm. Time to get to The Junction and speak to Danny about their CCTV.

Brook guessed the barman in front of him was about a dozen years his junior – early to mid-20s. Black jeans, black polo shirt and that tousled, blond, beach look that left him in no doubt he was about to hear an Australian accent.

'Danny?' said Brook, extending a hand.

'That's right, mate,' came the reply. There it was.

'DC Brook Deelman,' said the detective, flipping open his warrant card. 'I hear you're the man to talk to about CCTV.'

'I'll definitely see what I can do. I take it you're a rugby man with an accent like that?'

Brook smiled at the way they had both instantly profiled each other.

'Armchair fan these days,' he replied.

'Well, plenty of comfy chairs and cold beer here when there's an international on. Normally a decent atmosphere too.'

'Sounds like heaven,' said Brook, and meant it.

'Only when the Wallabies win,' smiled Danny.

Common ground established, they were soon crammed into a narrow office marked 'Staff Only' – scribbled rosters and Polaroid party photos pinned to the wall around an old computer monitor. A few clicks of the mouse brought up last night's footage from the camera above the main entrance. As the images rewound in the search for Victor, a steady stream of customers began walking backwards into the pub with jerky double-speed movements. The clock rolled back from 21:55 towards 21:52 – the time Jonboy had given for Victor leaving the pub and appearing on the nearest street camera.

'Can I ask who we're looking for?' enquired Danny, as the reverse marching drill continued.

'Old guy with a walking stick. Tweed suit.'

'Seriously?'

'Yep. Do you know him?'

'I think so. If it's who I think it is.'

The clock retreated past 21:52 and into the 21:51 range. At 21:51:37, Victor Watson appeared on the screen, seeming to quick march back into the pub while tapping his stick on the ground.

'There!' said Brook, pointing.

Danny clicked Play and Victor's speed and direction reverted to normal. He made his way steadily towards the main doors, leaning slightly on his stick with each step. The barman paused the footage as Victor passed beneath the camera.

'This guy?' he asked, making no attempt to hide his surprise.

'That's him,' said Brook.

'He's your suspect?'

'Not a suspect,' said Brook. 'He was found dead.'

Danny's eyes settled back on the screen.

'You're kidding me.'

'I take it you remember him then.'

'Yeah, how could you forget that neck scar? Even spoke to him. How'd he die?'

'I'm not entirely sure yet,' replied Brook, choosing his words carefully. 'Would you mind if I took a statement before we do anything else? Better if it's your own recollection rather than influenced by CCTV.'

'Course, mate… So do you think he was bumped off?'

Brook absorbed the question while smoothing out some statement forms from a jacket pocket.

'It's not being treated as suspicious,' he said, keeping his eyes down. It seemed the easiest way to put it. Even if it did sound a little suspicious.

As it turned out, Brook was impressed by the younger man's power of recall. He described in some detail the old guy's physical appearance, adding that he hadn't appeared drunk, that he wasn't aware of him smelling of whisky, and that, as far as he could tell, he had arrived and left on his own. Brook scribbled it all down in note form to write up neatly at the end. But it was the conversation between the two that interested him most.

'So, I made some kind of comment about how he was really getting through the beers and he goes: 'It's my birthday'. So I say: 'That's great. How old are you?' and he holds out his fingers – you know he only has half a pinky on his left hand, right? And he goes: 'I lost count'.'

Brook caught up with his notes then wrote down two dates… *28th April* and *21st April*. The first was the date on Victor's birth certificate – the day he was left at the Foundling Hospital in 1923. The second was the date on which Victor had told Danny it was his birthday. Fair enough. If he didn't know the exact date he was born then maybe he had picked one. It was within a reasonable margin.

What's more, it might explain the old report that had led them to Victor's home address – the drunken singing shortly before midnight on 21st April 2005. A few too many birthday tipples, perhaps.

'Sorry,' said Brook, realising he had been staring at the dates while Danny sat in silence. 'Carry on.'

'So I asked him how he lost his little finger and he goes 'Mousetrap'. So, obviously, I didn't know if he was kidding. Then he starts laughing. I mean, I still didn't know if he was kidding. Anyway, the crowd at the bar was getting pretty big at this point and my manager starts getting on my case for chatting so much. So I just say to the old guy something like 'I hope you got lots of birthday cards'.'

'And did he say anything to that?'

'Yeah, he said he didn't like cards. I mean, I guess you might not when you get to… Am I allowed to ask how old he was?'

'Early nineties,' said Brook.

'Jeez… Anyway, then he headed back to his table with his pint and that was the last time I spoke to him. Didn't really notice him again until he was leaving, a few minutes after the game.'

'How about his accent?' asked Brook.

'I guess all I could say is it was kinda posh-sounding. English but… sort of old-fashioned? I remember thinking it sounded like actors in old movies.'

Brook's eyes stayed down for a little longer as his notes caught up with the conversation.

'Perfect,' he said, leaning back. 'This will take about twenty minutes for me to write up. Would you mind if I use this office?'

'No, of course not, mate. Go for it.'

The detective was glad to be on his own again. He had a lot to consider. Like how someone who was 'kinda posh' ended up looking like a prizefighter. Quick-witted enough to make jokes about his finger, excellent at handling his drink, pretty steady on his feet… Wow, they had been so far off the mark with the idea of a shambolic, whisky-soaked drunk. Was that bottle of Tesco Value whisky beneath Victor's hand even his? And if the Lumberjack had been right about the 'big gold coin' then what about that other, even stranger, comment he had made – that it was the old man who had the knife?

What the hell was that all about?

Chapter 13

A panic attack? Doctor recommends complete rest? No visitors? This wasn't ideal. Not ideal at all. Why would a care home resident in his nineties be having a panic attack? Every day must be pretty much the same as the last, right?

He recalled the words...

'Sorry, love. Doctor's orders. 'Ee can't do 'owt but rest fer't time being.'

Debbie, her name was. Jesus, he needed a fucking interpreter to understand these people.

No, this could only mean one thing. The first target had spotted his surveillance and got a message to the second, who knew what was coming and was freaking out about it. And why wouldn't he? The end was nigh. Very fucking nigh.

Not for the first time, he was cross with himself. It was bad enough that the first target had nearly pulled a knife on him. Now it felt like he had been outwitted all over again. A landline call, he imagined, since the first target didn't seem to own a mobile phone. There was no denying it now – he had underestimated an opponent. Something he swore he would never do.

Look, it was a rush job from the start, he told himself. He would have taken more time and done it better had his contact in the police not been retiring in a few days. The contact was his safety net. His 'Get Out of Jail Free' card if things went wrong. He always felt better operating in the UK with him there. Not that he would tell him that. He preferred to keep the balance of power between them a little more nuanced. As was only natural, when one man's power was official and the other's came from a willingness to take lives in the shadows.

Yet again, he tried to emphasise the positive. So… at least things were well set for tomorrow. Once the second target's ridiculous panic attack was out of the way. And his cover story to the care home seemed to have been a success.

'I'm the grandson of one of his old army friends… I'd love to meet him and discuss some of the stories my late grandad used to talk about…'.

The reply suggested that a meeting would be suitably facilitated.

'Ooh, that would right cheer 'im up after all this funny panic business today.'

Only one other thing bothered him as he sat in the hire car and flicked through his phone for a hotel in which to spend the night. The words that 'Debbie' had uttered next.

'Actually, you might be able to 'elp me since you mentioned army. D'you know if he were ever in Middlesex Regiment by any chance?'

He had feigned ignorance. But that question… Why the sudden desire to find out if the second target had served in the Middlesex Regiment? Someone had been asking questions. Someone was 'getting involved'. He didn't know who, and he didn't like that.

He finished the tedious business of booking a room, then called his contact in the police. So who was it? Who was snooping around? 'The idiot' or 'the drunk'? He waited for the return call, drumming his fingers on the steering wheel, then answered on the first buzz... Ah, it was the drunk.

'What's his name?'

'You don't need to know his name.'

'I didn't say I need to know it. I want to know it.'

'Look, he's a serving police officer. You can't just–'

'Blah, blah, blah. What's his name?'

'Okay… it's Brook Deelman.'

'What kind of a stupid name is that?'

Chapter 14

In the end it was Danny who came looking for Brook. A pile of four or five neatly handwritten statement pages now lay on the desk. The detective was glued to the computer monitor. He looked at his watch as Danny came in.

'Shit. Sorry. Completely lost track of time.'

'No worries. Find anything interesting?'

'Not sure.'

The barman pulled up a chair while Brook used the on-screen controls to select *Camera 7* – a behind-the-bar view, looking out at the waiting customers.

'What can you tell me about this guy?' he asked.

Danny leaned in a bit closer. He was looking at a man in his mid-40s, dark brown hair cut short and sensible, a solid jaw and muscular neck beneath a navy blue sports jacket. The last man Victor Watson ever saw.

'Blimey, not much. Served him once, I think.'

'Can you remember his accent?'

'Nothing specific. I guess we only said a few words. If you had to push me I'd say he was English-speaking, but not actually British. What's the deal with this guy anyway?'

Brook had been asking himself the same thing. The answer, in terms of hard evidence, was 'not much'. The man on the screen had entered shortly after Victor and taken a position slightly behind him (but so had a few others), he had sent some glances Victor's way (a fairly common occurrence thanks to his scars), and he didn't seem overly concerned by the action on the big screens (not that this proved anything). At a push, Brook would say he adjusted his position slightly when people stood between him and Victor. He had also left just after him, albeit along with plenty of others.

'Just a feeling, I suppose,' said Brook. It seemed a fair summary.

He looked a little closer. There was just something of *the other* about him. Was it his comportment? His clothes, maybe? This 'smart casual' get-up that made him look like he should be on a yacht. He just wasn't entirely in his comfort zone. Someone in a strange place or a foreign country. A tourist, perhaps.

He let the image play. A member of staff that Brook was yet to meet placed a drink down on the bar and took payment from the Tourist.

'That's Craig, the manager,' said Danny, pre-empting Brook's question.

As Craig moved away, the drink was revealed as a bottle with a black and yellow label.

'What's that beer he's drinking?' asked Brook.

'Well, I suppose you could call it beer. It's one of those non-alcoholic ones.'

'You sell many of those?'

'Not that particular one. The other type sells a few – the Becks Blue. But this one? I'm not sure why we stock it, to be honest.'

'Did he have the same when you served him?'

'Yeah, the same. If I had to guess I'd say that Craig's served him first and the bloke's just asked for a non-alcoholic beer, so he's flogged him the ones that don't sell.'

Brook's mind was already adding the non-alcoholic beer to the list of tiny details that aroused his suspicion. The implication was obvious. At least if you chose to see it that way. A man with a task to complete. A need to stay sharp and focused.

'How many of those do you think you sold last night?'

'When I re-stocked the fridge there were only four to replace.'

'And you think he had..?'

'Three, but the footage would show you for definite.'

'Where do bottles go once they're collected?'

'First into a bottle bin at the end of the bar. Then that gets emptied into a big wheelie bin of bottles out the back when it's full.'

'And how often does that get collected?'

'Once a week. Next time is tomorrow morning.'

Brook fell silent for a moment and rubbed his chin through the heavy, night shift stubble. He was thinking how that wheelie bin must be a forensic nightmare. All the bottles pushed together, dripping dregs over each other, smearing fingerprints and mixing DNA.

'You want to look at those bottles for prints or something, don't you?' asked Danny.

Brook smiled. His comment about it not being treated as suspicious had clearly worn thin. Yes, he was curious to find out who the Tourist was. But his curiosity was no match for the protocols he would have to overcome to get those bottles submitted to the lab. Without any other evidence against this guy, forensic tests would never be authorised.

'Okay, listen,' said Brook. 'I know the bar must be filling up, but is there any chance you could burn this footage onto a disc for me while I make a quick call? And maybe just have a check of that statement and whack a signature at the bottom of each page if you're happy.'

'No worries,' said Danny, putting a blank disc into the computer and whirring through some more key tapping and mouse clicking. 'The police can compensate me when I get fired.'

Brook took out his phone. At some point in the last thirty seconds, it had dawned on him where the additional evidence to get those bottles submitted was going to come from. It was quite obvious now he had the answer. If the street CCTV on which he was waiting showed the same guy in the navy sports jacket entering the churchyard shortly after Victor, then it might just be enough to get the bottles he drank from analysed. Not enough for a charge on its own, of course. Let alone a conviction. But little steps were still progress.

Brook tapped on the number for the CCTV office while Danny worked away on the computer. He recognised the voice of the same civilian worker as earlier. Some guy called Steve.

'DC Deelman! Good timing. I was just about to call. Have you picked up your disc?'

'I didn't even know it was ready.'

'Well, in that case, someone must have picked it up with their own by mistake.'

'Brilliant,' said Brook, sarcastically. 'Has anyone signed the book for it?'

'No. I checked. The entry for your disc is blank.'

Brook rolled his eyes and took a deep breath.

'Look... Don't worry about it. I'll get Jonboy to do me another copy when he's in tonight.'

'Slight problem with that,' said Steve. 'That camera's fucked.'

'Since when?'

'Some point this afternoon.'

'You'll still have the thirty days of stored footage though, won't you?'

'By fucked, I mean fucked. Nothing.'

Now even Danny was wincing at the overheard conversation.

'How often does this happen to cameras?' asked the detective.

'Now and again. The whole system needs replacing, really. The fault has been logged.'

Well, that's wonderfully comforting, thought Brook.

'So how many of them have gone wrong today?' he asked.

'This and one other. The one here, covering the building entrance.'

'The one that might show who left with my disc.'

'If you're into conspiracy theories.'

Brook fell silent. *Right now I bloody am*, he thought.

'Anyway, sorry about that,' added Steve. 'It was only non-suspicious though, right?'

Brook hung up. He had nothing useful to say to that. Sure, there would be other cameras on Holloway Road. Private cameras covering shops and apartment entrances. But a nice high overview that could trace Victor and any follower through the post-match crowds and show the key moment of them entering the churchyard one after the other? Highly unlikely.

Danny had finished creating the disc of the pub's footage (at least this one wasn't about to go missing) and was busy reading his statement. Brook spent the time mentally running through the investigation so far…

The crime scene was gone. The key witness was gone. The street CCTV was gone. And now any chance of submitting the bottles was gone too. Four missed tackles. Had it been a rugby match, he would be 28–0 down already. He had to find a way to start scoring points.

The barman filled in his details on the statement and handed it over with the CD. Brook did his best to smile. Since ordering a pint from a witness seemed a tad unprofessional, he made his way over the road to the Hen & Chickens, forced his way through the Friday evening crush and drank at the bar. After a few big swigs, he was surprised to find himself having to suppress a laugh at his own investigation.

Ignoring the fact he still hadn't found a next of kin, what did he have to show for it all? Some footage of an unknown man drinking non-alcoholic lager and not paying much attention to the big screen sport. Well, naturally, the beer-guzzling, sports-mad, investigating officer had decided he must be the fucking culprit. How could a jury ever disagree?

As Brook drained some more of his pint, his gaze settled on a blackboard showing a list of cocktails. The top one was clearly mocking him with the name '*Smoking Gun*'.

In a crowded bar, DC Brook Deelman told a blackboard to fuck off.

Chapter 15

Sunday, 15th April 1945
Stalag IV-B, Mühlberg, Germany

Lance Corporal Victor Watson followed Oberst Lührsen towards the towering main gates of Stalag IV-B, uniformed guards flanking him all the way. With turret-like structures on either side, the gates looked like something from a medieval fortress (albeit, on this occasion, designed to keep the enemy in). The salutes thrown up by the guards as the colonel approached were crisp and quick, a world away from Blondie's half-hearted effort.

'Wohin gehen wir?'… *Where are we going?*… asked Victor as the small party was allowed to pass through.

'Wir bringen dich zu von Eberstein'… *We're taking you to von Eberstein.*

The statement left him none the wiser.

It was not the first time Victor had been back through the gates since his arrival. On two previous occasions he had joined work parties of prisoners, allowed out under heavily armed guard to labour in nearby fields. There were some who refused to take part – citing the principle of not working for the enemy – but Victor had decided that his lacklustre digging was unlikely to sway the course of the war, though the change of scene might just help preserve his sanity.

Work parties were also the only realistic chance of escape for those who, unlike Victor, were interested in such a pursuit. The chances were slim, but not quite prohibitively so. It had been known for the odd prisoner – during a pre-planned disturbance by their pals – to slip away into undergrowth during the march back to camp. If the head count could then be fudged by way of further antics, and the escaper's dog tags and papers conveyed back into camp by sleight of hand, then his identity could be taken up by a stooge and the escape kept secret. Even when initially successful, the ruse was often swiftly rumbled – the stooge thrown in the cooler and a hungry escaper quickly recaptured for similar treatment or worse. But there had still been a few successes.

Outside the main gates, half a dozen large huts provided accommodation for the guards and officers who ran the camp. Far from luxury, but a thousand-fold improvement on the cramped, lice-ridden dwellings of the prisoners. Oberst Lührsen led the way to the furthest one.

'Warte hier'... *Wait here.*

He ascended the couple of steps to the door, knocked twice and entered. Victor heard the muffled sounds of a brief conversation before the door opened again and Oberst Lührsen beckoned him in. The space inside the hut was dominated by a large mahogany desk with a leather chair on either side. Third Reich themed pictures hung on the walls while, behind the desk, a man in Nazi uniform stood looking away from them, hands clasped behind his back.

'Danke, Oberst'... *Thank you, Colonel.*

Oberst Lührsen left the hut without a word. The man behind the desk switched to English.

'Please. Take a seat, Lance Corporal.'

The speaker was looking out of a small window that offered yet another version of the staple view. Featureless fields and a distant line of trees.

'Not thinking of doing a runner, are you?' asked Victor.

'Hmm?' replied the German, turning around.

'Joke,' said Victor, taking up the offer of a seat. A part of him wanted to stand defiantly, but he was still aching from his encounter with Blondie, and the padded leather chair – with a high back and arm rests – was practically begging him to enjoy a rare moment of comfort.

'Of course. The famous British sense of humour. You know, I rather miss it,' came the reply.

The comment was an obvious cue for Victor to make further enquiries, so he made a point of saying nothing. After a moment, the German realised no question was coming, raised an eyebrow and took the leather chair opposite.

The two men assessed each other in silence for a few seconds. The Nazi officer appeared to be no older than Victor – though the different ageing effects of personal wars made it hard to be sure. Slim to the point of sinewy, blue-eyed and clean-shaven, his hair was a touch fairer than the Englishman's, though still a little off the Aryan ideal.

The uniform was every bit as immaculate as Oberst Lührsen's. Polished buttons, elaborate epaulettes and a host of shiny crests, emblems and chains around the chest area of the tunic. There was a rumour among the Allies that Nazi uniforms were the brainchild of a German theatre company. It was easy to believe.

Victor's gaze quickly settled on one particular part of the uniform – two angular letters on the collar. The classic double lightning strike. He was sitting in front of an officer of the Waffen-SS. The Nazi Party's muscle. Hitler's enforcers. Victor remembered a French prisoner telling him and Harry how 'SS' stood for *'Sans Sentiment'*. Since 'Without Sentiment' didn't work in English, Harry had come up with his own version. 'Sick Psychos'. It made people laugh every time he said it, so no-one had ever corrected him.

'I am endlessly amazed by your capacity to laugh,' said the SS officer. It took Victor a second to realise they had already been on the theme of humour and his mind wasn't being read. 'Take this theatre that you have created in the camp. What other race of men, at its lowest point, decides to put all remaining energy into staging a comic performance?'

He spoke excellent English, far more lightly accented than his compatriots.

'Oh, I don't know. We can't take all the credit,' replied Victor, glancing up at a framed photo of a staring Hitler receiving his salute from a unit of grey, goose-stepping clones. 'You give us so much material, we have to do something with it.'

Von Eberstein's roar of laughter was so unexpected it made Victor jump – the size of his lungs apparently belying his slim frame. Then he punched the air.

'Yes! I love it.'

The laughter continued to come in waves until he managed to compose himself, dabbing at the corners of his eyes. At last he was quiet again. Victor had no idea what to make of this fellow.

'I believe Oberst Lührsen said your name was von Eberstein,' he ventured, as the man opposite re-folded his tear-stained handkerchief.

'Indeed,' said von Eberstein, now smoothing down the front of his tunic, as if the laughter might have creased it.

'May I ask your rank,' said Victor.

'SS-Sturmbannführer,' came the swift reply, delivered with the sort of dramatic flourish that so many Nazi titles seemed to demand. 'Do you have any more questions?'

'I have three.'

'Please.'

'Where is Private Harry Wilson? What am I doing here? And how does an SS officer whose rank equates to Major have Oberst Lührsen running errands for him?'

Von Eberstein took a deep breath, as if finally putting the laughter behind him. Then he was perfectly still. He smiled, eyes narrowing slightly as he looked at the prisoner with a new intensity.

'Interesting…' he said. 'Behind the jokes there is an alert mind.'

Victor sat in silence, waiting for answers to his questions.

'Well,' said von Eberstein at last. 'Your friend Wilson is not really my concern. But from what Oberst Lührsen tells me, he is on his way to the cooler for trying to start a riot.'

'Good grief. And you say the British have a sense of humour?'

'As for why you are here, I will come to that in a moment.'

'I'm in no hurry.'

'And as for me holding the hand whip over a higher rank…'

'The whip hand,' corrected Victor.

'Of course. The whip hand. As far as that is concerned, it is what you might call a question of circumstance. When an army is on the brink of defeat, a hierarchy can become a little more… flexible. Would you not agree?'

'If I'm ever in an army that's on the brink of defeat I'll let you know.'

Von Eberstein smiled again. He had to admit he liked the Englishman's spirit.

'Well, I'm sure you can imagine that if two different ranks know that in a few weeks they will just be two unemployed civilians, then the dynamic can shift somewhat.'

Victor continued to be impressed by the German's level of English, though he was not in the habit of praising Nazis. Even those who accepted that the war was lost.

'At that point,' continued the SS officer, 'everyone starts to think about life after the war. How they will survive. Their families. When a hierarchy is so weakened, what matters is not rank, but money.'

'So, Oberst Lührsen is on your payroll?' asked Victor.

'In a manner of speaking. As are many others. I am more than happy for Oberst Lührsen to be the official head of this camp, but in reality – the only reality that matters – people answer to me.'

'And is it money that explains your young age and impressive rank? Even if rank is now meaningless, of course.'

The SS-Sturmbannführer allowed a half-smile at the Englishman's irreverence.

'Money and connections, you might say. Perhaps you know of my uncle? Obergruppenführer Friedrich Karl von Eberstein. One of the founders of the SS and a personal friend of Himmler.'

'Lucky him.'

Stony-faced silence replaced the half-smile as von Eberstein realised the conversation about his uncle had come to an abrupt end. He had expected a reaction somewhere between interest and respect – maybe even awe – rather than mockery and dismissal.

'So am I allowed to know why I'm here yet? The suspense is killing me,' said Victor, rather regretting his choice of words.

Von Eberstein leaned down to his left and opened a drawer, coming up with a manila envelope.

'This is why you are here.'

He removed a letter from the envelope and briefly showed it to the Englishman (typewritten text and some official stamps) before turning it back to read.

'A direct order from SS-Brigadeführer Schwarzmann.'

Once again, the dramatic title and name were delivered with the obligatory flair.

'I am aware you speak some German, but allow me to paraphrase…'

Victor nodded.

'The Brigadeführer has seen a roll-call of the camp and noticed your name on it… He is concerned that you are a person of 'cultural significance'… He instructs that you receive the same treatment as the most senior of captured officers… He goes on to describe your impressive achievements… Finally, he states this gesture should serve as an indication of the Third Reich's continued belief in the great shared culture of the Anglo-Saxon race, in wartime and in peace.'

Victor leaned forward and listened with a deepening frown – part concentration, part confusion. Finally, he was able to decode the pompous language.

'He's a football fan,' he said. 'He thinks I'm Vic Watson the footballer.'

'Sehr gut!' exclaimed von Eberstein. 'I happen to know the Brigadeführer spent some time in England, at the same time as my family was living there, and had a liking for Western Ham United.'

'West Ham United,' corrected Victor, simultaneously absorbing the information that von Eberstein's family had lived in England. 'Well, I'm sure you can do the honours of telling the Brigadeführer he is mistaken and returning me to camp. Vic Watson the footballer must be in his mid-40s by now. I'm sure the war has aged us all, but you can see perfectly well I'm too young.'

'Very well,' said von Eberstein, delving back into the drawer and this time emerging with a fountain pen and writing pad. 'I will reply to SS-Brigadeführer Schwarzmann and inform him of your *exact* date of birth.' He hovered the pen over the writing paper and looked up at Victor with eyebrows raised.

Victor opened his mouth to give the date on his birth certificate, then paused for a moment. Something about the way the question was worded. How would von Eberstein know that his 'exact' date of birth was a mystery?

The German was clearly anticipating the hesitation.

'No? So be it.' He whisked the pad of paper from the desk and tossed it back in the drawer, slamming it shut. 'Since I have no way of contradicting the Brigadeführer's assumption, I will faithfully follow his orders.'

Victor was getting an unsettling sense of secret games, hidden agendas.

'Now what the blazes is going on here?'

Von Eberstein leaned back and opened his arms wide like a welcoming host.

'Please. You are not thinking properly. This is good news for everyone. In the days after the war, Herr Schwarzmann will be able to demonstrate to the occupying powers that he was generous towards the enemy. I will be able to demonstrate that I assisted in such kind deeds. And, if an innocent error of identification was made, then the spirit of the gesture remains the same. As for you? Well, you are able to enjoy much-improved living conditions and a touch more… humanity. The situation benefits us all, does it not?'

Victor didn't reply. He was trying to work out where the truth lay in this bewildering charade.

'We all have to think of the future,' added von Eberstein, going for a co-conspiratorial tone. 'It is closer than many will admit. I imagine you will not have heard, but the great camp of Bergen-Belsen fell today.'

'I think *liberated* is the word you're looking for,' said Victor.

'Ah. Liberated. Of course. I must learn the new language for after the war.'

They fell quiet again, Victor lost in thought.

'Excellent,' said von Eberstein, as if the prisoner's silence was a tacit agreement. 'Since we are now friends, I will tell you my favourite joke. Though I'm afraid it was not provided by an Englishman, but a Dutchman. An old, Jew-hiding Dutchman.'

Victor sensed a subtle darkening in the Nazi's expression despite the supposed subject matter of favourite jokes.

'Go on,' he said, his mind still on other things.

'I was in his house. Ugly little house. And he was at my feet. Badly injured, of course. He was crying like a baby and he said: 'Please. Just kill me. Let my family live.''

Von Eberstein's eyes seemed to lose focus as he spoke, his mind drifting back to the pleading Dutchman. Re-living every moment.

'I'm not sure that's really a joke,' said Victor, the chair no longer feeling quite as comfortable.

A look of fury came over the Nazi's face at having his daydream interrupted. He slammed a fist down on the desk, causing a low-level chatter outside to fade to perfect silence. The unfocused gaze had been replaced by something altogether wilder.

'A Jew-hider making a request of an SS-Sturmbannführer? This is the biggest joke EVER!'

As quickly as the anger filled the hut it vanished, replaced by a fond look of reminiscence.

'Besides,' he continued, calmly, 'if it is not a joke, then why could I not stop laughing when I killed him last of all?'

Victor felt a shiver rush down his spine – fight or flight hormones bouncing around with no outlet in the confines of his seated position. He clenched his jaw and waited for it to pass.

Sick Psychos.

'Or maybe you are right,' said von Eberstein, shrugging. 'I am sure I can find a better joke.'

Victor realised his fingers had been digging into the arms of the leather chair and released his whitening knuckles before they were noticed. He was beginning to think he preferred the simple thuggery of Blondie to the unpredictable lunatic in front of him.

The officer reached down to another drawer and produced a bottle of Scotch and two tumblers. He cradled the bottle in one hand as he examined the label.

'Six years old,' he said with evident disappointment. 'The deprivations of war.'

He poured two generous measures and slid one across the polished mahogany to Victor.

'As I was saying. This letter is good news for both of us. We should have some toast.'

'Raise a toast,' corrected Victor.

'Of course. Raise a toast.'

Victor glanced down at the glass then back at von Eberstein.

'I don't drink,' he said, sliding the tumbler back.

The Nazi retrieved the glass from the middle of the desktop – the limit of Victor's half-hearted push – and swirled the amber liquid under his nose before closing his eyes, downing it and smacking his lips. As his eyes opened, he caught Victor looking at the empty glass.

'Oh, I think you drink,' said the SS officer. 'A smoke, perhaps?'

A packet of cigarettes followed the same polished route as the tumbler. Victor trapped it beneath his left hand just before it toppled off the edge. He thought for a moment, then took a cigarette and placed it in the breast pocket of his army issue shirt.

'Maybe later,' he said, sliding the packet back.

'Very well,' said von Eberstein. 'How did you lose the finger?'

He nodded at the hand with which Victor had trapped the cigarettes.

'Mousetrap,' replied Victor, since he had no wish to discuss the events of that day. As soon as he heard himself say the word, he wondered if he might be in one right now.

The Nazi gave a broad smile. Then it became even broader. He gazed at Victor's left ear and tilted his head, examining the missing section, now beaming with delight.

'I have a joke!' he announced, swirling the whisky in his tumbler faster. 'I have a good one!'

Victor nodded. Von Eberstein seemed to be bursting at the seams of his uniform to get this joke out into the open.

'So… So… If you lost your finger in a mousetrap, then perhaps you also lost your ear in the same mousetrap because you crawled in to try and eat the cheese like a big mouse. No, wait. Like a big, English mouse. Who is in mouse prison.'

Victor grimaced.

'You don't like my joke?'

'Maybe it's the delivery.'

Chapter 16

Friday, 22nd April 2016
North London

'Hello?'

'Ello..? Is that..?'

'Hello..? Hang on a second…'

Brook pushed his way through the crowded bar to the exit.

'Hi. Sorry about that. Just had to step out of a noisy pub.'

'Oh, that's much better. Is that Brook?'

'Speaking.'

'It's Debbie from Peak View Care Home.'

'Debbie. Hi.'

'I just thought I'd give update on who your Victor might've rung. We've been running a right little detective agency 'ere.'

Brook looked back through the window of the Hen & Chickens. He had been just about to order a second pint. It would take a while now.

'So, have you cracked the case yet?' he asked.

It seemed like the sort of private eye language Debbie would appreciate.

'Well, not quite. But I think we're dead close.'

'That's great.'

The detective was finding it hard to match her enthusiasm having mentally checked out once the first pint went down.

'We're down to three possibles,' continued Debbie.

'Are they holding out against your questioning?'

'Ha! As if. More to do with dementia, poor souls.'

Brook closed his eyes and tapped the phone against his forehead.

'All three of them?' he asked.

'Well, just two, actually. Third one were tekken sick yesterday with racing pulse – like a panic attack – so I've not had chance to ask him. But I think he were in army from what someone said. Doctor finally gave him something today and he's been proper zonked out.'

'No dementia?'

'I don't think so. Just bit of a sad case, really. His son dropped him off a year ago. Off to live in Canada he were. And I know his wife died not long before. But he's not had any visitors and he says that little I couldn't even tell you where he grew up. Just spends whole time looking out across gardens at back, poor chap.'

'So three possibles.'

'That's right.'

'Well, you've done far more than I could have hoped for, Debbie.'

'Ooh, I'm not finished yet. Reckon I'll 'ave it down to just the one by tomorrow. Like one of them murder mystery weekends.'

'Couldn't have put it better myself.'

Brook gave his thanks and hung up, unsure what to think. Was anyone really going to know or care why Victor

Watson called Peak View Care Home? And, even if they did, was it going to be of any relevance to anything? A part of him wondered if he was just wasting Debbie's time (even if she did seem to be enjoying it).

On another note, he had – to his own surprise – been dragged out of the negative mindset that had begun to settle on him. He looked back into the Hen & Chickens once more… then set off walking in the opposite direction.

Not for the first time, some deep-set part of his mind had been working away at a riddle without him really thinking about it. That name… 'Judas Iscariot'. Why had the biblical character been in the Lumberjack's head?

With the light starting to fade, Brook approached St Mary Magdalene Church with a new purpose. In a rear corner of the building were glazed double doors with vertical bar handles – the only nod to modernity. Brook rattled them both… Nothing. Moving to the front of the church, he yanked on the ancient main doors, turning a ring handle this way and that… Nothing again.

Undeterred, he continued his route round the building, scanning the walls for another entry point. Three quarters of the way along the more secluded flank he found it – steps leading down to a door at basement level. The old door was small (the sort that always generates the comment *'People were much shorter in those days'*). More importantly, it was ever so slightly ajar.

A few moments later, Brook found himself emerging into the main body of the church. What was it called again? The nave? The lights were on, though the place seemed empty. Above him, the undecorated windows felt just as bleak from the inside as the outside.

Perhaps to make up for it, enormous Bible-themed tapestries were hanging on the walls, like an art display from Gulliver's Travels. Brook noticed one bearing the image of a hunched villain carrying a bulging purse. He was fairly confident it contained thirty pieces of silver… Judas Iscariot.

The detective looked over the pews to the back of the silent church. It was dimmer back there. Either a light had not been switched on or a bulb was out. But there was definitely a figure.

Brook took out his phone, selected the flashlight and advanced towards the shadows.

'Hello?'

No answer.

Then he could see him. Sitting in the rearmost pew.

Long hair… Big beard…

Dressed like a lumberjack…

'Hello, mate,' said Brook, aiming for light and friendly. The Lumberjack glanced his way then went back to looking straight ahead. Maybe he didn't remember him. After a few more seconds of Zen-like stillness, the homeless man reached out a hand and smacked the pew hard, twice. The sound bounced around the empty church. Brook waited for some territorial utterance in that piratical Cornish. Something along the lines of *'My bench!'*. It never came.

'Sit down, officer,' said the Lumberjack.

Now that was unexpected.

Brook overruled his nostrils and accepted the offer.

'How's the head?' he enquired.

The older man lifted up a curtain of dark hair and felt around for the injury, his thick fingers finally settling upon a bump and two stitches.

'How's it look?' he asked. The accent was still there, the voice gruff and the words a little slow. But the slurring and stuttering had disappeared. Brook pulled a sympathetic face.

'That's your modelling career gone.'

The Lumberjack let the curtain of hair flop back; the hint of a smile on his bearded cheeks.

'Well, this certainly beats your last bench,' said Brook, taking in their surroundings.

'Can't stay this late most days. Vicar's doin' some work in the office.'

'You spend a lot of time in here?'

'Much as I can, I s'pose. Longer I'm sittin' in here, longer I'm not drinkin' out there.'

Brook was grateful to the vicar for working late. It seemed he had caught the Lumberjack at one of his better times.

'We didn't give you a fair hearing earlier,' he said. 'I'm sorry.'

It was met with a shrug and an indirect answer.

'I was wondrin' if you'd be back.'

'So, how's your memory?'

'I remember your friend, all right. One who said I was full of… nonsense.' He turned to Brook. 'Not comin' here, is he?'

'No. I'm on my own.'

'Good.' The Lumberjack nodded as if to confirm it. 'I'm very good at turnin' the other cheek, but… I might just have to knock his block off first.'

Brook smiled. Without the combined influences of extreme inebriation and DS Kev Padmore, they seemed to be getting on okay.

'Adam,' said the Lumberjack, extending a chunky-fingered hand.

'Are you just picking another Bible name?' asked Brook, shaking it.

'Not this time.'

The handshake was firm. He was strong and stocky for a homeless person. All the same, Brook suspected the name 'Adam' was never going to replace 'the Lumberjack' in his mind.

'So… What are the chances of you telling me what you saw and I'll listen properly this time?'

The Lumberjack wiped some non-existent dust from the back of the pew in front, as if clearing the way for a fresh start…

'Church had closed pretty early. Never good news for me. I'd been drinkin' on the street but I made it to that bench. Laid out some papers and stuff, case it rained, then got my head down.'

Brook nodded. Bench theory confirmed.

'And then I s'pose I was aware of folk nearby. You get into a lot of scrapes out there so your senses are always kind of up, even when you're smashed. It was the voice that did it, mind. Close enough I thought it was in my own head at first.'

'What was said?'

'He called out… He said… said…'

Brook felt a moment's anxiety. The old hesitancy was returning. Then he broke through it.

'He said 'Victor'. What was it? 'Victor Watson'. Yep. Full name. Enough to make me open my eyes, anyway. Then there they are. Standin' in front of each other. And pretty much in front of me.'

Brook heard the clunk and scrape of a heavy door opening behind the pulpit. A fresh-faced man with curly hair, grey jumper and a dog collar appeared. He put a shielding hand over the top of his eyes and peered into the shadows at the far end.

'Everything okay, Adam?' he asked.

'All good, thank you, Rev. Just helpin' the local bobby.'

'Right you are. Remind me to get that light fixed.'

Brook gave a wave.

'What happened then?' he asked.

'The old man said something 'bout how he knew why the other fella was there, or what he was up to. Something like that. Then he asked if he could smoke.'

Brook cast his mind back to the scene. He hadn't noticed any cigarette butts.

'I s'pose that's when it all started goin' a bit weird,' said the Lumberjack.

He was glancing up and down to his left – a sign of *recollection* rather than *invention* if you believed the theory – as if watching the events play out on a big screen projected from his mind.

'It looked like the young fella tried grabbin' the old man's cigarettes. But then this thing falls to the ground, and it ain't cigarettes. It's a knife. Sticks right in on its end.'

Brook leaned forward and ran a hand over his stubble.

'I told you it started goin' weird,' said the Lumberjack.

'And then?'

'Well… I prob'ly miss a bit 'cos I'm staring at this knife. But the young fella shoves his hand in the other's jacket and pulls out this gold thing. Medal. Medallion. Whatever you wanna call it.'

'You called it a big gold coin this morning.'

'Did I? That does the job. So I'm listenin' again now, and the young fella asks why he still carries it. And he says something 'bout second chances in life.'

'His keepsake from the orphanage,' said Brook, moving the jigsaw pieces around in his mind.

'And then the younger fella says 'I got a message for you.''

'A message?'

'That's what he said.'

'Did you hear it?'

'I did.'

'Well, what was it?'

'He said 'Fiona wants this back.''

'Fiona?'

'I told you it was weird.'

'So who's Fiona?'

'How the h… How should I know?'

'And you definitely didn't mishear?'

'I'm not gonna mishear that. Was my wife's name.'

The Lumberjack sensed Brook's hesitation over whether to enquire and saved him the trouble.

'Well… Would you stay married to this?'

The detective couldn't think of what to say, so carried on.

'What happened after that?'

'The end. Young fella sweeps him up, slams him against the stone. Bang.'

For all that Brook had started to imagine this was how Victor Watson's life had ended – in some distant, abstract way – it still felt shocking to hear it from an eyewitness.

'Shit,' he said, completely forgetting where he was. 'What did you do?'

'You need to slow down,' said the Lumberjack. 'Or you'll miss something.'

The comment took Brook by surprise, shifting the dynamic between the two. He had been convinced he was running this show – winning the Lumberjack's confidence and directing his recollections. Now he realised the other man was far more than a hapless witness in need of guidance. He had a total grasp of everything that was going on.

'The whisky,' said Brook, suddenly aware of what he had nearly missed.

The Lumberjack nodded his approval.

'From his own jacket pocket. Poured some over the old man, then stuck it under his hand.'

Those fine single malts in Victor Watson's drinks cabinet… the little voice in Brook's head had been right. The Lumberjack carried on.

'So, by now I've seen enough of this. Adrenalin's cuttin' right through the booze. I go to get up and… That's the last I remember.'

'You banged your head on the bench,' said Brook.

'Think so.'

'The blood's still there.'

'Next thing the rain's wakin' me up. Comin' through the newspapers. Drippin' on me. And these officers are takin' down the tape like nothing's happened. One's even eatin' a chocolate bar. I wasn't havin' that, so I just… sort of… crawled out and threw myself to make 'em stop.'

'You did well,' said Brook, feeling a fresh embarrassment at the way they had treated him. The Lumberjack let his eyes settle on the pew in front.

'Anyway. There you go,' he said with a hint of a sigh.

The two men fell into silence as Brook processed all the new information. And there was a lot to process. It was the detective who spoke first.

'Look, if there's any way you could make a formal statement about this, then I could get Homicide to take on the whole investigation.'

'Not you then?' asked the Lumberjack, still staring at the back of the pew.

'I'm not with Homicide.'

'And if I don't make a formal statement?'

'Then I guess it stays with me.'

'I want it to stay with you. I don't like coppers. You seem all right.'

'Look... Adam... They've got the resources, the budget, the expertise.'

'I want you to do it,' said the Lumberjack flatly. 'If makin' a statement means it goes to them, I'm not makin' a statement.'

Brook decided to move on quickly from the impasse. There was one question he had deliberately been putting off because he knew a part of him would stop listening to anything else once he had the answer. But now was the time.

'What did the younger man look like?' he asked.

The Lumberjack looked up.

'I was wondrin' when you'd get to that.'

'Sometimes you have to slow down or you miss things,' said Brook.

The Lumberjack seemed to like hearing his own words repeated back to him.

'Short brown hair. Tallish. Forties, I s'pose. White, but he'd had the sun on him. Looked strong. Picked the old man up like he was nothing.'

'What about his clothes?'

'Pale trousers and a navy kind of jacket. Like a blazer.'

Bingo.

Brook took out his phone, went into Contacts and tapped a brief text to a friend in Forensics.

'Hi Marie. Favour to ask. Are you on lates? Brook.'

Then he pulled out Danny-the-barman's statement and dialled the mobile number on the back.

'Hello?' The familiar Aussie accent. A noisy bar in the background.

'Danny. Brook Deelman. Don't put any more bottles in that wheelie bin. I'm coming back.'

'Okay, mate.'

It was too loud to talk any further.

Brook put a hand on the pew in front and pushed himself upright, his mind already lining up the next steps of the reborn investigation.

'Maybe it's for the best that you knocked yourself out rather than confronting him,' he said.

For the first time, the Lumberjack fixed him with a full stare. There was something different behind his eyes, a new tempo to his voice when he spoke…

'I couldn't care less who that tough guy thinks he is. If he's come through Goose Green. If he's come through Wireless Ridge. If he's marched into Stanley. Then I'll respect him.'

'You were in the Falklands?' asked Brook.

'Parachute regiment. And you could have put twice as much liquor in me last night. You could have poured meths down my throat. If I still had a pulse and I'd managed to lay one finger on that bully…'

For the first time, he forgot his surroundings.

'…I would have fucking killed him.'

Chapter 17

It was fair to say Marie might have reacted differently had the request come from anyone else. An overworked scenes of crime officer was no different to an overworked detective when it came to avoiding extra jobs. And there were plenty of ways to refuse some forensically compromised bottles from a sticky wheelie bin. But Brook could be a charming devil. It was why Marie now found herself sitting in the SOCO office of Grovebury police station with four neatly packaged non-alcoholic beer bottles, wondering how best to word the paperwork that would accompany them to the lab. Brook had gone out to fetch coffees and call Homicide again.

The forensics officer gave up on the paperwork and allowed her mind to wander for a moment. In the ten years she had known Brook, he had probably tested her 'no dating police officers' rule more than anyone else. Okay, *definitely* rather than probably. She used to like the way he would turn up for work sporting whatever bumps, bruises and black eyes he had picked up playing rugby. Sometimes it was more serious. Slings. Crutches. But he always met her expressions of concern with a crinkly-eyed smile and a 'You should see the other guy'.

Marie knew a bit about rugby from the Irish side of her family, even if the Barbadian side were more interested in cricket. She knew, for example, that Brook had played flanker (he once described his role as '*tackle anything that moves*') and that he had played to a decent level – a division or two beneath the pros despite the demands of policing. She suspected his love of the 'social' side of the game would have stopped him ever going any higher.

Despite literally ruling herself out of dating him, Marie still had to confess to a touch of jealousy whenever Brook had a girlfriend. The relationships never seemed to last very long. Brook being on his own somehow seemed the natural way of things. An indivisible unit, like Ayers Rock or Big Ben. In any case, there was no point thinking about it too deeply now. Things had worked out well, she reminded herself. She was marrying Neil in a couple of months. And that was a good thing.

She smiled as Brook re-appeared with two coffees and placed one in front of her before easing his big frame into an office chair. It creaked its objections.

'Still one sugar?' he asked.

'Still one sugar,' confirmed Marie in a gentle Irish accent. 'So how did the call to Homicide go?'

'Badly. As expected.'

Brook had deliberately avoided asking to speak to DS Beckford, with whom he had fallen out in the churchyard. Instead he had run it by a different DS who answered the main phone number. He had no trouble recalling his withering conclusion:

'Just so I've got this right. You've got an old dead bloke and a homeless drunk you've dismissed as a fantasist. Then you've watched some CCTV, decided some fella looks a bit dodgy, so

you've returned to the drunk fantasist you dismissed earlier, and – lo and behold – he's now given a perfect description of your guy on the CCTV. But he won't give a statement. Look, do I even need to say what a defence brief would do to this? Not that it would ever reach court. Sorry, mate…'

'So it's still non-suspicious?' asked Marie.

'Yep. It's a non-suspicious brutal murder. Clever, eh?'

'That's okay. We can work around this. Let's just look at what we've got and have a think.'

'Well, I wouldn't bother about the bottle with half the label picked off. If our suspect drank three of these, then that'll be the one that's not from him.'

'You sure?'

'He wasn't picking any labels on CCTV. That'll be from someone's bad date. I guarantee it.'

'Oh, so you're a dating guru now?' laughed Marie.

Even after ten years, Brook wasn't sure which he liked more – the soft Irish accent, or the contrast between the green eyes and the flawless mocha skin.

'Hey, I'm only a guru of bad dates,' he replied. 'That bottle has got awkward fidgeting written all over it. Either its owner moved on to hard liquor or they gave up and went home.'

'Okay. That makes things twenty-five percent easier,' said Marie, moving the bad date bottle to one side. 'So, are we looking at fingerprints or DNA for these three?'

'Not sure about fingerprints. You'll have the member of staff who stocked the fridge, the barman that served him, the bad guy and then whoever collected the bottle. How about we just ask for DNA testing around the rims? I know it's challengeable on its own. But if it provided a name that led to more evidence…'

'You're not wrong about it being challengeable,' said Marie, turning again to the paperwork. 'But… I can probably fudge it through.'

'Great,' said Brook, downing his coffee and pushing himself out of the creaking office chair. 'And thanks. I owe you.'

'You always owe me.'

Chapter 18

Brook left the police station via the back door and began the street-lit walk to Kings Cross and the tube journey home. It was over eight hours since he'd demolished the pancakes in Alfredo's – definitely time to start considering the takeaway options on his route. A text from Jonboy interrupted the burger-versus-burrito dilemma:

'Number One! Just heard about the balls-up with the Holloway Road footage of your dead bloke. That's a bugger, isn't it? Mainly as I won't get my donuts now, but a little bit for messing up your investigation too. Anyway, there's a few of us in tonight so I'm heading round to a kebab place, couple of doors down. Think one of their cameras reaches our front door here. Curious to see who was coming and going when your disc went walkabout. Also just fancy a kebab.'

It was good to have a couple of allies.

Soon the bright pedestrian plaza outside Kings Cross Station came into view – plenty of people out for a night on the town, putting their work worries behind them. Brook decided he needed to do the same. He knew just the place…

London's last 'pound-in-a-pot' strip bar was not going to be around for much longer. It was closing down, never to re-open – part of the grimy Kings Cross of the past rather than the shiny vision of the future. Brook couldn't remember the last time he had been on the other side of its frosted glass windows but, whenever it was, he certainly hadn't been this sober. He nodded at a towering, steroid-fuelled bouncer and headed straight to the bar to rectify that.

Far from the high value notes that flew out of bankers' wallets at other strip clubs, things were different here; the next dancer on stage passing among the punters with a pint glass into which the princely sum of one pound was duly expected and deposited. With around twenty people in tonight, no-one was making big bucks. Brook was well aware that the whole thing was not exactly edifying, but scruples and sobriety had a habit of disappearing at about the same rate. As he directed the barman towards a bottle of Budvar, a pretty brunette appeared at his shoulder.

'You're staying to watch me?' asked the dancer. A black lacy top and short skirt covered a hint of curves. She was around 5'5" and well put together. Late 20s with an East European accent. Just around the corner, in the main room, one of her colleagues was receiving applause and whistles for her routine to a Shakira soundtrack.

'I am,' replied Brook, dropping a pound coin into the pint glass to complete the formalities. It joined a dozen others and a rogue Scottish pound note. He looked up and noticed the dancer was still staring at him. Did she know him? The barman slapped the bottle down on the bar.

'Four pounds, please, mate.' Brook turned to pay and the brunette moved on. Appreciative applause and some indecipherable shouts signalled the end of the current dancer's routine.

The detective took his drink and moved from the small bar area to an adjacent room, scarcely any bigger. There was a raised stage at the back – the height difference between the two levels creating a baying, bear pit feel (one that the drunk punters seemed only too happy to embrace). Where the end of the main bar poked through to serve the larger room, he propped himself against it, settling in just as the brunette he'd spoken to appeared on stage.

Brook didn't recognise her chosen soundtrack. Something slower than Shakira anyway – more of a Burlesque feel. It had the strange effect of making the bear pit quieter with every item of clothing that came off, until it was in a concentrated silence. There was definitely a stage presence. And she was certainly very… athletic.

At the same time, her repeated glances over to Brook were not going unnoticed – either by their recipient or others in the room, who flashed him a few *'who the fuck is this guy?'* looks. Brook was still a little bemused by her interest in him. Still, as mysteries went, he would definitely take the one involving a naked dancer over the one involving a dead guy in a churchyard right now.

After the concentrated silence, the routine came to an end to cheers and enthusiastic applause. Brook joined in as the dancer left the stage with a final glance his way. Some of the drunker occupants of the bear pit were looking his way too. He raised an eyebrow and gave them all his best *'it happens'* expression before downing the remainder of his beer. All the same, he thought it might be prudent to head through to the other room to order his next one.

Just as when he ordered his first drink, the brunette soon appeared at his shoulder. The lacy top and short skirt were back on, but there was no pint glass of pound coins in her hand this time. Instead she pulled up a bar stool and sat down next to Brook, her elbow nudging him and a foot brushing the back of his knees as she adjusted her position. He refused to hurry a long, lazy swig before looking the stripper's way.

'Nice routine,' he said.

The comment was met with a smile but no immediate reply. Instead his new companion leaned in conspiratorially, sliding her elbows along the bar and tilting her head coquettishly.

'Shouldn't you be out arresting people, officer?'

Never what a policeman wants to hear in a strip bar.

'Even superheroes need time off,' replied Brook, before heading back to his previous spot and dropping a pound into the pint glass of a passing blonde. Purely in terms of getting fleeced for extra money, he would have been suspicious of any stripper flirting with him. But one who mentioned his job activated a whole different set of alarm bells. He was beginning to regret staying for a second drink.

Glancing back, he saw that the brunette had followed him, now clutching a beer of her own. Whatever she was after, she was determined. After a few seconds, a new soundtrack kicked in and the blonde took to the stage, her chosen music much faster than the swingy number that had preceded it.

Brook felt a tap on his elbow as the bear pit whistled at a bra flying through the air. He only half turned, keeping one eye on the action, unwilling to fully engage.

'I'm better than her,' said the brunette.

'At what?' said Brook, with a show of indifference.

Undeterred, she leaned in close enough that her breath was on his ear.

'So, if you're a superhero, what's your super power?'

Brook kept his eyes on the stage.

'Normally, I'd say X-ray vision. But you don't really need it in this place.'

No reply.

After several seconds, his curiosity got the better of him. He turned to see that the brunette was now looking behind the bar, an anxious expression on her face.

The detective followed her line of sight to the mirrored wall behind the array of bottled spirits. Staring back, from the reverse angle, the steroid-addicted bouncer at the main door. He was too stupid to realise Brook was now looking at him too.

'You're being a real asshole,' said the stripper, leaving it open to interpretation as to whether it was directed at Brook or the bouncer. The guy had a ridiculous ponytail, shaved at the sides, and a knee-length leather coat over a black t-shirt, deliberately too tight. As Brook observed him, the barman began clicking his fingers and pointing at a drunk bloke in a suit staggering through the entrance.

'Hey! Tomasz!' he said, trying to get the bouncer's attention. Brook made a mental note of the name as 'Tomasz' finally turned back to his job and sent the drunk tumbling into the street with the minimum of effort. The barman shook his head.

Brook returned his gaze to the stage. Whatever was going on between the brunette and the bouncer, he really didn't want anything to do with it. This drink would definitely be his last. As the routine continued, he polished off the beer and moved the empty bottle across the bar, holding up a flat palm of 'no thanks' when the barman looked interested.

'Well, nice to meet you,' he said, stepping past the stripper who had latched onto him.

'Wait!' she replied, pinching the elbow of Brook's jacket and pulling down in a *don't go* gesture. The detective looked at his elbow, then at the brunette. It took her a second to meet his eyes, too busy looking at the bouncer again with some kind of awkward reassurance *('It's okay. I've got this').*

For the first time, something else caught Brook's eye. High up on the stripper's right cheek, and again, on the jawline. Two rows of bruises were just visible through the camouflage of make-up. Irregular circles in a row, separated by gaps of unmarked skin – the distance between knuckles. Surprisingly wide gaps though.

It must have been a colossal left fist that had done this.

The stripper caught the detective looking at the bruises and any trace of a smile disappeared. As the bear pit roared some more approval, Brook turned back towards the mirrored wall and found the bouncer again – eyes wide, jaw clenched, a flush of colour in his face. What was going on between these two? Brook scanned down to the point where he could see the bouncer was clutching a bottle of Coke. It looked tiny in his fist. His colossal left fist.

'Actually, I told a lie about X-ray vision being my super power,' said Brook.

The stripper's smile returned at his apparent willingness to engage. She moved closer.

'Really?' she said, pressing her hip into him. 'You prefer to see things for real?'

'My super power is mind-reading,' continued Brook, ignoring her question. This time it was he who leaned in and spoke into an ear… 'You're in a violent relationship with the bouncer at the door. He's on bail for beating you up, but you both want the case discontinued. He loves you really, he'll never do it again… Whatever. The pair of you thought that compromising a police officer might give some good leverage to get the charges dropped – even if he does have to control his jealousy in the process.'

Brook nodded down to where a hip was still being pressed against him, albeit with less enthusiasm than a moment ago. 'I wonder where all this would have ended.'

The stripper restored the space between them.

'You must already know the case,' she said. 'I noticed you at the police station when I came in to change my story.'

'Nope. Just good old-fashioned mind-reading. But thanks for explaining how you know I'm a copper…' The blonde on stage finished her routine as Brook leaned in one final time to make himself heard. '…It was bugging me.'

He left the bear pit behind him and walked back towards the only way in and out. The bouncer watched him coming. He had taken off his leather coat to display his physique like a parading stag. Brook scrutinised him more carefully this time. Watching him in the mirror hadn't really conveyed his true size.

The man was drawn to a different scale – four inches taller and fifty pounds heavier than the detective. His skin seemed to strain under the sheer volume of chemically enhanced muscle. Prominent veins around his temples looked like rivers on a map, while his face displayed the acne scars of extreme steroid abuse and an artery pulsed in his neck. The guy was a cardiac arrest waiting to happen, but his poor long-term health would make him no less destructive in the next few moments. He took a step into the middle of the doorway, blocking Brook's path.

'Is there a problem?' asked Brook.

The bouncer angled his head slightly to one side and looked down at the detective. He was chewing gum in time to the metronome artery in his neck – the cocky look of an alpha male on home turf.

'Yez. There iz problem,' he replied, flexing his pecs. Thick, Slavic tones (Brook couldn't help but think of Bond villains). No doubt this was where the smaller man was meant to start apologising for any misunderstandings, to meekly ask to get past and catch his train, to hope that a display of sufficient subservience might save him from a beating…

'Actually, there are three problems, Tomasz,' said Brook, meeting the contemptuous stare. The authoritative tone and unexpected use of his name tweaked the balance of power, putting the bouncer back in the classroom.

'The first problem is that, if you fight me, the cops who come will find you're on bail and you'll never get bail again.'

The bouncer's chewing slowed but he neither spoke nor moved.

'The second problem is that, if you fight me, the owner of this place will lose his licence and you'll never get security work again.'

The bouncer finally stopped chewing, which Brook thought was a shame. It freed up the nine-tenths of his brain taken up by the task. The giant used the new-found computing power to speak.

'And what iz third problem?' he asked, looking Brook up and down with his best sneer.

'The third problem, Tomasz… is that if you fight me, you'll lose.'

The bouncer began chewing again. The tempo quickened. Then a smile broke out, turning into a full-blown laugh. He glanced left and right, looking for people to join in.

'Okay, funny man,' he said at last, stepping to one side. 'For make me laugh, you can go.'

Brook shook his head and tutted as confusion spread across the bouncer's acne-scarred face.

'Uh-uh,' he said. 'The first problem, remember? Your bail conditions not to contact your girlfriend over there?' There seemed little doubt by now that his understanding of the situation was correct. 'I can't leave you here. Either you fuck off or I'm arresting you.'

He showed the way to the exit with an open palm then clapped his hands together at the lack of movement. 'Come on. Chop chop. No goodbyes tonight, Tomasz.'

The bouncer's bully boy confidence evaporated as he seemed to visibly shrink before Brook. He turned to face the door, not quite believing how quickly this had all gone wrong. Then, with a final look back at his battered girlfriend, the alpha male was ushered out of his bar. Through his door. Off his turf.

'Spare me the romantic glances,' said Brook, tossing his leather jacket after him. 'And I don't want you coming back for that.'

'So…'

Brook held up a forefinger to signal 'quiet'. Then he tapped the screen on his phone a couple of times and held it to his ear. He scanned the surrounding lampposts for cameras as he pretended to wait for an answer to the non-existent call.

'Hello?' he said to no-one. 'Right, I need you to call up Camera 57 on the main screen.' He waved up at the nearest camera pointing vaguely his way. 'You got me? Great. Now, see this guy?' He pointed at Tomasz. 'Get a good zoom. Bail conditions not to return to this venue. Yep. Domestic. High priority. How many have you got working CCTV tonight?

Fifteen? Right, dedicate one to this camera. If he comes back I want two units here to arrest him ASAP. Have you matched him to his custody photo? Yep. That's him. You've got the crime report? Home address? Yeah. Tomasz. That's right. Check his bail date. Make Camera 57 a fixed camera until then. Thank you.'

It was all absolute nonsense but the Met could have some amazing resources when you were playing make-believe. He put the phone back in his pocket and turned to the massive bouncer.

'Are you still here?' he said.

Tomasz turned wordlessly and trudged away, his leather jacket swinging from one of those massive fists. Brook felt no sympathy. A wave of tiredness suddenly crashed over him. Was getting quietly drunk too much to ask? His phone began ringing in his pocket… Christ… Lucky that hadn't happened during his 'conversation'. Jonboy again.

'Hello, mate.'

'Number One! Where are you?'

'Strip bar.'

'Very funny. Listen, I've had a fantastic chicken sheesh while looking at this camera that shows the front door of the CCTV office.'

'I'm happy for you.'

'Enough of your sarcasm. I've even been comparing the arrivals and departures to our visitors' logbook.'

'Okay. You have my attention.'

'Only one person came into our building at a time when no-one officially signed in.'

'Have you got a description?'

'Course I have, Number One. Who do you think you're talking to? Tall, thin white bloke. In his fifties, I'd say. Long, black trench coat and bald as a coot. Proper shiny head. Do you know him?'

'I know him,' said Brook.

Now, he thought… *Why would the same Homicide DS who steered everyone towards 'non-suspicious' in the churchyard be stealing my CCTV?*

Chapter 19

It felt good to close his own front door behind him. The flat wasn't much – the only one-bed amongst the fancier pads on the top floor – but a balcony overlooking north London made up for its modest dimensions. Brook threw his burrito wrapper in the bin, grabbed a beer and the TV remote, then slumped onto the sofa.

As the relaxing commentary of some live baseball washed over him, he found his eyes drifting to a framed photo on the wall – the last trip back to his hometown of Maun. Drinking sundowners at the Okavango River Lodge, the final rays of sunlight hitting the water just right. He could almost hear the hippos and their belly laughs.

Sure, the trip had been tinged with sadness – his parents packing up for their retirement project of a farmhouse in southern France – but Botswana would always be *home*. And it had been too long. He vowed once again to rectify that.

Taking his beer, Brook turned the baseball to mute and walked over to one of the two large items he had insisted on rescuing. A sun-faded, and slightly out of tune, upright piano. On top of it was an equally faded photo of an 8-year-old Brook sitting at the same piano, a decade before moving to England for university (a joint honours degree in 'Rugby and Beer' was the old joke).

Not surprisingly, he had copped some serious stick from his dad for the financial cost of getting the 'fokken thing' shipped over. Still, it was only half as much as he'd copped for the other item. That one had needed salvaging from the local scrapyard. It was several storeys beneath him in the underground car park.

After a decent rendition of *Mad World* – the title seemed appropriate – Brook stretched the final note with the sustaining pedal until he was sitting in front of the yellowing keys in silence. The piano had always been a good place to get his thoughts in order. A place of patterns, sequences and bum notes that didn't fit. The anatomy of an investigation.

He took out his phone and looked at the screenshot from Jonboy, moving his fingertips over the image to make the man in the centre bigger… Yep, there he was. The bald Homicide DS from the churchyard. The only person to enter the CCTV office without signing in at around the time Brook's disc went missing.

The chances of an innocent explanation seemed slim. First, there was the cloak-and-dagger subterfuge of not signing in. Then the 'coincidence' of those two cameras dying – eliminating both the images of Victor's last known movements AND the theft of the disc that was their last refuge. Had Jonboy not known about the kebab shop camera, that would have tied up some loose ends very nicely (Brook had no idea how you went about sabotaging a CCTV system, but it was safe to say it had something to do with the dark arts of hacking).

He remembered Sandy reading out the name from her scene log… *'DS Chris Beckford'*. Maybe he could get in touch with a couple of old acquaintances at Homicide to get the lowdown on this guy? Then again, there was no way of knowing where new loyalties might lie. As for taking the whole thing to a senior officer, the balance of 'provable' versus 'deniable' was hardly in Brook's favour. No, chiselling the truth out of this one was down to him.

He finished the beer and – after all the mental gymnastics – decided on one more before bed. No more thinking about the case, though. Just the final relaxing beer of a long day in front of that soporific baseball commentary. This time he lay down on the sofa. *Ten more minutes of this*, he told himself. He was fast asleep in thirty seconds.

Chapter 20

He said the words out loud just to hear them.

'Detective Constable Brook Deelman.'

Why was this pest still making a nuisance of himself? He was meant to be 'a drunk' with a flatlining career. Not to mention a stupid name. Why wouldn't he just go away?

The only consolation was that Deelman's actions were, as far as possible, being picked up by his police contact and reported back to him. The contact had set up an alert for any mention of Deelman's name on police systems, as well as having a few other tricks up his sleeve. Which was comforting in one sense. Though it also meant that his own slip-ups – the ones the detective seized upon – were being reported back to him too. Which was not so comforting.

And now it seemed this Deelman had somehow found him on the pub's cameras (he did nothing suspicious in that pub. Nothing!) and three bottles of non-alcoholic lager were winging their way to a laboratory for analysis. So much for his contact's promise that one of his men would 'take care of the CCTV'. Even if that were true for the street footage, the detective had clearly discovered the link to the pub and got there first. The 'drunk' had been one step ahead.

What made it even more annoying was that he had actually considered whether to order drinks in a bottle or a glass. So it wasn't so much an oversight as just a bad decision. The staff had been falling behind with the glass collection. Even ones returned to the bar were being piled up at one end. He didn't like the thought of something with his prints and DNA on it hanging around for so long, maybe even getting overlooked until the end of the night. Bottles, on the other hand, were being swiftly chucked into some kind of bin at the end of the bar. The staff seemed to enjoy the noise it made. So that's what he had gone for. The bottles. A mistake, as it turned out.

The decision to stay away from alcohol… no, he couldn't regret that. The slightest reduction in his reactions and he would have been stabbed in that churchyard. But allowing himself to be palmed off with some unpopular brand by the barman? Yes, that was on him. And the worst of it was that, for all his connections throughout the police, his contact didn't currently have anyone in place at the lab. Which meant there was no way of heading this one off at the pass.

He lay back on the adequate bed in the adequate budget hotel – the place he was tolerating for the only night of his life he ever planned to spend in Sheffield – and permitted himself to consider the worst case scenario. It was more embarrassing than dangerous. On the one hand, he knew his name WAS on that national DNA database. At least the name he used when operating in the UK. It had been there since a bit of an issue with the first job he carried out here a few years ago.

On the other hand, far from being a liability, having his DNA on the system had actually turned into another part of the safety net that his police contact provided. It effectively created an early warning system, being linked to a Police National

Computer entry with explicit instructions for anyone reading it to call his contact. Similar instructions were par for the course – attached to records by detectives in case their suspect got name-checked in another matter. In this instance, however, it was so that any investigation could be nipped in the bud.

And when your contact's title was Deputy Commissioner of the Metropolitan Police, it was amazing the problems he could make disappear.

So, the worst case scenario? Yes, it was embarrassment. The embarrassment of having to rely on someone else to get him out of a sticky situation. But his confidence in his contact's ability to do exactly that was absolute. At least until the Deputy Commissioner's retirement next week. It was why all of this had needed to happen in a hurry. After that, well… he needed to focus on the task at hand.

Talking of which… he opened his palm and looked again at the three small tablets of MDMA. Ecstasy they called it in this country. Surprisingly easy to obtain. They weren't for him, of course. No, these were for someone else. The idea had begun to take shape while he was in a dark mood about the 'panic attack' and 'racing pulse' that the second target was suffering, preventing him from seeing him today. All that pressure on his heart. At his age. Well, anyone would be forgiven for thinking he was… on the brink of a heart attack. It's amazing how an obstacle can be turned into an opportunity.

Until hitting upon this method, he had been mulling over a few different ways of accomplishing the job. The way in which he dispatched the first target was not going to be an option in the middle of a care home. But this seemed perfect. After all, his cover story to 'Debbie' was that he would be having a nice long chat with the second target about his old army days. And that was bound to involve several cups of tea. The target's final one might just have an extra kick to it. There should even be a nice little delay for him to bid everyone a cheery farewell and be on his way before all the drama. No-one was going to do toxicology tests on a 93-year-old who had been suffering a racing pulse in the past 24 hours. In all likelihood, one tablet would be plenty. Three was probably, well... 'overkill'... but there was nothing wrong with that.

He smiled at his unintended pun.

And then he carried on smiling because there was no point denying it...

He was looking forward to killing Harry Wilson.

Chapter 21

Thursday, 19th April 1945
Stalag IV-B, Mühlberg, Germany

Four days now. Four days since Lance Corporal Victor Watson was summoned to von Eberstein's hut. He had not been back into camp since. The order from a senior Nazi that he be removed from the squalor and given the sort of treatment befitting an Anglo-Saxon cultural treasure was being strictly adhered to. He should have been ecstatic. But those little voices… the leftover traces of primeval survival instincts… shadowy senses no longer fully understood… They were having a field day.

Victor was certainly being given plenty of time for his mind to explore the endless theories. Not only had he not been back into camp in the past four days, he had barely left the hut. As well as the main space, dominated by the altar-like mahogany desk, there was a separate room to the rear where he had been told he could sleep. The single bed had a thick palliasse, fresh pillow and warm blanket – a level of comfort superior to the Foundling Hospital, let alone the lice-infested bunk beds of Stalag IV-B.

If he wanted to shower or use the guards' toilet block, Victor followed von Eberstein's instructions – a couple of knocks on the inside of the hut door and then a short wait, until an external bolt slid open and two guards escorted him there and back. Then the bolt slid shut again. And the theories began to clutter his mind.

Food was delivered by a guard every morning. Black bread, butter, cheese, potted meat and tinned fruit, along with a jug of water and a mug of ersatz coffee. In the evening a sort of meat and vegetable broth was also provided. Victor remembered to save some bread for it after the first time. Not exactly the Ritz, but after the past year and a bit, it may as well have been.

The old guard who delivered the food obviously felt the same, judging by the way he looked longingly at the tray as he placed it down. Victor recognised him as one of the kinder ones – he had tried his German vocabulary on him a few times in camp and received a genial response. The guard must have been in his sixties, maybe older. Another example of the 'all hands on deck' approach as the Third Reich sank along with all of its citizens. On the third day, Victor gave him a tin of fruit.

When not eating or trying to rationalise the feelings of unease, Victor passed the time by perusing a handful of German books and newspapers on a small table against one of the walls. A German translation of Hans Christian Andersen's fairytales was the only book he could manage for any length of time, on account of knowing some of the stories already. Thus he had discovered that *The Ugly Duckling* was *'Das Hässliche Entlein'* while *The Emperor's New Clothes* was *'Des Kaisers Neue Kleider'*. The newspaper articles were generally easier to digest, even if their propaganda wasn't.

Von Eberstein had been coming to the hut for a couple of hours each afternoon, insisting that Victor join him at the desk. He seemed keen to talk about all manner of subjects, though the Englishman's reluctance to fully engage was clearly a growing irritation. Victor also resisted the repeated offers of whisky – a drink to which von Eberstein seemed practically immune – though he did relent on the offer of cigarettes. Nevertheless, he made a point of not 'mirroring' or allowing his own actions to be 'mirrored' as they smoked. He was aware of the more subtle tricks of interrogation and manipulation.

Victor was reading his favourite book at the window when he heard the door open. He turned to see von Eberstein entering the hut, his uniform as immaculate as ever and a fresh bottle of whisky in his hand.

'Zwölf Jahre,' he said with a smile, holding up the bottle. 'Twelve years, this one. Civilisation is not dead after all.'

He sat down on his side of the desk and placed the bottle and two clean tumblers on the polished wood. Then he leaned back in the comfortable chair and linked his fingers behind his head.

'Please,' he said to Victor, nodding at the chair opposite. Victor put down the Hans Christian Andersen stories and joined the sinewy Nazi. There was nothing to be gained by refusing.

'I trust you slept well,' said von Eberstein.

'It's a comfortable bed,' said Victor, not entirely answering the question.

As always, von Eberstein poured two generous measures of whisky into the tumblers and slid one across the shiny desktop to Victor. The Englishman slid it back. Then the German swirled the liquid round the glass, inhaled deeply and downed it in one. The little routine never changed.

'Have you told the Brigadeführer that he's made a mistake with my identity and I should be returned to camp?' asked Victor. It was a theme he returned to on a daily basis. For all the extra food and comfort, he wanted to be in camp with his own people when liberation arrived – be it from the Russians, Americans or British.

'I will refer you to my earlier answers,' said von Eberstein, moving the newly emptied tumbler to one side and bringing the remaining drink closer. 'Communications are somewhat sporadic at this stage and, in any case, I suspect the Brigadeführer has more important things to worry about than whether or not you played for his Western Ham United.'

Over the space of four days, Victor had gradually tired of correcting von Eberstein on the issue of *West* Ham United.

'It seemed to matter a great deal to him a few days ago,' he replied.

'Well, I think we can all agree that his intention with this exercise has been achieved. I dare say a copy of his kind-hearted letter is already with his lawyer should he find himself on trial after the war for his… patriotic acts.'

'Sounds like quite the charmer,' said Victor, trapping a packet of cigarettes just before it slid off the edge of the desk. Von Eberstein sent the box of matches skidding after it. The Englishman lit himself a cigarette before sliding both back. Then the Nazi joined him – two ashtrays already in place from the previous day.

'I have this funny feeling that I am doing most of the talking in our little chats,' said von Eberstein. He drew deeply on his cigarette and fixed Victor with a blue-eyed stare as he exhaled the swirling white clouds.

Victor met his gaze with an equally blue-eyed stare and exhaled his own swirling white clouds. The two mini weather fronts met above the desk and engaged in tumbling combat.

'You forget how a poor diet has affected my memory, old chap. I'm sure if you just bring me up to speed on everything you've told me, I'll be able to contribute a little more.'

Von Eberstein took a sip of his whisky, then allowed a thin smile.

'Very well. I will humour your request. On the understanding that, as a proud Englishman, you will honour your commitment to be more talkful.'

'I will be more talkful,' agreed Victor.

'Well… In the past few days you have learned that the von Ebersteins are German nobility. That my father is a successful banker who moved the family to London in the early twenties. Which is also where I spent the first nine years of my life before our return to Berlin…'

He took another long drag on his cigarette.

'…You have learned that my uncle is Friedrich Karl von Eberstein. A double Iron Cross recipient from the Great War, senior member of the Nazi Party and great friend of Himmler. Oh, and when not fighting wars, also a banker like my father. You have learned that, thanks to a somewhat swift elevation through the ranks and impeccable connections, I have been able to pick and choose where I fulfil my SS duties, from Greece to Norway, before finding myself here. By choice, naturally.'

'All the time reserving the worst of your punishment for the same three groups,' said Victor. There was nothing wrong with his memory.

'Sehr gut,' said von Eberstein. 'You remember – cowards, those who tell lies to the SS, and those who accept the humiliation of being a prisoner.'

'So why am I still alive?' asked Victor.

'Well, unless you tell me which category you are in, I cannot say.'

The two men observed each other through the smoke. A new smile came over von Eberstein's face. He topped up his own tumbler, then filled the empty one with a triple measure before sliding it across the desk. It was sliding back to him less than a second later.

'And how did you become such a bloody psychopath?' asked Victor.

The SS officer swirled the returned whisky, absorbed the aroma, then downed it.

'Oh, I'm sure I am a classic case. A psychiatrist's dream. Distant, super rich parents, an emotionally cold nanny… I have no doubt I'm a walking cliché.'

Victor resisted the urge to point out that a lack of parents and affection in his own upbringing hadn't turned *him* into a psychopath.

'Now!' announced von Eberstein with sudden enthusiasm. 'You just asked two questions in a row… Why are you alive and why am I a psychopath… So we are having a conversation at last! If you are able to ask a third to re-enforce this new friendship, then you will earn yourself a reward.'

Victor closed his eyes and pulled on the cigarette, wondering what type of madman was sitting across from him. Von Eberstein saw only a man thinking hard about his next question.

'I'll keep it simple,' said the Englishman.

'As you wish.'

'What's your full name?'

'Ah! Just the question for pleasant chats. My full name is Karl Friedrich von Eberstein.'

'I thought that was your uncle's name… Himmler's mucker.'

'Why would you think that? Neither our first names, nor our second names are the same. You were obviously right about the poor diet affecting your memory.'

'So what was his name?'

'Friedrich Karl von Eberstein.'

Victor descended into a hybrid cough-laugh on his cigarette, the spasms of his lungs creating bursts of white smoke around him.

'I think you just made a joke,' he said at last.

'Excellent. Then we are making progress.'

Victor managed to take a proper breath.

'Progress towards what?'

'Well, let me put it like this…' said the Nazi, tapping the ash off the end of his cigarette and leaning forward. Victor braced himself for some self-indulgent, philosophical claptrap.

'The von Ebersteins have always had an ability to adapt and overcome. In wartime and in peace. What other family spent the time between two wars making a fortune in the capital city of the enemy?'

'Congratulations,' said Victor with heavy sarcasm.

'And now, here we are once again. Just as in 1918, the British are about to find themselves at the head table. Master of ceremonies, do you say? The key to succeeding in post-war Europe for a man such as me will be understanding the Englishman, knowing how he behaves, how he thinks. And here I have a real live one in front of me to study. So, perhaps you understand my enthusiasm for our little situation.'

'Well, your whole family sounds quite bonkers to me,' said Victor, pricking the pomposity.

'Many millions of pounds says quite the opposite,' replied von Eberstein.

'I wouldn't know about that, old chap. An Englishman finds it rather poor form to discuss financial matters.'

'Excellent advice! This is exactly what I am talking about. Thank you.'

Victor frowned at his unintended assistance as he tapped the ash off his cigarette.

'Come now,' said von Eberstein. 'I promised you a reward for three questions…'

Reaching down to a drawer, he unlocked it and produced two items, tossing both onto the desktop. One was a rather tatty calendar. Victor didn't pay much attention to that because the other was a gold medal. It bore the motto *'Ad Victoriam'*.

Von Eberstein tried to read the prisoner's expression as he looked at it.

'The medal was in your possession when you were processed on arrival,' he said, matter-of-factly. 'I like it.'

He stubbed out his cigarette, picked up the medal and turned it around in his fingers, examining it. The words were surrounded by a circular design of some sort – the delicate impression somewhat worn down. A ring of flames maybe? A laurel leaf crown? The two words were cut deeper and remained legible enough. It was a fair assumption it had started life as some kind of sporting prize.

'I have a little cousin who collects medals like this. Normally better quality, of course,' said von Eberstein, weighing it in his palm. 'Still, I think she would like it. She actually has three medals from the Berlin Olympics. I mean to say, they were won by Jew athletes, so at least they have a proper home now. I wonder… does this mean a lot to you?' He kept his head down, while raising his eyes to see the Englishman's reaction.

'I found it,' said Victor, keeping his gaze off the medal to feign a lack of interest. Some kind of mind game was going on. He wasn't about to give up any emotional ammunition.

'How?' came the instant reply, trying to trip Victor up.

'Wadi Akarit. Tunisia. Forty-three. We were busy giving Rommel's mob another sound thrashing and there it was in the sand. Couldn't even say if it came from one of our chaps or one of the fleeing Hun. Seemed a shame to leave it behind.'

'I see,' said von Eberstein, placing the medal carefully on the calendar. For the first time Victor looked at this other item… February was on display and two dates were marked with red crosses – the 8th and the 17th. Victor recognised them.

The dates of the last two escapes by prisoners out on work parties.

On account of the improving news over the radio, there had been no escape attempts since, but these two had been celebrated as successes. A Scotsman and a Kiwi. As far as anyone knew, the Germans were unaware of their absence (and the fact they hadn't been returned to camp suggested things might have gone well – maybe even a home run to Blighty).

But here were the dates of their escapes staring back at Victor. He did his best to give nothing away. As it happened, the Nazi wasn't finished with the account of finding the medal.

'You lied,' said von Eberstein. 'You told me a lie.'

Victor said nothing.

'I thought an Englishman was true to his word.'

Silence.

'Why is the Englishman lying to me, please? WHY?'

He slammed a fist down on the mahogany desk. Victor narrowed his eyes.

'An Englishman can make an exception for Nazis.'

Von Eberstein leapt to his feet, sending his leather chair crashing backwards. He leaned over the desk, pounding it with his fist on every word.

'LIE! LIE! LIE! LIE! LIE! LIE! LIE!'

Victor tilted his chair back to avoid the worst of the whisky breath and waited for von Eberstein to stop. He had known bullies since his earliest memories of the Foundling Hospital. He had known them during basic training. And he had known them more than ever among his captors at Stalag IV-B. It had all left him with a thicker skin than most.

When von Eberstein had grown tired, he stood upright, breathing hard. Victor let his front two chair legs return to the floor. After a few seconds, the SS officer turned, retrieved his own chair, righted it and sat down again.

'Besides,' said Victor. 'I was telling the truth about giving your boys a good hiding in North Africa.'

He knew he was pushing his luck.

In keeping with von Eberstein's total lack of predictability, he showed no reaction to the taunt. Or maybe he was just too tired from his tantrum. He was still breathing heavily as he spoke.

'The medal was with you when you were left at the Foundling Hospital on 28th April 1923… The staff allowed you to have it when you were seven or eight and it has been on your person ever since… Until your capture and arrival at Stalag IV-B… For some reason you treasure it as the only link to the mother who abandoned you… And you have never had any intention to escape because you refuse to leave it behind… Now, perhaps when you consider my knowledge of your life, and my knowledge of recent escapes, you will be able to realise my source…'

Victor's heart quickened. There was only one explanation.

'You're torturing Harry,' he said.

Von Eberstein clapped his hands together and grinned.

'Wunderbar! A true Sherlock Holmes! I prefer to say that Harry has been persuaded to talk.'

Victor leaned forward to make his appeal.

'Look, there's no need. Whatever information you want about me, I'll give it to you. You can let Harry go. Give the order.'

'Your request is noted,' said von Eberstein, cheerily.

He put the calendar back in the drawer, slipped the medal and cigarettes into his tunic, and grabbed the whisky bottle. It was considerably lighter than when he'd arrived. Then he stood up with a broad smile and dusted down the front of his immaculate uniform with his free hand.

'Tomorrow, I will return. And we will have a chat about whatever I wish to talk about to explore the English mind. And your performance, and your honesty, will be better. I am sure. Lance Corporal Watson.'

SS-Sturmbannführer von Eberstein walked round the desk, past Victor, and over to the hut's door. He paused just before reaching it.

'Ah! I almost forgot to say. A different guard will deliver your food tomorrow. I caught that lying old man trying to hide a tin of peaches in his pocket and had to discipline him. He offered the absurd defence that you *gave* it to him.'

'I did,' said Victor.

'Really? Amazing. You see? Even now I am learning about the Englishman's strange ways.'

He opened the door.

'If he survives his injuries I will give my apologies.'

Chapter 22

Saturday, 23rd April 2016
North London

Brook took his morning coffee through to the bedroom, recalling how it had been around 3am when he finally dragged himself the short distance from sofa to bed. He put the mug on the bedside table, swung his arms a few times, then dropped to the floor and hooked his feet up on the edge of the mattress. Ten ultra slow motion press-ups followed. He tried to focus on every working muscle on the way down, then their opposites on the way up. The aim was always to be totally spent after the tenth – any more press-ups left in the tank and the slow-mo tempo had not been slow enough. His arms quivered as he forced through the tenth. Then he was done. He finished his coffee and headed for the shower. That was enough exercise for a while.

A home-made breakfast of fried eggs and more coffee didn't last long. Brook had just put down an extra two slices of toast when his phone began buzzing on the counter... *Marie.*

'You're up early,' he said.

'I could say the same. I wasn't sure if I'd wake you.'

'As if I'd ever complain about being woken by you.'

'Whatever, Deelman.'

The soft Irish accent conveyed the hint of a smile.

'Anyway,' she continued. 'I'm on the quick change-over shift. Plus, I had a text to say the results from the bottles were ready.'

'You're kidding me. How did you manage that?'

'Well, the night shift cover at the lab may just have been an ex-flatmate of mine. You know, dealing with the urgent submissions.'

'And?'

'And for the first time in forever there were no urgent submissions. So there was no point them having idle hands now, was there?'

'Marie, you're a miracle worker.'

A pause indicated it was time to move on to the point of the call. Brook felt as if there was a lot riding on the next few seconds.

'So were they able to get a DNA profile?' he asked.

'They were.'

'And is there a hit on the database?'

'There's a hit. Are you coming in to the station?'

'I bloody am now…'

The forensics officer was sitting at her desk as Brook put his head round the door, unnoticed. Marie's hair was still wet from the shower, brushed straight back to a horizontal cut just beneath the nape of her neck. In her mid-30s, she barely looked any different from when Brook had met her a decade ago.

The detective tapped the door with his foot so as not to surprise her if she looked up.

'*Déjà vu*,' said Marie, smiling at Brook's second delivery of coffee in the past twelve hours.

She was wearing a white blouse beneath a light green cardigan that matched her eyes. Just like the previous evening, she was the only one present of the dwindling number of forensics officers who worked at the station. Brook placed the coffees on her desk.

'So, is this staying then?' she asked, reaching up and lightly brushing his heavy stubble with the back of a finger.

'Not sure. What do you reckon?'

'I'll need a bit longer to think about it. You've definitely got a few hints of silver fox though.'

That sounded much better than *grey*. Maybe he would keep it after all. He looked for the coffee cup with an 'S' and pushed it towards Marie.

'One sugar,' he said.

'Perfect. I hope I'll be able to train my husband this well.'

They both took a sip of their drinks to mask the slight awkwardness that followed the remark.

'Right,' said Marie, clicking through her e-mails, keen to move on. 'Here it is.'

Brook selected the same office chair as his last visit. Once again, it creaked its objections. A dense report of scientific terms and lengthy statistics was on the screen. He squinted at it for a moment before leaning back and taking the easy option.

'Can I have the edited highlights?'

'You're getting old, Deelman.'

'Tell me about it.'

'Okay. The edited highlights are… that the first bottle gave a gazillion mixed profiles, so had probably been dripped on by all sorts of things in that wheelie bin.'

'I love it when a scientific report contains the word 'gazillion.''

'I thought you wanted the edited version.'

'True. I'll shut up.'

'The second bottle was better and gave a partial DNA profile from one individual, but not enough to compare it to the database.'

'Third time lucky then?'

'Just like Goldilocks, isn't it? The third bottle gave a full DNA profile from one individual. It matched the partial one and was also good enough to run through the national DNA database. Bringing back a big… fat… hit.'

'So that will be our man,' said Brook, leaning closer to the screen now.

'I'd say so… Here he is.'

Marie brought up the final page of the report. Brook didn't need any edited highlights for this:

Logan Baird

6'0"

M

13/08/71

Dunbartonshire, UK

LKA: 1 Station Road, Bexhill-on-Sea, East Sussex

'What do you think?' asked Marie.

Brook stared at it for a moment longer.

'I think it's an alias. Scottish-sounding name. Born in Dunbartonshire. The barman at The Junction got the impression he wasn't British. I think he would have recognised a Scottish accent. Or even an English one, depending on how long this East Sussex place has been his last known address. Interesting name…'

He got out his phone, tapped in an internet search and scrolled through the result.

'Tell me,' he said, 'if you had to name one famous person that comes to mind when you see *Logan Baird*, who would you say?'

'Ooh, an early morning pub quiz? Okay… John Logie Baird. Was he the telephone or television?'

'Invented television. The man responsible for me falling asleep on the sofa every night.'

'So what about him?'

Brook turned his phone around.

'Born in Dunbartonshire on the thirteenth of August. Died at 1 Station Road, Bexhill-on-Sea, East Sussex. I think someone was having a bit of fun when they gave those details. At least they didn't give 1888 as their year of birth.'

Judas Iscariot's reign as the world's most obscure fake details had lasted barely a day.

'Oh, for fuck's sake,' said Marie.

'Hey!' said Brook, nudging her arm. 'No defeatism allowed. Let's look at his full PNC.'

Marie rose from her slump to call up the Police National Computer and entered Logan Baird's details. The identical information came up, but with a couple of additions. A single crime report number from 2013 – the point at which the DNA sample must have been taken – and a footnote:

'IN THE EVENT OF ANY DEALINGS, CONTACT DEP. COMM. BARNES BEFORE PROCEEDING ANY FURTHER.'

It was accompanied by a phone number.

'Dep. Comm…' read Marie. 'The Deputy Commissioner?'

'I guess so.'

'Are you going to call him?'

'Maybe… Or maybe we should just take a look at that crime report first.'

Marie gave him a look before punching in the solitary crime report number. The result did not take long to read:

'REPORT RESTRICTED BY DEP. COMM. BARNES 22/04/16.'

'A report that's three years old but was only restricted yesterday,' said Marie. 'And by the Deputy Commissioner, no less. Whose name is also all over your suspect. I get the impression you're treading on some big toes with all this, Deelman.'

She was only saying what both of them were thinking.

'Interesting timing, isn't it?' said Brook.

'It is, but… there'll be an explanation. I take it you're still going to call him.'

'Sure.'

'Brook.'

'Eventually.'

'Do you think that's what he meant by *'Before Proceeding Any Further'*?'

Brook pushed himself out of the chair and took his coffee for a wander around the office. He hadn't yet brought Marie up to speed on the full strangeness of DS Beckford's behaviour and, as such, on why he was so wary of taking the Deputy Commissioner's instruction at face value.

At the same time, a new thought dawned on him… Nobody ever called DS Beckford to the scene. What was it he had said? *'Just grabbing a coffee round the corner. Heard this come out over the local channel and thought I'd see if we were needed.'* How had he missed that little coincidence?

Marie's voice broke the silence.

'Look, Brook. You know I pulled some strings to get these results so quick. I guess I would just feel more comfortable if you called the Deputy Commissioner. You don't really want us both getting sacked just before my wedding now, do you?'

Brook's impromptu wander around the office meant he had his back to Marie as he replied.

'That wedding's on your mind a lot today, isn't it?'

He immediately felt embarrassed by how petty and ungracious it sounded. When he turned around, he saw Marie's expression had changed.

'You know, that's actually not entirely unusual, Brook. Maybe you'll find out one day.'

Now it was Marie who felt bad for how much harsher the comment sounded once it was verbalised. Brook tossed his empty coffee cup in the bin.

'Maybe,' he repeated, heading for the door.

The printer in the corner began chuntering as he passed it.

'That's your lab report and your PNC for Logan Baird,' said Marie, joylessly.

Brook stood in awkward silence by the printer, his back to the room, the seconds passing painfully slowly. At last, the final page scuttled out and the printer stopped grumbling. Brook gathered them all up unceremoniously.

'Thanks,' he said, half turning back towards Marie.

'Welcome,' she replied, her green eyes a little duller than before.

Chapter 23

'Well done, Brook… That went really well… You're a genius.'

The detective muttered sarcastically to himself as he wandered the police station's corridors.

'Have a medal… In fact, have Victor Watson's fucking medal.'

Far from helping, the monologue was only annoying him even more. He told himself to shut up and focus. Apart from falling out with Marie, he had learned a lot in the last few minutes. Not least that DS Chris Beckford appeared to have an ally in Deputy Commissioner Barnes when it came to obstructing the path to the man who killed Victor Watson. A man who went by the alias 'Logan Baird', or at least once had. That was a lot of new pieces for the jigsaw; if he could just stop beating himself up about the Marie stuff.

Brook turned into the central stairwell just as a particularly tedious DI appeared at the far end of the corridor. He hoped he hadn't been seen…

'DC Deelman!'

Shit.

He reluctantly stepped back and watched as Detective Inspector Julian Self approached. He was about ten years younger than Brook. Maybe more. A beneficiary of the new Direct Entry Scheme that catapulted those with 'special skills' straight into a position of power (DI Self's special skills had something to do with scraping a degree in Media Studies).

'Just the man,' he said, approaching. That didn't sound good – there was clearly some point he was dying to make.

'I'm not exactly in work today,' said Brook, pre-empting any request to help with prisoners or take on a new investigation.

'Funny,' said the DI. 'I could swear I can see you.'

You're fucking hilarious, thought Brook, giving something between a smile and a grimace.

'I'm just doing a bit of overtime in relation to a non-suspicious death.'

'Overtime for a non-suspicious death? Who authorised that?'

Petty little prick.

'Don't worry,' said Brook. 'It's not coming out of your budget.'

'Glad to hear it,' replied the DI, looking genuinely pleased at the saving. Maybe that was his equivalent of winning a big case. He was a skinny man, a few inches shorter than Brook, with a ruler-straight side parting in his fair hair and a smooth, weak chin. He never quite seemed to fill his expensive Italian suits. Standing in front of Brook – with his untamed dark hair, heavy stubble and sturdy frame – it must have looked like the first meeting between homo sapiens and Neanderthal man.

'So, you'll be out making enquiries, will you?' asked the DI. 'Dealing with members of the public? Representing the Metropolitan Police Service?'

Brook knew where this was going but let it play out anyway.

'That's the idea,' he replied.

'So you'll be wearing a–'

'A smile?'

'A suit, DC Deelman. You'll be wearing a suit. Because that's what we do.'

We. Nice one. Brook had about as much intention of changing his attire as the Lumberjack, but the DI was on a roll…

'I take it you also saw the e-mail about the change of clothing policy surrounding night duty. I hear you and DS Padmore also failed to wear suits during your week of nights.'

'We did catch a lot of bad guys though.'

'That's not the–'

'Not the point?' offered Brook.

Some colour came into the DI's cheeks.

'Look…' he started again. 'What I was going to say before I got sidetracked by the whole suit issue, was that you're moving to us in the CSU next week.'

The Community Safety Unit – domestic and racial violence.

'That's fine,' said Brook. Another e-mail he hadn't read.

'Now, we're going to need everyone on board to get our detection rate up to the combined target of thirty-seven percent. So I expect you to play a full part in our reaching that challenging but achievable goal.'

Christ. The chip had been implanted deep with this one. As the DI launched into some more leadership-speak, the sound of Brook's ringtone offered a welcome escape route.

'That's all great, Sir,' he agreed, whipping out the mobile and making for the stairwell. 'Got to take this, I'm afraid. Very important.'

'Actually, I haven't fin–'

'Hello..?' shouted Brook, drowning out the DI and heading down the stairs. 'Hello..?'

Only when he reached the ground floor did he actually listen to the voice at the other end. It had a Yorkshire accent.

'Ooh, blimey, can you 'ear me now, Brook, love?' said Debbie.

'Debbie. Sorry about that.'

'Seems whenever I call up, you're shouting *'ello* at me.'

Brook remembered her last call that had caught him in the Hen & Chickens.

'You're right. Still, better than shouting Goodbye.'

'I'll give you that much. Anyway, I thought you might like to know that Peak View's finest team of detectives 'ave come up with an answer for you.'

'You have?'

'Don't sound so surprised, Brook. I told yer we would. Right… that bloke who were 'aving panic attack yesterday? I were able to talk to him this morning. Turns out he grew up down there in London and served in't Middlesex Regiment during war. Went a bit quiet when I asked about Victor Watson, and I didn't want to push things after his funny turn. But it's got to be 'im, don't yer think? Harry Wilson his name is.'

'Brilliant work,' said Brook, his thoughts turning to getting a local police officer to talk to this Harry. There was a limit to what he could request of a civilian.

'What's he doing today?' he asked.

'Well, right now, he's with a nice chap I'm hoping will cheer 'im up. The one who called and said he'd like to chat to Harry 'bout his army days. Said Harry had served with his grandad or summat like that.'

Brook's pulse went up a notch. That sounded like a cover story. Or, to put it another way: Bullshit.

'I don't suppose you got his name did you?' he asked.

'Ooh, 'ang on a sec. Let me check visitors' book.'

It couldn't be, could it? *Logan Baird?* Brook heard the brief clatter of the receiver being placed on a hard surface, then faint voices. Debbie was talking to a colleague. They started laughing about something. Then another brief clatter as Debbie lifted the receiver back up.

'Sorry about that,' she said, through the tail end of the laughter. 'We were struggling to read writing… It looks a bit like *Yogi Bear*.'

Chapter 24

The industrial 'clunk, clunk, clunk' of the winding mechanism came first. Then, as unseen wires tightened, the metal strips of the roller shutter appeared to stand to attention, each overlapping panel presenting a little prouder. Finally, the bottom edge lifted from the tarmac, the slatted steel curtain coiling itself around an overhead axle as the ramp to the underground car park greeted the outside world with a mechanical yawn. The whole process took about ten seconds. For the driver waiting on the ramp side, it felt like an eternity. He didn't wait for the clunking to finish. As soon as the gap was high enough for his vehicle to squeeze through, he floored it.

The 1980 Land Rover Defender roared into the daylight like a liberated beast. The second item Brook Deelman had shipped over from Botswana. The growling 4x4 had a navy blue body with a white roof to reflect the worst of the African sun. Right now, however, it was off to Sheffield.

Brook had always felt too much of an affinity with the old family vehicle to leave it in that Maun scrapyard. A powerful unit with a few creaking joints – they had plenty in common.

Now it just needed to get him to Peak View Care Home in world record time. The Defender tore through a couple of amber lights and treated the speed bumps with the sort of contempt befitting an off-road legend that had earned its stripes on dirt tracks.

It was fifteen minutes since Debbie had said the words 'Yogi Bear', and a few seconds less since she had confirmed the name in the visitors' book was 'Logan Baird'. Brook had rushed straight to the back yard and flagged down a departing patrol car to beg an unauthorised lift home. He was relieved to recognise the driver from a recent case in which Brook had smoothed over a couple of fuck-ups. Whether it was eagerness to return the favour, or just the look in the detective's eyes, the driver had slapped on the blue lights and his new passenger wasn't about to complain about the breach of protocol.

Staying on the phone to Debbie, he had managed to establish that Logan Baird had in fact just left. Harry Wilson was now in the communal lounge and seemed fine, enjoying a nice cup of tea. If that was good news, it posed a brand-new question – why was Victor's killer meeting Victor's friend a couple of days after his murder? Another question followed hot on the heels of that one – was Harry Wilson *really* fine?

Brook made one lightning quick pit stop on the 150-mile journey to grab a takeaway coffee. It was all conducted at such speed he almost flattened a guy trying to sell him breakdown cover. Now that he was closer to Sheffield, he dug out an ancient satnav and typed in Peak View's postcode. The stern female voice reminded the bachelor why he rarely used it.

Nevertheless, Brook was soon rolling past a street name he recognised from the care home's full address, leaning forward and scanning left and right for the building. In the end, he spotted it at the exact moment as the two questions on his mind were answered…

Was Harry Wilson *really* fine after his meeting with Logan Baird?

Answer: No.

Why was Victor's killer meeting Victor's friend a couple of days after his murder?

Answer: To kill him too.

Brook pulled the Defender over to the kerb and brought it to a halt in front of a cluster of three vehicles. A police car. An ambulance. And a coroner's wagon.

The satnav had a message for Brook and Harry alike…

'You have reached your destination.'

Chapter 25

He watched the Land Rover pull up from his vantage point and checked the dashboard clock. Deelman had made good time. The powdered ecstasy tablets had taken longer than he thought to kick in – and longer than he thought to finish off Harry's old heart. He was glad now that he'd gone for the 'overkill' of using three.

Having opted for a taxi to travel to and from Peak View – keeping his hire car sterile – he felt confident no-one would notice the black Ford Fiesta now he'd returned to monitor events from a handy side road. Sheffield seemed to be made entirely of hills. It made for a host of good surveillance spots.

The dead-end residential street was what they called a 'cul-de-sac' in this country. Nobody had bothered him as he sat there in the instantly forgettable vehicle. Of course, he hadn't been sure if this DC Deelman would show up – even though he had an idea he was poking around when Debbie asked that question about Harry serving in the Middlesex Regiment.

At that point, it was still possible that the detective was just going through the motions – making a tick-box enquiry and writing up a banal report to show some bored supervisor. That was the usual way in any police force. But a call from Barnes had confirmed that Deelman's phone was travelling north on the M1. And now here he was. A long way from home. He was clearly one of those annoying police officers who believed in getting things done.

Barnes had already informed him of the detective's private vehicle in case he came across it. Probably not the hardest thing for a man in his position to find out. Still, the phone tracking and vehicle description were all confirmation of his usefulness, even if things had been a bit tense between them (not least because Barnes' initial dismissal of Deelman – as a drunk who was nothing to worry about – seemed worse by the day. If the detective was an alcoholic, he was a fucking high-functioning one).

Anyway, he was in an upbeat mood. All in all, the day could hardly have gone better. Harry had been... what was the word?... 'compliant' throughout. Sure, the old bastard he killed in the churchyard had managed to get a call through to him – he had been right to think that was the source of his panic attack. But Harry also seemed to accept there was nothing he could do to outrun this. The funny thing was, that after coming through the panic, he appeared strangely serene. It was as if he had made his peace with what was going to happen. Maybe, even, his peace with everything that had happened in the past.

He recalled his words as they sat down with their cups of tea after a walk round the gardens – a walk during which Harry, resigned to his fate, had told him everything...

'There's something in there, isn't there?' he'd said, looking at the hot drink.

If there was one lesson to take from the last few days, it was that these ninety-somethings were not to be underestimated. He hadn't bothered to lie.

'There is. You can drink it, or I can come back tomorrow and we'll do this another way.'

He knew it wasn't the threat that had made him drink it. He was just… ready.

'Don't worry, guv,' Harry had said, the Cockney accent still there, even though the voice was thin and weak. 'You won't have to come back.'

Fast-forward to his vantage point, and the drop in urgency among the various people in uniform told him that Harry had been true to his word. Any lingering doubt was removed when the guys in suits from the Coroner's office turned up.

It was done.

And now… now he was looking at a navy blue, long wheelbase, Land Rover Defender with a white roof. There was no need to check that the licence plate matched the one Barnes had given him. He knew this was Deelman. His first glimpse. He seemed to be taking his time getting out of the vehicle – no doubt taking in the scene and weighing up how best to approach it. Still, even from this distance, it was clear he was a big guy.

He had left a little surprise for the detective. In a deliberately obscure way.

The taxi firm he had used were the unwitting custodians of it.

If Deelman was good enough, he would find it. And if he wasn't then, well…

Then maybe he was nothing to worry about after all.

Chapter 26

Brook sat in the Defender for a couple of minutes, staring at the three vehicles in front of him and considering his options… 'Just wing it,' he said to himself, stepping down. He nodded at a couple of paramedics unhurriedly completing some paperwork in their ambulance. Yep, Harry was dead all right.

A paved path with lawns either side led up to Peak View Care Home – a functional, two-storey building, set back from the rows of suburban semis either side. Brook entered via clunky automatic doors, finding a pine reception desk to his left and a floral-patterned carpet beneath his feet. The whole place had the feel of a slightly dated budget hotel, albeit with the addition of a cloying, chemical sweetness that could be tasted as much as smelled. Behind the desk, a phone was ringing with little prospect of being answered.

The only life Brook could see was in some kind of day room beyond a glazed dividing wall at the back of reception. Five people were in there: two suited Coroner's officers, a male police constable and two women in staff-issue polo shirts – dark blue with matching logos. Brook made his way into the new room, meeting the group's silent appraisal with a simple 'Hi'.

He noticed more detail now he was inside. Such as how every coffee table was strewn with half-eaten biscuits and cake, half-drunk teas and coffees. It looked like a police canteen following a call for urgent assistance (even if this place had likely emptied at a somewhat slower rate). He could see the five people better too.

The Coroner's officers both had shaved heads and big jowls. They looked like an older and younger version of the same person – a father and son team, no doubt. The uniformed PC was a cheery looking, red-faced fellow. Finally, the two female members of staff appeared to be in their mid-40s. A stocky blonde, with forearms perfect for any lifting of residents, and a neat brunette with her hair tied back in a ponytail and lively eyes. All five formed a rough semi-circle around a body bag on a gurney. The brunette spoke first as Brook approached.

'Sorry there's no-one out there at minute, love. We'll be with you in just a sec if you don't mind waiting.'

Brook recognised Debbie's voice and flashed his warrant card.

'Debbie, isn't it? Brook Deelman.'

'Oh, my Lord,' said Debbie. 'I were going to call you. That's your Harry Wilson in there, poor chap.' She added a few words of explanation for the others: 'Brook's a detective in London. Been trying to trace someone's next of kin and thought Harry might be able to 'elp.'

Brook sensed five sets of eyes upon him as he looked down at the body bag. He realised he hadn't shown the faintest reaction to the news that, of all the residents, the one on the gurney was the one he had come to see.

'I thought it might be him,' he said, keen to break the silence but only making things worse. 'You know…' he quickly added, turning to Debbie. 'After what you said about him having those panic attacks and a racing heart.'

'Oh, right. That's right,' said Debbie.

Brook felt the intensity of the group's attention move away from him. Good save.

'Well, I think I'm done here,' said the PC in broad Yorkshire tones, snapping his pocketbook shut and shoving it into the back of his trousers. 'I'll get doors for you, lads.'

'Cheers, pal,' said the Coroner's officers in stereo, beginning to manoeuvre Harry's gurney around the tables and chairs. Debbie's blonde colleague followed them out, as if bringing up the rear of a mini funeral procession – albeit one with a wheel that had picked up a bit of Victoria sponge and was now laying down a broken line of icing sugar and jam.

'I'm sorry you've had a wasted journey,' said Debbie. Brook thought he could see a faint sheen in her eyes. 'I know it's daft, but I never get used to them dying.'

'I can understand that,' he replied, a little distractedly, scanning the coffee table closest to them. It appeared to be lacking the food and drink remnants of the others.

'Was Harry having tea as well?' he asked, hoping the question could squeeze under the radar as idle chitchat, rather than a specific interest in murder methods.

'He were, yeah. Right there,' said Debbie. 'It all got knocked over when he turned a funny colour and we were trying to 'elp him. I think Tina cleared it away while we were waiting for that lot.' She nodded to where the mini funeral procession was now trying to negotiate the automatic main doors. The Victoria sponge road markings had finally come to an end halfway across reception.

Brook looked at the empty coffee table, thinking how any chemical evidence in food or drink was now in a bin or down a plughole. A beeper went off in Debbie's pocket.

'Sorry about this, love,' she said, taking out the device. 'Someone's had a fall. I'll be back with you soon as I can.'

'That's... fine,' said Brook, the second word to himself as the glazed doors closed behind Debbie. He looked around the empty room. A quick check told him there was no CCTV in here. Maybe HD quality footage of the Tourist slipping something into Harry's tea was too much to ask.

There was nothing to be gained from staying where he was, but the heavy silence held him there for a moment. The empty chairs all seemed to be saying: *'Well, we all saw what happened. What are you going to do about it?'*

Brook noticed a new member of staff was on duty in reception.

'Let's start there,' he told the chairs.

Chapter 27

Friday, 20th April 1945
Stalag IV-B, Mühlberg, Germany

It was towards the end of the fifth day that it came to Victor. Halfway through the meat and potato broth. He put the spoon down and stared into the middle distance as the realisation settled in. 'What the devil..?' he said to himself.

The evening food had been delivered by a new guard – his second delivery of the day after the usual assortment of bits and pieces in the morning. This guard wasn't as friendly as the last one, spilling broth as he slammed it down on the small table (Victor recognised him from the vicious beating of an Indian prisoner who had 'refused' to stop shivering during a January roll-call).

'English, Russians, Americans, Jews…' said the Nazi through gritted teeth, as Victor wiped some broth from the Hans Christian Andersen book. Then he spat at the prisoner's feet, barely able to contain his loathing, desperate for just one punch.

'Ein Moment,' said the Englishman… *One moment.*

He went to the sleeping quarters at the back of the hut and returned with a small tin of peaches he had been saving for pudding. He held it out to the guard and tried to look as meek as possible.

'Freunde?' said Victor… *'Friends?'*

The guard looked between Victor and the peaches with a quizzical expression. Then he grunted, grabbed the tin and shoved it in an overcoat pocket. He clearly hadn't heard what happened to the last chap. Victor watched him leave and looked forward to a new guard in the morning.

The light bulb moment – and the 'What the devil?' that accompanied it – arrived shortly after. It was all down to one phrase. *'In wartime and in peace'*. Von Eberstein had used it the previous day when describing how his family had always adapted to either circumstance.

Even at the time, the words had sounded familiar to Victor. Not just in themselves, but when spoken in that light German accent of von Eberstein's. Nevertheless, it had taken him more than a day to realise exactly when he had heard the SS officer use that phrase before. And, if he was right, then those primal instincts telling him the situation was not as it seemed had been correct all along.

The afternoon had been spent engaging in von Eberstein's attempts at conversation far more freely than before. He had asked about Victor's early life, the Foundling Hospital, his joining the army, his war before Stalag IV-B and what he hoped to do when the war was over – small talk about anything and everything. The fact that any answer Victor lied about could be exposed by torturing Harry – who knew all the answers – meant there was little choice but to be truthful, while giving away as little as possible.

Von Eberstein had seemed delighted at the new openness. Even if it had been achieved by blackmail. The whisky tumblers and cigarettes had skidded back and forth across the polished mahogany with greater frequency than ever before.

But now… now Victor knew when the SS officer had used those words before… *'In wartime and in peace'*.

Tomorrow's chat would be different.

One way or another.

Chapter 28

Saturday, 23rd April 2016
Peak View Care Home, Sheffield

Brook headed back out to reception and introduced himself to the new person at the desk. The member of staff's name was Nick. It turned out he had only just started his shift and had missed all the drama. Floppy hair, black-framed glasses and in his early 20s. He would have looked at home in some 'tech start-up' company.

'So, you're the detective from London who Debbie fancies?'

He didn't beat around the bush.

'Umm… I'm a detective from London. I wouldn't know about the rest. You don't sound like you're from round here either.'

'From Cheshunt, originally. That used to be part of the Met but it switched to Hertfordshire Police when they changed the boundaries.'

'Good knowledge,' said Brook.

'Yeah, I'm up here studying criminology at Sheffield Uni. This job's just part-time for some extra money. I'd quite like to do what you do, actually.'

First Debbie, now Nick. What was it with this place and people wanting to be detectives?

'I'm sure you'd be more successful than me,' said Brook. 'Listen, since the person I came to speak to about this next of kin search has… died… I was wondering if you might be able to help me find the guy he met this morning. It's one step removed, granted, but he still might be able to help.'

It sounded plausible enough in a vague kind of way.

'Sure,' said Nick, opening the visitors' book and spinning it round to face Brook. It took only a moment to see that the Tourist's entry was both helpful and unhelpful in equal measure.

Each line of visitor information comprised seven columns – date, time, resident name, visitor name, phone number, address and signature. In the case of *'Logan Baird'*, the phone number was one digit short while the address, once again, was John Logie Baird's old house *(1 Station Road, Bexhill-on-Sea, East Sussex)*. The signature was a meaningless scribble. He had apparently arrived at 10.05am.

The useful part was that it showed a link between Victor's and Harry's deaths. After all, here were the same details (one lot obtained via DNA) in venues over 150 miles apart where both dead veterans had spent final or near-final moments. In terms of finding out who Logan Baird really was, however, it was entirely useless.

'Is this filled out by the visitor or staff?' asked Brook.

'Visitor normally.'

'I think he forgot a digit in his phone number.'

'Shit. Sorry. At least you've still got his address.'

'Mmm.'

Brook glanced up and noticed a CCTV camera above the desk.

'Perhaps I could ask another favour…'

Moments later, he was standing next to Nick, both men hunched over a monitor with a quartered display – the camera in reception, another one covering the front path, and a third over the patio that led to the garden. The final quarter of the screen stayed black.

'Not exactly *Big Brother*, is it?' said Nick.

He went back to Logan Baird's recorded arrival of 10.05. The front-facing camera was angled in such a way that it only picked up the bottom half of people walking past on the pavement. It meant the Tourist's pale chinos and smart brown shoes appeared first.

As he turned onto the path, the navy sports jacket entered the frame, followed by the wide, muscular neck and dark hair, cut short and sensible. He waited for the automatic doors to do their tedious admission ceremony and then he was through to the camera in reception, standing with his hands behind his back while Debbie's blonde colleague with the strong forearms finished a phone call.

'Do you know him?' asked Nick.

'Kind of,' replied Brook.

'Okay. That's Tina on the phone,' he added, pre-empting Brook's question.

The phone call came to an end, at which point there was a brief exchange of words between the two before Tina lifted the visitors' book onto the reception desk and offered a pen. The Tourist took a pen of his own from an inner breast pocket and filled out his bogus details (maybe he was being more careful about forensics this time). Tina gave the details a cursory glance, then made a gesture towards the Tourist's lapel.

'She's saying she'll get him a visitor pass,' said Nick.

Sure enough, Tina walked over to a box of badge holders and began filling out the visitor's details on a card. As she did so, the Tourist leaned over the desk a little, tilting his head to one side as if reading something. Brook and Nick both spotted the subtle movement and looked around to see what had caught his eye. Nothing obvious. Then Brook lifted up the moveable keyboard – beneath it was a yellow Post-it Note, apparently written by Debbie:

'DC Brooke Deelman re. Victor Watson next of kin?? Met Police (!)'

It was followed by the mobile number he had given.

Brook looked back at the screen where Tina was still writing the visitor's name on a card to slide into the guest pass. The Tourist was now staring straight into the CCTV camera. A part of him must have known Brook might end up watching this. The detective found his jaw muscles clenching. It was a curious feeling – the two adversaries occupying the same space but in different time zones. A challenge laid down through the fourth dimension.

Nick seemed to sense the change in atmosphere.

'Is something wrong?' he asked.

'Huh?' said Brook, dragged back to his own timeline. 'Yeah, Debbie put an 'e' on the end of my name. Makes me sound like a girl.'

Nick's smile suggested he accepted the explanation. Even so, Brook could probably have done without his name and number being offered on a plate to the bad guy. They watched as Tina handed over the guest pass then showed her visitor to one of the accommodation corridors.

A couple of minutes later, the Tourist re-appeared on the camera over the patio with a shuffling old man beside him.

Brook's first sight of Harry. He was wearing a grey cardigan over a yellow shirt with brown trousers and plaid slippers. Every yard was hard won – planting his Zimmer frame and making his feet catch up with grim determination.

After nearly twenty minutes, the pair re-appeared on the same camera, heading back into the building. And then, finally, on the reception camera as they made their way to the lounge for the fatal cup of tea. Harry looked small next to the Tourist but had lost none of his mop of hair, even if it was now completely white. In the brief moments when he wasn't looking down, he seemed to have a distant air about him. A thousand yard stare in those old eyes as he moved the Zimmer frame with a metronomic resolve.

Fifteen minutes after going into the lounge, the Tourist emerged alone, left his guest pass at reception and waved a cheery farewell. There was just the hint of another glance up at the camera. Then he was on the outside footage, walking along the path and turning left onto the pavement.

Nick hit fast forward again and scrolled through the next hour… Debbie appeared, making her phone call to Brook, and everything seemed normal for a while. Then the explosion of activity amongst the carers, the frantic 999 calls and evacuation of the residents, the arrival of the paramedics… and the gradual return to normal. Game over.

'That's it, I guess,' said Nick.

Brook didn't reply straight away. He was thinking.

He was thinking that only a man with the backing of someone as powerful as the Deputy Commissioner could throw around his ridiculous alias and lay down challenges by staring into cameras like that. He didn't like the arrogance. The sense of entitlement. A murderer creeping around in the shadows was one thing. One who delighted in parading his bullet-proof credentials was something else.

'You think he's a suspect, don't you?' suggested Nick, catching Brook by surprise.

'Look, if everyone who spoke to someone before a heart attack was a suspect, we'd have a lot of investigations going on,' said Brook, swerving the question.

'You still think he's a suspect though, don't you?' came the reply. They were certainly a tenacious bunch at Peak View.

'Well, let's just put it like this,' said Brook. 'Since I've come all this way… it would probably be rude not to get a copy of that CCTV, photocopy the visitors' book and seize his guest pass for forensics. And is there any chance I could take a quick look in Harry's room?'

Chapter 29

So his DNA had come back on those bottles. A phone call from Barnes confirmed it. An inconvenience, but not a major problem. There were systems in place to deal with these things. More worrying than the DNA hit itself, was the fact that Deelman had clearly chosen to ignore the on-screen instruction to call Barnes. Even the safest systems could be bypassed by someone not playing by the rules. If the detective drifted into 'rogue' territory then that… changed things.

It made him even more relieved that he had left that surprise for Deelman with the local cab firm he had used. Barnes knew nothing about that. It was his own little safety net. A way of snaring a rogue copper rather than one playing nicely. It meant that all eventualities were covered.

As he held the phone to his ear, a passing resident glanced at him and the black Ford Fiesta. He wasn't worried. They would choose one of the many innocent explanations. None would be 'chatting to the Deputy Commissioner of the Metropolitan Police about covering up some murders'.

Deelman was taking his time in there. He wondered if he had seen the CCTV yet. Hopefully, it would remind him of the power dynamic here. There was a cat. And there was a mouse. And even a determined and capable mouse was little more than a curiosity to a cat.

He recalled a documentary he had seen about a remarkable brain parasite found in rodents. Given a choice, the parasite preferred a feline host, so – by some miracle of nature – it could make its rodent carrier attack cats in the suicidal hope of being eaten. The name came to him just as he was growing tired of Barnes' update.

'Don't worry,' he said. 'I think your officer is just suffering from toxoplasmosis.'

'Toxic what?'

'Never mind...' He cut the call and tossed the phone on the passenger seat.

Chapter 30

'This is it,' said Nick, pushing open the door to Harry's bedroom. The modest room had an en suite bathroom, with various support bars and pull cords, and a window looking onto a patch of grass. Brook stepped in behind his tour guide and the door swung shut on its weighted mechanism. The cloying sweetness of Peak View's favourite air freshener was present in the bedrooms too.

A framed photo on the bedside table seemed to be the only personal touch. From what Brook had seen on the CCTV, he would say Harry was about ten years younger in it. He was sitting in a deck chair next to a white-haired lady Brook guessed was his late wife. Using a few more guesses, there appeared to be three younger generations around them…

The son that Debbie had mentioned – now in Canada – was there with his wife. And then there was their daughter who was holding a baby. Despite the sunshine, no-one was really smiling or had any joy in their eyes. Even the baby had been captured with a stern expression. Brook found himself frowning. Harry's life didn't seem very happy.

'So, what are you looking for?' asked Nick.

'Well…' Brook wondered how best to put it. 'When you join the police you'll hear some searches described as a bit of a fishing expedition. They're generally discouraged, but can be surprisingly useful.'

'What does that mean?'

'It means I have no idea what I'm looking for.'

'A clue,' said Nick. Brook smiled at how the student's two little words had summarised the situation far better than his rambling explanation.

'Well put,' he agreed.

Emboldened by Nick's tacit approval, the detective nudged open the wardrobe doors. Hangers of shirts and slacks didn't seem to offer much. The chest of drawers was a similarly clue-free zone of folded clothes. Brook closed everything back up and moved over to the bedside table.

'We should probably check he didn't have any midnight snacks that might go off,' he said.

'I agree,' replied Nick.

The top of the small unit was home to a lamp, radio and big-button telephone. Beneath that was a drawer and cupboard. Brook opened the drawer – some spare batteries, a packet of mints and a few pens. Nothing of interest. Then he forced himself into a crouch and opened the cupboard.

'Was that your knees?' winced Nick at the loud click.

'Yep. I'll let you know if I need one of your Zimmer frames.'

The cupboard contained a row of books – a mix of thrillers and history. Brook almost closed the door without noticing the thin brown envelope slotted between a couple of paperbacks. Had it not been a few millimetres out of line he may never have seen it. He plucked it out and pushed himself upright.

'Catch anything?' asked Nick, peering over from his position by the door.

'Catch? Oh…' The fishing expedition metaphor. 'Not sure.'

The front of the envelope displayed the handwritten Peak View Care Home address and a stamp with a robin in the snow. It was franked with *'Melbourne'* and the date it was posted, just before Christmas 2015. Brook could feel there was a card inside – he slid it out through the envelope's torn top edge and laid everything on the bed.

The card showed a nativity scene on the front, while what little writing there was inside appeared to be in the same hand as the address. *'To Harry'* was in the top left, followed by the pre-printed *Happy Christmas* halfway down. Beneath it, *'21st December'*, followed by *'VICTOR'* and a brief message: *'See you soon'*.

'Funny place to put the date,' said Nick, still peering over.

He was right, but it wasn't Brook's first thought… That was the fact that Victor – a guy in his nineties with seemingly no traceable friends or family – had apparently spent Christmas in Australia.

'If I tell you I'll speak to Debbie about seizing this, then you can watch me take it with a clear conscience, can't you?' said Brook, raising an eyebrow in Nick's direction as he slipped the card and envelope into an evidence bag.

'Totally clear,' said Nick, with a conspiratorial wink.

All right, don't overdo it, thought Brook.

'Now,' he said, stuffing the evidence bag into his jacket. 'I'd really love to see the garden.'

'You think there'll be clues in the garden?' asked Nick.

'Nope. Fresh air.'

Five minutes later – after saying his goodbyes to Debbie – Brook climbed back into the Defender. The visit had given him plenty to think about. Still, he didn't want to do it while sitting outside the care home, drawing attention to himself. He fired up the engine, swung the vehicle around so he was pointing towards home and looked for a quiet side street to pull into.

After less than fifty yards, a cul-de-sac rose steeply to his left. Brook turned into it, just as he began wondering what to do about the Tourist having his phone number. He was so lost in thought, he almost crashed into a black Ford Fiesta that had chosen that very moment to come tearing out. At least it had left a useful parking spot.

Brook cruised past it, turned the old 4x4 around and tucked into the empty space. He felt more comfortable being able to see any people or cars coming up from the main road.

Not that the Tourist was likely to show up in a random Sheffield cul-de-sac.

He was probably miles away by now.

Chapter 31

Saturday, 21st April 1945
Stalag IV-B, Mühlberg, Germany

The extra creaking of the hut's floorboards gave the first clue as to the new guard's identity. Victor knew of only one man in the whole of Stalag IV-B who was heavy enough to put that much strain on the wooden planks. Maybe if he just stayed on his bed, out of sight, the new guard would deposit the morning's food and be on his way. He heard the metal tray clang down on the small table and waited. One minute. Two. Three. There were no more creaking floorboards. No sounds to indicate the guard was going anywhere. After five minutes, Victor got to his feet and walked to the doorway.

'Hello, Blondie,' he said.

The psychopath looked up from the table. After all the hours Victor had spent in front of the sinewy von Eberstein, it felt strange to see such a bulging Nazi uniform. Blondie had helped himself to a seat and now he was helping himself to the food.

The cheese was already reduced to a few crumbs, while the jar of potted meat was empty, as was today's tin of peaches. Half of the final piece of black bread hung from his big lips. He grabbed it and threw it back onto the plate. Then he finished his mouthful in one enormous gulp and gave a big smile. Victor regretted setting up the second guard with that tin of peaches.

While still smiling, Blondie washed it all down with the mug of ersatz coffee. He thumped the metal mug down on the table and burped as if he were in a Bavarian Bierkeller.

'Das war mein Essen,' said Victor… *'That was my food.'*

'Ja. Das war dein Essen,' replied Blondie… *'Yes. That was your food.'*

'Übrigens, du wirst heute sterben,' he added… *'By the way, you're going to die today.'*

He leaned back in the wooden chair, testing its Teutonic craftsmanship to the full. Victor stayed in the doorway, embracing the illusion of security it offered – for he was well aware it was only an illusion. He was in a hut with a man who killed prisoners for fun. His exact location in that hut didn't matter a great deal. Unless he could outwit his enemy, the Englishman's fate was entirely in Blondie's hands.

'Und was soll ich jetzt essen?' asked Victor… *'And what am I going to eat now?'*

He avoided the whole issue of dying and forced himself to hold Blondie's gaze. He knew displaying weakness only encouraged psychopathic tendencies and, as a self-styled *Übermensch*, Blondie no doubt considered it his duty to eliminate the weak. After a few seconds, a new smile spread across the bigger man's broad features. He wiped the traces of coffee from his mouth with the back of a hand and pointed at the prisoner.

'Gute Frage!'… *'Good question!'*

Reaching into the left pocket of his tunic, he produced a tin of peaches, placed it on the table, then tilted his fist to show bruised and swollen knuckles. The mirror image of the same action followed. Right hand into the right pocket… a second tin of peaches placed on the table… battered knuckles of the right fist displayed.

'Man darf nicht stehlen,' he said… *'One mustn't steal.'*

Well, at least that explained who von Eberstein had employed to discipline the two guards caught with the tinned peaches.

'Nimm,' said Blondie, pushing the tins across the table… *'Take them.'*

Victor ignored the peaches and nodded at the half slice of black bread.

'Und das?' said the Englishman... *'And that?'*

Blondie picked up the bread and flung it on the floor in front of Victor. Then his Aryan eyes flickered between the prisoner and the scrap of food. The tactic was obvious. An invitation for Victor to show weakness by eating food from the floor. No doubt it would bring back joyous memories of the Russian who dived on a splash of muddy soup before Blondie stamped him to death. The anticipation was racing through him, adrenalin kicking in. He began licking his lips.

Victor stared at the bread, thinking. Then he scurried the few feet over to it, grabbed it and scurried back to the doorway.

'Genau,' said Blondie, nodding slowly… *'Exactly.'*

He got to his feet, knocking the chair over backwards, and approached his prey across the creaking floorboards. He was almost drooling now. It was time to add to his tally…

Victor took a mouthful of the bread and began chewing quickly, backing up into the sleeping quarters. Blondie stalked him, savouring the moment, cracking the swollen knuckles of both hands as he closed the gap.

Then the Englishman stopped retreating, a look of confusion in his eyes. With a violent spasm, he coughed up half the bread he had been wolfing down. Blondie took a step back as it landed between them. Raising a hand to his mouth, Victor coughed up more bread with a strange hacking sound. It landed even closer to Blondie.

The prisoner's eyes began to swim upwards and he steadied himself with a hand on the side of the hut. The coughing continued, turning into dry retching and desperate wheezing. Victor dropped awkwardly to one knee, banging his head on the panels of the hut wall and drawing blood. His eyes were looking right through Blondie now. He raised a hand to the head injury then covered his mouth, smearing blood around it. More retching. He sank further, tears running from his eyes. Blondie took another step back as Victor raised what remained of the bread to his nose, then threw it away with as much force as he could muster.

'Von Eberstein,' he growled through gritted teeth. 'Von–'

'Was? Von Eberstein was?' said Blondie… *'What? Von Eberstein what?'*

Victor struggled to get the words out, hugging the wall with one arm while beating the floor with the other.

'Gift!'… *'Poison!'*

He ardently hoped a couple of things were going through Blondie's mind at that moment. The first being that he weighed twice as much as Victor, so any poison in the food would need a little longer to take effect. The second, that he did indeed have the hint of a funny feeling in his tummy (after devouring cheese, potted meat, peaches and black bread in a few short minutes of gluttony).

Victor was just beginning to feel faint from the exertion of his own acting when Blondie clutched his stomach and ran headlong for the exit, sending one of the outside guards tumbling head over heels as he charged to the toilet block to make himself sick.

The Englishman lay on his back for a couple of minutes, composing himself after the intense theatrics. Then he stood up, dusted himself down and had peaches for breakfast.

Von Eberstein arrived early. And by a different method. Victor heard the motorbike approaching at speed just as he was sipping the last of the syrupy juice from the tinned fruit. Moments later, the hut door flew open and the SS-Sturmbannführer burst in – a helmet, cream scarf and leather gloves over his regular uniform. The prisoner matched the bustling energy of the new arrival, leaping up from his chair and jabbing a finger in the officer's direction.

'Now, look here! I want a bloody word with you. You're playing fast and loose with the Geneva Convention. I could have been killed earlier!'

Von Eberstein waved a dismissive hand, keeping up his quick pace over to the mahogany desk and his regular chair. He left all of the motorcycle kit on, even the helmet, as he leaned to one side and began fumbling with the key to one of the locked drawers.

'Ja, Ja, Ja,' he said. 'Could have, could have…'

He was jittery and growing increasingly agitated with the little key.

'SCHEISSE!' he shouted, the frustration mounting. When the lock finally clicked, he flung the drawer open with such force it came clean out of the desk and skidded six feet across the floor. Victor watched in baffled silence.

The SS officer went after the drawer, finally grabbing the bottle of whisky that had seemingly been the object of his frantic behaviour. He whipped the top off and poured it down his neck – a quarter of the bottle in one go. Then he squeezed his eyes shut and grimaced before slowly opening them again in a series of hard blinks. The blue eyes were bloodshot and watering.

'Besser,' he said, taking a deep breath.

Von Eberstein returned to his chair and collapsed into it, gripping the whisky bottle in his right hand and staring straight ahead. He looked as pale as a Nazi ghost. Finally, he turned towards Victor, who had barely moved during the whole strange episode.

'Sit,' he said, gesturing at the chair opposite.

Victor stayed where he was.

'I want to see the letter from the SS-Brigadeführer. The chap who ordered my removal from camp.'

The wraith-like von Eberstein managed a patronising expression.

'Your German is not sufficient to understand.'

'Then there's nothing to lose by showing it to me,' said Victor.

The Nazi frowned as if considering the statement. He took another massive swig of the whisky. For mid-morning he was really going for it.

'Very well,' he said at last.

His hand was marginally less shaky this time as he opened the relevant drawer and pulled out the manila envelope. He spun it through the air to Victor, wincing at the small physical action of throwing. The prisoner kept his eyes on his captor as he retrieved the envelope from the floor, only looking down once he had removed the letter and unfolded it. He scanned the typed text. Then he took his regular spot opposite von Eberstein.

'Satisfied?' asked the SS officer.

Victor tossed the letter across the desk.

'*You* wrote that,' he said.

Von Eberstein took another big swig with a gloved hand and banged the bottle down on the desktop. The little grimaces kept on coming. He was clearly in some kind of pain.

'Explain,' he said.

'In Kriegszeiten und in Frieden. In wartime and in peace,' said Victor.

'Meaning what?'

'It's in the letter. The bit about showing respect for our shared Anglo-Saxon culture. You used the same phrase when describing how you von Ebersteins always adapt and succeed. I think you like that phrase.'

'They are common words. It proves nothing.'

'Maybe not. But *Western* Ham United does. You're the only bugger who uses that. Yet there it is in the letter. I thought this Brigadeführer who wanted Vic Watson protected was meant to be a fan from his time in England. Such a fan that he doesn't even know their proper bloody name?'

Von Eberstein opened his mouth to give another rebuttal and then changed his mind. He looked down at the letter and placed a gloved hand on top of it as if accepting ownership. Then he looked up at Victor with bloodshot eyes.

'Oops,' he said.

The two men stared at each other in silence, their minds running through the implications of the new situation. Finally, von Eberstein shrugged.

'It makes no difference.'

'It makes every bloody difference! It means the reason I'm here has nothing to do with mistaken identity or some superior of yours trying to look generous. It was all a charade. You arranged the whole little ruse yourself. Now, what the devil would you want with *me*?'

The Nazi took his time in replying, examining Victor.

'Clever,' he said. 'Clever, clever, clever... You truly are an English fox.'

With another swig, and another wince of discomfort, he reached down to unlock a new drawer, pulling out the calendar he had shown Victor once before.

'You remember this?' he asked, holding it up. Victor remembered the crosses – the ones marking the dates of escapes... escapes previously thought to have been secret and successful.

'Look more closely,' instructed von Eberstein, tossing over the 1945 calendar. 'And this one,' he added, taking a 1944 version from the same drawer.

Victor worked his way back from the current date to his arrival at Stalag IV-B in February '44. There were more crosses. Every one at the time of a supposed escape 'success'. In a camp with so little to do, each one had been a major event. A big morale boost. And, even if Victor couldn't quote all the exact dates, he knew to within a few days. Here they were. A dozen or so crosses. The vast majority of the escapes they thought their captors had never known about. The ones where the escapee had never been returned to camp.

'Why are you torturing Harry for useless old information? These people are long gone,' said Victor, returning the calendars. 'I want to see him.'

Von Eberstein drained the remainder of the whisky and blinked hard again. Just under a whole bottle in five minutes. Then he threw the calendars over his shoulder, followed by the letter and the empty whisky bottle. It smashed on the floor.

'Excellent idea,' he said. 'I'll drive.'

Chapter 32

Saturday, 23rd April 2016
M1 southbound, Derbyshire

Brook came off the motorway at the same services he had visited on the way up and found an empty bay next to a yellow VW camper van. It reminded him of the film *Little Miss Sunshine*. There was no urgency to his pit stop this time. Harry Wilson had joined Victor Watson on the list of victims. Killed in the lounge. With the tea. By the Tourist. If only this was all a game of Cluedo.

The detective's stop in the Sheffield cul-de-sac had been dominated by a phone call from the press officer at work. She wanted to know if he'd found a next of kin for the lonely World War Two veteran in the churchyard. *'It would make a great story. Real tug-on-the-heartstrings stuff. Not to mention that the publicity might actually help you find a next of kin.'*

Brook didn't like the idea of extra attention on a case he was struggling to get to grips with. All the same, short of mentioning murder, conspiracy and cover-up, he could think of no official reason to knock back the request. In the end, he managed a compromise. 'Can you just hold fire for a few days? I've got a couple more leads to chase up. Always best if the next of kin doesn't find out through the press if possible.' That seemed to do the trick. For now, at least.

With the Defender's tank still half full, Brook focused on his own refuelling in a window seat of the food hall, examining the card from Harry's bedroom as he ate:

'To Harry... Happy Christmas... 21st December... VICTOR... See you soon'.

It wasn't exactly a wealth of information. And, it went without saying, if it was from a different Victor then it offered nothing at all. But Harry didn't seem to be suffering from a surfeit of friends. Brook flipped the evidence bag and looked at the envelope facing out the other side – the Peak View address and the stamp of a snowy robin with the Melbourne frank on it (he liked how so many hot parts of the Commonwealth still chose frosty Christmas scenes). He looked at the date on the frank... *'15.12.15'*. Then he looked inside the card once again... *'21st December'*.

Now, what was that all about?

Even in Brook's most hungover state, he rarely got the date wrong by more than a day or two. Six days? That was quite a stretch. If the wrong date were part of some in-joke between Victor and Harry, then he would never know now. If not, why was it even in there at all? Especially in that strange position, beneath the printed *'Happy Christmas'* and to the top left of *'VICTOR'*. The name wasn't brilliantly written, the first two letters somewhat bigger than the rest.

What was he missing? Was there a unifying reason for the little anomalies? He imagined the 21st December date in different forms. 21/12. Or 12/21 in some countries... 2112...

1221… The number 2112 felt vaguely familiar, though his brain could just as easily be playing tricks on him. He soon gave up and shoved everything back into a pocket. There were more pressing matters.

Brook took out his phone and laid it on the table. He had been quietly considering his options from the moment it was compromised by the Tourist seeing his name and number on Debbie's Post-it Note. One possibility was to simply change the number, but someone with the right connections and authority could still trace and track a handset even with an old number (and Deputy Commissioner Barnes would hardly be lacking on that front). Brook didn't like the idea of effectively carrying a location beacon for the other side to keep tabs on him. Of course, given that his number was hardly top secret at work, it was quite possible they already were.

On the back of his food receipt, he transcribed the few phone numbers he would actually miss from his Contacts. Then he went into Photos and sent all the ones he wanted to keep to his e-mail account – everything related to the case and a handful of others of friends and family. That was all he needed to do. It took about five minutes.

Before he got rid of the phone, there was one last call he wanted to make… DS Chris Beckford in Homicide. That bald weirdo of surprise churchyard appearances and CCTV stealing fame. Brook would play it dumb, of course. Totally dumb. Just an innocent call from the dumb local DC investigating the dumb non-suspicious death. Enough to try and get a feel for the man. As he picked up the phone, it began buzzing in his hand – a number he didn't recognise on the screen. Brook twisted to look around the food hall, then scanned the car park before answering.

'Hello..?'

'Hi Brook, it's Danny from the pub. I helped you with the CCTV?'

The detective relaxed.

'Danny. Hi. How can I help?'

'I just thought I'd give you a heads-up. Not my fault, but the manager's just had a bit of a barney with one of your colleagues. He wanted to see the same CCTV you took the other day.'

'Was he a tall, bald guy by any chance?'

'Yeah, that's him. It was in the middle of the lunchtime rush, so he and the manager didn't exactly hit it off. Is there a problem with the disc?'

Brook didn't answer. He was beginning to see the outline of how this little operation worked. Barnes as the boss man, the Tourist as the hitman, and DS Beckford as the handyman, assessing what evidence was left behind and sweeping it away where possible. Even though Brook already had the footage from the pub, Beckford had gone there to find out exactly what it showed. Exactly what scraps of evidence were out there.

'Are you still there?' asked Danny.

'Yeah, sorry about that,' said Brook. 'He's a strange one. I'll have a word with him. Sorry if he caused any trouble. But thanks for the call.'

'No worries, mate.'

Interesting. Very interesting. If he'd wanted to speak to Beckford before, he definitely did now. He swirled his remaining coffee and looked through the window at the Defender and the Little Miss Sunshine camper van as he dialled the main Homicide number. A female detective answered and Brook introduced himself before getting down to the reason for his call.

'I was hoping to speak to one of your DS's there. Chris Beckford.'

'You'll have a bit of a wait, I'm afraid.'

'Why's that?'

'Maternity leave.'

'Sorry… Chris Beckford.'

'Yeah, that's right.'

'Chris Beckford is a woman?'

'That's normally how it works with maternity leave. DS Christine Beckford. She's always called herself Chris. It does create a bit of confusion.'

Brook made his excuses and hung up. He hadn't seen this one coming. There were only two possibilities. Either Sandy Sanderson had somehow recorded the wrong name in the scene log, or it was the bald guy's warrant card that was 'wrong'. A fake. He recalled the phone call he'd taken in front of them… *'Tell them to keep it warm. I'll be back in two minutes. Yeah, nothing for us here.'*

What a great bit of acting and manipulation.

Yes, they were all linked – Barnes, fake Beckford and the Tourist.

Each with their role in the killings and the cover-ups.

All the while, Brook had been staring out at the Little Miss Sunshine camper van. It was the only yellow vehicle in the car park. Unusual colour. Memorable too. A little voice in the back of his head was trying to tell him something. Maybe he would make one more call before ditching the phone. He tapped on the number for Peak View…

'Nick, it's Brook.'

'Oh, hi. Did you miss something?'

'Not sure. I might be imagining things. But I have this vague recollection of seeing something on the CCTV that didn't really register at the time. I won't be able to check until I'm back in London so I thought you might be able to help.'

'I think I can manage that,' said Nick, keen as ever. Brook heard the lightning-quick clatter of fingers on a keyboard. 'Right… What am I looking for?'

'Go to the point when you first see Logan Baird on the camera at the front.'

'Got it.'

'Now rewind from there, it won't be more than a minute, and keep your eye out for a yellow flash at the top of the screen where you can just see the edge of the road.'

'Hang on… Yep, I see it. It's a yellow car driving past.'

'Okay. Good. I'm less sure about the next one. But go to the point when he leaves and walks off to the left on the pavement. Tell me if there's another yellow flash at the top of the screen.'

'Right… One moment… Watching him leave now…'

Nick was doing a good job of ramping up the suspense.

'Yep, there it is. Just after he goes out of shot. Another yellow car going past.'

'I'm thinking they're taxis,' said Brook. 'I hadn't even considered how he got to and from your place.'

'Just a sec. I know exactly who that will be… One of their cards is here somewhere… Got it. They're called New York Cabs. All sorts of different vehicles but they put a yellow paint job on them all.'

'Nick, you're a bloody genius,' said Brook, as he took down their number.

Time to finally ditch the phone.

After entering the wrong passcode enough times to block the handset, Brook turned it off, snapped the SIM card in half and dropped the whole lot into his takeaway coffee cup, pressing down the lid. Then he visited the Gents and chucked it in a grubby bin.

Heading over to one of the ubiquitous little phone shops in service stations, he used cash to buy their oldest iPhone and a pre-paid SIM, persuading the guy to put some charge into it while he got another coffee. A text to Jonboy was the phone's inaugural message *('Hello, mate. New number. Long story. Free for a beer later? Brook')* while the honour of the first call went to the number Nick had just given him… New York Cabs.

A gruff-sounding Yorkshireman answered and Brook explained he was a police officer trying to find someone who had visited Peak View Care Home earlier. It was about the death of an elderly resident and the contact number this guest had left was a digit short (all true, in a way). He had a hunch they had used New York Cabs to get to and from the care home…

'Would it be possible to find out if I'm right in thinking that?'

'No need to find out, pal,' said the Yorkshireman.

'Oh, right. You remember the booking being made?'

'Never mind booking. It were me what drove 'im.'

Brook's fortunes were suddenly looking up.

'Did he say much?'

'He certainly did, pal. We had quite a chat...'

Chapter 33

As victorious homecomings went, returning to a bland London chain hotel after one night away was not quite in the ticker tape and marching band category. But there was a certain quiet satisfaction in a job well done. He lay back on the bed and flicked through some Saturday evening television in a fruitless search for a history or wildlife documentary. There seemed to be no shortage of excruciating game shows. He paused long enough on one to see a contestant guess that the biggest country in South America was 'Africa'. Once the answer was revealed, she promised the host that Brazil was going to be her second guess. The television went off. Truly, evolution had come to an end.

The silence in the small room led naturally to another mental check of everything that had happened in Sheffield. Barnes had assured him that the local police could scarcely be less interested in Harry Wilson's death. That was good to know. To have some northern version of Deelman poking around would have seriously tested his patience.

Talking of Deelman – which he seemed to be spending far too much time doing these days – he was still none the wiser as to what had made him drive up that little street overlooking Peak View. For a moment, he had been convinced he was coming for him. That they were going to have this out in a... what was it?... a 'cul-de-sac'.

Obviously, he had no concerns about losing such a confrontation. But, at the same time, it was an unnecessary complication. At least at this point. It was why there had been a degree of relief when the detective simply drove straight past, seemingly lost in thought. Still, if Deelman refused to give up, despite being way out of his depth, then it looked increasingly likely that a meeting was what it would come to. Well, a meeting or a confrontation. He was easy either way.

In a sense he had already made the invitation. It was just a case of whether Deelman was smart enough to find it. If he was, then by now he should already be in touch with New York Cabs. No doubt he would be congratulating himself on being so clever.

His phone started buzzing beside him on the bed... Barnes.

'Yes?'

'Just to let you know it looks like he's ditched his phone.'

'Smart guy. I presume you can still track his vehicle on the ANPR cameras.'

'On his way back to London last time I checked. But once he's out of the vehicle, I won't be able to give you any updates.'

'What's your point?'

'That you might just want to watch your back.'

'I assure you, it's not me who needs to watch their back.'

'Look, I told you before. He's a serving police officer. You can't just–'

'Yeah, yeah, yeah. I have it under control.'

'Is there something you're not telling me?'

'It's under control.'

'That's not an answer. Give me an answer.'

'The biggest country in South America is Africa.'

'What's that?'

'It's an answer.'

He hung up and turned the TV back on. Barnes really needed to trust him more.

Chapter 34

Brook stood in the doorway to The Lamb and cradled a dimpled pint glass – the same type from which Victor Watson had been drinking in the footage of his final night. It wasn't the only thing making the detective think of poor Victor. He was staring at the original gates to the old Foundling Hospital, thirty yards along the street to his right. Black iron railings between stone gatehouses – the only part of the orphanage still standing according to the eccentric Theodore.

Beyond the gates were lawns, paths and some kind of bandstand. No trace of the old building. But they were the gates all right. The same ones through which an infant Victor Watson was taken on the day of the 1923 FA Cup Final, wrapped in a West Ham scarf and with a strange gold medal. Brook had wanted to come back to where it all began.

The detective was in a good mood – and not only because his jacket was now considerably less cumbersome (the investigation's array of discs and paperwork re-homed in a new Lonsdale shoulder bag slung across his back). The phone call with the cab driver who remembered the Tourist had gone surprisingly well.

Mehmet his name was, though from his accent he was clearly anything but a new arrival in Yorkshire. More importantly, he had a good memory. Apart from his passenger repeating the same line he had given Debbie – about going to Peak View to meet an old army friend of his late grandfather's – it turned out they had talked mainly about football on both journeys. Not what Brook was expecting.

Mehmet explained he was a fan himself, so had been happy enough with the topic. He said his passenger was looking forward to watching Spurs play West Bromwich Albion back in London on Monday night before leaving the country. He apparently only made it to a couple of games a year, but he loved the pre-match atmosphere in The Elbow Room pub before heading over to the stadium…

GOT HIM.

A time, a venue, and right next to Brook's regular north London patch. Just two days from now this whole thing was going to come to a head.

'Did he say where he was actually from?' Brook had asked.

'He just said he'd moved around a lot,' Mehmet had replied.

Even a good memory couldn't provide an answer that wasn't there.

Apart from telling Brook that the passenger had asked to be picked up and dropped off at a street corner in the city centre, Mehmet didn't have access to the full booking details – the name and number that had been provided. Those would be with the dispatchers, but… he lowered his voice… if Brook waited until 9pm then his sister would start her shift and she wasn't too fussed about all that 'Data Protection Act' stuff. Brook decided he would happily wait to avoid the extra paperwork.

The detective stopped staring at the Foundling Hospital gates to look at his watch. 7.20pm. Jonboy was late. Given that his route from the tube would take the former Royal Military Police officer past two other pubs, Brook wasn't entirely surprised. Alcohol and Jonboy had been closely interlinked ever since he first clapped eyes on him – blind drunk, in his boxer shorts, and handcuffed to the Borough Commander's chair amid a growing puddle of drool (drinks with old army friends, it seemed, could get even messier than police ones). The fact he had somehow saved Jonboy's skin had turned a stranger into a friend for life.

Brook finished his first ale and headed back into the 18th century pub for a fresh one, making his way round to the side of the horseshoe-shaped bar so as not to have his back to the entrance. An extra level of caution was definitely prudent when in the business of pissing off a murderer and the second most powerful cop in London.

After tapping a quick text of '*You lost?*' he tried to recall the last time he had seen Jonboy. A couple of months ago, maybe. Their last really big session had been at the England v Wales game in the Rugby World Cup. He remembered Jonboy threatening to arrest an Englishman who took a shine to his inflatable sheep (for the offence of 'cultural appropriation'). Still, such antics were small fry compared to the famous meltdown that had seen him shuffled into the CCTV office.

The death of two old friends in Helmand Province seemed to have been some sort of trigger. In any case, Jonboy had come to work drunk for a week and decided to conduct various police activities while wearing a giant chicken head from a fancy dress shop (it had been kicking around the locker room for years after some prank or other). The drug addict whose flat was searched by a giant police chicken was probably still telling friends about his bad trip.

Word of Jonboy's activities had eventually reached the Senior Management Team and a Superintendent had hauled him in for 'a meeting without coffee' as the expression went. For fifteen minutes, Jonboy had launched a vigorous defence of himself against the scurrilous accusations, while wearing pristine full dress uniform. And a massive chicken head.

Only several years of good service and the suggestion the Met had ignored some underlying 'issues' from Jonboy's own tour in the desert saved him from the sack. Nevertheless, it was thought best for everyone that the public and Jonboy be kept on opposite sides of CCTV cameras after that.

The hipster-bearded barman took Brook's order, grabbing a new pint pot and filling it with the golden ale. The detective must only have looked down for a second or two to sort out the payment. But that was all it took. On looking back up, he realised someone had almost fully covered the distance from the entrance…

Brook began to raise an arm to protect himself from the rapidly approaching figure, but it was too little too late. A great Welsh bear hug came crashing through his half-hearted defence and engulfed him.

'Number One!' roared the booming South Wales baritone, no doubt to the total confusion of everyone else in the pub.

'Christ. You walk like a fucking cat,' wheezed Brook, as the bear hug turned into some hefty pats on the back. Jonboy adopted a Karate Kid pose in his British & Irish Lions rugby top.

'It's all the training, boyo. Just takes over, doesn't it?'

Then he lost his balance and grabbed hold of the bar. Brook's theory about Jonboy nipping into a couple of pubs en route from the tube was looking pretty solid. The barman had no idea what to make of it all.

'I'll have what he's having,' said Jonboy upon regaining his balance. 'I trust him.'

He grabbed his pal's shoulder.

'That's lucky,' said Brook.

At about an inch taller than Brook, and with fifteen pounds of extra padding, Jonboy was certainly built for bear hugs. His upcoming fortieth birthday drinks would no doubt add a couple more pounds all on their own. And with a laissez-faire approach to the combing of hair and shaving of stubble that surpassed even Brook's, the pair of them looked more like a couple of bouncers who had fallen on hard times than the Met's finest.

A snug off the main bar provided a handy place to discuss the case in relative privacy (their only company a framed photo of a young Prince Charles pulling a pint in the same pub). Jonboy had remembered to bring the laptop Brook requested – saved from being crushed in the bear hug by virtue of being in a backpack. Not that the old computer didn't have enough damage in the form of a scratched screen and several missing keys.

'Told you I wouldn't forget,' said the Welshman.

'Bloody hell, Jonboy. Did you crack the Enigma code with that thing?'

'Oi! Even old wrecks have something to offer. Just look at…'

'Don't say the Defender.'

'…you.'

'That's better.'

Over the course of the next couple of hours and several more drinks, Brook walked his old friend through the entire investigation until Jonboy knew the case almost as well as Brook himself. Every statement and exhibit… Every connection and anomaly… Every bit of forensics and CCTV… (When the footage from The Junction was on the screen, he used his phone to take a photo of Victor – he didn't want a scratched disc deleting the last ever images of the man).

It was towards the end of their third pint that Brook finally slumped back, happy there was nothing left to tell.

'So what do you think?' he asked.

'I think you've got yourself quite a situation.'

'I knew I could rely on you for a pearl of wisdom.' He checked his watch. 'I've got a call to make while you figure it all out…'

Standing with his back to the pub in the slightly quieter surroundings of the street, Brook re-dialled the number for New York Cabs and introduced himself.

'That's right,' said Mehmet's sister. 'He did mention it. Said some copper might call 'bout booking details for chap he took to Peak View. Obviously, you'll get Data Protection paperwork to me at earliest opportunity.'

'Obviously,' agreed Brook, going along with the pretence.

'Well, no point delaying your investigation then. Let's take a look…'

Paperwork bypassed. Just as Mehmet had predicted. Some 150 miles north of Brook, the taxi dispatcher brought up the details on her screen and relayed them in the same Yorkshire accent as her brother.

'Right… Well, there's no address as such, because pick-up fer't first trip to Peak View were a street corner in city centre. And then it were same trip in reverse an hour later. I can give you street corner if you like.'

'I'll come back to that. How about a name and phone number?'

'I've got phone number he gave, though we didn't have to use it to find him or 'owt. He were always where he said he'd be.'

The dispatcher began reading out the number as Brook fumbled for a pen in his jacket. Halfway through he stopped fumbling. There was no need to write it down – he already knew it off by heart. Up until a few hours ago, it had been his.

'Thanks,' he said, managing to hide any surprise in his voice. 'And how about the name that he provided?'

There was already a sense of inevitability about the coming answer.

'He said his name were… Brook Deelman. Hang on a sec. What were your name again?'

'Detective Constable Brook Deelman.'

'Ooh, blimey. Either someone's playing a game with you or that's got to be world's biggest coincidence then.'

'I think I'll go with your first guess,' said Brook, experiencing yet another step-up in paranoia. He should be getting used to it by now.

He thanked the dispatcher for her help, looked up and down the street once more, then headed back inside to the snug, retaking the seat across from Jonboy.

'How did that go?'

'Good news and bad news, I suppose.'

'Go on.'

'The good news is I needn't have worried about him seeing that Post-it Note with my name and number.'

'And the bad news is he already had it,' said Jonboy, one step ahead.

'Yep. Gave my name and number when booking his taxi.'

'Christ.'

'There's me feeling smug for discovering his chat with the cab driver and the pub he's going to be in… He always wanted me to find out. It's not a slip-up, it's an invitation.'

The pair weighed up the shifting playing field.

'Right,' said Jonboy at last. 'Better make it count on Monday night then. Surveillance team, arrest team, search team for any vehicles or properties linked to him, interview team, briefing beforehand. Get Homicide back on board now that you know Beckford doesn't work for them…'

'Nice idea. But totally impossible to organise without Barnes getting wind of it all.'

'What's your master plan then?'

'I'm just going to fucking nick him.'

'Bloody hell, boyo. That certainly simplifies things. So what's my role?'

'You sure you want to be involved?'

'Course I'm bloody sure. Only so much CCTV a man can look at.'

They both took a long swig as if to confirm their agreement. It was Jonboy who spoke first.

'You do realise there'll be the mother and father of all shit-storms after this? Whatever happens. I've got the excuse of being mental already, but it might not be great for *your* career.'

'True. But when the Deputy Commissioner is relaying your personal details to a murderer, I think you have the right to respond as you see fit. Beyond that, we'll just have to see how it pans out.'

'Nicely put. But you still haven't given me a role.'

'I suppose you're the entire cavalry, you fat bastard.'

Jonboy headed back to the bar for another round.

'It's the horses I feel sorry for,' he said.

Brook let his mind drift to Monday night. Jonboy was not wrong when he said his actions would stir up a shit-storm. A borough DC unilaterally nicking a multiple murder suspect on the back of a secret little op with the Met's resident mental bloke was not exactly official procedure. But the arrest would still be lawful. And the aftermath should force the truth to the surface. When Jonboy returned with the fresh pints, he had clearly been doing some thinking of his own.

'Right then,' he said, sliding the ales to their respective sides of the table. 'Two points. One detailed and one general.'

'Let's hear the detailed one first,' said Brook, making a start on the new pint.

'So… Victor told the barman in The Junction it was his birthday,' said Jonboy.

'Yep. Thursday just gone. The 21st April.'

'Which is a week before the date he was abandoned on Cup Final day, and a week after the date he was believed to be born. But doesn't actually match either.'

'True.'

'And he's definitely got a thing for that date, hasn't he? Because that's the date when he was doing all that drunken singing in 2005 when the neighbour called the police. So why choose that date to celebrate on?'

'I feel there's a theory coming along in a minute…'

'All in good time, Number One.'

Jonboy took another sip of ale, enjoying holding court.

'Right, I think you should use your new phone to check when Stalag IV-B was liberated. It must have been around then, so I'm going with 21st April. If you've got a floating birthday around that fortnight, then the day you got your life back would be a good time to celebrate it.'

Brook entered the search into Google and scrolled down. As a former Royal Military Police Officer, Jonboy's knowledge of military history was usually spot-on. Relevant details located, Brook read them out loud.

'Stalag IV-B was liberated by Russian forces on 23rd April 1945.'

'Bugger. Two days out. It would have been perfect, you see? His drunken singsong in 2005 would have been the 60th anniversary if I'd been right. Just a bit too perfect maybe.'

'Unless he did somehow get out two days early on the twenty-first.'

'You're just trying to make me feel better now.'

'Probably. So what's the other point you mentioned? The general one?'

'That, Number One, is far simpler… Why are these old boys being killed and what the bloody hell is going on?'

Chapter 35

Saturday, 21st April 1945
near Mühlberg, Germany

A hundred yards… Fifty… Twenty… Victor closed his eyes. The odds against a head-on collision with the overloaded lorry barrelling towards them were diminishing as quickly as the gap. At the last possible moment, von Eberstein either realised the danger or finally got his whisky-addled body to respond. He swung back to his side of the carriageway, miraculously managing a further adjustment to cling to the edge of the road surface. The lorry sped past within a matter of inches on its sagging suspension, horn blaring. Wherever von Eberstein was taking Victor to see Harry – and it clearly wasn't the camp cooler – it was very much in the balance as to whether they would make it in one piece.

Indeed, 'balance' was something of a key word in their current predicament. Even though Victor had heard von Eberstein arrive at the hut by motorbike – before bursting in wearing a helmet, scarf and gloves – he had still expected the Nazi's offer of *'I'll drive'* to involve a change of transport to something four-wheeled. Instead, his choice of vehicle had remained the same. Not a motorbike as such – but a motorbike and sidecar.

A shackled Victor was in the sidecar, trying hard not to lose his mind with terror as von Eberstein took another blind bend on two wheels. The passing blur of countryside suggested they were avoiding the local town of Mühlberg. While Victor clenched his teeth, the only thing silencing von Eberstein was the buffeting air-flow, whipping away his maniacal cries of 'HAHAAAAAA!'

At last the speed began to drop, accompanied by a shifting down through the gears as Victor's hearing returned to normal. An old farmhouse, surrounded by a scattering of outbuildings, appeared to be their destination – an array of German military vehicles stationed in the courtyard. Von Eberstein rolled their three-wheeled deathtrap to a stop in front of them and lowered the top edge of the scarf covering his face and neck.

'Exciting, no?' he said with a grin.

Victor raised his shackled hands to his face and wiped away an assortment of dead insects before staring back wordlessly.

'So, now it is the Englishman with no sense of humour,' said von Eberstein, dismounting from the motorbike. He motioned for Victor to get up.

'Du willst Harry sehen, oder?'... *'You want to see Harry, don't you?'*

The prisoner clumsily exited the sidecar and reminded himself of the journey's original purpose – his demand to check on Harry's welfare. The fact they were now at a farmhouse in the middle of nowhere did not bode well for his friend.

Von Eberstein kept a certain distance, a gloved hand on the Walther P38 sidearm holstered at his hip, just in case his passenger decided upon some suicidal act of fight or flight. For now, Victor's only fight was against dizziness. He took a deep breath and nodded at his captor.

'Harry,' he said. 'Jetzt'... *'Now.'*

The SS-Sturmbannführer ushered Victor ahead of him to the oak front door.

'Knock,' instructed von Eberstein.

Victor obliged, a little awkwardly due to the iron bindings on his wrists. The internal screen to a spyhole slid open, paused for a moment, then slid shut again. There followed a series of clunking and scraping noises as locks and bolts were released. Finally, the door opened, revealing yet another dramatic Nazi uniform with double lightning strikes on the collar (judging by his waistline, this new SS man had done pretty well out of the war). Victor was trying to figure out his rank from the various insignia when he snapped a salute. Well, somewhere beneath SS-Sturmbannführer then.

'Please. Enter, Lance Corporal,' said von Eberstein, pushing Victor firmly between the shoulder blades. The prisoner stepped inside, his threadbare Middlesex Regiment uniform brushing past the saluting Nazi.

'To your right,' said von Eberstein.

Despite the vast amount of whisky he had consumed in the hut, the adrenalin of the journey seemed to have restored some clarity to his actions. The fact he was even still upright was a minor miracle in itself.

Victor followed the instruction and headed down a dim passage, ancient flagstones beneath his worn-out boots. As von Eberstein's footsteps followed him, his mind began to race...

Was this whole adventure really to reassure him of Harry's welfare? Or was he here to join Harry in being tortured? Or perhaps in being dead.

The Englishman passed an unoccupied room on his right, a huge elk hide on the floor in front of a fireplace. Next came a kitchen on the opposite side. A silent elderly couple in peasant clothes were peeling potatoes. Victor guessed they were the tenants of the farmhouse, kept on to cater for these strutting SS officers. The husband and wife stared blankly at the stranger.

'Heil Churchill!' said Victor, before von Eberstein shoved him in the back again.

There was only one door remaining. At the far end of the passage, a few inches ajar. Victor could hear music and some low level German chatter mixed in with the occasional laugh. There was too much competing noise to make out many individual words, but the general atmosphere seemed to be one of bonhomie. He reached the door and stopped.

'Enter,' ordered von Eberstein behind him.

The door made no sound as it swung on its hinges, the music and chatter continuing undisturbed. The fire was lit in this room, even though the spring day scarcely required it. At the far end, three high-backed armchairs were arranged in an arc around the crackling flames.

While the smoke from the fire disappeared up the chimney, the haze hanging in the air came from the cigars being enjoyed by each of the armchairs' occupants. A gramophone in the far corner was playing a female German singer.

Von Eberstein nudged Victor again and he stepped closer to the three chairs, starting to pick up bits of the conversation now. It sounded like the unseen men were chatting about matters of finance or business. A bottle-carrying hand appeared to the side of the centre chair as its occupant reached left, then right, to top up his companions' Cognac.

As each recipient leaned over to offer his glass, Victor saw their SS uniforms. Both noticed the new presence in the room and stared back at the prisoner. The occupant of the centre chair had no such angle from which to view the new arrival.

For a moment there was no discernible activity from the final member of the Cognac club. Then Victor heard the hiss of a cigar being extinguished and the wispy smoke above the middle armchair began to dissipate. Its occupant slowly stood up and turned around to face Victor over the back of the chair…

'All right, Vic?' said Harry.

Chapter 36

Sunday, 24th April 2016
North London

Brook could swear the hill got steeper every day. Steeper and longer. He used to barely notice it ten years ago. But he was still determined not to take the bus for the half-mile journey from Kings Cross to Grovebury police station. Which was why he now found himself trudging the familiar route once again. It felt as if the bailiffs for his sleep debt were finally banging on the door.

The day ahead held a couple of tasks – the first, retracing something he had already done; the second, preparing for something he was yet to do. Top of the list was re-visiting Victor's flat to see if he and Kev had missed anything that first night. The second activity was checking out The Elbow Room pub ahead of the Tourist's invitation to talk, ingeniously made via New York Cabs.

Brook wasn't sure of the right word for the upcoming event. A meeting? A rendezvous? It all sounded a bit too friendly when his intention was to arrest the other guy for murder. As for the Tourist's intentions… who knew what they were?

Still, first things first. It was the Christmas card in Harry's room that had got him thinking about searching Victor's flat again. He and Kev really hadn't done a thorough job the first time. Understandable perhaps, given how little they had known back then. But it still felt like a weak point in the investigation until done properly.

Jonboy had agreed to help in return for a simple payment plan – one doughnut for every new piece of evidence found. It seemed a fair price for getting up early on a Sunday morning.

Alfredo's café, round the corner from the police station, was their agreed meeting point. Approaching with Victor's flat keys tucked in his pocket, Brook saw that Jonboy was already well-settled with a cup of tea and a window seat. He had gone for the radical wardrobe change of swapping his 2009 British & Irish Lions rugby top for a near identical one from their 2013 tour. At least the team had won in the new version – maybe it would bring some good luck with it. It certainly seemed to be bringing Jonboy luck with the Polish waitress. She had abandoned the poker face to laugh at one of his jokes.

Brook was halfway across the road, planning to ask how he had done it, when a voice stopped him in his tracks.

'Where do you think you're off to, Deelman?'

It was female. And Irish.

He turned to see Marie walking his way – looking good in black jeans and a white top. She was carrying a folded newspaper and appeared far happier than the last time they had seen each other. Brook returned the smile, silently regretting he hadn't spent a couple more seconds looking in the mirror.

'This is a surprise,' he said.

'You're meant to say it's a *nice* surprise,' replied Marie. 'Jeez, you look tired.'

'Thanks.'

'Whatcha up to?'

Brook nodded over at his big Welsh friend in the café.

'Jonboy's just helping me out with a few things. You remember Jonboy?'

'Who doesn't?' said Marie, returning Jonboy's wave. 'Anyway, I just saw you through the window and thought I'd chase you down. I've been trying to call you.'

'Ah. Yeah. New number. Sorry about that. I'll text it to you.'

'You sure I'm not blocked?'

'Only on the old phone,' teased Brook. 'I might offer you a fresh start on the new one. It all depends if you still want to beat me up.'

'You got lucky. I decided to let you off with a caution.' She gave a little wink. Brook was relieved the awkwardness of their last encounter had been dealt with so quickly. He nodded at a few sheets of A4 paper just visible in the fold of Marie's newspaper.

'So, is this a new friendship contract in case we fall out again?'

'I think we can take our chances, don't you?'

The forensics officer grabbed Brook's shoulder bag and pulled him towards her until there were just a couple of inches between them. Then she slipped the newspaper inside the bag and stepped back.

'... It's the crime report that Barnes restricted on Logan Baird. From when his prints and DNA were taken in 2013.'

Brook's skin tingled as he looked up and down the street.

'Christ, Marie. I thought you didn't like the idea of getting sacked just before your wedding.'

'Well, I'd still prefer not to be. But there's nothing in any marriage vows about turning into a complete wuss now, is there?'

'I suppose not. But how–'

'Just good old Irish charm.'

Brook raised an enquiring eyebrow.

'Okay, maybe I know someone with administrator access who agreed to open it in View mode for me.'

'They must be quite a friend.'

'Not really. I just know something bad he did. Anyway, I didn't do anything as stupid as print it at work and leave a digital trail. Just took screenshots on my phone and printed them off at home.'

'Brilliant.'

'It was a tad rushed when I took them though, so you've only got the main body of it there. No Victim or Witness pages. Just remember that VIW1 is an 88-year-old man called Paul Fisher and VIW2 is your Logan Baird.'

'So Logan Baird wasn't a suspect?'

'Officially just a witness. Only had his prints and DNA taken for elimination purposes.'

'Weird.'

'I know.'

The pair were interrupted by Jonboy banging on the café window. As they looked over, he beckoned the Polish waitress and whispered something in her ear. She opened the front door to the café and leaned out into the street.

'He says you must big kiss!' she called over to them.

Behind her, Jonboy dissolved into fits of laughter.

Brook turned back to Marie, glad to see he wasn't the only one trying to hide a smirk.

'You got time for a coffee?' he asked.

'No, you're all right. I've… got some things to do in the office.'

'Okay. Well… thanks again for this.' He patted the bag at his side.

'You're welcome. I hope it helps.'

They exchanged little smiles and nods then walked off in opposite directions, Marie back to the police station, Brook to Alfredo's. Both glanced back at different moments, missing the other doing the same. When Brook pulled up a chair opposite Jonboy, his friend was still laughing.

'You're an idiot,' said Brook, shaking his head.

Jonboy watched Marie disappear round the corner.

'So are you,' he said.

Chapter 37

Saturday, 21st April 1945
near Mühlberg, Germany

'Meine Herren. Lassen Sie uns bitte alleine,' said von Eberstein…

'Gentlemen. Leave us alone, please.'

The SS officers in the armchairs either side of Harry Wilson got to their feet and left their fireside spots, taking their drinks and cigars with them. Just three men in the room now – Victor, von Eberstein and Harry. The gramophone needle reached the edge of the record and the singing faded to a static hiss. Then silence flooded the room.

'That all looked very cosy,' said Victor to his old friend. 'And your German has certainly come on in leaps and bounds.'

The two men appraised each other over the middle armchair. Harry was wearing civilian clothes – a white shirt and grey trousers held up with braces. He took a sip of his Cognac.

'You know 'ow it is. Just clicks after a while, don't it, Vic?'

'Funny. We all thought you could barely speak a word of it.'

Victor glanced between Harry and von Eberstein, the pain of his shackled wrists overtaken by more pressing thoughts.

'Is someone going to tell me what the hell is going on? I come here to check on my mucker's welfare and find him hosting a bloody SS house party.'

'I'm afraid there is no easy way of putting it,' said von Eberstein, steadying himself against the back of the armchair to Victor's left. 'Harry is not exactly… well… perhaps he should explain.'

'I think he should too,' said Victor, turning back to the friend he had made on that daunting first day at Mill Hill Barracks in 1940.

'It's just survival, Vic. You understand that, growing up in that bloody orphanage. You see a chance, you take it. Even if other people get… Look… No-one's gonna do you any favours if you don't do yourself any, are they?'

Victor tried to make sense of the weasel words coming out of Harry's mouth.

'The St George Legionnaire,' he said. 'That traitor who came into camp a week after we got there…'

Von Eberstein seemed to delight in Victor's comment.

'Wunderbar! He is so sharp, your friend!' he beamed at Harry.

Victor ignored him.

'You threw a bucket of shit over him when he was scouting for more traitors and you both got hauled out of camp. Great laugh, we all thought. But that was the start, wasn't it? My best friend… a bloody collaborator.'

'A survivor,' protested Harry.

'Genau,' agreed von Eberstein, raising a forefinger… *'Exactly.'*

Harry was looking far too at home in the SS house – left hand in the pocket of his new trousers, right hand cradling the glass of Cognac. A fresh realisation dawned on Victor as to just how such acceptance must have been earned.

'Those crosses on the calendars weren't made after the fact, were they? You were giving up our men all along.'

'I knew I couldn't hack that camp, Vic. I would have done myself in. Don't be all holier than bloody thou about it. It's a war for God's sake. The aim is to survive.'

'So you played up every time you had new information to pass on. And we all thought you were just a joker getting thrown in the cooler again and again.' Victor looked around at the old farmhouse – the comfy chairs, the booze, the warm fire. 'And all the time you were here. Building your reputation with every escape you grassed up, until… Look at you. An honorary bloody member of their little club.'

Von Eberstein had moved a little unsteadily over to the fireside table while Victor was speaking. He produced a cigar and lit it from the flames.

'The hardest thing was stopping him growing fat and giving the game away,' he said. 'Lots of good food, but only little bits. Right, Harry?'

Victor took no notice. He had bigger questions.

'So how many escapers did you give up?'

'Dozen maybe,' said Harry with a shrug.

'Fifteen!' exclaimed von Eberstein, jabbing his cigar in the air as if in triumph.

'And how many were recaptured?'

'Fifteen!' cried von Eberstein again, repeating the celebratory action.

'I knew a lot of those men,' said Victor. 'How many were executed?'

'Fifteen!' bellowed von Eberstein, punching the air a third time with his cigar.

No-one spoke for a few moments as the full scale of Harry's treachery sank in.

'What a bloody hero,' said Victor at last.

'And how many millions have died in the war?' countered Harry. 'What's fifteen?'

He was unable to hide a more plaintive tone – trying to convince himself as much as Victor.

'Whatever the number is, you can add fifteen good men to it thanks to you, you bloody coward. And that business with Blondie when he wanted to throw you over the wire? Was that just another ruse to get taken out of camp and back to your SS pals?'

'Actually, that was quite real,' interrupted von Eberstein. 'Schmidt – or Blondie as you call him – was not fully…' He circled his cigar in mid-air, looking for the right phrase. '…on board, at that point. Things have changed since that near miss. I actually owe you a debt of gratitude.'

'What difference would it have made? You'd already squeezed all the usefulness out of this little turncoat by then.'

'Not quite. In actual fact… his usefulness is only just beginning.'

Victor addressed his response to Harry.

'What the hell does that mean?'

Harry threw back the last of his Cognac and grimaced.

'This don't end well for you, Vic.'

'And it was all looking so bloody rosy,' said Victor, raising his shackled wrists.

'No… I mean it really don't fuckin' end well,' said Harry.

Victor looked at von Eberstein for an explanation. The Nazi had given up a brief search for a fresh brandy glass and was now swigging directly from the Cognac bottle.

'Excuse my manners,' he said. 'You know, just for a moment, I thought you were going to work it out. You saw through the letter, but you didn't pursue your questions to the end.'

'Enlighten me,' said Victor.

'You see… developing an agent who helps in the elimination of fifteen escapers earns one great credit in war. Unofficially, at least. But the same actions do not look so good in peacetime. In fact, thanks to the Geneva Convention, such patriotic acts get you hanged. Crazy, no?'

Von Eberstein took another swig and shook his head.

'Too many people know of my wartime successes, Victor. Too many. In such circumstances, one needs a plan for when the peace arrives. Otherwise, it's the gallows. Harry mentioned you one night and it just seemed too perfect. I invented the… the… *confusion* with this footballer Vic Watson simply to study you for a week.'

'I still have no idea what you're talking about,' said Victor.

'In a way I'm disappointed. You liked the Hans Christian Andersen book, no? The stories of illusion. Of new beginnings…'

Von Eberstein raised his hands to the bottom edge of the motorcycle helmet he had been wearing all day and awkwardly edged it upwards until it was clear of his head.

The top third of his left ear was missing.

He tossed the helmet into an armchair. The leather gloves followed. Then he raised both hands, palms facing forward, fingers splayed, like a magician showing the crowd he wasn't hiding anything.

The left little finger was missing beyond the first knuckle.

'What the..?'

Victor looked over to Harry, then back to von Eberstein – and the wounds that mirrored his own. Each had a layer of crusty blood. They were fresh.

'Are you out of your mind?' blurted Victor, now straining against the shackles. 'You want to escape your war crimes by impersonating me? That's... bloody ridiculous!'

'Were the subject anyone else I would agree,' replied von Eberstein, gently feeling along the top of his newly reduced ear. 'But with you there is actually a chance of success. And I will take even a small chance over the certainty of the hangman's noose.'

'And what makes *me* so special?' demanded Victor, giving up the brief and fruitless struggle against his restraints.

'Think about it. You are not just *special* as far as my requirements are concerned – you are perfect! No family... No fräulein waiting for you... Your only close friend standing right here... You have been a forgettable member of two institutions – an orphanage and the army. There is no life of any substance for you to return to. Plus, you have these unique wounds that identify you. Well, that is to say, they *were* unique.'

He allowed himself a little chuckle. Yes, he would count that as a joke...

'The basic physical resemblance is acceptable. Height, eyes, frame and phrenology. Naturally, I have reduced my food intake on account of your time in camp...'

'You're bloody mad.'

'...but none of that would have been enough without the ear and the finger. Man is a lazy beast. We look for simple markers. And, of course, the wounds are not the only thing that identifies you as being you...'

He put his uninjured right hand into a pocket of his decorated tunic and inched it back out, looking at Victor with eyebrows raised as if playing a game with a child.

'Surprise!' he said at last, holding up the gold medal with *'Ad Victoriam'* engraved into it. 'A token from the mother who abandoned you. Now, who else would have this other than the real Victor Watson? Hmmm?'

With a roar of frustration, Victor kicked the back of the armchair that separated them. The SS officer stepped aside as it struck the low table and pitched forward into the fire, the flames taking hold immediately. Harry dragged it out and began patting them down.

'Fuckin' hell, Vic. You can't treat other people's stuff like that.'

'You can't.... What?' Victor couldn't even bring himself to explain the clunking irony of the comment. His heart was thumping. Blondie had been right after all. He was going to die today.

'And what's your role in this?' he yelled at Harry, as his old mucker got the singed armchair under control. 'You've already told him all about me. Why would he keep you alive just to spill the beans on all this one day?'

Von Eberstein saved his new English friend the trouble of answering.

'He will vouch that I am you,' he said with unerring calm. 'What greater insurance than Victor's best friend to crush any doubts? Even better than the medal and the injuries, no? In return, I will keep quiet about his actions of the past year.' He brushed a hot cinder from the sleeve of his uniform. 'There is also the small matter of one hundred thousand pounds and a sizeable annual payment for life. Not that Harry would need such an incentive to keep his word, I'm sure. But a little extra security can't hurt.'

'Nice to know what my life is worth,' said Victor, looking Harry up and down in disgust.

'It's just survival, Vic,' said Harry, sticking to his theme.

'Not for me it bloody isn't.'

Von Eberstein tossed some small, metallic object to Harry, who caught it.

'Do it,' he commanded. 'Now.'

Harry lifted Victor's wrists and used the small key to finally release them from their iron bindings. The shackles clattered to the flagstones. The condemned man held each wrist in turn and began rubbing life back into the nerve endings, all the time staring at his former friend. His right fist slowly clenched and unclenched.

'Go on then,' said Harry. 'Hit me if you–'

He didn't quite reach the end of his sentence before Victor spun and charged von Eberstein, slamming a punch into the middle of his face. The Nazi staggered backwards, landing in an armchair on top of his motorcycle helmet. Victor dived on him, slamming home another punch, then a third as soon as the right hand could be pulled back and unleashed again. The chair rocked back with the SS officer pinned to it. He made no attempt to fight back.

As Victor drew back his bloodied fist for a fourth punch, Harry grabbed it and hauled him off, both of them falling to the ground. An exhausted Victor made to scramble to his feet before freezing... von Eberstein was pointing his Walther P38 pistol straight at him. The Nazi spluttered a little, blood pouring from his shattered nose, then pulled the helmet from beneath him and sank into the chair.

'I am so glad I'm drunk,' he said.

He tentatively felt the damage to his nose, before giving up with a sharp intake of breath.

'Oh, this is ideal,' he said. 'I was going to ask Schmidt, but I had a feeling you might oblige. The nose plays such a vital role in recognising a face – you have just blurred the lines between us. Thank you.'

Victor inched himself back until he was leaning against the armchair opposite von Eberstein. He was still breathing hard. Right hand swelling up fast. His play having failed, he managed a resigned laugh.

'Always wanted to break my hand on a Nazi's face... Sick psychos, eh, Harry?'

The voice was no longer raised. The energy in the room was dropping. Harry slumped into the middle armchair, the top of it still smouldering.

'By the way,' said Victor, raising his eyes to von Eberstein, the blood finally spoiling that perfect uniform. 'You don't even sound like me.'

Von Eberstein lowered the edge of the scarf he was holding to his nostrils as a claret stain spread through the cream fabric.

'Your voice? Ha! Films, films, films... So much easier to copy than some regional accent... But I agree it may take time. The only sure solution is silence. Perhaps for a number of years at least.'

'Not suspicious at all,' said Victor, sarcastically.

'Well, if no-one even expects a man to speak...' replied von Eberstein.

Keeping his pistol trained on Victor, he began to remove the bloodstained scarf with his free hand, twirling it up and away. As the final loop was pulled clear, it revealed the Nazi's neck – a sickening horizontal cut, closed up with big, ugly, vertical stitches. Victor stared at the butchered skin, transfixed by both its appearance and the audacity of the plan it represented.

'You're insane,' he said at last. 'And so is whatever Nazi doctor carved you up.'

Von Eberstein's pained behaviour in the hut now made perfect sense.

'The doctor may be insane, but he is now also rich. His co-operation was not cheap. But, come now. It is important Harry and I remember our story.'

'Which is?'

'I – Victor – was being horribly tortured by SS officers in this big old farmhouse when Harry here helped me escape. Luckily, we had overheard that the Americans were just a few miles to the west, so headed that way. All very plausible, no? In any case, it has to happen. The Russians are even closer than the Americans. In a few days they will take the camp, and God help any German who is still here for that.'

Insane or not, they were really going to do this.

'Of course,' continued von Eberstein. 'I imagine your country will be in some chaos when I arrive there. Millions of men returning to civilian life. All of which will be of great help to me. And a numbered Swiss bank account goes a long way. I confess that a background in banking and considerable wealth is not exactly a hindrance for the purpose of this project.'

Victor was tiring of the boastful monologue. He glanced at the door leading back to the passage as surreptitiously as possible.

'He's thinking about it,' said Harry.

'Don't,' said von Eberstein. 'Schmidt is already out there… I have a task for him.'

Victor realised he had been vaguely aware of a vehicle pulling up in the courtyard while everything else had been going on. He looked at Harry and shook his head.

'Listen to yourself,' he said. 'Good God, man! A few weeks from now we would have been getting drunk in an English pub. Now you'll have a hundred thousand pounds to spend all on your own.'

Harry didn't reply at first, choosing simply to stare into the flames.

'It's already settled,' he said at last.

Victor sensed him wobbling.

'For Christ's sake, it's not too late, Harry. Two of us will have a chance. Come on. Forget what you've done. It was the stress of war. We can be chasing girls in Leicester Square next month. Think about it.'

Harry finally turned away from the flames to look at Victor. His old friend was right to think he had been wavering. A moment's indecision over the choices he had made. But only a moment.

'Vic…' he said. 'I'll be able to buy a bleedin' pub in Leicester Square.'

The finality of the words sent a chill through Victor.

'Don't look so sad,' interjected von Eberstein. 'You fought a good war. In fact…'

He stood up and moved over to a drinks cabinet in the corner, keeping Victor in his sights.

'I saw the way you looked at the whisky during our chats,' he said, clumsily pouring a generous measure. 'There is really no need to deny yourself any longer.'

'I agree,' said Victor, looking at the heavy glass of the tumbler… a potentially lethal projectile. Then he glanced down at Harry's empty brandy glass. At some point while pulling the armchair from the fire, he had left it on the edge of the low table. An altogether more delicate object, though perhaps it could still be useful.

'You have to do something for me first,' added von Eberstein. 'I can't very well turn up at the American lines dressed like an SS-Sturmbannführer. Your uniform and your boots. Give them to me.'

Victor wanted that heavy tumbler. He also wanted his captor to mentally lower his guard. He wearily got up from the stone floor and began untying his laces, easing off each boot and casually tossing them over to the SS man. The shirt and trousers of his patched up uniform followed, leaving him standing in his underwear. He was glad of the warmth from the fire.

'Good,' said von Eberstein, pleased by the lack of resistance. He nodded at the thin chain round Victor's neck. 'Now those dog tags.'

Victor pulled them over his head – yet another way for von Eberstein to 'prove' his new identity.

'Out of interest…' he began, throwing the tags onto the rest of his uniform, '…why did you bother explaining all of this to me? All you had to do was kill me when I got here.'

Von Eberstein nodded at the rational question.

'What can I say? When you have come up with a plan of such perfection… one that will have to stay hidden forever… it seems a shame not to show it off just once.'

He handed Victor's whisky to the seated Harry, then sank into his own armchair. The traitor avoided eye contact as he passed the tumbler on to his old pal. Victor took it in his broken right hand – it was still his throwing hand, after all. And his only hope now was to blind von Eberstein, thus forcing Harry to switch allegiance once again. A blind von Eberstein would never be able to make it cross-country to the American lines. It was a long shot, but the only one on offer.

Victor stared into the tumbler. Swirling the whisky. Judging the weight.

'I never asked if you were a religious man,' said von Eberstein. 'Perhaps you would like to say a few words?'

'I honestly don't know,' replied Victor, raising the glass to breathe in the aroma. 'Hard not to have a few doubts when you've seen so many good men killed, wouldn't you say, Harry?'

His old mucker stared straight into the fire.

'But there is one bit I once memorised. Just before we shipped out for the first time… Ephesians 6:10. The Armour of God.'

Victor stopped swirling the whisky. Reciting the verse didn't seem such a bad idea. On the one hand, von Eberstein would see a man accepting his fate. Surely that would dull his reflexes a little. On the other, if this really *was* to be the end, then, doubts or not, it still couldn't hurt.

'As you wish,' said von Eberstein, the Walther P38 relaxing ever so slightly in his hand.

The Englishman raised his eyes to a small window just behind the Nazi – a scrubby field and a distant line of trees. Crows were gathering on the neglected land. It seemed an appropriate view for the occasion. Victor had spent the last year looking out at a similar line of trees through the wire fence of Stalag IV-B. They were always just out of reach. If the heavy tumbler didn't hit home in about thirty seconds time, they always would be.

He invisibly tested the grip of each finger holding the glass in his damaged hand. From the nights of silent repetition on the troop ship to North Africa, he knew the passage contained exactly ninety-five words. He kept his eyes on the distant trees and began…

'Finally, be strong in the Lord and in His mighty power. Put on the full armour of God so that you can take your stand against the devil's schemes…'

Sixty-six words to go.

'For our struggle is not against flesh and blood, but against the rulers, against the authorities, against the powers of this dark world and against the spiritual forces of evil in the heavenly realms….'

Thirty-two words.

'Therefore put on the full armour of God, so that when the day of evil comes, you may be able to stand your ground…'

Eight.

'…and after you have done everything…'

Two.

'…to STAND!'

Victor downed the whisky and kicked a table leg, diverting eyes downward to the topple-and-shatter of the brandy glass while simultaneously drawing back the empty tumbler, focused on the point between von Eberstein's eyes.

Only Harry was distracted by the shattering brandy glass.

Von Eberstein raised his Walther P38 and shot Victor in the head.

The heavy tumbler fell vertically from the point at which it was about to be launched, reaching the ground with a smash at the same time as a crumpled Victor.

The deafening echo of the shot gradually gave way to the sounds of Harry throwing up over the side of his chair and startled crows squawking skyward. Von Eberstein slowly got to his feet to inspect the scene.

He looked down at the motionless heap of Victor, his hair a bloodied mess with glimpses of white skull beneath. Then he stepped over him, intrigued by the way the gramophone's brass horn had created a blood-free silhouette on the spattered wall.

A knock at the door.

'Ja?' answered von Eberstein.

The door to the passage swung open and Blondie entered, the big elk hide from the other room under his arm. He showed no reaction to the sight before him. Blood, injuries, death… it was all very mundane to him.

'Fertig?' he asked… *'Ready?'*

'Fertig,' replied von Eberstein.

With impressive speed, Blondie rolled out the animal skin next to Victor, then pushed and pulled his limp body onto it, before rolling it all up. Easier transportation.

'Wie immer,' said the new Victor… *'The usual place.'*

Chapter 38

Sunday, 24th April 2016
North London

Brook ordered the American-style pancakes while Jonboy asked for the 'full Welsh breakfast', before pointing to the full English on the menu to alleviate the waitress's confusion. He never tired of that one. With none of the neighbouring tables occupied, Brook risked slipping the restricted crime report out of his bag for a first look.

'I'm guessing that's the top secret document Marie handed you in a folded newspaper,' said Jonboy, any chance of being overheard drowned out by the nearby espresso machine.

'Maybe I need to work on all that Cold War spy stuff,' replied Brook.

'Go on, then. What is it?'

Brook leaned a little closer.

'The crime report on Logan Baird that Barnes restricted.'

Jonboy nodded approvingly at Marie's clandestine skills.

'Interesting,' he said, before grabbing Marie's newspaper and turning to the sports pages.

'Hopefully,' agreed Brook, starting to read. He reminded himself of Marie's words: *'VIW1 is an 88-year-old man called Paul Fisher and VIW2 is your Logan Baird…'*

The crime report described events in the borough of Westminster, central London, in June 2013. It explained how two uniformed PCs had been on an evening foot patrol in Hyde Park when they turned the corner past a wooded area to find an elderly white male (VIW1) lying on his back. Another white male of around forty (VIW2) was a few yards away. He stated: *'Thank God you're here'* to the officers, before rushing to the elderly male and attempting CPR.

One of the PCs took over resuscitation attempts while another summoned an ambulance. VIW2 expressed surprise that police had *'arrived so quickly'* as he had only just asked a passing female to call them. The female *'could not be located'*.

VIW1 was pronounced dead at the scene. VIW2 was *'helpful and co-operative'*. He described coming across the elderly male on the ground while walking in the park and asking the unknown passing female to call police while he tried to resuscitate him.

He was apparently doing this when he got up briefly *'to check on the whereabouts of the female'* and bumped into the officers coming round the corner. No call about this incident could be found on the system. There was *'no CCTV in that area of the park'*.

Owing to recent robberies in the area, this Crime Related Incident report had been created until it could be established that VIW1 was not the victim of an offence prior to being found by VIW2. Due to the physical contact during resuscitation attempts, *'VIW2 was asked to provide elimination fingerprints and DNA, in case evidence of an earlier offence emerges and a forensic strategy is required'*. He agreed to the request.

The deceased's details came from a wallet on his person, including photo ID. His next of kin was located after reporting her husband missing. The couple had been visiting London from their home in Florida.

VIW1's wife had viewed the items in his possession and did not believe anything had been stolen. Medical reports found no obvious signs of foul play. Intel reports and the closest CCTV cameras had also been checked and gave no indication that any offences played a role in VIW1's death, which was believed to be heart-related... *'Report submitted for closure'*.

A single line from a supervisor approved the conclusions.

Brook leaned back in his chair, shuffled the report back together and pushed it across the table to Jonboy, who was shaking his head at all the multi-millionaire footballers in the sports pages. He began reading the crime report as the Polish waitress arrived with their breakfasts.

'Are you cross with me for 'big kiss' shouting?' she asked Brook.

'Very cross,' replied the detective with a wink. The waitress smiled back. Jonboy had clearly cracked the code where that smile was concerned. Brook began dissecting everything he had just read, while Jonboy took it all in for the first time. It turned out he was an even quicker reader.

'Well now then,' he said, pushing the report back across the table.

'So what do you think?'

'I think this Logan Baird fella was disturbed just after killing the old boy and styled it out to perfection. You?'

'The same,' said Brook. 'But none of that's provable now. The official record is that he's a Good Samaritan, tried to save someone and helped the police.'

'Okay. You're saying the official version does more to prove his good character than his bad character, so why did Barnes go to the trouble of restricting it two days ago?'

'Exactly. I think there's something in there we're not seeing.'

'Bit weird about the elimination DNA ending up on the database, isn't it?'

'True. Though I guess you only had to tick the wrong box on those old green forms.'

'But it's not as if it hasn't been spotted. Barnes has got those instructions to contact him written all over it. If it started off as a mistaken entry on the database, he seems happy enough to leave it up there. Seems he's quite invested in this fella one way or another.'

Brook began to read it again, but the smell of pancakes easily defeated his remaining willpower. He slid the report back into the bag.

'Quite right,' said Jonboy, skewering a Cumberland sausage. 'These things come to you when you stop thinking about them.'

Brook tried to heed the good advice as he ate, looking at the framed sporting photos to give the police parts of his brain a rest. Behind him, a customer was chatting to the waitress as he paid. He asked her to give his best to the owner.

Brook dropped his cutlery on the plate.

'Fiona,' he said.

'Or just Jonboy is fine.'

'Fiona wants this back… The Lumberjack misheard him.'

'How's that then?'

'It never made sense, did it? Our killer saying 'Fiona wants this back' when he took Victor's medal. It didn't make sense because he didn't say it.'

'So what did he say?'

'He said *The owner* wants this back…'

'You sure?'

'The Lumberjack said he would never mishear his wife's name, but it's the exact opposite. It's exactly why he *did* mishear it. He was preconditioned to hear the name in his head.'

Jonboy nodded cautiously. It did seem to make more sense than Fiona. Though it still left an obvious problem.

'You realise you're only replacing one question with another, don't you? If Victor has had that medal since he was a baby and his killer says *the owner* wants it back, then who's he talking about? I'm guessing Victor's long lost mum didn't hire a hitman on her hundred-and-fifteenth birthday to whack her son and take her medal back.'

'I think I'm with you on that.'

'So what's the answer, Number One?'

'Patience, Jonboy. All we do is acknowledge that there's some sort of dispute over the medal and toss that jigsaw piece back into the mix.'

'So it doesn't get us anywhere?'

'But it stops us getting nowhere.'

'Bloody hell.'

When the waitress collected their plates, Brook ordered two double espressos.

'Come on. I'm in a problem-solving mood…'

He reached back into his bag and pulled out the Christmas card from Harry's bedroom.

'This old chestnut,' said Jonboy.

'There's an answer to this. I'm convinced it's to do with that date inside the card. Six days out from the official frank. It's deliberately chosen, so it's saying something. The twenty-first of December… Twenty-one twelve… Two, one, one, two… It feels familiar.'

Jonboy was staring at the card in silence so Brook shut up. Espressos duly arrived at the newly becalmed table. Jonboy tipped three sugars into his, gave it a stir and downed it in one.

'Have you transferred all the photos from this job onto your new phone?' he asked.

Brook called up the photos and handed over the mobile. Jonboy scrolled through them, forward and back, pausing here and there. Then he slid the card and phone across the table, leaned back in his chair and casually opened the sports pages again.

'Giving up already?' asked Brook.

'Au Cointreau,' replied Jonboy, deliberately mangling the French. 'It's not giving up when you've figured it out, is it?'

'You're kidding me.'

'Nope… You said it looked familiar, didn't you? If the twenty-first of December was turned into digits. Have you got the dog tags in that bag?'

'I've got everything in that bag.'

'Take them out and have a look.'

Brook fished around until he had the evidence bag with the dog tags from Victor's flat. He laid it on the table and looked at the inscription:

STALAG IVB 211251

'Two, one, one, two,' said Brook, staring at the dog tags. 'The first four digits of Victor's prisoner number.'

'Exactly. Like the twenty-first of December. That's why it seemed familiar. I don't know if it helps us though. It's not even an exact match, is it? The first four digits of a six-digit number. Could just be a coincidence.'

Brook tutted. 'You know my views on the C-word.'

He placed the dog tags alongside the open Christmas card and looked between the two, rubbing his heavy night shift stubble. After a minute or two, a smile began to emerge.

'Humour me with this,' he said, placing a pen and paper in front of his friend.

'I hate it when you're smug. Go on then.'

'Write *fifteen* as if you were writing about a rugby team – the first fifteen.'

Jonboy picked up the pen and wrote 'XV'. Brook carried on.

'Now write *eleven* as if you're writing about a cricket or football team.'

Jonboy wrote 'XI' next to the 'XV'.

'Now get rid of all the Xs. What are you left with?'

'V and I.'

'Which is?'

'Six. Or a five and a one.'

'Now look at the card again. And the name next to the date.'

Jonboy looked once more at the date of *'21st December'* and then, beneath it to the right, the name *'VICTOR'* in capitals, the *V* and *I* bigger than the other letters. The penny dropped.

'The last two digits of the prisoner number are in the name,' he said. 'V and I. Five and one.'

'Two, one... one, two... five, one... Victor's entire POW number encoded in the card.'

Jonboy scratched his head. 'Am I allowed to point out that you've just replaced one question with another again? It's signed from Victor anyway. Why go to all the effort of secretly confirming which Victor it is?'

'You don't need to have all the answers straight away. It's–'

'I know, I know. Another piece of Brook's never-ending jigsaw.'

'You're getting the hang of this.'

'Would Harry even have noticed it in there? It took us long enough to figure it out.'

'But we knew there was *something*, didn't we? The little anomalies flagged that up. Plus, these old soldiers lived in a world of codes and secret messages. Not like us idiots.'

'So let's accept all of that. It's included deliberately and it's meant to be noticed. But… why?'

Brook took a deep breath, then let all the air out in a sigh.

'Not sure,' he said.

'Brilliant.'

He finished his espresso and put everything back into the shoulder bag.

'So what are we looking for at Victor's flat?' asked Jonboy. 'And you're not allowed to say *any pieces of the jigsaw*.'

'I think we're looking for two things,' said Brook. 'Victor told the barman he didn't like cards. It was so insignificant, I almost didn't include it in his statement. But, since there's something funny going on with cards, let's look for cards.'

'What's the other thing?'

'Any pieces of the jigsaw.'

Chapter 39

He felt a certain amount of satisfaction as he watched the two of them approach. Okay, he admitted it, a massive amount. The fact he was watching them had nothing to do with any tip-off from Barnes. This was all his own initiative, and his hunches had proved right.

Firstly, that Deelman would find the 'invitation' he had left for him with New York Cabs in Sheffield. He was very confident of that now. Secondly, that the detective would want to squeeze in another visit to 'Victor's' flat for anything he had missed before their little tête-à-tête tomorrow. Some time after breakfast had always seemed the most likely window. This Deelman seemed to like his food. And here he was. Right on cue. Hadn't he told Barnes he needed to trust him more?

Whoever was walking alongside Deelman didn't look shy of a square meal either. Tall, too. Where were the Met Police getting these giants from? Assuming this new guy was police, of course. Which seemed highly likely since he was heading towards the flat with Deelman. He didn't recognise whatever red sports jersey he was wearing, but it definitely seemed the Met had ditched their shaving requirement.

He raised the can of super-strength cider to his lips as the two police officers walked past his bench on the other side of the street. With a grey hoodie, stained baseball cap and copy of the Daily Star, there was little danger of being recognised as the man they had seen on CCTV. Amazing the character you can create when you put your mind to it.

He took a good look at them now – he had only seen Deelman from afar at Peak View and, obviously, it was his first view of this other big lump. But assuming they would be operating as some kind of team tomorrow, this was an invaluable head start.

He still had no idea how this whole thing would end. A lot of it would depend on what layer of truth Deelman had drilled down to by the time of their meeting. Because there were many, many layers, and he was genuinely curious to see how deep he would get.

If they foolishly decided to go for him then they would regret it, of course. Being a big, burly London 'copper' was one thing. Even being two big, burly London coppers. Having five percent body fat and twenty years of intensive hand-to-hand combat training under your belt was something else. It was up to them if they wanted to make the mistake.

As the two police officers passed beyond his position and approached the flat, he was glad to lower the can of super-strength cider from his lips.

How did people drink that shit?

Chapter 40

'This is it,' said Brook, as they reached 64 Duke Crescent. He took in the scene for a moment. With everything that had happened, it was hard to believe it was only a few days since he had been here with Kev. A loud click focused their attention on the front door just before it began to open. A blonde of around thirty came into view, struggling to manoeuvre a buggy with off-road wheels.

'Yummy mummy,' whispered Jonboy, before making light of his bulk to dance up the steps and assist with the door.

'Thank you so much,' said the blonde, blowing a disobedient fringe out of her eyes. 'I always struggle with that.'

'Pram's too big,' said Jonboy, helpfully. 'You could fit a massive baby in there and you've only got a little one.'

Brook bit his lip and winced as he presented his warrant card...

'Would it be okay if we came in? We're from the police station down the road. Just dealing with the death of the old man in 1A.'

The resident couldn't quite hide her surprise that Jonboy also presented a warrant card.

'Of course,' she said, closing the door softly enough that it rested against the latch. 'Yes, I saw that you were looking for his next of kin on the local police Twitter account.'

The two men gave each other a glance that said '*We have a Twitter account?*' at the same time as Brook realised his request for the press officer to hold fire had been totally ignored. Oh well. Too late now.

'I'm so sorry we haven't been able to help more,' the blonde continued. 'I suppose nobody really knows their neighbours these days, do they?'

She moved the buggy towards the top of the steps.

'I'll get that for you,' said Jonboy, hoisting the contraption skyward before whisking it down to street level. The yummy mummy followed with just a hint of concern on her face.

'There you go, little fella,' said the big Welshman, handing over control.

'Thank you,' replied the baby's mother. 'Though she's a girl, actually.'

'Oh, right. I just thought with all the blue stuff and the… other blue stuff.'

'We don't believe in gender stereotyping.'

'Quite right,' said Jonboy. 'Quite right. Very bad business indeed all that gender… business.'

'You coming, mate?' called Brook, mercifully, from the top of the steps.

Jonboy took them three at a time while the yummy mummy walked off with a strange story to tell at baby yoga.

'I don't know what you're laughing at, Number One.'

'Shall we just stick to searching the flat from now on?'

'Good idea.'

Victor's home looked exactly the same as before. Dated yet meticulously maintained.

'Not a bad place, is it?' observed Jonboy, taking himself on a quick tour… 'And he owned it?' he called from the dining room, staring at the photo of Stalag IV-B's theatre.

'Looks like it. But the version of the land registry database I checked only went back fifty years. Still, it hasn't been bought or sold for half a century at least.'

'Blimey. Just think of the increase in value.'

'Yep… You'd think there would be no trouble finding a next of kin.'

They both looked around in silence for a moment.

'Right then,' said Jonboy. 'Let's get cracking.'

It would be fair to say that Brook had known easier searches, but plenty of harder ones too. After about ten minutes, he was close to completing the kitchen – taking infinitely more care than he and Kev had shown the first time – when a familiar baritone shattered the silence. It filled the flat with a single triumphant word.

'Doughnuts!'

Brook headed through to the bedroom, where Jonboy was standing in front of an open wardrobe. The top drawer of its internal unit was open too – some neatly arranged socks, underwear and handkerchiefs inside. Brook looked down at them, then across at Jonboy.

'You're not getting doughnuts for finding his pants.'

'We'll see about that,' said Jonboy, sliding the drawer out and placing it on the bed.

Whatever was hiding in there, he'd clearly already seen it.

Brook began removing the small items from the drawer, soon revealing a white envelope. It had the same handwriting as the one in Harry's room and a similar Christmas scene on its stamp. The frank told him the card had been sent from Perth in 1992.

He lifted it out of the drawer… another envelope was beneath it. He tilted his head to look in from an angle… plenty more beneath that one. Brook tipped them all onto the bed.

'Okay,' he said, 'doughnuts it is.'

They spread out the envelopes. Eleven in total. All addressed to *'Mr Victor Watson'* at the flat in which they were standing and all franked in Australia… Brisbane, Cairns, Adelaide, Bundaberg, Canberra, two from Perth, two from Sydney and two from Melbourne.

The most recent was from Melbourne in 2015. The oldest from Sydney, sent in 1954. The others were from the intervening decades, each slit envelope still holding its contents.

Brook pulled out eleven Christmas cards and laid them open. Apart from changes to the generic printed greeting, the writing inside was always the same. *'To Victor... 21st December… VICTOR… See you soon'*. The *V* and *I* were always a bit bigger than the other letters – exactly the same coded message as Harry's card. The Stalag IV-B prisoner number of one Victor Watson.

Brook checked the frank on the Melbourne envelope from 2015. It matched the one on the card in Harry's bedroom. Sent together.

'I'm guessing Harry received matching cards for all these other ones too, but one way or another they didn't survive his move to Peak View.'

'This is making my head explode,' said Jonboy.

Only the oldest card contained any additions – the different ink and handwriting suggesting they were the work of the recipient rather than the sender. The date and the first two letters of *VICTOR* were ringed, followed by the same 'answer' Brook and Jonboy had arrived at in the café… *211251.*

Victor Watson's POW number was followed by a couple of words.

'You speak a bit of German from your time based over there, don't you?' asked Brook.

'Often mistaken for a local,' said Jonboy, staring at the words being pointed out:

Er lebt??

'He's… in love?' he offered.

Childhood holidays in Namibia and a varied home schooling meant Brook was, fortunately, not reliant on Jonboy's translation skills.

'He's alive,' he said.

Jonboy ran a hand over his face, ruffled his hair and grunted.

'Right… Just… Right… So the Victor who phones Harry does so from this flat. But the Victor who sends Christmas cards to Harry does so from the other side of the world. And *that* Victor also sends cards to *this* Victor. And both Victors lay claim to the same POW number. Because one puts it in his cards, while the other has it here on his dog tags and Red Cross record.'

He closed his eyes and rubbed his temples as he spoke.

'But logic says Victor can't be two people. So we must have one Victor and one nut job. And if the nut job is the guy who lived here, then… who the hell is he? And what's with the German?'

Brook stayed lost in thought while Jonboy continued his monologue, trying to rationalise everything before his head went pop…

'It would be nice if the cards said a bit more. I mean, *See you soon* is pretty standard fare and, apart from that, they're just saying 'this is me and this is you'.'

'Or put that another way,' said Brook. 'I exist and I know where you live.'

Jonboy noticed the distant look in his friend's eyes.

'You're shuffling those jigsaw pieces again, aren't you?'

'Think motive and opportunity,' suggested Brook, returning to the flat's only photograph... So why this one? Why this as your one and only photo? He read the caption again:

'Stalag IV-B, Christmas 1944, 'The Empire' Theatre'

Just four months before the camp was liberated and the captors became the captives. Motive and opportunity. He examined the image once more. The uproar of the stage show, the mixed crowd of prisoners and guards... But he looked at it differently this time.

There was a Nazi officer nearest the camera. Immaculate uniform. He was throwing his head back and laughing even more than most (he clearly liked the jokes). One could almost have been forgiven for thinking the photo was all about him.

Brook took out his phone and found the solitary shot he had taken from The Junction's CCTV – 'Victor' passing under the camera, momentarily glancing up at someone holding the door open. He put the images side by side and tried to mentally undo the injuries and years of ageing.

'What is it?' asked Jonboy.

'I think it's called an epiphany.'

Chapter 41

Saturday, 21st April 1945
near Mühlberg, Germany

Darkness.

Is this what it was like, then? Being dead?

He was pretty sure his eyes were open. But it was hard to tell. Just… darkness.

Odd that he was aware of the physical sensation of opening his eyes though. Do you still have sensations like that? When you're dead?

There were other feelings too. Like a vague sense of movement. And his head felt strange. Cold. Different.

He tried to raise a hand to it in the darkness. If he could raise an eyelid then surely he could raise a hand. Ah… No… It didn't move at all. Dead then. And yet he was aware of the muscles trying to move the arm and meeting some kind of resistance. Strange.

Light.

Blinding light everywhere.

So this was it. The moment of ascent. Two questions answered in the affirmative: Was heaven real? And would he ever see it? He hadn't expected the ascent to be this loud though. It sounded like an explosion.

And flames? Flames were everywhere now.

No. Not this way. Not down. Come on! Hey! I did my best!

Blue sky.

Better. Much better. Now, this was more like heaven.

Serene blue sky with some fluffy white clouds just ambling by. Take your time, clouds. This was far more pleasant than the flames.

And now a new shape up there. He knew this… A plane! Not the glorious curves of a Spitfire, but some other fighter. Russian maybe. Flying low and looking for targets of opportunity. Funny thing to be doing in Heaven.

Still, it looked like it had nailed one. Some thirty feet away. The burning shell of a vehicle. Hard to say what it once was. A Kübelwagen maybe. The German army Jeep.

Now what… what was this beneath him? An animal skin rug? All scorched and smoking. So would this animal have been killed on Earth or in Heaven? This was all very confusing.

Ah! A face! A face he recognised. What was his name again? Come on, Victor… Think now… Think… Blondie! That was it. But how did he get up there when he was so heavy? All the way up in that tree?

Of course! It was obvious once you realised. He had left the bottom half of his body behind. To make himself lighter. Clever Blondie. He didn't look very happy up there though. Maybe because he was on fire.

He tried again to lift a hand to his cold head. It worked this time. But… his head wasn't how he remembered it. There was a channel all the way along the scalp. A furrow, an inch or two off-centre. The hair either side felt like he had just stepped out of a shower. Except it wasn't water. The pain of touching the injury began to chase away thoughts of the afterlife. It was as if…

…As if a bullet from the Walther P38 of a drunk man had caught the top of his forehead and traced the surface of his skull, collecting skin, flesh, blood and hair like a snowplough before throwing it all out behind him.

The wound was deep. Horribly deep. Along much of the furrow, the white of the skull itself was exposed. But that, too, had saved him. It had been enough to distract von Eberstein when he should have been noticing the shallow movement of lungs somewhere in the crumpled heap. It also satisfied him instantly that Victor was dead. Nobody survives having their skull on display. Well, almost nobody.

Then there was Blondie. So quick and efficient at wrapping him in the animal skin that he too had missed the faint signs of life. The multiple rolls of thick hide had surely helped save Victor when he was thrown clear of their blown-up vehicle.

Of course, if he ever met the regimental pastor again, the clergyman would no doubt have a different explanation for his survival. Nothing to do with a freak of physics or the poor aim of a drunken shooter. His answer would be simpler… *'The Armour of God'*.

In any case, there would be no need to check for signs of life where Blondie was concerned. His flaming upper body had started to burn through the branches in which it was lodged. Victor heard them start to crack and saw the semi-charred remains slipping from the canopy above him.

For a moment, a wrist became stuck, giving the eerie impression that the fiery half-corpse was trying to hold on. Then the final restraining branch gave way and the burning top half of Blondie came plummeting towards Victor. He rolled out of the way as fifty percent of a Nazi psychopath slammed into the ground beside him. Still trying to kill prisoners. Even in death.

The sudden movement and smell of burned flesh made Victor's head spin. He took a long time to compose himself before trying to stand up, only to fall straight back down, confused. He looked at his legs – it was easy to assess them since he was only in his underpants. There was something wrong with the left one. Nothing seemed to line up properly. He tried to rise again, putting all his weight on the right leg, only to lose his balance and hit the ground once more. Maybe his luck had run out after all.

He was becoming more aware of the throbbing pain from his head wound now. The shock that had been protecting him from the full horror of it was starting to wear off. From his position flat on his back he looked around, for the first time seeing beyond the immediate surroundings of smouldering metal and gently crackling undergrowth.

There was a farmhouse away to his left, at the top of an incline. Not the SS house. A different one. If he could somehow haul himself through the hedgerow then it was just the other side of a sloping field. Why were things always the other side of a bloody field? There was no point wondering about the political sympathies of its occupants for now. He just had to get there.

Rolling onto his side, Victor tried grabbing a section of branch that had been brought down by Blondie. His right hand refused to grip it, swelling badly after its violent encounter with von Eberstein's face. He rolled onto his other side and grabbed the piece of wood in his left. Then he began using it as an ice pick – pulling hard, while pushing with his good leg, and digging in his right elbow for a third point of thrust. He was able to cover a short distance with each combined effort.

Negotiating the ditch at the side of the road was every bit as painful as expected. The broken left leg tumbled down into it. With gritted teeth, Victor hauled himself up and out the other side. Hedgerow next. He looked up and down for a weak point, finally settling on some kind of badger run a few yards away. A few more heaves and he could see through the little tunnel to the farmhouse. But the route through the dense hedgerow was narrower than he had thought. Foxes perhaps, rather than badgers.

He heard the distant sound of a vehicle approaching. A decision to make… Take his chances with the vehicle or take his chances with the farmhouse? Von Eberstein had told him how close the Americans and Russians were. Maybe the vehicle was one of theirs. The occupants of the farmhouse were bound to be German. But not all Germans were friends of the Nazis.

The engine noise grew louder. Victor made his decision. The age-old scenario of a weary traveller throwing himself upon the mercy of strangers seemed the best bet. He began dragging himself through the hedgerow, realising almost immediately that its mesh of twigs was stronger than he had anticipated. It pinned him to the ground, making progress almost impossible. Soon he was wriggling desperately.

Nearing the point of exhaustion, he managed to get his left hand out the other side and dig the piece of wood into the ground, hauling himself forward. The twigs scratched and scraped at his head, sending bolts of lightning through him. All the time, the engine noise got closer – at any moment they would be able to see his legs still poking out.

Victor dug the 'ice pick' in again and pushed with his good leg at the same time. Then again. And again. Gritting his teeth to the point of damaging them. The hedge's grip moved down his body and then it was gone. He was in the field. He rolled away from the tiny tunnel and lay flat on his back, eyes closed, exhausted.

On the other side of his hedgerow shield, the fast-approaching vehicle pulled up at the scene of the explosive devastation. Victor heard doors opening… male voices speaking German… fast, angry German. It was hard to understand, but one word seemed to be repeated more than any other – '*Schmidt*'. They all knew Blondie. Nazis. Victor had made the right choice.

Unlikely though it was that they would hear him, the Englishman tried to lie still and breathe silently. It was an approach that created its own problems. After a minute or two, the blood and lack of movement attracted a crow that mistook him for carrion. Its wing grazed the gaping head wound as it came in to land for its feast. Victor muffled the scream of pain and swatted it away, hoping that its squawks would not draw attention.

After a few more minutes of angry disagreement over what to do with the two bits of Schmidt, the hum of more aircraft in the area caused the Nazis to retreat to their vehicle. They sped away amid more slamming of doors. Victor took a deep breath and steeled himself for the long and painful crawl to the farmhouse. And whatever fate awaited him there.

But something had changed. It had crept over him during those minutes of stillness. A weakness – physical and mental. He had gone to the well one too many times and now it was empty. He opened his eyes but his vision was blurred. He was starting to drift, returning to the fingertip grip on reality he had experienced earlier. He could feel the world spinning beneath him, wanting to spin him right off into the void. He didn't know whether to hold on or let go.

Then the Angel appeared.

He had heard about them in stories from the Great War – appearances over battlefields, the famous 'Angels of Mons', legends told by old soldiers in pubs. He had never been sure if they were real. But here was one now, just for him, looking silently down. She was blonde and wearing a white dress. Of course she was. She was an Angel. And she was beautiful. Obviously. A part of him was sad he hadn't made it to the farmhouse. Never mind. He was safe now.

But why was the Angel looking scared? That wasn't meant to happen. She was staring at his head injury and then turning back to the farmhouse, beckoning urgently. Calling other Angels, perhaps.

Victor gave up on trying to work out if this was real or not. If it was life or afterlife. Heaven or Earth. He gave up on everything other than converting the last vestiges of hope, the last scraps of his battered spirit, into two short words.

Because, whether his broken body was dead or alive, the words he needed to say to the Angel were the same.

'Help me.'

Then darkness returned.

Chapter 42

Sunday, 24th April 2016
North London

At just a couple of hundred yards from Tottenham Hotspur's White Hart Lane stadium, 'Big Dave's' was a café designed to survive any match day trouble between rival fans. The five white Formica tables along each wall were bolted to the tiled floor, while their red stools appeared to hover in mid-air – attached to the underside of the tables by rigid crossbars. It all amounted to a café with no 'throwable' furniture (though a wall mirror covered in special offers was something of an oversight).

Brook and Jonboy had chosen the place on account of its proximity to The Elbow Room pub – for their pre-Tourist recce – and because it looked quiet enough for Brook to make the two phone calls he promised were 'the final pieces of the jigsaw'.

Marie answered the first. Back home early rather than stuck in the office for a change. After the greetings, Brook got straight to the point.

'You said that VIW1 in the crime report was called Paul Fisher – the old guy who died in Hyde Park after meeting Logan Baird. How was Fisher spelled?'

'Hang on,' said Marie. 'I've just got out of the shower, but I wrote it down here somewhere.'

'We could switch to FaceTime if you want me to help with the search?'

'You're hilarious, Deelman.'

It didn't take long for her to find the bit of paper and read out the exact spelling. It was as Brook expected. An extra 'c' between the 's' and the 'h'... *'FISCHER'*... The first old man to die after encountering the Tourist had a Germanic name.

'There's something else I was going to call you about,' said Marie. 'I spotted it on the Intranet just before I left work.'

'Oh, right?'

'I don't know if it's important, but Barnes retires in a few days. It was right there in Notices.'

'Interesting... Thanks.'

They said their goodbyes and hung up.

'Just one more call,' said Brook.

'No hurry at all,' replied Jonboy, nodding at one of the many Spurs photos. 'I'm learning all about how Tony Parks saved a penalty to win the 1984 UEFA Cup.'

Brook detected a heavy dose of sarcasm. He switched from his Contacts to the internet and called up something he had found while researching Stalag IV-B – the home page of a museum dedicated to the old POW camp. The place had sprung up next to the original site, while the camp itself had been reclaimed by nature; a new forest gobbling up the wooden huts that had once housed twenty thousand men. Only the layout of the 'streets' and a concrete shower block remained.

The website told him the museum was usually closed on Sundays but would be open throughout this weekend on account of the anniversary of the camp's liberation. He tapped on the phone number and simultaneously tried to access the mothballed German language files at the back of his sleep-deprived mind – not fluent like Afrikaans, but kicking around with half-forgotten French, bits of Setswana, and later additions in which he could order a beer. A female voice answered and Brook switched to German mode...

'Hello. Is that the Stalag IV-B museum?'

'It is.'

'Do you speak English, perhaps?'

'Only a little bit. But your German is not bad. Can I help you?'

(That could have gone better).

'I have a strange question.'

'Yes.'

'I have a photo of Stalag IV-B's theatre. Christmas '44. A musical. There are, umm, prisoners and German soldiers... together sitting.'

'Yes, I know that photo. It's actually quite well known. One moment. We have it here in one of our books.'

As the helpful assistant went off to find the book, Brook puffed out his cheeks and gave Jonboy the thumbs up. After a minute, he heard the receiver being picked back up.

'So, I have found it. And your 'strange question' has something to do with this photo?'

'Exactly. There is a German officer. Not far from the camera. He is laughing. He is laughing... a lot. Do you know who that is?'

Brook pressed the phone harder to his ear. The assistant made him wait a moment longer.

'So, I know a few names of people in this photo. Sometimes a visitor can help us with such things. And this officer... Yes. This officer, I know.'

Brook grabbed a pen and paper from his jacket.

'What can you tell me?'

Amid the note taking that followed, the detective repeated the two key details by way of confirmation – a name, and an English phrase that the museum assistant was clearly familiar with.

'Karl Friedrich von Eberstein'... 'Missing, presumed dead.'

Then he gave his thanks and hung up with a degree of relief – speaking German was draining.

'Well?' asked Jonboy. 'Are you finally going to tell me what I'm missing here?'

'I am,' said Brook, standing up. 'In The Elbow Room. You'll need a pint to hear this.'

Chapter 43

He didn't like not knowing. Not knowing meant uncertainty. Uncertainty meant risk. Risk was something to be managed and minimised. So he didn't like not knowing. And, right now, he didn't like not knowing what had been in those evidence bags that Deelman and his friend had brought out of the flat.

The flat was always a weak point in the operation. The fact he had never been inside to search it meant he didn't know what secrets it held. Given a more generous time frame, he would have liked to gain access before the first kill (he doubted it would have unduly tested his range of skills). But he had always known that compromises would have to be made due to the small window of opportunity before Barnes retired.

The alternative was to do this without the safety net Barnes provided. And that meant greater risk. So, yes, he had been right to take out the first target when the opportunity in the churchyard presented itself. But that didn't stop him really wanting to know what was in those evidence bags.

His curiosity was such that he'd considered taking a table in the café to which he had followed the two officers. 'Big

Dave's'. But even if his new appearance gave him a chance of not being recognised, it was too much of a risk. This Deelman was... above average.

No, he would just have to live with the curiosity for now. And at least where some new uncertainty had emerged, some old uncertainty had been erased – the moment he watched them walk into The Elbow Room. There was no longer any trace of doubt. They would be there tomorrow evening. Looking for him.

He felt his phone vibrating and checked the screen... Barnes... He let it ring out. Safety net or not, he was bored of speaking to him. He was going to do this his own way.

Chapter 44

Monday, 25th April 2016
Brook's apartment

You can never tell when a hippo is going to surface nearby. But when it does, you fucking know about it. At the midpoint of a sleepless night, Brook Deelman was almost certainly the only Londoner pondering that thought as he stepped onto his balcony and looked out over the lights of the capital. For once, it wasn't the investigation on his mind, but a childhood memory. One that had chosen tonight to re-announce itself after a quarter of a century. Talk about timing.

The 11-year-old Brook had certainly known all about it when a hippo decided to surface nearby. Or directly beneath, to be precise. The narrow 'mokoro' ferrying him across the Thamalakane River was flipped in an instant, its six occupants pitched into the dark, reed-filled waters. The river was about 100 metres wide at that point. They were halfway across.

As soon as he hit the water, the young Brook had started swimming for the shore – ignoring the option of clinging to the upturned boat, his legs on offer to the crocs. He was a good swimmer and already getting strong, yet, to this day, he had never been able to recall a single sight or sound between that first stroke and reaching the bank. All he could see was an image of himself from below. Arms windmilling. Legs thrashing. Even the details of his school uniform. A croc's eye view.

Only upon reaching the side did regular senses kick back in. He recalled seeing the other occupants of the mokoro dragging themselves across the same fast-flowing currents. He remembered wading out to help haul them in, a long way down river from where they had entered the water. Everyone was exhausted. Staggering in the shallows. Splashing. Collapsing. Just one more, then they would all be safe. Just his school friend Vincent…

Brook took a sip of the decaf coffee, washing down another sleeping pill for good measure.

It was a week before they found Vincent. What remained of him, at least. He had been a year younger than Brook. Small for his age and not much of a swimmer. He used to have a *Ghostbusters* lunch box. Downstream, two different police forces announced on the same day that they had found 'the body'. Then there was an unseemly row over who had the biggest chunk. It was home school for Brook after that.

He still recalled the strange look in the eyes of Vincent's parents at the funeral. Just at the moment that he shook their hands wearing a suit that was too big for him. Their eyes were saying the things they weren't allowed to verbalise. Not to an 11-year-old… *'Why didn't you do more, Brook? Why didn't you help him?'*

…He finished his coffee.

'Sorry, mate,' he said into the night.

Then he turned and looked back at the clock in the flat. It was just after 4am.

Brook watched it in silence. Out in the darkness. On the other side of the glass doors. And he realised he had been wrong. The memory *was* about the investigation. The paranoia it had generated in him. His name, his phone number, his actions – all of them known, seen and foreseen by those operating against him. They were watching him. In the dark. The croc's eye view.

Chapter 45

Jonboy caught the overworked barman's eye and ordered a bottle of Corona, watching in dismay as it was poured into a cheap plastic cup due to match day regulations. He looked at his watch. Thirty minutes to go until the 8pm kick-off. Still no sign of the Tourist.

The Elbow Room was barely recognisable from their recce the previous day. Right now it was packed to the gunwales with loud, thirsty Spurs fans, confident their team could brush aside West Brom and still pip Leicester to the title. Not that yesterday's recce had been without its merits – establishing the layout, the lines of sight, and the fact that the rear smoking area was being renovated, forcing smokers to stand at the front. They had also gained a degree of familiarity with the bar staff.

All while Brook filled Jonboy in on everything.

Now, just over 24 hours later, the Welshman eased his way out of the crush at the bar and took his beer to a spot in the corner. He scanned the place once again, then looked out of the front windows to where Brook was standing with the smokers.

The loose plan had been working pretty well – Brook and Jonboy swapping their inside and outside positions every fifteen minutes or so. It increased the area under observation while also allowing for a second set of eyes if the Tourist somehow made it past the outer watchman or, indeed, had been managing to lie low inside the whole time. The possibility he might have changed his appearance meant nothing could be ruled out.

Although neither officer was a smoker, both had found they could play the part for surveillance purposes during their careers. Far harder was drinking their beers at super-slow speed (two new faces sticking to lemonade gave way too much of a 'plain clothes police' vibe). Conversation with the regulars had been just about often and light-hearted enough to earn the right to be ignored, while the Sky Sports pre-match waffle provided something in which to feign interest.

...Just twenty minutes to kick-off now. The crowd in The Elbow Room was already past its peak as more people made their way to the stadium. Brook finished his cigarette and headed wearily back inside, tripping slightly on the threshold. He looked like he could fall asleep at any moment.

'Not coming, is he?' said Jonboy as they crossed.

'Doesn't look like it.'

The wait to be served was shorter now. Watches were being checked, hands shaken, drinks downed. Brook got himself another – only his third in nearly two hours. But it was true what they said about tiredness multiplying the effects of alcohol. And Brook hadn't slept much last night. Not for a long time, in fact. He continued to survey the scene in front of him. Jonboy was right. After deliberately revealing exactly where he would be, it now looked as if the Tourist had been playing with them.

…Fifteen minutes to kick-off now. For the first time Brook could see everyone in the pub. About thirty people left. None of them the Tourist. He tapped a quick text to Jonboy *('Stay where you are. I'll join you for last few mins. Then we'll call it a day')*… Bar staff were starting to visibly relax, looking forward to a couple of quieter hours before the post-match rush. A sense of de-escalation was in the air.

Brook made his way outside and scanned the street again. No Tourist. Then he looked at the remaining smokers clustered in front of the pub's windows. No Jonboy. He glanced at the text he had just sent him… *'Unread'*.

'Fucking hell, Jonboy,' he muttered, checking a couple of nearby fast food vans. He peered back into the pub in case he had somehow missed him. Nope. His phone was still in his hand as it started to vibrate… *'Jonboy'*… Brook swiped the screen.

'So was it a burger or a hot dog?' he asked.

For several seconds there was only silence. Then, finally, a response.

'Hello, DC Deelman.'

Many moments in the past few days had caused Brook's pulse to rise. Surprisingly, this wasn't one of them. The Tourist's voice restored the prospect of bringing this situation to a conclusion, and that sense of finality brought with it only a Zen-like calm in Brook. No more pre-match anxiety. The game was afoot. And, on the rugby field, he had always loved that first whistle.

The detective moved one building down from the pub and backed up against a closed retail premises… still scanning the street… still trying to pick out anyone on a mobile…

'Where's the owner of this phone?' he asked.

'You mean Jon? Or is it Jonboy?'

Brook said nothing.

'Don't be surprised. It's quite easy to find someone's name once you have their phone.'

Brook still didn't reply. Let the other guy speak. Besides, he could sense the Tourist's confidence edging towards arrogance and that was fine by him.

'Actually, I'm not sure where he is,' the Tourist continued. 'I last saw him chasing the kid he thought stole this phone. Amazing how fifty pounds can buy you the perfect decoy runner around here.'

'Clever,' said Brook, feeding the Tourist's pride.

'Not really. The clever bit was getting close enough to see your friend's passcode before picking his pocket.'

'Well, aren't you talented? I would give you a medal but I've a feeling you picked one up just a few days ago.'

'Ah. A comedian too?'

Brook stayed silent. He could hear a police siren approaching from the south of Tottenham High Road. The response vehicle sped past him and a few seconds later he heard it down the phone. The Tourist was a couple of hundred yards to the north. He stepped out for a better view. Still no sign.

'You don't say much do you, DC Deelman?'

'I tend to loosen up after a few beers. Why don't you come join me in The Elbow Room like you said?'

'I changed my mind. We're not all functioning alcoholics.'

'That's okay. I can check if they've got your favourite non-alcoholic bottles.'

The Tourist took a shade too long to reply. Brook felt he had scored a minor point.

'I think I'd prefer a café. How about Big Dave's where you and Jon had coffee yesterday?'

Point regained.

'I'm on my way,' said Brook. 'Don't run away this time.'

The line went dead.

Brook made one final visual sweep of the area for Jonboy, then began walking. The strange calm that had come over him remained in place. Senses heightened. Pulse normal.

Chapter 46

Wednesday, 25th April 1945
The Ackerman Farm, near Mühlberg, Germany

Victor wasn't sure exactly how long had passed. A few days was his best, vague guess; largely spent drifting in and out of consciousness. He was aware that his head wound had been cleaned, dressed and re-dressed (the excruciating pain of each process meant there was no way of sleeping through that), but he still hadn't seen the damage in a mirror. Only – through half-closed eyes – the facial expressions of those looking at it. It was enough to know it wasn't pretty.

At some point he had woken to find himself in a pair of pyjamas; any embarrassment at how this had been achieved soon eclipsed by the feel of the soft material. He tried to focus on it to distract from the pain of his head and a broken left leg. He had no idea if its rudimentary splint had been attached with any medical know-how.

The farmhouse had three occupants. A heavily bearded man and his silver-haired wife – both quiet, stoic, around sixty – and their daughter… 'the Angel'. A relatively late arrival by the looks of things. She couldn't have been more than twenty. Sometimes Victor woke to find her sitting beside the bed, forcing him to relive the blurry question of whether she was a vision. As if to add to the effect, she seemed to have a whole wardrobe of white and cream dresses, not to mention an effortlessly pretty face with a hint of freckles, framed by loose blonde curls. There was a sense of tranquility about her.

If his new carers said little during the rituals of changing bandages and providing porridge or soup, then Victor said even less. In fact, he was yet to utter a single word. And with good reason. The first thing he had heard in the house was an argument about him (it was then he learned the Angel's name was Gerti). From what he could gather, there were three points of view – all stemming from the impossible task of identifying the nationality of an unconscious man in his underwear.

The father (or '*Vati*', as his daughter called him) said the stranger could only stay if he was German – anything else would expose them to too much risk if the local SS came knocking. The mother (or '*Mutti*') said anything but a Russian soldier was fine by her – she had heard stories of gruesome reprisals as they approached from the East and wanted nothing to do with them. Gerti seemed happy at the thought that Victor was British or American.

'Ich glaube daß er 'Help me' gesagt hat. Das ist englisch, oder?'... *'I think he said 'Help me'. That's English, isn't it?'*

Then she backtracked upon seeing her father's expression.

'Aber ich bin mir nicht sicher'... *'But I can't be sure.'*

Since there was no way of knowing which argument would hold sway, Victor had chosen the tactical option of playing dumb, beyond the occasional thumbs up when an empty food bowl was taken away. For a while he wondered why they didn't ask him more direct questions. Then it dawned on him. By not knowing the truth themselves, they were avoiding the need to lie to whichever nation's forces came knocking first. Doing a kind deed for an unknown soldier saved them from more complex political realities.

The room containing Victor's makeshift bed was on the ground floor, off the kitchen. When doors were ajar, he could see through to the main room where a creaking wooden staircase led to the floor above. His own room may even have been some kind of pantry in times of plenty – hooks, shelves and dusty ceramic pots. But these were definitely not times of plenty.

Whatever the farm's land had once supplied was now reduced to a vegetable garden and a few chickens. Essential equipment had been broken up for parts by local army units, farmhands conscripted to the frontline, market places deserted or destroyed… All that remained here was Mutti, Vati and Gerti scraping a hand-to-mouth existence. And, now, handing a little bit of that existence to an extra mouth.

Despite the hardships, it was enough to give Victor his first ever glimpse of family life. The smells and sounds of the kitchen drifted into his room, while the chickens created a comforting background chatter – their coop just beneath his small window. As well as heavier topics, he heard conversations about day-to-day trivia, fond reminiscences and moments of laughter. The strict routines of the Foundling Hospital and the Army had kept this world of families a secret from him.

Since arriving, he had left the bed just a couple of times – to awkwardly drag himself to the water closet using a chair as an improvised crutch. Both times he had slept for hours after making it back, only adding to his confusion over how long had passed. Whenever he woke, he went back to listening to family life; sometimes wishing he could speak freely to Gerti, sometimes dreading how he must look thanks to that Walther P38 bullet.

Victor told himself that if he could somehow avoid an infection in the wound, he may be able to get some kind of skin graft to repair his scalp. He had learned the term from a poor RAF chap. Mostly, however, he was just glad to be alive. He felt… lucky.

It was on the fourth day that the Russians came.

The chickens outside Victor's window sounded the alarm first. The people in the house noticed something was wrong too – everyone falling quiet as the hens grew louder. Raising himself on his elbows, Victor saw the father get up from his chair, going out to check on the commotion. As his palm settled on the front door handle, the entire structure burst inwards, sending him flying. The Russian soldier on the other side still had his boot raised at the point of impact. He looked nothing like the poor wretches Victor had seen in camp. Six-foot-six of Red Army muscle. The elaborate epaulettes on his trench coat suggested his rank was every bit as high as he was.

Gerti and her mother screamed and ran over to where Vati was trying to gather his senses. Then they turned on their heels, screaming again as three of the Commander's underlings came pouring in past his giant frame. These three were smaller, fast and feral in green uniforms.

As mother and daughter ran up the creaking staircase, only one of the underlings pursued. Maybe they had drawn straws. The other two began slamming their way through every cupboard in the house, turning over furniture, ripping open storage boxes, looking for whatever resources this place had to offer. They were already swinging dead chickens in their hands. No wonder there had been a commotion in the yard. The massive Commander watched over everything with a seen-it-all-before indifference.

Gerti's father nearly managed to regain his feet (before being encouraged to stay down by a Russian Army boot) as Victor cursed his injuries and looked around the small room for a weapon. No-one had checked back here yet. From upstairs, he could hear shouting, screaming and laughing. He didn't have long.

While the two foraging soldiers filled a sack with anything useful they could find, the yells from upstairs suddenly grew closer. Victor picked up the rapid creak of the old staircase again. People charging back down.

Craning his neck for a better view, he saw Gerti's white dress flash across his field of vision followed by a furious Russian, bleeding from his forehead. Both were pursued by Gerti's screaming mother as the injured man's friends laughed hysterically at his predicament. The whole thing was a scene of total chaos. Yet still the mountain range of a Commander watched impassively from the shattered front door.

Gerti's bloodied pursuer turned briefly to send the mother tumbling into her floored husband with a backhanded smash across the face. Then Gerti was on her own, backing into the kitchen, tripping over cupboard contents strewn over the floor. Victor's room was the only place left for her to run, but still she didn't enter – determined not to give away the location of the badly injured stranger she knew nothing about. Nothing beyond a feeling.

With both parents in a concussed heap, the frantic laughing, screaming and shouting gradually subsided, replaced by the simpler sounds of heavy breathing. All three of the lower rank soldiers had their attentions on Gerti now. One of them swung his dead chicken casually by the neck as he looked her up and down… Then the bird's head came off in his hand, sending the detached body skidding across the kitchen floor and into the shadows of Victor's room.

The accidental chicken decapitator made some *Oops*-like utterance and held up the severed head as all three men had a chuckle about it before turning back to the cornered Gerti. Victor could no longer see her, but he could hear she was crying.

'Bitte,' she said… *'Please.'*

The soldier with the bleeding forehead took a step towards her. A crooked smile was spreading across his scrawny face, defined by a deep scar running from mouth to ear. He pointed to the fresh injury on his forehead and began wagging a finger at Gerti, making a tutting sound…

Then a headless chicken hit him between the eyes.

He flapped at it in shock for a moment, assuming it was alive rather than a lifeless, feathered missile. His friends saw exactly where it had come from. They pointed at Victor's door and shouted in Russian as Gerti grabbed a frying pan and ran into the small room first, turning to face them as she reached Victor's bed.

The three soldiers rushed in after her, then stopped in their tracks at the unexpected sight. The adrenalin rush had caused Victor's scalp to start bleeding again, the bandages sodden as he tried to lever his splinted leg out of the bed. In front of him, a tear-stained Gerti wielded the frying pan like a lethal tennis racket, shouting out the threat of yet more decapitations to go with the headless chicken.

'Wer wird der erste? Komm schon! WER WIRD DER ERSTE?'

'Who's first? Come on! WHO'S FIRST?'

The same soldier as before stepped forward. The one Gerti had whacked in the forehead upstairs. The one who had got a chicken in the face. The one with a growing score to settle. He drew back his fist at the same time as his two colleagues drew their pistols on Gerti and Victor. Gerti drew back her frying pan.

As everyone's time perception entered slow motion, Victor and his broken leg finally managed to get upright at the side of the bed. He thrust a raised palm into the space between the warring parties and roared his first word in four days – the only Russian he had learned in camp.

'NJET!'... *'NO!'*

The single word froze everyone in position. Even Gerti recognised it as Russian. All in the room were now staring at Victor. All asking themselves the exact same question: Who the hell *was* this guy? For the first time, the hulking Commander pushed himself off his shattered door frame and walked slowly towards them with echoing footsteps, stepping over Gerti's dazed parents. He had to duck to enter the room.

The two underlings on either side moved out of the way and lowered their weapons. The third kept his fist pulled back, poised to punch Gerti in the face. Victor stepped in front of her, momentarily – and excruciatingly – putting weight on his broken leg. Gerti was between him and the bed now. He reached both hands back, grabbing the thin mattress and forming a protective triangle around her. The Angel pointed a finger over Victor's shoulder at her tormentor-in-chief, while raising the frying pan a little higher.

'Der erste...' she said, nodding at the scar-faced soldier and breathing hard... *'The first...'*

Christ, she's got some spirit, thought Victor. Taking on the Red Army with pots and pans. He raised his gaze to the Commander. Then he raised it some more. Finally, he was looking him in the eye. His left leg strained against the splint, wanting to return to the random angles at which it had broken. He couldn't tell if it was sweat or blood stinging his eyes.

'You speak English?' he asked the huge Russian, refusing to let his voice quiver.

'A little,' replied the Commander, heavily accented. He raised a hand to the poised fist of the angry underling and lowered it without resistance. He could have killed everyone in the room in a heartbeat. The swell of Gerti's chest seemed to press into Victor's back a little more at the sound of him speaking English. He took a deep breath and urged his creaking leg to keep him upright as he held the giant's gaze.

'My name is Lance Corporal Victor Watson... Middlesex Regiment... British Army... Combined Allied Forces... We're on the same side.'

The Commander looked at Victor. The blood oozing from his bandages. His broken leg. His thin body being used as a shield to protect Gerti. Then he extended a massive hand. Victor took it in his broken right hand and shook it without flinching.

'Good people?' asked the Commander, nodding at Gerti and back at her parents.

'Good people,' said Victor. 'Very good.'

That evening, a crate of food was left on the doorstep. Enough for four to eat well.

For Victor, the war was over.

Chapter 47

Monday, 25th April 2016
Big Dave's Café, North London

Brook approached the café along the opposite pavement to give some distance and a wider field of view. Smells of fast food and cannabis mingled with traffic fumes as he passed kebab houses, bookies and payday loan shops. Some places that had closed for the day were now hidden behind graffiti-covered roller shutters. The megabucks of Premier League football rarely extended beyond the players' car park.

The neon sign outside Big Dave's was still illuminated (or the neon sign outside *'Bi Dav s')* while a police carrier was parked up fifty yards beyond it. Brook knew from experience that the driver and sergeant in the front seats would be joined by half a dozen colleagues once the match kicked off. He could probably borrow their manpower to ensure a swift and smooth arrest of the Tourist.

But this case wasn't that simple. If he ever wanted the full picture… if he ever wanted the truth… he had to go in there alone.

The detective was opposite the café now. He made no attempt to conceal himself as he looked into it from the other side of the street. The Tourist looked different in his grey hoodie as he returned the silent appraisal. No wonder Jonboy hadn't noticed him – especially if his hood had been up. But here he was. Dark hair cut short and sensible, solid jaw, and that wide, muscular neck. Action Man made real, sitting in a Tottenham greasy spoon.

Brook's strange sense of calm remained as he crossed the road and pushed open the café's front door. He was already familiar with the bolted-down tables, fixed stools and special offer-covered mirror along the right wall. The counter at the back housed a cash register between two curved glass units (hot snacks and cold drinks) while the general clutter suggested pre-match trade had been brisk. An armful of plates was being whisked away by the same battle-hardened waitress as yesterday – blonde ponytail with grey roots, blue jeans and a yellow blouse.

'Take a seat, darlin'. I'll be wiv you in a sec!' she shouted, disappearing through the hanging beads to the kitchen.

'Thanks,' said Brook, maintaining an air of normality.

Apart from the Tourist, only the two rearmost tables were still occupied. The one on the left by a man of about eighty – flat cap, cup of tea, copy of the *Racing Post*. The one on the right (behind the Tourist) by two teenage girls. They were talking about a fight outside their school gates. Something about someone filming it for YouTube.

Brook wanted their table with the minimum of fuss.

He took out his warrant card and let it flap open as he looked at the special offers – making a big play of struggling to extract the emergency tenner he kept tucked in the holder.

After a few seconds, one of the girls kicked her friend and the whisper of *'Fed'* told Brook his warrant card had been spotted. They got up and left in exaggerated silence, starting to run and laugh as they reached the door. Brook strode past the Tourist and sat down at their table.

'Cup of tea?' asked the waitress from behind the counter.

'Please,' replied Brook, looking at the Tourist's back.

Your move now, mate.

As it turned out, he didn't have to wait long. The Tourist may not have been happy at the prospect of turning his back to the entrance, but having his back to Brook for too long wasn't much of an option either. With unhurried movements, he got to his feet – twisting to his right on the fixed stool then standing up.

Brook noticed the total lack of any hands on the table as he completed the manoeuvre. It was the total opposite of how the detective tended to haul himself in and out of position with a clicking back and reluctant knees. The impression was one of controlled power. Then the Tourist stood there, still facing away from Brook, staring out of the café's window and into the street.

Was he checking if the detective had backup? Letting him know he didn't consider him a threat? Showing that he would do things at his own speed? Perhaps an element of all three. Brook waited in silence.

Finally, the Tourist turned around.

He gave a contemptuous snort to show Brook what he thought of his little game and reluctantly took the seat opposite, placing his elbows on the table with exaggerated precision. As he brought his hands together, his right made a fist that his left enveloped. Up close, there was a leathery quality to the tanned skin. He spoke calmly over the top of the triangle created by his forearms…

'Why are you harassing me, officer?'

The detective's forearms were also forming a triangle. Horizontal rather than vertical. His fingertips lightly touching on the table in front of him. Guarded. Ready.

'Where is that accent from?' asked Brook, ignoring the Tourist's question.

'You must get asked that a lot yourself.'

'All of us Japanese do.'

Not a flicker.

'You do realise no-one's laughing at your jokes, detective?'

'They're too busy laughing at your attempts to be a competent hitman.'

The old man at the adjacent table gathered up his coat and left in a hurry, dropping the *Racing Post* but deciding against going back for it. Now they were alone.

'Hitman?' asked the Tourist, smiling for the first time in either CCTV form or real life. 'I take it back. People *do* laugh at your jokes.'

'What term would you prefer?' asked Brook, impassive.

The Tourist opened his mouth to speak then closed it again as the waitress came round the counter, carrying a mug of tea and a glass of Coke. She placed the mug in front of Brook and the Coke in front of the Tourist. He must have ordered just before Brook arrived.

'There you go, my darlin's,' she said.

'Thank you,' said both men, staring straight ahead.

'What's happened to your other friend then?' she asked Brook, referring to the big Welsh bloke she had taken a shine to yesterday.

'That's a good question,' he replied.

The waitress took a step back and glanced between the two men, easily noticing the atmosphere between them.

'Oh dear,' she said, turning and retrieving the *Racing Post* from the floor. 'You boys.'

They waited until she was out of earshot.

'You were about to tell me how you're not a hitman,' said Brook.

'Well, let's see,' said the Tourist, his arms and upper body staying almost unnaturally still. 'On Thursday I had a pleasant evening in a pub, watching some soccer. The Junction, I think they call it. Then, the following morning, I'm in a café and some police officers are talking about this poor war veteran who was found dead after leaving that same pub.'

'Well, isn't that a coincidence.'

'Middlesex Regiment, they said he was. It got me thinking how sad it is that we don't really speak to these people while they're still around. I'm into history, you see. So, I was able to find this other veteran of the same regiment. Harry Wilson. In a care home in some place called Sheffield. It's amazing what you can do with the internet these days.'

'Isn't it just.'

'So, I head up there and spend this fantastic hour with him as he tells me all about his war and the POW camp. Amazing, really amazing. I call back later to see if we can to do it again and they tell me the poor guy's had a heart attack. Just horrible news. But as if that's not bad enough, I have some psycho detective chasing me who's got it into his head that I *killed* these heroes. You're a sick man, DC Deelman.'

Brook used a single hand to slide his mug of tea to the far end of the table while keeping his eyes on the man opposite.

The Tourist did the same with his glass of Coke. Neither was going to risk taking a sip from an object that could be smashed straight into their face.

'Don't stop now,' said Brook, 'you've got the jury in the palm of your hand. Why don't you tell them how you know my name?'

'Your name? Well, it seems to crop up everywhere, doesn't it? Those officers were using it as they spoke about the dead veteran. Then it was on some kind of note at the nursing home. And now it's all over your own force's website with some search for a next of kin.'

That bloody enthusiastic press officer. All the business about overhearing the case was total bullshit of course, but vague enough to be hard to disprove among the other nuggets of truth about Post-it Notes and police appeals.

'You're doing well,' said Brook. 'You must have seven or eight jurors on your side by now. Why don't you tell the others why you used my details to order that taxi?'

'*Your* details? Did I? That's weird. I mean, I already had them from one of those officers in the café. I told him I'd been in the same pub as the poor veteran and he said I should call you if I had any information. I remember looking at that bit of paper as I was booking the taxi and… How ridiculous of me. I guess I just wasn't concentrating. It's funny how the mind works.'

'Nine jurors on your side… What made you say I was harassing you?'

'Isn't it obvious? When I called Peak View to see if I could meet Harry again… And when I went back to The Junction… They were all telling me the same thing – 'There's this detective, Brook Deelman. He thinks you're a murderer'. I couldn't believe it.'

'Ten jurors… Who's Paul Fischer?'

'Fischer? Wait. Is that the poor old guy I tried to save in Hyde Park a few years ago? God, that was awful. The cops actually wanted to give me some sort of citizen's award for my efforts, but I just wanted to put it all behind me.'

'Eleven jurors… How did we come to be in this café?'

'I wish we weren't. I've got a ticket to the match. I was having a smoke outside The Elbow Room and there was this big, drunk, Welsh guy mouthing off about work. Obviously an off-duty police officer. Everyone was sort of embarrassed. At one point he tried to put his phone back in his pocket and dropped it. I was just picking it up for him when this young kid bumped past us – twelve, thirteen years old, maybe. The drunk cop patted his pocket, decided the kid had stolen his phone and set off after him. Obviously the terrified kid just ran away as fast as he could.'

'Obviously.'

'Well, the lock screen hadn't kicked in yet, so I thought I would call one of his contacts to let them know I had the phone. And who should I see up there near the top? Brook Deelman. Under 'B', you see? Near the top.'

'I get it.'

'So I think to myself: Great! I can get the phone back to a friend of his at the same time as explaining this whole other… you know… misunderstanding. And maybe even get to see the rest of the game.'

'Boom. Twelve jurors on your side. You win,' said Brook, leaning back.

'Oh, it's not a case of winning or losing. I'm just trying to stop a valued officer of the law wasting any more time. I mean, you've probably been running around gathering forensics and

CCTV to place me in the pub and the nursing home. But I've just explained all of that.'

'And that stuff you said when you rang me? About stealing Jonboy's phone and standing close enough to see his passcode?'

'Well, a mad detective with some kind of vendetta against me would say that, wouldn't he?'

'I guess so.'

The Tourist lowered his defensive forearm triangle, now placing his hands on the table. He looked more relaxed. Tension evaporating.

'I'm glad we didn't have to fall out,' he said.

'Sure,' said Brook.

Senses heightened. Pulse normal.

'You never did tell me where that accent was from,' he added.

'Around,' said the Tourist, a hint of steel returning to his expression.

'Well, mine's from Botswana. You know that already, of course. There wasn't much on TV when I was growing up, but my second favourite show was *Columbo*.'

'Is this where I ask what your favourite was?'

'*Batman*,' replied Brook. 'The original. Adam West and Burt what's-his-name. You see, *Batman* was good, but those really long explanations by the bad guys were just so fucking boring. I was thinking about that a moment ago when you were talking.'

The Tourist began returning his forearms to their vertical triangle, then became aware it was too obvious a defensive movement. Brook raised an eyebrow to let him know the indecision had been noted. Then he carried on.

'Columbo was better at cutting to the chase, wasn't he? What was it he used to say?'

'You know what he used to say.'

'I know that I know. I just want to hear you say it.'

'And why would I perform for you, detective?'

'Because if you don't, I won't tell you what you're missing. And the not knowing will drive you mad.'

Both men fell quiet as the Tourist weighed up his two options… Either say Columbo's catchphrase at Brook's behest, or refuse and risk not finding out what he was 'missing' just to avoid a momentary loss of face. Somehow both seemed to be a victory for the officer. The Tourist's stare seemed to increase in wattage as he forced himself to say the well-known words.

'Just… One… More… Thing…'

'The cards,' said Brook.

'The cards?'

'The cards.'

'I have no idea what you're talking about.'

'Congratulations. That's the first truthful thing you've said in the past five minutes. But don't beat yourself up about it. If it's beyond your skill set then it's hardly your fault.'

The Tourist thought back to those evidence bags he had seen Brook and Jonboy carrying out of the flat. The ones that had made him so curious.

'Okay,' he said. 'So tell me about the cards.'

Brook leaned in a little, sacrificing some of the reactionary gap in order to dominate the space between them. It was his turn to hold court now.

'Both of your victims this week were receiving Christmas cards from a 'Victor' in Australia, with a coded reference to the POW number of one Victor Watson. Which throws a bit of a spanner in the works, doesn't it? Considering the first dead guy was meant to *be* Victor Watson.'

The Tourist gave nothing away. There was no need to worry yet.

'Fascinating,' he said, with undisguised sarcasm.

'Just look at the basics,' continued Brook. 'Seventy years after the war, those two men were still being prodded and poked by someone letting them know he was still around. Victor Watson. The real Victor Watson. Not that Nazi you killed in the churchyard.'

The Tourist continued to hold his nerve – the corners of his mouth turning up in a show of amusement and disdain.

'Nazi, you say? I do love a good conspiracy theory. And what about Harry Wilson? Was he a Nazi too?'

'Looks like I won't get the chance to ask him now. Ideology? Money? Who knows? But the two were in touch and received identical treatment – the cards then the killing. Which is a pretty good sign Harry Wilson was in cahoots with Karl Friedrich von Eberstein.'

Brook dropped the name with all the relish of a big reveal in interview – that key bit of information the other guy wasn't counting on. A tiny muscle beneath the Tourist's left eye gave the faintest of twitches and his jaw set a little firmer. Brook welcomed the confirmation of his theory.

'You killed them both on behalf of Victor Watson. And he found you, or Barnes, or your little team, because this is what you do. Just like you did in Hyde Park a few years ago. How hard would I have to look into this *Paul Fischer* before I found he was another on the wrong side of history?'

For the first time, the Tourist lowered his gaze, looking instead at Brook's hands resting on the table. He made a shape with his mouth as if trying to dislodge something stuck in his teeth. Trying to get rid of an irritant. He was thinking. Considering options. He looked up.

'I hate to spoil your little world of guesswork and supposition. But I'm going to drag you back to that annoying little thing called evidence, detective. You have none. I mean, fucking zero.'

It was the first time Brook had heard him swear.

'And to be perfectly honest…' he continued.

'You should always be honest,' said Brook.

'…You're getting in my fucking way.'

The detective let the Tourist's loss of cool hang in the air. He was rattled. The waitress put her head through the hanging beads, picking up on the first edge to the measured tones in which the men had been talking.

'Are you two playing nicely?' she asked.

'Just talking about *Columbo*,' replied Brook, without turning around.

'Good. No falling out allowed.'

The swishing of the beads was replaced by the faint sounds of a debate between waitress and chef over whether Columbo had a glass eye.

'I'll give you some credit,' said Brook. 'Two bodies in three days and neither police force calling it murder. A defence lawyer would fancy your chances even if you did get brought in. Your only worry would be if someone proved the bigger picture, and for that they'd need to find Victor.'

The Tourist stayed quiet this time. He was curious…

'New Zealand,' said Brook, cutting straight to his best guess in the hope of catching another micro-reaction. The rogue nerve ending beneath the Tourist's left eye did not disappoint. The detective continued, emboldened…

'A Christmas holiday in Australia every few years by the looks of it. That's when he sends the cards. Nice little trick if you don't want the others tracking you down. I doubt he'd be impossible for New Zealand police to find though. Pretty small population, especially when you get to Victor's age bracket.'

The Tourist blinked in annoyance at his twitching 'tell'. He had never been aware of it before. For the first time in his life, he wondered if he was past his best. The last couple of minutes had not gone well.

'Tell me, Brook,' he said, using the detective's Christian name for the first time. 'When you watched war films as a kid, did you want to be the guy who got the Nazis? Or the guy who got that guy?'

'I wanted to be the guy who did the right thing.'

'What a lazy answer.'

They fell quiet as the waitress emerged from the kitchen again to clear the last of the clutter.

'I was right,' she smiled over another armful of plates and mugs. 'Googled it. Columbo *did* have a glass eye.'

Brook waited for the beads to stop swishing before seeking to capitalise on the shifting balance of power.

'That bald guy claiming to be DS Beckford. What the fuck was that all about?'

The Tourist opened his mouth to reply, then decided he had nothing useful to say.

'Ex-police, maybe?' suggested Brook. 'He blagged it pretty well. Came close to shunting this whole thing into a siding right at the start. But all that business sabotaging the CCTV when the opening gambit didn't work – pushing his luck a bit there, wasn't he? And that name of a random Homicide DS for his fake warrant card...'

Brook allowed himself a smile.

'That was just picked off the e-mail system, wasn't it? DS Chris Beckford – had to be a man, right? You lot really don't give me much credit, do you?'

'I'm sure you appreciate that not everyone is involved in every decision.'

The implication was easy to detect – *that fuck-up is on Barnes.*

'And the fascination with John Logie Baird? Or are you blaming that on Barnes too?'

The Tourist hesitated, before deciding that knowledge of his Logan Baird alias was all that mattered – the reasons behind it were pure trivia.

'It felt like a good fit at the time. I'd just seen a documentary on him. Television means *far sight*, you know? Seemed appropriate for someone making old Nazis pay for their crimes.'

'So what's your real name?' asked Brook.

'I think you're well aware that you'll never know that.'

'And how did this little team of yours even come to exist?'

'Same answer.'

'How many of you are there?'

'Yet another thing you'll never know.'

'Then tell me how there are even enough Nazis left to keep you going?'

'Oh, we're very good at diversifying,' replied the Tourist, sensing he was back on more comfortable ground. 'Balkan war criminals, African warlords, the henchmen of Arab dictators… You'd be amazed how much evil is out there. How much can be wiped out in the time it takes for one show trial at The Hague. Now…'

He leaned a little closer and lowered his voice to give the impression of earnest advice.

'...You need to do what you should have done on that first night. Just walk away, DC Deelman. Have another beer. Watch some fucking sport. Let this all become an urban myth. And stop threatening to drag a brave, old war hero like Victor through a murder trial.'

Brook reflected the earnest tone straight back.

'My issue's not with Victor. It's with you. I couldn't be sure until I spent some time with you. But I'm good at getting a feel for someone. And now I'm sure.'

'You're speaking in riddles again.'

'Then I'll make it simple. I'm not buying the heroic avenger bullshit. I don't know about the rest of your team, but you're not a man weighed down by some moral crusade. It's the killing you like. Pure and simple. I've seen you on camera before and after – totally relaxed. That's a talent, and I think you're a man who makes the most of his talents. If you were charged and remanded for any of these murders while Interpol picked over your life, they would find bodies galore. The good, the bad and the ugly.'

The re-appearance of the waitress allowed the Tourist to look to his left as she rounded the counter. It stopped Brook seeing the little twitch beneath his eye. The detective was right, of course. Well, half right. The jobs he did with Barnes, he did for free. He stayed in the cheap hotels, drove the cheap cars, lived a monastic life for a few days and killed people who thoroughly deserved it.

But he did all that in a vain attempt to balance the scales on Judgement Day.

In every other aspect of his life, it was only the price that mattered. No questions asked. And he had become a rich man out of killing all over the world. Very rich.

Sure, some of the big money, no-questions-asked victims were probably bad people. He liked to tell himself that. And if he didn't take a job, it would only go to someone else with the same end result. He liked to tell himself that too. But the law of averages said many of his victims were good people who didn't deserve it. Political rivals, whistleblowers, embarrassing witnesses…

Not asking questions was just part of the job. And, in turn – like a Foreign Legion recruiter – Barnes chose not to ask about the Tourist's life beyond the role he fulfilled for him. However much he suspected.

The waitress walked through the café to the front door, opened it, reached up and pulled a metal roller shutter two thirds of the way down before heading back.

'You'll have to duck on your way out, I'm afraid. You can have a few more minutes while we finish up in the kitchen though.'

'Thanks,' said Brook, still keeping up the appearance of normality.

The Tourist withdrew his hands from the table. Disengaging.

'Well, I haven't got time to sit here while you deal with your moral dilemmas. For what it's worth, it's pretty clear your case ended the moment that homeless bum in the churchyard refused to give you a statement.'

The comment confirmed just how much Barnes was all over the investigation, relaying it all to the Tourist. It was increasingly clear that everything was an open book.

Brook's mind turned to the handcuffs in his jacket. The *now-or-never* moment was fast approaching and he was still in two minds as to whether to make the arrest. He had no desire to go into battle on behalf of old Nazis. Or against Victor Watson. But he was still a cop with a warrant card, sitting in front of a murderer… The Tourist's voice cut through the conflicted jumble of Brook's thoughts.

'If you'll excuse me now,' he said, calmly.

He stood up with that smooth action. All controlled power. Brook kept his eyes on him, waiting for something to nudge his decision-making process one way or the other.

'Good luck doing the right thing, DC Deelman. Whatever that means.'

It was a good sign-off. Dramatic. Thoughtful. Yep, the Tourist would be happy with that as a parting shot. He turned towards the front door just as the hanging beads swished again.

'You off, darlin'?' called the waitress. 'That's just eighty pence for the Coke then.' She glanced at the table. 'Even if you didn't drink it.'

Such small things.

On which so much can pivot.

Had the waitress never appeared, an undecided Brook would almost certainly have watched the Tourist open the front door, duck under the roller shutter and disappear forever. But his perfect sign-off had been spoiled. And small things can have big consequences.

'Right,' said the Tourist, patting the pockets of his unfamiliar hoodie. He found a few coins and took them out, dropping a couple on the floor.

'Ninety pence, right?' he asked, stooping to pick up one coin and giving up on the other as it rolled around on its edge.

'Eighty,' said the waitress.

'Eighty. Right.'

He sifted the coins in his hand, the cinematic coolness of his parting comment now very much a thing of the past. This was all very awkward. Losing face in front of Brook. At last, he stepped towards the counter, leaning in towards Brook as he passed. He couldn't quite let the dent to his pride go – not without a clumsy attempt at restoring it.

'Besides,' he whispered. 'Even if you got the homeless bum to make a statement, I'd make sure he never made it to court.'

It was a comment heavy on bravado. But that didn't make it an empty threat. Brook gave no visible reaction. The Tourist continued to the counter where the waitress didn't appear to have registered the hushed remark. She was clattering through some old CDs, choosing which music to put on while she and the chef completed the final tasks of the day.

'Ta, sweetheart,' she said, taking the small sum of money.

Relieved to have finally completed such a petty transaction, the Tourist turned to leave as the waitress disappeared with her chosen CD. At the counter, he was in the only public part of the café behind Brook's table. As he took his first step, the detective's eyes panned right in readiness for him. Then a hand landed on Brook's shoulder.

'You did well, officer,' said the Tourist. 'But you're out of your depth.'

Still trying to reclaim that lost pride.

Brook raised his left hand from the table and brought it down over the patronising palm on his shoulder, his fingers wrapping tightly around the thick, well-trained wrist. The Tourist tried to wrench his hand upwards, but Brook was expecting it – and his coiled muscles were in a stronger position than the Tourist's straight arm. The hand lifted an inch or two before the detective managed to reverse the movement, slamming the Tourist's hand down flat on the table.

Both men silently recognised they had just passed the point of no return.

It was a whole different ball game now…

Chapter 48

'You really need to think about this,' said the Tourist.

Brook responded with the clear authority of someone who had gone through the formalities a thousand times before. Albeit never quite like this.

'I'm arresting you for the murders of Karl Friedrich von Eberstein and Harry Wilson…'

'Walk away, detective.'

'…You do not have to say anything but it may harm your defence…'

'Walk…'

'…if you do not mention when questioned…'

'Away…'

'…something which you later rely on in court…'

'Now.'

'…Anything you do say may be given in evidence.'

For a moment neither man spoke or moved, frozen in a strange sculpture.

'Sit down,' said Brook, nodding at the seat opposite. His voice was firm, flat, indifferent. The universal don't-fuck-with-me tone of cops the world over. His mind was moving on from moral dilemmas to physical practicalities – getting the handcuffs from his inner jacket pocket onto the Tourist's wrists.

'Sit down,' he said again, tone and volume identical to the original instruction. The Tourist stayed still. Thinking. All those times he had ignored Barnes. All that stuff about dealing with this on his own. It was never meant to get messy.

A static crackle came over the café's four ageing corner speakers – the waitress in the kitchen clearly oblivious to the new developments as she hit 'Play'... Then Benny Andersson dragged a finger down a keyboard and the opening bars to *Dancing Queen* filled the air.

If the two men had any reaction to their new ABBA soundtrack, they hid it well. With his left hand still pinned flat to the table, the Tourist took a half step towards the stool in front of him and began to flex his knees as if to sit down. As instructed. Compliant. Brook silently urged him to *keep going*.

His inner voice hadn't quite finished the second word when he realised the Tourist was spinning the other way, pivoting around his trapped left hand and flashing his free elbow towards Brook's temple. With so little time to react, the detective's only defence was to duck his head and lift a shoulder.

The block was only partial but probably prevented an instant KO – the lightning-fast strike deflecting upward off the shoulder and delivering a glancing blow to the corner of Brook's forehead. No more phoney war. This was on. Twenty years of close combat military training versus 230 pounds of blunt force and will-to-win. ABBA signalled their approval of the fight with '*You can dance. You can jive...*'

The elbow had barely finished cracking open the skin of his forehead when Brook gave up his prize of the Tourist's wrist and surged up from his seat like an unleashed rodeo bull.

His shoulder crashed into the other man's sternum as he drove him back at speed, crossing the open space down the middle of the café and slamming him into a table on the far side. The combined mass and momentum was more than the fixtures could take as the table ripped itself free of both floor and wall, throwing up plaster and broken tiles.

Brook kept driving his opponent back, the detached table clattering towards the one behind it. Off balance and unable to resist Brook's barrelling progress, the Tourist switched tactics, going with the direction of movement then pushing off from the ground to launch himself out of Brook's grasp. He skidded across both tables on his back before executing a neat backward roll and landing deftly on the far side.

Brook could feel the blood from his split forehead beginning to pool above his eyebrow and run down the side of his face. He moved down the centre space to cut off the escape route from the Tourist's new position and pointed straight at him.

'Hands on your head! Hands on your fuckin' head NOW!'

Over the speakers, Agnetha and Frida were nonplussed by the commotion.

The Tourist gave no hint of complying as his eyes flickered over the bloodied officer, formulating an attack strategy. He closed the gap between them quickly.

Brook tried to grab a handful of hoodie, but a swift backhand to his outstretched arm made him lose his grip, leaving him upright and exposed. The Tourist was on him, blasting a flat right palm into the centre of his chest that removed all the air from Brook's lungs.

The aggressor withdrew the same right hand and followed up with a forearm smash to the throat. It was half an inch too low, the fearsome impact taken partly on the collarbones rather than fully on the throat. Even so, it knocked Brook backwards, prolonging the struggle for breath. The Tourist closed the gap again.

In an act of instinctive defence, the doubled-over officer managed to raise his left hand into the hitman's face to fend him off – pawing, pushing, reopening some of the gap between them. As a partial gulp of air reached Brook's lungs, he threw everything into a straight right. Once again, the Tourist was too quick, leaning smartly to one side as the fist sailed harmlessly by.

With Brook overbalancing, his opponent snapped a bladed hand into the bridge of his nose, flattening the bone a little more where a stray rugby boot had laid the groundwork years earlier. Capillaries burst in the skin around Brook's eyes and he saw nothing but white, followed by a dream-like falling sensation.

Somewhere deep inside his spinning mind, some piece of consciousness endured. A safe house in the white-out. Aware that his knees had buckled and he was falling to the ground, it sent out a counter-intuitive message to any muscles still receiving… *Head-butt the table.*

Whether the instruction had any effect or not, Brook's cheek slammed into a stool on the way down. The fresh jolt had the effect of bringing him round, albeit with the side-effect of opening up a new cut beneath his left eye. It started to bleed at a similar rate to the forehead. He was conscious again. But down. And taking damage.

Brook had always been good at taking damage.

Head still bowed, he gathered his limbs beneath him, blood from his injuries seeking out the lowest points of his face. A whole carrier of police officers may have been just fifty yards away, but the roller shutter and music ensured no-one was coming to Brook's aid. Raising an arm to one of the fixed stools, he dragged himself round so he was at least facing the Tourist – even if he was still on his hands and knees.

'I told you to walk out the door,' said the unscathed man.

Brook spat out some blood.

'I will when I'm dragging you in cuffs.'

The Tourist was standing a little more flat-footed than before. He had mentally checked out of fight mode and the springy alertness that came with it. Understandable, when the other guy was a bloodied mess. For good measure, he swung a parting 'stay down' kick into Brook's midriff, just in case he thought about coming after him when he left the café.

The strike was delivered without the snap of his earlier actions – a bullying sense of punishment replacing any respect for his opponent. It was only a ten to twenty percent drop in standards, but enough for Brook to see it coming. He tensed his stomach muscles as the kick hit home, instantly wrapping two vice-like arms around the ankle before ignoring every ache to spring to his feet.

The Tourist's eyes betrayed a flash of panic. He was definitely back in fight mode now.

'Hold tight,' said Brook, not quite finishing the words before throwing everything into forward momentum. Propelled back by his captured leg, the Tourist could only manage a couple of desperate hops before becoming totally airborne and slamming into his second table of the fight.

Thanks to Brook's standing start the momentum was even greater this time. He couldn't tell which part of the other guy made contact with the table first. Back? Hip? Arse? He didn't much care. Once again, the fittings blew apart; wall cracks spreading even further now. The table hit the one behind with such force that the explosive process was nearly repeated – stressed mountings creating rivulets of damage in the plaster.

This time there was no wriggling free and fancy backflip as Brook gripped handfuls of the grey hoodie and slammed the Tourist onto the table top, his left arm pinning him like a felled tree as he finally got a punch in. What the haymaker lacked in precision it made up for in power, somehow managing to strike eyebrow, cheek and nose as it smashed into the Tourist's face. The effect on the leathery skin was less than Brook might have hoped – and the muscular neck seemed to cushion the impact like a column of industrial rubber – but the eyes still lost focus for a moment. A result. However small.

The Tourist grabbed at Brook's army surplus jacket, trying to pull him in and deny the space for another punch. The blood-covered cop flexed a straight left arm to restore the gap and drew back his fist for a second strike… at which point, the right edge of his world started closing in.

The ruined plasterwork caused by tables tearing free had swallowed up key fixtures for the big wall mirror and its sheer weight had done the rest. It had effectively been standing on its bottom edge since the massive collision. Now it toppled towards the two men. Eight-foot by four-foot of accelerating glass.

Brook aborted the second punch and grabbed the Tourist, hauling him off the table and throwing both of them to the floor in front of the main counter. The air was forced out of the hitman's lungs as his back hit the ground just as the mirror crashed onto the tables, scattering razor-edged shards.

'What part of *arrest* don't you understand?' growled Brook, his winded opponent grappling with him more weakly than before. The Tourist was running out of ideas. Brook found he could hold him down with one arm and the weight of his body, while his right hand moved inside his jacket for the handcuffs. For a moment they didn't want to budge – one of the bracelets having come open and snagged on the pocket's lining.

Out of the corner of his eye, Brook saw a huge figure emerge round the end of the counter. A 22-stone man with a mullet and goatee, wearing all black beneath a blue-and-white striped apron. The chef. Maybe even 'Big Dave' himself. He had a fire extinguisher in his right hand and was looking nervously at the two men destroying his café to a 70s disco classic.

'Wait there!' ordered Brook, briefly interrupting his attempt to free the handcuffs to bat away a grip the Tourist had established on him. Then he began ripping out the entire jacket pocket to try and release the snagged restraints. Big Dave continued to hover nervously with the fire extinguisher. Maybe the waitress had told him to 'do something'.

The Tourist saw one final chance.

On the blind side from Big Dave, he managed to snake a couple of fingers into the pocket of Brook's jeans, feeling for the officer's warrant card… Then he turned his head towards the chef, held the police ID aloft and forced out a few desperate words.

'POLICE! HELP ME!'

Big Dave stepped forward with sudden purpose as Brook opened his mouth to protest. Too late. The fire extinguisher smacked into the side of the detective's head, instantly knocking him sideways off his stricken opponent. Brook's vision turned to reds and greens and the sides began to close in like theatre curtains as he was sent rolling onto his back…

The Tourist composed himself for a moment. Then he got to his feet with just a hint of unsteadiness, dusted himself down and turned to his accidental saviour.

'Thank you,' he said, tossing the warrant card on top of Brook.

Big Dave dropped the fire extinguisher with a clang and ran back to the kitchen as fast as 22-stone could move, shouting out his mistake to the waitress.

'TRACY! TRACE! I HIT THE WRONG ONE!'

Brook tried to concentrate on little more than staying conscious as his hearing developed a distant quality to accompany the distorted vision. His senses were going into basic mode to avoid total shutdown, the blood from his injuries now trickling down his neck and chest. In all the destruction, his left foot had ended up dangling over an errant crossbar that used to attach one of the fixed stools to a table.

The Tourist had seen enough Lazarus-like comebacks for one day. He stepped over to where the foot was hanging over the crossbar and stamped down on it, snapping the ankle and turning the foot most of the way round. Brook made only a muffled 'Nnnng' sound through gritted teeth, the black theatre curtains closing in a little more.

Primitive survival instinct still compelled him to push back with his hands on the floor, moving a pathetic distance away from the threat until he was pressed against the counter. He refused to direct his increasingly blurred vision towards his ankle, knowing that would be the end of whatever scrap of consciousness he was clinging on to.

The last man standing looked down and shook his head at the struggling detective. He didn't care about Queensbury

Rules. A win was a win. Brook began reaching around for a way to pull himself up as ABBA entered their final chorus. He felt anything but *young, sweet* and *seventeen.*

'Just stop trying,' said the Tourist, the area around his eye starting to swell, even though the leathery skin refused to give up a speck of blood.

'You first,' said Brook.

His right hand found the counter above him and he began hauling himself upright on one leg. Some sort of automatic pilot was kicking in. Fifty points down with moments to play. Victory impossible… Never give up. Never give in.

As his right hand slipped on the counter top, he blindly swung out his left in a vain attempt to stop himself falling back down. It smashed through one of the curved glass display units, sending cans of Coke, 7 Up and Fanta cascading out. Unable to find a grip, he slumped back to the ground as the soft drinks tumbled around him.

In the clatter, and through his half-functioning vision, he was vaguely aware of a figure ducking under the roller shutter and opening the café door. Any noise they made was masked by the last moments of ABBA and the waterfall of cans.

The Tourist had seen enough. It had gone badly – and he would have a lot of explaining to do to Barnes – but it could have gone worse. Just about. He watched in disbelief as the blood-covered detective with his mangled ankle reached up for the counter once again.

'You've got some kind of problem,' he said.

Brook blinked away the blood to hold his gaze. ABBA faded out.

He could see the new figure now.

'You too,' he replied.

The Tourist turned to finally leave the madman behind.

He never completed a step towards the front door.

The clunking right fist of Jonboy sent him slamming into the counter as if attached to a recoiling bungee rope. His body arched back, opened the cash register with a ping, then slid down next to Brook. Spark out…

The detective weakly elbowed his nemesis away from him.

'Bloody hell, Brook. I don't think your foot's meant to look like that.'

'I'm not looking,' said Brook. The fact that Jonboy had called him by his first name rather than 'Number One' told him it must be bad.

'The cavalry took their fucking time,' he added.

'Sorry about that,' said Jonboy, taking in the devastation. 'Partly my fault.'

A boy of about twelve ducked under the roller shutter and pushed open the door. He stared wide-eyed at the ruined café and injured men, then caught the phone that Jonboy tossed back to him and ran off.

'Had to catch that little shit first and figure out he hadn't really nicked my phone. Used his *Find My iPhone* tracker thingy to see that mine was in here – just wish I'd remembered my password a bit quicker.'

The black theatre curtains closed in a little more on Brook's vision. He reached into his jacket and finally un-snagged the handcuffs, tossing them towards Jonboy as the Tourist began to stir.

'You'll have to help me out here.'

The new last man standing picked up the handcuffs from the floor.

'Have you nicked him then?' he asked.

'For everything.'

'Right you are.'

Brook's senses shut down one more level as the adrenalin faded.

'And I hate to be a nuisance…'

'Go on.'

'But you might want to get me an ambulance.'

Then the curtains closed.

Chapter 49

Three days later
University College Hospital, London

Not for the first time Brook woke to find Jonboy in a bedside chair, stuffing his face with the grapes he had bought on his way to the hospital. The detective pushed himself into a sitting position, wincing at the pain caused by such a simple movement.

'You know I'm not a massive fan of grapes,' he said, once he was settled.

'That's why I buy them,' said Jonboy, throwing another five into his mouth.

Before Brook could complain, his friend nodded at a separate collection of goodies he had placed on the bedside table.

'Cheers, mate,' said the patient, the skin beneath his eyes a rainbow of bruise colours and nine stitches shared between forehead and cheek. 'I take it they haven't changed their beer policy then?'

'Maybe tomorrow.'

The doctors had kept Brook in for observation on account of Big Dave's unconventional use of a fire extinguisher. Given that the concussion checks allowed time for some of the swelling around his re-aligned ankle to go down, he was going to be passed straight from the head trauma experts to the brave surgeon who would try to rebuild the shattered joint. He had been told to expect pins, screws, wires and staples. It was best not to think about it too much.

The Tourist… The Tourist was long gone. He had spent just under an hour in custody. Less than sixty minutes for Murder, Resisting Arrest and Grievous Bodily Harm to Brook's ankle. He had never even been questioned – surely some kind of world record considering the offences involved. Barnes must have played an absolute blinder behind the scenes.

Nearly as strange was the total silence surrounding the events. Just at the point that Brook and Jonboy might have expected to be bombarded by phone calls and visits from senior officers wanting to know what the hell had gone on… Tumbleweed. Not a single attempt to make contact in any way.

A tiny 'News in Brief' in a local newspaper said that Big Dave's had been damaged by a small number of Spurs fans, angry at the 1–1 draw with West Brom that scuppered their title chances. The common theme was clear – the events of Monday night were being airbrushed from history.

The Tourist's custody record had naturally been restricted, but Marie had used her resourcefulness to get hold of screenshots once again. Jonboy had brought them in for Brook to see for the first time… The battered officer scanned the pages of A4, the text ending abruptly with a few cut-and-paste lines about 'No Further Action' and the letters 'DI' in brackets.

'So, what nameless DI has the authority to release a murder suspect?' asked Brook.

'That's what I thought at first. Then I realised it probably doesn't stand for Detective Inspector.'

Brook thought for a moment. He still wasn't firing on all cylinders.

'Diplomatic Immunity,' he said at last. 'What a load of bullshit.'

'Course it is. But authorised bullshit beats unauthorised truth every time. He was out of custody before I'd even finished writing my notes.'

A nurse doing the rounds with hot drinks came past the end of the bed and was polite enough to smile at Jonboy's request for an Irish coffee before both men accepted a cup of tea. They drank in silence for a moment, contemplating the documented proof that all their efforts had amounted to a big fat zero.

'Look, maybe… maybe it's for the best,' said Brook, taking a sip.

'The alcohol ban?'

'The way things turned out.'

'Seriously? Have they upped your morphine?'

'Or, let's just say, it's not all bad. I didn't exactly relish the prospect of Victor getting dragged through a murder trial. Besides, they know we won. We figured it out, gathered the evidence and got the suspect into custody. What more can you do?'

'Bastard broke your ankle.'

'Double break and dislocation,' said Brook. 'Yeah, don't worry – that's being filed under 'Unforgiven'. Fucking cheap shot.'

Even before he had finished talking, his attention was being drawn to the television above his neighbour's bed. All patients had the option of one, on a big adjustable arm and activated once you had paid ten quid for a card. Brook's neighbour was asleep while the local news ate up some of his credit. It was the strapline across the bottom that caught Brook's eye:

'Lonely Funeral Fears for WW2 Hero'

He pointed over Jonboy's shoulder to alert him, before the more mobile of the two cranked the TV their way and turned the volume up to Max in the headphones – the only way of listening in. With the earpieces at the full extension of their wire, the report was just about audible.

It seemed that one little thing had, after all, slipped through the net that Barnes was trying to throw over events. The media had picked up on the next of kin appeal from the police press officer and were running with it. A young female reporter in a red jacket was nodding as the studio anchor finished his link to her. She was also standing outside 64 Duke Crescent. Brook and Jonboy knew it well. With a final nod, she began her piece to camera…

'That's right. Lance Corporal Victor Watson served with the Middlesex Regiment during World War Two, was captured in early 1944 and spent the rest of the war in the notorious Stalag IV-B prisoner of war camp. He lived here, on his own, without other residents knowing anything of their quiet neighbour's past. Since his death last week, a police appeal to find a next of kin has failed to yield a single call. After learning of the case via the local police Twitter account, one neighbour has now started a Facebook appeal for Victor Watson to be given the send-off he deserves. In just 24 hours, it has been viewed and liked by over half a million people.'

Jonboy immediately recognised the yummy mummy opposed to gender stereotyping who appeared next. They were able to hear her opening line of *'I just felt I should do something...'* before someone pulled the alarm cord in the toilet and prevented them hearing any more. After thirty seconds, the camera went back to the young reporter who handed back to the studio with her best 'sad and sincere' face. Jonboy returned the TV to its sleeping owner (turning the volume down so as not to give him a brand new head injury).

Neither man was quite sure what to make of what they had seen.

'Well, that was weird,' said Jonboy, eventually.

'The law of unintended consequences,' said Brook. 'They've killed an old Nazi and turned him into a national hero.'

Chapter 50

Ten days later
Otago Peninsula, New Zealand

The young doctor brought his rattling 50cc scooter to a stop and tried to check the map on his phone. No reception. He dug out a paper version, unfolded it in the strong breeze, and looked up and down the coast road. Had he gone past it? There didn't seem to be any more dwellings before the road disappeared into grassy dunes and the crashing surf of the South Pacific. He pulled his jacket collar tighter – winter came earlier near the bottom of the South Island. Medical school up in Auckland seemed positively tropical by comparison.

He squinted harder towards the end of the road and made out one more dwelling. The grey wood of an 1860s settler cottage, almost totally invisible against an equally grey sky. A few hardy trees obscured the single-storey structure a little more. He stuffed the map away and set the scooter in motion once again – volcanic hills rising to his left, sandy scrub merging into a blustery beach on his right.

Pulling up in front of the cottage, the newly qualified GP could see that the land around it had been reclaimed from the scrub. There was a small lawn, a couple of flower beds and the neat geometry of a well-tended vegetable patch. When he took off his helmet – unleashing a floppy-haired reminder of his student days – he could hear chickens round the back.

Carrying a letter, he knocked on the door. It didn't take long for it to be answered. An old man looked back at the young doctor – thinning white hair and a blue fisherman's jumper.

'Can I help?'

'I'm Dr Taylor. I just started at the surgery in Portobello. Is it Mr Ackerman?' He extended a hand. The old man shook it.

'That's right… Unusual to have a personal visit.'

'Well. It happened to be on my way, so…'

The doctor was trying to play down his 'new boy' enthusiasm to visit everyone in the community of his first posting. The old man looked down the coast road to the dunes.

'What was it on your way to?'

A little colour came into the doctor's cheeks.

'Well, not exactly on my way but… not too far out of it.'

The old man smiled. He didn't mean to make him uncomfortable.

'Anyway…' Dr Taylor started afresh. 'Your latest test results arrived at the surgery and I thought I'd bring them over rather than ask you to come in.'

'Very kind of you,' said the old man, without any great anxiety.

'I can give you the headlines to save you worrying. It's good news. I know you had a couple of scares there, but the results are very positive. Remarkably so. It seems you just… keep on living.'

The old man accepted the letter.

'It's a habit,' he said.

The pair stood in silence for a moment. The doctor intrigued by the old man. The old man aware that he intrigued the doctor. It was the younger of the two who spoke first.

'Ackerman? Is that some German heritage you've got there?'

'The name is German, but the heritage isn't mine. I took my wife's name.'

The GP smiled a little distractedly, his focus on something else…

'If you don't mind my asking, Mr Ackerman – just from a medical perspective – how did you..?' He nodded at the head injury that had captured his attention.

'I was shot by an officer of the SS during World War Two.'

Dr Taylor opened his mouth, but found he was incapable of forming an adequate response.

'Don't worry, old chap,' said Victor. 'These things happen.'

The young doctor smiled and had another go at speaking, still not fully composed.

'I heard about your recent… I mean, I'm sorry about… At the surgery… They told me your wife recently–'

'Thank you,' said Victor.

Both men became aware of a very different engine sound coming down the coast road – the restrained thunder of a Harley Davidson. The rider was wearing a brown leather jacket and no helmet. As he got closer, they could see he had dark hair, cut short and sensible, and a wide, muscular neck. He pulled over beside the 50cc scooter, instantly making it look like a child's toy.

'A friend?' asked Dr Taylor.

'An acquaintance,' said Victor.

He had never seen the man before, but he had a fair idea who he was. He had received the message. It was done. The young doctor saw it as a good cue to take his leave (while he thought about just what Mr Ackerman's generation had been through). He exchanged greetings with the Harley rider as they passed. It was turning into a busy day for the little cottage.

'I think I know who you are,' said Victor.

'I definitely know who you are,' said the Tourist.

'You had better come in.'

Victor led the way through his home to a kitchen at the rear. He walked with a limp but otherwise moved well for a man his age (the time of year had moved beyond the annual indecision over his exact date of birth – allowing him to know for sure he was ninety-three years old). The kitchen had an oak table with a view out to sea. Victor pulled out a chair for the Tourist then went to the fridge, cracking open two bottles of the local Emerson's Pilsner and setting them down.

'Thank you,' said the Tourist, taking a sip. When not working he allowed himself alcohol. In strict moderation, of course. Victor sat down opposite and took a sip of his own beer. From across the table, the Tourist had a good view of the injury that had so fascinated Dr Taylor...

A primitive skin graft ran the length of Victor's scalp from front to back, an inch wide and an inch or two off-centre. No hair grew on it. The graft couldn't quite hide a groove that followed the same path. The whole thing had a melted plastic quality to it – enough to distract the observer from the missing top third of the left ear. For a moment, at least.

'I've got something for you,' said the Tourist, reaching a hand inside his leather jacket. He took out the precious cargo that had accompanied him from London and placed the item in front of his host.

Victor looked at the old medal and read its simple inscription for the first time in over seventy years… '*Ad Victoriam*'… It was home. The only tiny link to a blood relative he had ever had. The only connection to the unseen eons of ancestors that had resulted in his existence.

He had last seen the medal on the day he was shot by von Eberstein. The day he learned of Harry's betrayal. The day he met his wife… the Angel. He left it where it was on the table and walked to the back door, stepping out into the small garden. The Tourist watched through the window as the old man stared out to sea. Then the telltale rise and fall of the shoulders.

After a while, the shoulder movements slowed, then stopped. He saw Victor raise both hands and rub his face. Then he fed the chickens, using the practical task to compose himself before coming back inside. He sat down and slid the medal into a drawer at the side of the table.

'Thank you,' said Victor, taking a long sip and raising his beer in acknowledgement.

'You're welcome,' said the Tourist, raising his in return. He looked around. 'So, this is where you came after the war?'

'Not this very place. But the area, yes. A farm on the other side of the peninsula. I don't know how much you know about my past.'

'A bit. I'm allowed to ask questions. When I'm doing this type of job.'

Victor noted that his guest did different 'types' of jobs and carried on.

'Well, it took the best part of a year to patch me up. The leg was never quite the same. And the head… well… you can see the head. The Ackermans had a cousin who knew a surgeon in Leipzig. He did his best.'

'I never even noticed,' said the Tourist, raising a smile from Victor.

'Of course, the long recovery worked in my favour in the end. Gave me time to get to know Gerti. She never seemed bothered by the injuries. As I got better, I started to help around the farm. Did whatever I could.'

'Surely you wondered what was going on with Harry and von Eberstein? Whether they had actually pulled it off?'

'I thought about it. A great deal for a while. But other things were happening. Gerti seemed to be showing interest, even though I kept telling myself not to get my hopes up. Every day, my new life seemed better than the one they'd stolen. In the end, she actually proposed to me. Can you believe that? How many women did that in 1946? Best day of my life.'

The Tourist saw a film of moisture return to Victor's eyes. For a moment, it looked as if the chickens might be about to get another feed.

'Anyway… We got married out there. Paperwork had to be fudged a bit due to my lack of documents. But it wasn't all a bed of roses. The farm was struggling to make any money and then there was the… politics… of a German girl marrying a mystery Englishman. Let's just say it didn't meet with universal approval from the locals.'

'And the parents?'

Victor sipped his beer then shook his head.

'The parents couldn't have been happier. I suppose the thing with the Russians had put me in their good books.'

The Tourist raised an enquiring eyebrow.

'It's another story,' said Victor. 'In any case, in the end they sold some family jewellery. Heirlooms, I suppose you might say. They didn't really like to discuss it. But they scraped together enough for us to move out here. A new start away from everything. A Kiwi soldier had told me about this area, though he didn't live to see it again, poor fellow. We had just enough to buy the worst bit of land on the whole peninsula. Leakiest farmhouse...'

A smile began to spread as the flickering home movie of Victor's mind spooled through the happy footage.

'Gerti turned it around. She knew her stuff when it came to farming. Arable. Like the farm in Germany. Not so common out here in sheep country. She got a tune out of that land for over half a century before we rented it all out and moved down to this cottage.'

The Tourist leaned in a little.

'But you could never quite let it go, could you?' he said. 'Harry and von Eberstein, I mean.'

Victor's brow furrowed in thought for a moment.

'You mean the cards?'

'Let's just say they came as a bit of a surprise when I found out.'

Victor sensed an element of restraint in the comment.

'Well, you're right, of course. It was always going to be hard to totally forget. I had a permanent reminder after all.' He gestured to his head. 'The idea that it might all have gone swimmingly for those chaps didn't sit comfortably with me. Call it pride if you like, I don't mind.'

'I would just call it being human.'

'I knew I couldn't risk what we had here. Couldn't stick my head above the parapet and start shouting about *the truth*.

The bastards had already killed me once. I would have spent my whole life looking over my shoulder. Plus, I had something to lose now.'

He looked out of the window, as if the permanence of the sea might provide a link to the old memories he was trying to access.

'It came to me when we started talking about visiting Australia for the first time. Fifty-four, was it? Fifty-five? We were doing a bit better by then. I managed to find a private investigator in England – he had a small ad in one of the London papers that made it over here. I told him all I could about who I was looking for and he eventually wrote back with two addresses, just before we left for Australia.'

'So you decided to let them know you were still alive.'

Victor drank some of his beer before continuing. He hadn't talked this much in a while, but it was hard to deny there was a certain therapy to it.

'As they always say, there's more than one type of prison. The physical and the mental. I realised I could build a mental one for them. A mental Stalag. I could make sure they were the ones who spent a lifetime looking over their shoulder. For a man they'd seen shot dead. For a ghost.'

He shrugged.

'I don't know how much it worked. Sometimes we went years without a holiday. And I always felt it was too risky to send a card from round here, even if I had the camouflage of a different surname. But I like to think that the next one always arrived just as they were beginning to forget the last.'

'What did your wife think of it?'

'Gerti? Ha! She loathed them more than me. She was the only other person who knew the whole story from top to bottom. Would have killed them herself given half the chance. With a frying pan probably.'

He tried to focus on a point on the horizon.

'We knew Christmas would be our last trip. Gerti was… Anyway… She still insisted that we went. I got news of Harry's move into that home just in time to send the last cards.'

Victor's mind drifted to that final holiday with Gerti. Then he brought himself back.

'So they kept the cards, did they? Good. I'm glad it was playing on their minds. How did you come across them?'

'I didn't. Some detective was poking around. He found them.'

The Tourist took a swig, using the bottle to disguise any hint of mixed emotions in his face.

'There were problems?' asked Victor.

'Nothing that couldn't be handled.'

'I take it no-one got hurt. No-one else, I mean.'

'The detective will be okay.'

Victor frowned. Unintended consequences. The Tourist moved on quickly.

'So you were still keeping tabs on their addresses after all these years. Not the same private investigator, surely?'

'Not quite. His son. And not private. Police. He took over the little checks from his father when he retired. Unusual for police to do private work on the side, of course, but this chap was a bit different.'

'I'm intrigued.'

Victor took his beer and stood up.

'Join me in the garden. The sun's trying to come out.'

The chickens greeted them as they came through the back door. Half a dozen were roaming free while a couple more were keeping warm in the hen house. It was just beneath the bedroom window. The Tourist tilted his head at the strutting birds.

'Good layers these,' said Victor.

'Doesn't the noise drive you mad?'

'I find it comforting.'

The yard was surrounded by a white picket fence with a gate to a path leading down to the sand. The Tourist sipped his beer and gripped the fence as he looked out over the beach. It was sturdy. Victor had built it well.

'You're breaking all the movie rules here, Victor. Everyone knows that soldiers who dream of white picket fences never make it to the end credits.'

'I like to be different.'

'You're succeeding.'

Victor walked over to him. He loved this view.

'You were going to tell me about the PI and his son in the police,' reminded the Tourist.

'Ah. That's right. Memory isn't quite what it was.' He took a moment to organise his thoughts. 'Well… this private investigator who first helped me with the addresses. We became good friends over the years. Nice chap. Another ex-soldier as it happened, though Korea was his big one. Lost an eye out there. I suppose there was some sort of natural kinship between us.'

'Another unbreakable type.'

'Or another lucky one. In any case, he had a son. Early sixties he must have been born. He went on to join the police and be a real high-flyer. Top of his class. Climbing the ranks. His father couldn't have been prouder.'

The Tourist began to suspect where this was going.

'They fell out in the end. It was strange. No amount of justice ever seemed to be enough for the son. He had this obsession with it. Or at least, his version of it. Trying to right every wrong. His justice. His punishment. They like the word *vigilante* these days, don't they?'

A nearby flock of gulls that had been pecking around the beach went squawking into the air. Victor waited for their cries to die down.

'He was good at it, mind. His father used to call him a crafty operator. He was the perfect officer when he needed to be. Played by the rules. Got the promotions. But all the time, out of sight, he was circumventing the whole game. Righting the wrongs in his own way. With a bit of help from men like you, of course… *Sudden* heart attacks, *random* accidents, *unexpected* suicides… Whatever it took to make bad men disappear. His father blamed himself – thought he'd told him too many of his war stories when he was young. Too many tales of injustice. Who knows? Anyway, the father died last year… His name was Alfie… Alfie Barnes.'

The Tourist showed no surprise. He had seen it coming. But he had still found himself enthralled. Victor had a gentle and engaging way about him.

'So you decided to point Barnes junior in the direction of Harry and von Eberstein? After your wife died?'

'Funny thing is, I don't even remember it being a decision. It seemed as natural as finally calling in pest control. The idea of a world where those two were still breathing after Gerti was gone…'

Victor gave a little laugh at the absurdity of the idea.

'…No. No way. I'm sure plenty would preach to me about forgiveness. Well, I allowed those bastards a life, didn't I? Even after everything they'd done… betraying those fifteen escapers, executing them, Harry selling my life and von Eberstein damn near taking it. They lived a lifetime. How's that for forgiveness? And then I called time on it. For every one of those poor sods who never got the chance.'

He raised his eyes to the overcast sky where shafts of sunlight were now poking through and dancing on the waves.

'You see that? If all of that is nothing more than science, then I was right to do what I did… If no higher power was waiting to deal with them.'

'And if there's something more than science?'

The old soldier's back straightened and his lungs sucked in the sea air.

'I'm happy with my choices,' he said.

For the first time, the Tourist saw the hint of steel in Victor's eyes. The steel that had got him through his youth as a Foundling, through the battlefields of North Africa and Italy, through Stalag IV-B and the pain of all his injuries. He had been so lulled by the old man's gentle manner he had almost forgotten he was standing next to one of the toughest men he was ever going to meet. As quickly as the edge appeared it was gone, replaced by something altogether softer.

'And what's your story?' asked Victor.

Even with such a simple question, the Tourist chose his words carefully.

'Well… Let's just say there are some people who leave the military and soon find they are surrounded by medals and commendations… but flat broke. And maybe some of those people take the skills they have acquired and put them to use in the shadier parts of the private sector – building that 'money' column up to the max, while the 'honour' column slips down to zero. Then, at some point, they may realise they need to seek… a balance. So they can live with themselves.'

Victor got the gist of it. Even if his visitor understandably preferred to talk about his activities in vague terms. He tried not to think about what the Tourist must have done. About the murky world he was rubbing shoulders with.

'I imagine finding a balance isn't easy. For those people, I mean,' he said.

The Tourist realised his avoidance of first person pronouns was starting to sound a little silly.

'I knew the person who did this role for Barnes before me. Pest control, as you say. When he stopped doing it, I thought it might help me. To balance out the other things.'

'And is it working?'

The Tourist puffed out his cheeks and thought of his fight in a London café.

'Not really. Somehow real life always tends towards being a fucking mess. Anyway, that was my last job with Barnes. I mean, it would have been even if he wasn't retiring. It could have gone better.'

Victor didn't press him any further. Along with the earlier oblique comment about an injured detective, it was beginning to sound as if – end result apart – things hadn't exactly gone to plan. He limited himself to one more question as he finished his beer.

'So where are you actually from?'

The Tourist finished his bottle at the same time and went to speak, before hesitating. He liked Victor. But not that much.

'Around,' he said.

Both men left it at that as they watched the sea in silence for a couple of minutes. The shafts of light appeared, faded and re-appeared elsewhere as the clouds shifted.

'Do you ever swim in that?'

'Every day.'

'Really?'

'Really. Good for the leg.'

They headed back into the cottage, leaving the empty bottles on the oak table as they passed through the kitchen and into the living room. Framed photos of Gerti and Victor were everywhere – backdrops of coasts, mountains and cities. The couple grew steadily older as the technical quality of the photos improved, from black-and-white, to faded colour, to perfect high definition. They were smiling in all of them. Big, genuine smiles. Gerti was stunning, maintaining an air of glamour all the way into old age. In two of the more recent ones, she was wearing a pink bandana. Still smiling.

Victor let the Tourist look around.

'Any children?' his visitor asked.

'Never quite happened for us,' said Victor. 'How can I complain? Seventy years of happy marriage after being shot at point-blank range while in my pants. I'll take that.'

The Tourist nodded, his eyes moving over to a television in the corner of the room. It was showing a BBC World News report, the pause symbol suggesting Victor had been watching it before the knock at the door. It wasn't the first time he had watched it…

The scene was a London street, lined on either side by a large crowd, three or four deep. Some old soldiers with polished medals were in the front rows, while a hearse carriage drawn by two black horses was frozen in motion. The Tourist read the strapline:

'Huge Turn-out For Lonely WW2 Hero'

His brow furrowed as he stared at the screen.

'Not many people get to see their own funeral, do they?' said Victor.

The Tourist processed a lot of information very quickly and then relaxed a little. Seeing the results of his handiwork turned into television news was undeniably disconcerting. But the fact von Eberstein was being buried – and the story was about well-wishers rather than murder – suggested any suspicion had passed. After all that had gone wrong, that was worth a sigh of relief.

'It's not too bad,' said Victor, as they both stared at the still image. 'And the stuff about the early years is true at least. Funny to think he was Victor Watson for three times longer than me.'

'I like the name Ackerman.'

'Me too. Means ploughman. Had to be farmers, really, didn't they? Talking of names… What was the name of the detective who got hurt?'

'Why do you want to know that?'

Victor's response was a little too slow to avoid a slightly awkward silence. The honest reply would have been 'because a very anonymous donor might pay for any treatment he needs'. But he knew that sort of interference would not go down well.

'Just… indulge me,' he said.

The Tourist thought about it for a moment. Hadn't he once used a similar line on Barnes?

'DC Brook Deelman,' he replied.

'Interesting name.'

'That's almost what I said.'

Victor's guest looked around the room a final time.

'Well… Good luck.'

He didn't offer a handshake as he saw himself out. He could sense Victor had mixed feelings about him – about what those hands had done. Not making him shake hands was his final gift. He was gone before the old man could reply.

Victor heard the deep growl of the Harley Davidson, followed by the fading drumbeat of its departure down the coast road. Then he turned off the television – he had seen his funeral enough times. Walking through to the kitchen, he put the kettle on (he was still an Englishman, after all). The cloud outside was really breaking up now. The chickens sounded happy.

He opened the drawer containing the medal and rested his hand on it for a moment, before reaching beyond it. To a pink bandana. He pulled on its near edge until it was covering the medal. Then he lifted the whole bundle.

Victor closed his eyes hard and held it tight as sunlight flooded the room.

Chapter 51

One week later
Grovebury Police Station, North London

Brook paused to look up at the Union Jack and Met Police flag fluttering above the municipal brick of his police station. Something felt different this time. Different from the thousands of times he had been here before. Nothing about the police station had changed, so something about him must have. The same surroundings that had felt so mundane a few short weeks ago now seemed strangely alien.

He balanced between one crutch and one good foot as he slid his warrant card through the electronic reader, punched in his code and swung the back door open. Inside, a couple of uniformed officers greeted him as they walked past.

'Playing rugby?' asked one, nodding at Brook's left leg. The plaster cast rose from his foot to disappear into the three-quarter length khaki shorts he was wearing (the operation on his ankle had gone well, though airport metal detectors might be a bit of an issue from now on).

'Doing a jigsaw,' replied Brook.

Making his way to Marie's office, his triceps strained against the black fabric of his t-shirt – arm muscles pumped up by the daily effort of getting about on crutches. The constant calorie burn had also tightened his belt a notch or two, assisted by the fact he hadn't touched alcohol in three weeks. He knew it wouldn't last, but he had decided to see how long he could stretch the enforced detox of his hospital stay. His liver was probably already composing a letter of thanks to the Tourist.

Marie wasn't the official purpose of today's visit – that was a meeting about some 'return to work plan' with DI Julian Self, the Direct Entry Scheme poster boy. But seeing Marie would definitely make such a tedious appointment more bearable. There had been a few phone calls and texts, but they hadn't seen each other since Brook's starring role in Fight Night at Big Dave's. He had a suspicion their friendship might be the source of some tension between Marie and her fiancé.

All the same, his favourite forensics officer had sent a very nice Get Well Soon card. It arrived the same day as an unexpected one from PC 'Sandy' Sanderson. Yep, that was a good morning. The nurse had even asked Brook if he was looking so happy because the friend who ate all his chocolates was no longer around. Even Jonboy couldn't avoid work forever.

As Brook approached Marie's office, she came round the corner, zipping up her stab vest and clutching a police radio, an agitated voice at the other end. On her way out to an urgent job. Caught by surprise, she ignored the radio and took in the sight before her.

Brook's clean shave and short haircut had definitely reduced the creeping hints of 'silver fox', but any chance of looking fresh faced was somewhat dented by the healing stitches in cheek and forehead and the dying embers of two black eyes.

'Jesus, look at you,' said Marie.

Brook gave a crinkly-eyed smile.

'You should see the other guy.'

They stared at each other as the radio garbled away. Then a male forensics officer came bustling round the corner. Brook didn't recognise him. A new guy. He was zipping up his own stab vest and swinging a set of van keys on a finger.

'Let's go,' he said, passing Marie.

She grabbed the keys off him.

'I'll drive.'

Suddenly key-less, he stopped bustling.

'I'll see you in the yard,' said Marie, sending him on his way. He took the hint. She turned to Brook and shrugged apologetically.

'Aggravated Burglary. Some inspector's having a hissy fit that we're not there already.'

Brook nodded, then used a crutch as an oversized pointer.

'It's that way,' he said.

Marie gave a sad smile and then began walking, squeezing his arm as she passed.

'I'll call you,' she said, looking back.

'I might answer,' said Brook, teasing her.

Then he was alone.

After a few seconds, a different face appeared at the far end of the corridor – DI Self in one of his perfect Italian suits. Brook muttered *'from the sublime to the ridiculous'* as he gave a fake smile.

'I thought I heard your voice,' said the DI. 'Shall we get this out of the way?'

'Let's,' agreed Brook.

The door to DI Self's office was open. Brook followed him in and saw someone else was already there. He was looking very comfortable in a padded chair with curved wooden arms. DI Self took a chair with fancy suspension behind the desk, leaving only a plastic one in front of it.

Brook exchanged a look with the third man as he hopped over to the cheap seat and lowered himself onto it. This other guy was in his mid-50s, a cropped widow's peak of grey hair and a neat grey beard, edging towards white. He was wearing a dark suit and some kind of private members' club tie. The language of power.

But he looked pale and tired.

Brook recognised him from the police intranet and occasional television interviews. In an age where senior officers were all pressed from the same media-trained mould, he had always found him to be something of a throwback. Nevertheless, he waited for DI Self to do the introductions.

'I'm sure you know our recently retired Deputy Commissioner Barnes. He's on a bit of a farewell tour of a few stations.' He gestured towards his guest. 'He heard about your injury and said he would like to meet you.'

Brook wasn't sure what account of his smashed ankle the young DI had decided to believe, but it was a fair guess he was ignorant of the truth. The injured detective nodded in Barnes' direction.

'Thought I recognised you. What's your first name again?'

DI Self interjected with a cough.

'Err, I think *Sir* might be more appropriate, DC Deelman.'

'I thought you said he'd just retired.'

'I… Yes… But, out of courtesy…'

The sycophantic DI was floundering. Unlike the military, high ranking police officers didn't get to keep their rank after retirement. They were just ex-coppers with first names. Unless their political manoeuvres had earned them a place in the House of Lords.

'It's Terry,' replied Barnes, cutting through the bluster. He had the voice of a smoker.

'Good to finally meet you, Terry,' said Brook.

DI Self was aware of some kind of familiarity between the two men but didn't quite understand why or how.

'I wonder if you might give us a moment,' said Barnes, directing the question to his host and then returning his eyes to Brook.

A part of Brook relished the DI's awkwardness. Having just insisted that Barnes' retired status be ignored, he was now being turfed out of his own office by a civilian. The Detective Inspector's eyes darted between the two men, trying to find a way of saving face.

'I'll get us all a coffee,' he said, looking relieved at hitting upon the perfect way out.

Barnes wasted no time in moving round to the DI's side of the desk and sitting in his chair. He knew its owner didn't have the balls to complain. He looked around the room from his new position. Then his eyes settled on Brook.

'You really fucked things up for me,' he said.

'You really fucked things up for my ankle,' said Brook.

Barnes leaned forward, jabbing a finger onto the desk to make his point.

'Do you have ANY…' his voice was too loud. He glanced at the closed office door and started again. 'Do you have *any* idea how many favours I had to burn to clear up that fucking mess you created?' He jabbed the desk one more time. 'A fucking career's worth.' Then he leaned back.

So much for introductory pleasantries.

Brook let the post-rant silence do its ever-reliable job of holding up a mirror to anger. Then he provided the added emphasis of a raised eyebrow.

'Finished?' he asked, calmly.

Barnes' eyes were firing lasers across the desk.

'WELL?' he asked, losing control of his volume once again.

'Well what?'

'Who are you running to with all of this? Press? Local MP? Commissioner? Or are you just going to put it all out on social fucking media for your fifteen minutes of fame?'

'I'm not running anywhere,' said Brook, stating the obvious, at least from a physical perspective. Even as he said the words, he was re-calibrating his understanding of the situation.

He had spent three weeks making his peace with the idea that the Tourist would walk free in exchange for Victor being left alone. Three weeks coming to terms with the fact that there were things he would probably never know. Like the true identities of the Tourist or the fake DS Beckford, or if there were any other clandestine players behind the scenes.

In Barnes he had identified the 'director' and understood his brutal, real-life morality play. Beyond that, murderous conspiracies tended not to come with a souvenir programme of cast and crew. All the time, Barnes had seemingly been waiting for him to blow the lid off the whole thing. As Brook wondered how to respond to the new situation, his thoughts were interrupted.

'You're a smart man, Brook. In some ways, at least. I'm sure you realised I'd have to take out some kind of insurance once you started threatening me like this.'

'Insurance?'

Barnes scoffed.

'You're playing in the big leagues now, son. I thought I would have to go digging for something, but in the end it fell right into my lap.'

Brook could think of plenty of minor misdemeanours and rule bending he could be accused of, but nothing that would justify the smile spreading across Barnes' face. The older man didn't keep him in suspense.

'There are some CCTV images kicking around of an unknown police officer in a Kings Cross strip bar. The old pound-in-a-pot place.'

Now it was Brook who smiled.

'That's it?'

'Not exactly. He needs to be spoken to about how he dealt with a bouncer's breach of bail conditions for a domestic assault on his girlfriend. She worked there as a stripper. It seems this officer just moved him off the premises when he clearly needed to be arrested for the breach.'

A little worse, but not calamitous. Although it did beg the question…

'How does anyone know this?' asked Brook.

'Oh. Sorry. From the bouncer himself. When he was being questioned over killing that stripper girlfriend of his. About a week after you fobbed him off with some unofficial warning.'

Brook was about to say that he'd only ever been guessing about the bouncer's bail conditions. Blagging it. But he realised how weak it sounded even before the words came out.

'That's right,' continued Barnes. 'Very tearful confession to the murder by all accounts. He blamed the bodybuilding. *'Roid rage'*. Said he wished the police officer in the bar had arrested him to stop it ever happening. Of course, he's got a fair point. Chances are he would have been remanded in custody for the breach of bail and the poor girl would still be alive. Needless to say, I could hardly believe my luck when I saw the CCTV… It's you, Brook. I even took the liberty of checking where your phone was that night. Suffice to say, you're bang to rights.'

Insurance.

The dynamic in the office had shifted completely. Brook stayed quiet. Barnes was on a roll.

'It's not a massive issue for his trial. He's going to plead at the first opportunity anyway. But the DPS would be licking their lips at something like this. I mean, let's not be naïve – it's a career-ender.'

The Directorate of Professional Standards. Barnes wasn't lying. They would have a feeding frenzy over it. Brook still didn't respond. He wasn't thinking about his career. He was thinking about the excellent English the brunette had spoken; her old bruises just showing through the make-up as she talked to him at the bar. Somewhere, many miles away, her parents had probably had to learn she wasn't working in a restaurant after all. What a fucking waste of a life.

'Where was she from?' he asked, blankly.

It wasn't the combative response Barnes had expected.

'Lithuania,' he said, letting go of the smirk. 'Look, it doesn't have to be a career-ender. I still have just enough leverage to get this kicked into touch. If you do the same with… the other thing.'

The office door opened and DI Self came in with the coffees. Barnes got up from the fancy ergonomic chair and moved back to his previous spot.

'Just reminding myself what it feels like on that side,' he said. 'I'll miss it. You're lucky.'

The DI smiled awkwardly and continued trying to tell himself that everything was normal as he handed out the drinks and sat down, a little irked that the seat felt a bit warm.

Brook downed his coffee in one, pushed himself up on his crutches and turned to leave.

'Nothing to say then?' asked Barnes, giving up on keeping their interaction secret from DI Self.

'There's no need,' said Brook. 'If you come for me, I'll come for you. And vice versa.'

'A stand-off?'

'Call it what you like.'

The detective swung himself towards the door. Barnes didn't like the lack of certainty in the answer – it still left him feeling wide open.

'What if we went for friendlier terms?' he offered. 'There must be something on your wish list.' He was thinking along the lines of a transfer to a specialist squad, a favourable promotion panel…

Brook paused at the door.

'There's a homeless guy,' he said. 'A former Para who sleeps rough around St Mary Magdalene Church. I'm sure a man with your connections could help him get back on his feet. Properly back on his feet. Long hair and a big beard. Wears a lumberjack coat. You can't miss him.'

Having used every trick in the book to monitor Brook's investigation, Barnes was already well aware of the man being described.

'And then we're quits?' he asked, betraying a little too much relief. The stakes were high for him. Brook had peeked behind the curtain at events that could earn him life in prison, however deserving he believed his targets were.

'One more thing,' said Brook. He took an item from his pocket and tossed it through the air to Barnes… 'I'm sure you'll find a way of getting that back to Victor.'

Then the detective pulled open the office door and left.

Barnes opened his right hand and looked at what he had caught. A thin chain was hanging from his palm – Victor's POW dog tags attached to it.

A confused DI Self followed Brook into the corridor and called after him.

'We still need to discuss your return to work plan!'

Brook replied without turning back.

'Ages for the fracture. Ages for the rehab. A full quota of annual leave and twenty-five rest days in lieu… I'll be in touch.'

The detective inspector didn't bother chasing after him. When he got back to the office, Barnes was still looking at the dog tags. He was happy with how 'negotiations' had gone.

'Smart kid,' he said to the returning DI. It took DI Self a moment to realise he was talking about Brook, who was nearly ten years his senior.

'Well… Not the easiest to deal with. But I could really do with getting him back to work as soon as possible. A combined end-of-year detection rate of thirty-seven percent is a challenging but achievable target if everyone is pulling in the same direction.'

Barnes stood up and straightened his suit…

'Do you really fucking talk like that?'

The lift pinged open on the ground floor and Brook began his rhythmical progress towards the police station's back door.

He focused on the physical process of using the crutches. It helped hold back any more difficult thoughts about events in the strip bar.

One way or another he would find a way of rationalising it, of dealing with it, of moving on. It wasn't the first time a well-intentioned act had gone wrong. Callous as it sounded, he would cope. Matters of life, death, regret – they all came with the warrant card. Let others judge who didn't walk in his shoes (or *shoe* as it was right now).

He had nearly reached the exit when he heard a familiar voice behind him. It was unaccented with a warm, friendly quality.

'Hey! Brook without an 'e'…'

He turned to see a smiling Sandy Sanderson. She was looking well. Blonde hair in a loose ponytail, casual jeans and a dark blue hoodie with 'FDNY' in yellow on the front. Out of uniform, she looked even more Scandinavian. Brook found himself smiling back.

'I thought it was you I saw sneaking out,' said Sandy.

'You got me,' said Brook. 'Thanks for the card by the way.'

'You're welcome.'

She looked at his leg, the crutches, the healing facial injuries…

'I've been hearing the craziest rumours about you since that night in the churchyard.'

'It's been interesting,' said Brook. He nodded at the letters on her hoodie. 'Fire Department of New York? Come on, Sandy.'

'What?'

'Everyone knows God invented cops so firefighters could have heroes.'

She rolled her eyes with a brand-new smile.

'Then why are their calendars so much better?'

Brook shook his head, secretly enjoying her quick wit.

'You're such a traitor,' he said, playfully.

'Listen, some of us are going for a few birthday drinks tomorrow if you're free.'

'Whose birthday is it?'

'Mine.'

'Twenty-one?'

'Ha! I wish. Twenty-seven.'

A couple of years older than Brook would have guessed. Maybe he didn't have to feel like such a lecherous old man after all... *Get a grip*, he told himself. *She's only being friendly.*

He tapped the cast on his leg with a crutch.

'Sorry. Having this off tomorrow afternoon. Moving on to an 'air boot'. Should be a bit easier to get to the itches.'

Sandy shrugged with her hands in the hoodie's pouch. Brook told himself he was imagining it when he sensed a hint of deflation.

'But happy birthday in advance,' he added.

'Thanks. I'll have one for you,' said Sandy.

'Have more than one.'

They turned to head in opposite directions with little nods and smiles. Brook shoved open the rear door while Sandy walked away down the corridor.

'How about Saturday?' she called back, half a second before the door closed behind him.

He caught it.

'A friend can't make it to the Comedy Store so I'm going on my own as it stands... Unless you can make it to Covent Garden on your crutches?'

Brook re-evaluated his overly defeatist assessment of things.

'I'm sure I can,' he said. 'I like a challenge.'

'Great. Me too,' smiled Sandy. 'See you at the Maple Leaf at seven?'

'Perfect.'

They went their separate ways, Sandy secretly hoping the Comedy Store wasn't sold-out.

Out in the street, Brook heard the door shut behind him and the faint whir of the electronic lock re-engaging. He took a deep breath and looked around. Nice day. The middle of May. He didn't look back at the police station as he set off down the street – he wasn't going to think about it for a long time. The slight element of tunnel vision that the crutches required meant he didn't see a *Daily Express* sandwich board outside a newsagent:

'Sheffield OAP Leaves £1.7m To Care Home Pals'

When he reached his bus stop, Brook patted his pocket. Just to feel the crinkle of the printed A4 sheet inside. Flight details. Tickets all booked. His first proper holiday in years.

In two weeks, he would be back in Botswana. Back in Maun. Sipping sundowners at the Okavango River Lodge, listening to the belly laughs of the hippos and watching the huge African sun kiss the horizon.

Home.

Epilogue

Saturday, 28th April 1923
Bloomsbury, London

Her feet seemed to freeze as she reached the iron gates, suddenly unable to take another step towards the looming symmetry of the Foundling Hospital. She had put it off for as long as possible, praying for time to slow down. But days had turned into a week, one week had turned into two, and now here she was. Out of time.

A fortnight was as long as she could possibly stay away from her job while pretending to be sick. Any longer and the family would simply get another local girl to carry out her menial tasks. God knows there were enough who needed the money.

And then there was her sister, having to take on so much more since the arrival of the baby. It was a lot to ask of a fifteen-year-old to look after their four younger siblings – even if she had barely been any older herself when Spanish flu took their mother. The Great War had already claimed their father by then. Her wage was the final lifeline.

She could see a group of children being led across the courtyard now. They walked silently, two by two, the Foundling Hospital their ark in a merciless world. She tried to read their faces. It was hard to tell. No laughter or smiles. But no tears either, she told herself.

As for the origins of her predicament… She had always known it was wrong. He was the master of the house; his wife the lady she took her orders from. But she couldn't deny she had been flattered by his attentions – especially as she considered herself the plainest of 19-year-olds. For just a moment, she had felt a faint connection to his world of luxury and lavish parties, even if she knew she could only ever be an embarrassing secret.

It was why she absolutely had to hide it when she found out she was pregnant, just as his attentions cooled. There was no way he would have kept her on – the potential for embarrassment now including a child. Hiding her condition had been a task in itself, but she had managed.

Her feet were still rooted to the spot as she became aware of laughter behind her… a group of daytime drinkers spilling out of The Lamb. One of them pointed at the baby in her arms.

'Is he playing today, love?'

Her dad's old West Ham scarf made up the outermost layer of the bundle. He'd given it to her the day he went off to war, asking her to be brave and look after her brothers and sisters. It somehow seemed right to leave it with the baby now.

But it still wasn't a traditional keepsake. It might get mixed up with other clothing and lost. As a true keepsake, there was only one option – the only thing she had ever won. She looked at the school cross-country medal and read the words in the middle for a final time… *'Ad Victoriam'*. A teacher had explained it meant *To Victory*. She liked that. Maybe the baby would know that his mum wanted him to be a fighter. To overcome whatever life threw at him. To just keep going.

Behind her, the drinkers from The Lamb were getting noisier and closer. It was the spur she needed to get her feet moving again. She tucked the medal into the bundle – it looked like the baby was holding it in his little hands – then she kissed him on the head and pushed open the iron gate.

The two by two parade of children had disappeared as she hurried down the path to the courtyard, heart pounding at the enormity of what she was doing. Somewhere on her right, a door opened – a nursemaid emerging with a new group of children. The young mother made sure she'd been seen, then placed the baby down and turned, half stumbling in the swirl of emotions. She picked up the pace as a voice called after her.

'Excuse me!'

Don't stop...

'Hey!'

Don't stop...

The tears began to sting as she hurried back through the gates and ploughed on, barging past people, charging across streets, attracting shouts and baffled stares. It was nearly a mile to the house where she worked. Only on rounding the final corner did she stop to compose herself, lungs working overtime to sift the poor London air. She smoothed her hair, straightened her pinafore and tried to force her thoughts forward... forward to the job she was returning to.

The family had always had two little girls since she started, but – as if things weren't bad enough – a son had arrived a few days before she feigned illness to give birth herself. She would be working in the same house as the little half-brother of the baby she had just said goodbye to.

It felt strange to think of the two boys, born just days apart into such different worlds. She wondered if their paths would ever cross. If they would ever know each other without either realising who the other was… the Foundling and the Aristocrat.

A postman was standing at the end of the gravel driveway that led to the house in which she served. He had a sack of letters over his shoulder but was squinting at one in particular, moving it back and forth. He looked up as she approached.

'Sorry, Miss. Maybe you can help. I'm having a bit of trouble with this one. I think I'm at the right place, but it's that funny foreign writing.'

Victor's mum looked at the envelope.

'Von Eberstein,' she said… 'I can take that.'

THE END

Acknowledgements

The first person I would like to thank is you, the Reader. It is only in the reading that the worlds of Brook and Victor come alive. Without you, all I have created is a bunch of text, paper and pixels. So thank you for being the other half of the process. For lending me your imagination.

To my family – the Midlands branch, Yorkshire branch, London, East Anglia, South-West and Wales branches – thank you for the shared genes and sense of humour. I'll say more about you throughout the series if you don't mind bearing with me and Brook.

To Mike and Paul – thanks for the anecdotes and nights out (both memorable and half-forgotten).

To Jo, Darren, Nicky and Nathan – thanks for all the rugby chat and job-related gallows humour.

To Angela, Caroline, Leah (and Ludo) – thanks for all your sage advice and support.

To Ed B and family (India's biggest Southend United fans) – thanks for the steadfast encouragement.

To Mark and Katie – thanks for showing the path from policing to writing.

To Jo Y, Rosa, James, Fifi and Liliana – thanks for keeping my spirits up on many occasions.

To my old journalist pals, Gav and Ste – thanks for all the beers, laughs and footie.

To Carrie and Reed – Skol Vikings. Go Badgers. And thanks for having such a good surname!

To everyone at Spiffing Covers – thanks for your artistic and technical wizardry.

To Dagmar – thanks for your language abilities (any mistakes are my own).

And to Jon(boy) – thanks for being the inspiration for, oh, I don't know, some character or other.

Finally, I would like to offer my humble appreciation to a WW2 veteran who recently passed away. New Zealander Tony Vercoe wrote "Survival at Stalag IVB" – an invaluable resource for me when it came to bringing Victor's world to life.

Thank you for your book and your service.

Printed in Great Britain
by Amazon

46773559R00218